ALSO BY JULIET E. McKENNA

THE ALDABRESHIN COMPASS
Southern Fire
Northern Storm
Western Shore
Eastern Tide

THE TALES OF EINARINN
The Thief's Gamble
The Swordsman's Oath
The Gambler's Fortune
The Warrior's Bond
The Assassin's Edge

CHRONICLES OF THE LESCARI REVOLUTION

IRONS IN THE FIRE

CHRONICLES OF THE LESCARI REVOLUTION

IRONS IN THE FIRE

JULIET E. McKENNA

SOLARIS

First published 2009 by Solaris
an imprint of BL Publishing
Games Workshop Ltd
Willow Road
Nottingham
NG7 2WS
UK

www.solarisbooks.com

ISBN-13: 978 1 84416 601 5
ISBN-10: 1 84416 601 5

Designed & typeset by BL Publishing

Printed and bound in the US.

For Chaz

ACKNOWLEDGEMENTS

This book sees the beginning of a new series, with a new publisher, through the good offices of a new agent. A writing life is always subject to change, so I'm grateful other things remain so constant.

Heading into the twentieth year of our married life, and my tenth as a published author, Steve always provides unfailing moral and practical support together with crucial insights whenever I'm hesitating over the best next step. Mike and Sue, best of friends, sister Rachel and invaluable pal Gill sustain me with timely reassurance and unflagging encouragement. These days, the next generation's lively interest in exactly what I'm doing with all the maps and notes and bits of research also keeps me keen.

Maggie Noach's untimely death robbed me and many others of a champion. Thankfully, working with new agent Sam sees me looking to the future with enthusiasm and optimism. Similarly, it's a tremendous pleasure to be working with the Solaris team, George, Christian and Mark, as their passion and professionalism spur me on. Lisa has done her usual sterling service polishing the blemishes out of my prose, for which I remain sincerely grateful. None of this would be possible without Marc's original vision and initiative so my profound thanks to him.

The community of SF & Fantasy writers and fans, through the Internet, through conventions and much else besides, provides support, inspiration and opportunity to grow as a writer. Listing half the people who deserve a mention would be impossible, so I'll content myself with acknowledging this book's particular debt to Pete Crowther. Writing the novella 'Turns & Chances' brought the Lescari Civil Wars into focus for me; the people, the places, the plots and calamities. Reading that, Chaz Brenchley was the first to see that resolution demanded revolution. Thanks for pointing it out, Chaz. This series is the result.

SOLITH

SOLURA
LIDRAFESS OTHILFESS
HATHALFESS
PASTAMAR FEYVAFESS
GRYNTH

GIDESTA

THE
GREAT
FOREST MEDESHALE
SEERIMA VANAM WREDE
ENSAIMIN
EYHORNE HANCHET SHOLVIN COVE
AMBAFROST FRIERN INGLIS
GULF OF PROME PEORLE DALASOR
COL DRYEA
TREBIN ABRAY DRAXIMAL ASHERRY BLACKLITH
CHANAUL
CARLUSE LESCAR TANNAT
DUSGATE COLEBRIDGE TRIOTLE SAVORGAN
KEVIL AST
FERL MARLIER PARNILESSE
CALADHRIA ADRULE SOLLAND ANGOVE
CARIF ZAFER BREMILAYNE
PINERIN TOREMAL
CLAITHE RELSHAZ NYME FEVERAD
MARKYATE KALAVEN
ATLAR THE VEYEN
GULF OF LEQUESINE
LESCAR MORETAYNE
DERRICE SIRALCA
REGIN LYOUTESSELI
ALDABRESHIN CAPE OF WINDS

BELIEVED POSITION OF
HADRUMAL
(THE WIZARD'S ISLE)

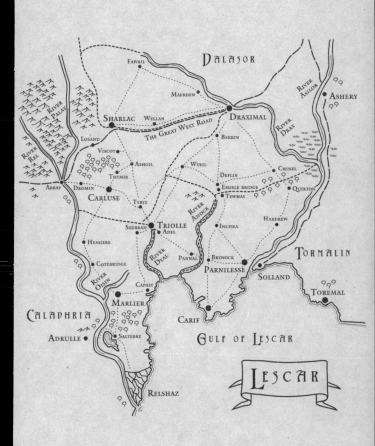

Taken from

The Political Almanac

*Being a description of the current
condition of those lands formerly
provinces of the Tormalin Empire
with notes on the status and
reputation of those of notable rank.*

*Compiled by Marol Afmoor,
Mentor and Scholar of the
University of Vanam*

Lescar remains a divided and fractious land with the prospect of unity beneath any undisputed High King as unlikely as it has been for these past ten generations.

Carluse continues to prosper thanks to its control of The Great West Road between the Caladhrian border at Abray and the border with Sharlac. Though it should be noted that merchant traffic from either east or west has not yet returned to the levels that generated such profitable tolls before the most recent conflict with Sharlac.

Prospecting for ores and quarrying stone in the hills between the Rel and Palat rivers continues. The horses bred by Duke Garnot's personal stable remain highly sought after, fetching the highest prices among discerning buyers.

Duke Garnot retains a force of mercenary troops but has not engaged in any military undertaking since the battle around the town of Losand where his troops engaged forces under the command of Lord Jaras, heir to Duke Moncan of Sharlac. The result of that battle was inconclusive, due to the deaths of both Lord Jaras and Duke Garnot's bastard son, Lord Veblen. However it is now clear that Lord Veblen would not have been lured into any incautious invasion of Sharlac's border, well aware that militia and mercenaries were ready to fall upon his forces. However it is widely believed that Carluse was preparing to follow the defence of Losand with a full-scale invasion of Sharlac, intending to cite this assault as provocation and justification.

The loss of Veblen, an able military commander much respected by the Carluse militia, put paid to such plans. His death has severely limited Carluse options. Duke Garnot knows he would be ill-advised to take the field himself until his noble heir, Lord Ricart, attains sufficient age and experience to rule with his father's firm hand, should Duke Garnot himself suffer injury or worse.

Relations between Carluse and Marlier remain tense, according to merchants engaged in shipping goods down the river Rel. Certain Caladhrian lords on the west bank of the Rel have reportedly warned Duke Carluse that any attempt to restrict trade or increase levies on river vessels while they travel between Abray and Marlier's border will incur their deep displeasure.

Rumours persist of threats of Caladhrian support should mercenary forces retained by Duke Ferdain of Marlier launch an incursion to secure both banks of the Rel all the way from Abray to the sea in the interests of open and secure commerce. Fortunately, there is no sign that any such attack is contemplated.

Duchess Tadira continues to promote close ties between Carluse interests and her brother Duke Orlin of Parnilesse. There is nothing to confirm or refute rumours of any greater understanding with Triolle.

Relations with Duke Secaris of Draximal remain cool given Draximal's long-standing alliance with Sharlac in order to deny Carluse control over The Great West Road. There have been reports that Duchess Tadira proposed a match between Lord Ricart and the eldest Lady of Draximal since Lord Jaras's death ended that bethrothal with Sharlac. It is widely believed that such an offer was soundly rebuffed.

Thus we can now discount Duchess Tadira's rumoured ambitions of securing the High King's crown for Lord Ricart through marriage alliances with Draximal and Triolle, her own ties with Parnilesse and the military defeat of Sharlac which would leave Marlier too isolated to oppose Carluse hegemony.

Sharlac shows no sign of resuming its military adventures against Carluse. If there was truly a plan to advance Sharlac's boundary to the eastern bank of the Palat river while Caladhrian forces advanced across the river Rel to seize the land running up to the Palat's western bank, that has most assuredly been abandoned since the battle of Losand.

It is now beyond doubt that Duke Moncan had no knowledge of Lord Jaras's participation and would never have permitted it, had he known. He would never have exposed his heir to such danger, even for the sake of luring pursuing Carluse forces back across the border and into ambush.

Since that abortive campaign, Sharlac militia forces have been much reduced and are little in evidence beyond maintaining the peace of The Great West Road. Duke Moncan has reduced his retained mercenary force to numbers merely sufficient to garrison the castle and town of Sharlac itself.

Duke Moncan has been living largely in seclusion since the death of his heir Lord Jaras and is believed to be dedicating himself to the education of his younger son Lord Kerlin.

There is no evidence of increased ties or commerce between Sharlac and Triolle following the wedding of Litasse, Lady of Sharlac, to Triolle's heir apparent. It would seem this match was merely one of family affection, arranged between the Duchess of Sharlac and her brother Duke Gerone, late of Triolle.

Triolle has seen a peaceful transition from the astute rule of the much lamented Duke Gerone to the unproven hands of his son Duke Iruvain. The youthful duke has done little of note thus far beyond reducing expenditure on mercenary forces, apparently in order to present a less belligerent aspect to Marlier on his western border and Parnilesse on his east, given his father's quarrels with both.

Such a reduction in readiness to bear arms might be considered unwise given Draximal's historic ambitions to annex land up to and including the silver-bearing hills on Triolle's north-eastern flank. There is no indication of such ambition at present, possibly because recent reports agree the mines are all but exhausted. Reduced income may be why Triolle is currently relying on seasonal militia drafts for patrols and garrisons along the border with Draximal.

Bridges and ferries across the rivers Dyal and Anock continue to be maintained at Triolle's expense. There is no sign of the increased river trade that Duke Gerone hoped to promote. It is believed the dukes of Marlier, Draximal and Parnilesse all made it clear to Duke Iruvain that encouraging any trade that would lead to a diminution of commerce along the rivers Rel, Drax and Asilor would incur their grave displeasure. Marlier and Parnilesse continue to dominate all coastal trade along the Gulf of Lescar.

There is no indication thus far of any child issuing from Duke Iruvain's wedding to Duchess Litasse. The succession remains secure through Lord Roreth, though rumours of his betrothal to one of the younger Ladies of Carluse remain unproven. This would be a prudent match. Carluse assistance would be vital if Triolle were to withstand any Draximal incursions or become the battleground for some resumption of old hostilities between Marlier and Parnilesse.

Marlier shows no sign of increased hostility to Parnilesse or Triolle. The previous alliance with Sharlac to attack Carluse from both north and south has been abandoned. Duke Ferdain's attention has turned entirely to the west. He is currently active in promoting trade up and down the river Rel, facilitating a boom in shipping between Abray and Relshaz. His relations with both the Relshazri magistrates, the Caladhrian lords on the western bank of the Rel and the guild masters of Abray remain excellent, to their mutual profit.

This is doubtless in no small part due to the numbers of Marlier exiles living in such places and all along the trading routes throughout Ensaimin. Remittances from such exiles continue to alleviate the poverty that their families still in Marlier would otherwise have to endure.

Dues and tolls paid along the river Rel enable Marlier to retain considerable numbers of mercenaries. Under the command of Ridianne the Vixen, these troops effectively curb Carluse ambitions along their common border. They also keep the peace in those riverside camps where unsworn mercenaries from across Lescar gather for rest and recuperation and customarily seek winter shelter. Rumours persist that Caladhrian lords pay Marlier to ensure such mercenaries do not cross the Rel to plunder their lands. This remains unproven.

It is beyond doubt that Caladhrian lords and merchants continue to profit from selling supplies to the mercenary camps, as well as from buying raw materials from Marlier and the rest of Lescar. They then return the finished goods that the disruptions and uncertainties of life prevent the Lescari from making for themselves.

Parnilesse interests continue closely involved with the noble houses of Tormalin who hold lands across the river Asilor on their eastern border, most notably the princes of Den Breche and D'Otadiel. Parnilesse exiles continue to strengthen such ties and to support their relatives still living under Duke

Orlin's rule. Tormalin merchants remain able to buy materials and sell their wares in Parnilesse under extremely favourable terms.

However Parnilesse pre-eminence as Tormalin's principal trading partner may soon be challenged by Draximal. Duke Secaris's envoys have been negotiating with the princes of Den Haurient, Den Breche and D'Otadiel.

Duke Orlin's ability to counter this threat to his Tormalin trade has been hampered by unrest within Parnilesse's own borders. Hostile pamphlets are appearing once again in all the ports and principal markets. Letters are nailed to shrine doors at night repeating the old calumny that the dowager duchess poisoned the late duke. Now the rabble-rousers are asserting that she did this with Duke Orlin's prior knowledge and full acquiescence. They cite the voluble dissatisfaction of the late duke's younger sons with the provision made for them on his deathbed as evidence of suspicions within the ducal family.

Duke Orlin has been using both mercenary companies and his own trained militiamen to suppress such rumour-mongering as well as paying handsome rewards to anyone identifying those responsible. All those discovered aiding and abetting the pamphleteers are closely questioned and flogged. The rabble-rousers themselves suffer far harsher penalties. There are rumours that the mercenaries of the coastal enclave of Carif have been selling prisoners to slavers trading with Aldabreshin warlords. Duke Orlin is inevitably accused of tacit connivance in this vile practice.

The princes of Tormalin are concerned both by the persistence of such accusations and the evident disunity between Duke Orlin and his brothers. There are indications that lords with border holdings are looking more favourably on trade with Draximal as a consequence.

Draximal is intent on making up losses of tolls thanks to the reduced trade along the Great West Road by increasing its trade with Tormalin. Ducal envoys are known to have visited the junior princes of many noble houses holding lands along Tormalin's western border.

This past winter, the Duchess of Draximal paid extended visits to the principal residences of the Den Haurient, Den Breche and D'Otadiel families, accompanied by her elder daughters. A marriage alliance with a cadet branch of the Den Breche family is widely expected.

Since this will clearly provoke Parnilesse resentment, Duke Secaris continues to maintain significant mercenary forces along his southern border. Vassal lords in northern Parnilesse accuse these companies of raiding their lands as well as skirmishing with mercenaries retained by their own duke in pursuit of private quarrels of their own. The danger of such conflict breaking into open warfare remains potent.

Draximal trained militias regularly patrol his borders with Triolle and with Carluse. Duke Secaris remains suspicious of Duke Garnot's ambitions despite the current lull in hostilities between Carluse and Sharlac.

There have been rumours of Draximal forces encroaching into Sharlac territory to deter raids from Dalasorian clansmen. This has prompted much indignation among the vassal lords of eastern Sharlac but there has been no response from Duke Moncan.

CHAPTER ONE

Tathrin

**The City of Vanam, Northern Ensaimin,
Spring Equinox Festival, Third Day, Evening**

HE STOOD STILL in the midst of the chaos. Fear threw his wits into utter confusion, robbing his legs of any strength.

"Make way! Make way!"

Voices bellowed, brutal with panic. Festival garlands of green leaves and spring flowers were knocked from doors and cornices to be crushed underfoot.

Sweat beaded Tathrin's forehead. His heart was racing, breath catching painfully in his throat. He felt as if he were choking.

This was how it had been when the gutters had run red and the agonies of the dying had echoed around the houses. Their cries had mingled with the murderous exultation of their assailants, so it was impossible to know which way to run for safety, or which way would take you straight onto the killers' sword-points.

Men and women, old and young, fought blindly to outstrip the others. There was simply no escape from the fleeing crowd confined between the tall wood and brick houses. Screams of pain pierced the hubbub. Tathrin saw a burly man trip on a loose cobblestone and fall to be trampled by uncaring boots.

A glimpse of a woman's stockings, petticoats hitched high as she jumped over the fallen man, recalled the dreadful sights he'd seen. The sobbing girl cradling the half-severed head of her lover, her brother or merely some friend. Whoever he had been, her skirts were sodden with his lifeblood, her bare legs exposed for all to see.

Hooves scraped on the cobbles. Horsemen were coming.

He'd seen what mounted warriors could do. Riding down the helpless and unarmed townsfolk, slashing at unprotected heads and shoulders with their heavy swords. Driving their frenzied steeds to trample those lying injured in the open. The leader's white mount had been splashed with so much blood it had looked like a painted sorrel.

He had to move. Blindly struggling, he fought his way up the sloping street, away from the approaching riders. A vicious elbow dug into his ribs and a hob-nailed shoe scraped down his anklebone, the sudden pain excruciating.

The only way to escape their murderous rampage was to find some recess too deep for their swords to reach, some alleyway so narrow that even their whip-scarred horses would baulk at entering it.

Dread lending strength to his already impressive height, Tathrin forced a path to the dubious shelter offered by the overhang of a house's upper floors. As soon as he reached it, though, he regretted the choice. Now he was trapped, the carved wood of the frontage digging painfully into his back.

"Saedrin save us!"

Two women shrieked hysterically, grabbing for their children as the swirling confusion of the crowd threatened to tear them apart. One of them, a little maid, wailed, her festival dress torn and fouled. Tathrin would have gone to help them but he couldn't move, crushed as he was against the building.

Saedrin had saved precious few before. The mounted mercenaries had shown the shrine of even the greatest of gods no respect. Throwing blazing torches in among those who'd vainly sought shelter there, the murderous scum had slammed the door and barred it shut. Every last person inside had died, their charred corpses crushed amid the funeral urns of their forebears when the shrine's roof had collapsed.

He heard a horse's whinny rise above some bestial noise halfway between a snarl and a squeal.

"Fair festival and Trimon's grace, if you please." A robust townsman and his wife, both too stout and too canny to succumb to unnecessary alarm, pushed past, arms linked as they made their way composedly up the street.

Others who'd been braving the muck of the cobbles joined those crowding the paved walk in front of shops and taverns. Tathrin finally saw what was happening.

"Make way for Talagrin's hunters!"

Cheerful voices shouted appeals in the hunting god's name. Their exuberant horns were deafening.

"Go shit on your own doorstep!" a surly householder shouted from an upper window, prompting laughter and agreement from the crowd.

A half-grown russet pig was running up the sloping street, two men on horses harrying it with lances. Already bleeding from gashes on its shoulders and hindquarters, the infuriated beast was unable to decide where to attack first.

"Get back! Get back!"

Budding sprigs of ash pinned to their tunics, hunters on foot rushed up to level sturdier spears and make an impromptu barrier between the infuriated beast and the jostling crowd. Others stood ready, their broad blades pointing downwards.

"You kill the beast and welcome, but don't you leave blood and guts spread all over here," a stern matron warned belligerently from her doorstep, "bringing rats and dogs to plague us!"

Some onlookers were cheering. More were still doing their best to leave the perilous hunt behind. Even a young pig could inflict murderous injuries.

Squealing with fury, the pig lunged, only for the nearest sweating horse to dance nimbly aside. The second hunter took his chance and stabbed at the pig's rump. The tormented beast whirled around, screaming with ear-splitting ferocity. The hunter wrenched his mount's head sideways to urge it out of the way. Bloody foam dripped from the horse's mouth as it half-jumped, half-stumbled on the slippery cobbles. The first hunter dug his spurs into his steed's sweating flanks. As the pig charged, he drove his lance deep between its neck and its bristling shoulders.

A cheer of relief went up as the pig fell, thrashing and squealing. One of the foot-hunters hurried up to dispatch the hapless animal with a thrust to the heart.

"Fair festival!" The first hunter waved his bloody lance exuberantly. "Fresh meat for the paupers' feast at the shrine of Ostrin!"

The cheers grew more enthusiastic as the crowd flowed back into the street.

Tathrin didn't feel the carved wooden post digging into his shoulder. He wasn't hearing the hunters' congratulations. Shrieks and curses and dying pleas still echoed in his ears. The scent of men's lives spilled out across a little town's market square filled his nostrils, not the mingled sweat and perfumes of this sprawling city's holiday crowd.

Instead of the hunters' jerkins bright with new ash leaves, Tathrin saw ragged leather tunics and chain mail clotted with muck and blood. He had cowered behind a stinking privy as the riders had passed by. Stained rags bound gashes on their arms, their legs, even their heads, but none of them seemed to care. All with their naked swords still gory in their hands, any one of them would still have killed him as soon as look at him. All he had been able to do was hide like a frightened child.

"Tathrin! Stay there, lad!"

Master Wyess's triangular black velvet cap headed towards him, fighting against the flow of people. If Wyess was a head shorter than Tathrin, he was broader in the shoulder and made short work of clearing a path.

At least being taller than most meant he was easy to spot in a crowd, Tathrin thought numbly. But he could not have moved even if no one had been standing in his way. Recollection of that earlier slaughter still paralysed him.

"Come on, lad, let's try a different route." The burly merchant puffed as he reached him.

Tathrin clenched his fists to stop his hands shaking. Why had this hunt brought back memories he'd taken such pains to stifle? He hadn't even dreamed of that appalling day for more than a year.

"No harm done and that's one less hog menacing the streets." Wyess's voice slowed, concerned. "Lad? Are you all right? You're as white as my lady's linen."

"Yes." Tathrin cleared his throat. "Yes, Master. I'm fine."

"Let's get there before all the good wine's drunk, then." Wyess urged him back down the sloping street.

Tathrin was about to ask why they were retracing their steps. Belatedly he saw that the way ahead was blocked by the hunters and their horses. Some of the householders had emerged to castigate the men trying to lash the pig's trotters together before slinging it on a spear for carrying triumphantly away. As he turned and followed Wyess, he swallowed, trying to ease the dryness in his throat. The shivers running down his back were slow to fade.

He looked up. With every storey of Vanam's tall houses built out further into the streets than the one below, only the barest strip of twilight sky was visible above. Torches already burned in nearby brackets. With the Lesser Moon absent and the Greater Moon rapidly shrinking through its last handful of days, this festival's nights were dark ones. The flames struck a gleam from the golden brooch on Master Wyess's hat.

"This way." Wyess caught Tathrin's elbow to draw him into an alleyway. There was no gainsaying him. The merchant was still strong enough to wrestle the barrels of furs in his warehouse should the need arise.

The cutting between two buildings might originally have been wide enough for two men to pass each other. Now Tathrin found his shoulders brushing plastered walls on both sides where the wooden-framed houses had warped and settled so closely together over the generations.

They reached a small courtyard with darkened windows looking down on three sides. In a door's recess on the far side, Tathrin saw shadows surround a candle lantern. Pewter clinked and a girl's giggles gave the lie to her coy protests. Not love, just festival's passing pretence of devotion. Such sweet nonsense wouldn't silence the echoes of distant death still ringing in Tathrin's head. He knew. He'd tried.

"Still got your purse and your ring?" Wyess pounded loudly on a solid wooden gate set in the wall on the fourth side of the courtyard. "Mind them both. The city's full of thieves at festival and any number could be drinking in here."

That prosaic reminder recalled more immediate concerns. Tathrin felt the solid silver of his scholar's ring secure on his finger and the discreet lump of his purse belted not merely inside his doublet but within his shirt. "Yes, sir."

A hatch in the wooden gate slid open. "Who's knocking?" someone growled in the darkness beyond.

"Lastel Wyess."

"Fair festival to you, Master."

The unseen voice turned cheery and Tathrin heard the bolts withdrawn.

"Come to drink Raeponin's health?" A grizzled man with a hefty cudgel opened the gate.

"Not tonight." Wyess shook a coin out of his glove and tossed it to the porter. "My compliments to Master Avin, but we're just cutting through."

As Tathrin followed Wyess through the narrow garden and into a paved yard, the damp scents of brick and soil were the closest he'd come to a breath of fresh air all day. The quiet after the cacophony of the festival streets prompted happier memories of peaceful days at home. He gathered his wits, resolutely setting aside the pig's death and the unwelcome recollections it had forced on him. "Master, where are we?"

"Taking the back way into the Dancing Stoat." Wyess laid a hand on the latch of a door. "Start learning your way around the back alleys of the lower town." He turned to wag a finger at him. "Make some friends among the lesser classes, especially among our countrymen. I'm relying on you."

"I know, Master." Tathrin found it ironic. He'd spent two years striving to soften his Lescari accent, finding it so often disdained by the university's mentors. Then he had completed his studies and been forced to look for employment, and his despised birthplace had proved to be as much of an asset in Wyess's eyes as his proficiency with mathematics.

Although Wyess's own voice no longer betrayed his Lescari origins. Did he ever think of whatever family he had left behind? Tathrin wondered. Did he recall the constant fear and uncertainty? The quarter days when paying the ducal levies meant everyone going hungry to bed? There were no festival feasts for paupers in Lescar.

But who was he to judge Wyess? How many days went past when he barely spared a thought for his own mother and father, for his sisters? Ashamed, Tathrin hurried through the busy kitchen after the merchant.

The noise in the vast taproom struck him like a physical blow. Every conversation seemed to be trying to outdo the ones on either side. Rune stones were cast in trios across the scarred tables, gamblers shouting blessings to Halcarion or pained laments that the fickle goddess's favour had deserted them.

"Fair festival! Come and join us!" Cries of delight from all sides greeted Wyess. Gesturing hands invited him to sit, brandished flagons slopping incautious ale.

"Fair dealings and Raeponin's blessings!"

As far as Tathrin could see, Wyess acknowledged every hail with a cheery smile and a wave. The merchant didn't slow, though, as he threaded through the crowded tables and benches. They soon emerged onto the wide thoroughfare in front of the tavern.

Tathrin took a moment to orientate himself. As the lower town sprawled around the great lake's margin, it wasn't always easy to see the slope of the land towards the water. It had been much simpler when he was living in the upper town. Streets either had to scale the undulating hills or bridge the steep gullies between them.

"That's saved us fighting through the crush around Misaen's shrine," Wyess said with satisfaction, straightening his hat, "but you do need to visit the booksellers before the end of festival. Buy a good book of maps and start making notes in it. A sound one, mind. The cheap ones are only good for wiping your arse."

"Yes, Master." Tathrin focused resolutely on the challenges that lay ahead this evening. He mustn't let anyone think him a fool, even if his two years at the university hadn't given him half the knowledge he was going to need in Master Wyess's fur-trading business.

These first two days in the merchant's employ had already taught him that much.

How could Vanam's scholars be so wilfully ignorant? Granted, they grudgingly respected their rival university in the southern city-state of Col and acknowledged some of the learned societies in Selerima and Drede. Beyond that, the mentors largely ignored the towns threaded along the high roads. Unless one of them happened to be the birthplace of some particularly notable scholar.

Whereas even the junior clerks in Wyess's counting-house could list every trader's speciality, not just in the major towns like Peorle and Drede, but in every remote corner of this vast region between the western forests and those countries to the east that had once made up the long-fallen Old Tormalin Empire. At least, that's what it felt like to Tathrin. Furthermore, as they laboured for the master merchants, those apprentices so scorned by the scholars of the upper town learned to cannily negotiate the complex web of obligation and alliance connecting the Guilds in Vanam with trading partners everywhere. And how to judge the likely outcome of a prospective business deal.

At least that was something Tathrin had learned from his father. A good innkeeper gets the measure of a man inside a few moments. But he was starting to wish he'd had the leisure to spend more time in the lower town when he was studying at the university. Then he might not have felt at such a disadvantage at that moment.

"Write down everything you've heard when we get home tonight, before you go to sleep." Wyess shot Tathrin a glance as a coach rattled past. "We'll discuss your notes tomorrow and I'll tell you what you've missed."

"Thank you." Tathrin recalled one of the other clerks assuring him that Wyess would examine him as closely as any of the mentors he'd studied under. Only the merchant's tests could happen at any time, not just at the quarter-year festivals, and mostly without notice.

As they crossed the high road something stung him sharply on the cheek. As he slapped a startled hand to his face, more pale missiles pattered on his chest and fell to the ground.

"Enough!" Wyess waved a hand at some giggling boys clutching lengths of reed. He chuckled as he tossed them a handful of halved and quartered pennies. "I take it there are no rains of peas at this season back home."

"No one would be so wasteful," Tathrin said curtly. Nor could anyone afford to discard cut-pieces, even if the Vanamese scorned tokens of such slight value.

Wyess halted and laid a hand on the younger man's arm. "Have you truly never come down to the lower town for any festival?"

"No, Master, on my honour." Tathrin cleared his throat. "The university prefects advise students to keep to the upper town."

"Short of a riot that gives them the excuse to lock the citadel gates, they can hardly insist." Wyess regarded Tathrin for a moment. "So you were a student who abided by the prefecture's wishes." He started walking again, chuckling. "That must make you as rare as a fox with no taste for ducks."

"I travelled home for any festival I could." Which was true, even if he'd only ever got home for Winter Solstice. It took him all year to save up the price of a seat on a courier's coach.

The merchant nodded. "Ah, yes, of course you'd want to see your family."

Tathrin hoped the shadows hid the colour rising from his collar. He didn't like being less than honest with Wyess, but telling him the full truth would mean questions, and avoiding awkward answers could mean lying outright and he really didn't want to do that.

"Scented hair powders." As the street broadened into a marketplace, peddlers eased their laden trays through the crowds. Horns and drums sounded above the din of the milling throng, different tunes rising and falling, competing with exuberant snatches of song.

"Ribbons and combs." A huckster planted herself in front of Wyess. Her hair was ornately dressed to display the wares in her basket. "A fairing for your lady?"

"Not today," Wyess said courteously.

Tathrin recalled the other clerks' gossip as they combed their hair and polished their shoe-buckles. If he'd thought they might envy him, the newcomer, for having this duty as Master Wyess's attendant tonight, he'd soon learned different. The other clerks had very different amusements in mind. His gaze followed the huckster as she accosted another prospective customer.

"Ribbons and combs is all that she's selling, in case you're wondering," Wyess commented. "If you're fancying a touch of lace, don't go looking for it on the streets, especially not at festival time. I can introduce you to an accommodation house with nice clean girls."

"No, Master." Embarrassed, Tathrin tried to explain. "I was just thinking I might buy some ribbons for my sisters."

He should have thought of that sooner, he chided himself. If he hadn't been so wrapped up in moving from his old lodging in the upper town to his new place in Master Wyess's counting-house.

Wyess didn't hear him, intent on pressing on. They soon reached the portico of the largest hall on the far side of the marketplace.

"Timing is the key to so many matters of trade, my lad." The fur merchant looked up with satisfaction as the bells in the tower united to proclaim the first of the night's ten hours. "Arrive too early at a gathering and people will think you don't have enough business to occupy your time. Arriving late smacks of disorganisation, and no explanation for that will do you any credit."

He shrugged to settle his mossy green mantle on his shoulders and smoothed the sable fur trimming the front. His amiable face turned serious.

"Now, lad, this gathering will be mostly those of us with Lescari blood. As a rule, we've left all those quarrels behind us, but sometimes wine reminds a man of old grudges. Think before you speak, and don't give too much of yourself away."

"Yes, Master." Tathrin tugged at the hem of his new grey doublet to make sure it hadn't ridden up to reveal his well-worn shirt.

The gates to the lower floors were all locked, the storerooms where visiting merchants could warehouse their goods securely barred. Only the stairway to the upper hall was open. A handful of Furriers' Guild servants waited by the door, warming their hands over a blazing fire-basket.

"Master Wyess, Raeponin grant you fair festival." The steward bowed low before studying Tathrin. "And this is...?"

Tathrin noted the quarterstaffs propped just inside the door. These men were ready to deter anyone keen to sample the Guild's hospitality without an invitation.

"Tathrin Sayron, newly accepted into my counting-house," Wyess said with satisfaction. "A scholar sealed by the university this last Winter Solstice."

"Master Scholar." The steward inclined his head.

"Fair festival to you." Tathrin bowed.

Wyess started up the stairs as a coach drew to a halt behind them. "Right, let's see who's already here."

Tathrin took a deep breath and followed.

CHAPTER TWO

Tathrin

The Furriers' Guildhall, in the City of Vanam, Spring Equinox Festival, Third Day, Evening

MOST OF THE merchants invited to this festival gathering apparently shared Wyess's opinion about arriving nicely to time. As Tathrin reached the top of the broad stair opening onto the long hall, he saw that four other men and two shrewd-faced women had also just arrived. They were still handing their cloaks and gloves to their own attendants.

"Shall I take your hat, Master?"

"No, we'll only forget to fetch it back at the end of the evening. Why do you think I said not to bother with a cloak?" Wyess was scanning the room. "Let's see what we can learn before dinner's served."

If Wyess hadn't told him this was an occasion for the Lescari living in the city to gather together, Tathrin would hardly have known it. All were dressed in Vanam fashions, few of the overlapping conversations betraying accents learned elsewhere.

As the merchant headed purposefully for a trio of richly dressed men, one of their attendants whispered in his master's ear. The man broke off from whatever he was saying. "Wyess, it's good to see you."

"Fair festival, Malcot. How's business in the cloth trade?" Wyess smiled and bowed, so Tathrin did the same.

The first merchant shrugged russet shoulders, his broadcloth mantle embroidered with scarlet. "Ask me when I know how many customers haven't settled their accounts by the fifth day of festival."

"Garvan, Kierst, fair festival." Wyess looked at the other two men. "Any news you care to share?"

"I hear the ice has broken above Ferile," a thin-faced individual in a black velvet robe observed.

Tathrin knew he must remember that. It meant that the first boatloads of raw skins would be coming down the river from the mountains. The stink of tanning and curing would soon hang over the city, reaching even the university's lofty halls when the wind was in the wrong quarter.

"There's talk of another levy for repairs on the roads around Hanchet, Trimon curse it." The third man scowled. "Why aren't the Hanchet Guilds bearing the cost? That's what I'd like to know."

"Spend a penny to earn a gold mark." Malcot the cloth merchant was philosophical. "We can't shift our goods if our wagons can't roll."

"We smiths will be paying," the black-gowned man agreed.

So the man was a smith, but all manner of metal working was done in the city. What exactly was his trade, and what was his name? Tathrin tensed as he realised he didn't remember it from Master Wyess's greeting. He listened more closely.

"You can afford to, Garvan. You and Malcot make more profit than Wyess and I do with furs, wagon weight for wagon weight." The dissatisfied man sniffed. "I shall be voting against it."

His long nose was red with the thread-like veins that Tathrin's father had warned him indicated an unwise drinker. He'd note that down against this man's name. Kierst, he remembered that one.

"You get the better bargain trading towards Selerima, Wyess," the disgruntled fur trader continued. "More than any of us who trade to the south and west. All those towns along the East Road know it's in their best interests to keep the highway in good repair."

"Wine, masters?" A Guild servant proffered a tray of goblets.

Tathrin waited to see the other three attendants each take one before doing so himself. As Wyess drank, Tathrin merely moistened his own lips. He wondered how he might go about learning the names of the other merchants' attendants since they evidently weren't going to be introduced.

"Aldabreshin glass." Garvan, the black-clad smith who'd heard that the mountain rivers were flowing again, studied the elegant goblet. "Does anyone know what the Guilds of Col are planning to do about those accursed corsairs plaguing the Caladhrian coast? I had a half-share in a cargo that left the Archipelago last Summer Solstice. It was lost somewhere, never to be seen again."

Tathrin listened carefully. He thought the smith was from Lescar, but whatever dialect coloured his words was so faint as to be unidentifiable.

"I hear the Justiciars are issuing licences to any privateer who can round up a ship and a crew," Wyess commented. "There's rumour the Guilds are planning to approach the Archmage, to ask him to send wizards to defend their waters."

"You don't have much to worry about," sniffed Kierst, the fur merchant who was so unhappy with the notion of a road levy. "No corsair ship has ever yet come as far north as Col and that's as far south as you trade." He raised his glass and drained it.

Tathrin wondered how much the man had already drunk that evening. His accent wasn't Lescari, nor yet of Vanam. Was he from one of the unschooled city-states like Friern, to which the university paid little heed for all the volume of their commerce?

"Rumour?" Garvan shook his head, his black hair sleek with perfumed oil. "I'll believe in wizards getting their hands dirty when I see it."

Malcot, the russet-clad cloth merchant, was more hopeful. "This Archmage has interested himself in mainland affairs more than most of his predecessors. He might be persuaded it's in everyone's interests to send those corsairs to the depths. Let them explain themselves to Dastennin." He lifted his glass in a salute to the god of the sea.

"I'll gladly see them all drowned," Wyess agreed. "But even if the Guilds ask, I cannot see Archmage Planir breaking with so many generations of tradition and sanctioning the use of magic against them."

Kierst the other furrier was still aggrieved. "The Guilds of Col will squeeze as much coin as they can out of us to cover whatever costs they claim to be bearing to ward off these corsairs. Why aren't the

Caladhrian lords unlocking their strongboxes to buy in some mercenaries?"

"The coastal lords would hire in swords and ships readily enough," Malcot the cloth merchant protested, "but they cannot do anything without a majority vote and a decree sealed by that parliament of theirs."

"While the inland lords won't agree to financing ships they don't need," Garvan the smith observed.

"So they carry on as they have done for countless generations," Kierst scoffed. "No individual lord will undertake anything of substance on his own initiative because they're all bound by their oaths to Ostrin and Drianon to uphold harmony and unity." He snapped his fingers to attract a lackey with a tray of full goblets. "Hidebound and hobbled, more like. Fools and farmers, the lot of them."

At least if all the Caladhrian lords do is talk, Tathrin thought bleakly, it keeps them from fighting each other.

Malcot was clearly thinking along similar lines. "Your dukes of Lescar and their endless quarrels are all the warning the Caladhrians need of the dangers of uncontrolled dissent among their lords."

That remark merely confirmed Tathrin's initial conclusion that the cloth merchant was Vanam, born and bred.

He watched the Guild servants covering trestle tables with snowy linen cloths, bringing out the first of the rich dishes. The merchants would be feasting on rabbit and bacon pies, braised fowl, minced mutton, artichoke hearts stewed with beef marrow, cinnamon wine-sops and apple fritters.

His father and the guildmasters back home might share a bottle of wine over a dish of stewed herring, if they had managed to save some coin after paying their spring rents. They couldn't vote on the need for road repairs. If they didn't pay up, the dukes would send their militias to collect the coin. Or worse, sell the right to collect the levy to some mercenary band who would ransack houses and break open strongboxes and seize whatever silver they found over and above the sums owed.

Tathrin regarded the freshly garlanded statue of Talagrin at the far end of the hall with dislike. The Furriers' Guild might honour the god of the wild places but Tathrin couldn't forget how many mercenaries claimed his sanction for their abuses. Had the sight of Talagrin's tokens on the men hunting the lower town's feral pigs sparked such hateful memories? he wondered.

"Caladhrians." Kierst drained his second glass and handed it to his silent attendant. "When it's *our* wagons left with broken axles and *our* horses lamed by ruts in the Great West Road, they're so sorry but they cannot make repairs without the vote of their parliament. Come the turn of For-Autumn, when their cattle are fat and their fields and vineyards are ripe for harvest, they're quick enough to find the money."

"It's a good thing wheat and cattle don't need the parliament's permission to thrive," Garvan commented dryly.

That prompted a laugh from Wyess and Malcot and dutiful smiles from the other merchants' attendants.

Tathrin struggled to match their expressions. These people mocked the Caladhrians but that wouldn't curb the trade each merchant did with Caladhrian lords. The guildmasters and merchant families of

Ensaimin's greatest cities of Col, Vanam and Selerima didn't much like each other. They didn't have to. They all knew the value of cooperation as surely as they knew the value of every coin struck in each different city's mint.

Which is why these people can waste peas and beans on children's festival games, Tathrin thought bitterly, instead of hoarding every last one for spring sowing and then praying their crop doesn't get crushed by a battle before summer's end.

If the dukes of Lescar could only set their differences aside, just for a while, surely they'd see how peace and trade could improve life for everyone, from highest to lowest?

"Does anyone have news about the state of the high road beyond Caladhria?" Wyess asked casually. "Or the current relations between Lescar's dukes?"

"You're looking eastwards?" Garvan studied him with raised brows. "Thinking of expanding your trade into Tormalin?"

Wyess smiled easily. "It never hurts to keep one's ears open."

"And one's options." The black-gowned smith nodded. "I hear some ill-feeling boiled up between Draximal and Parnilesse over the winter. Though I've yet to hear any two explanations that agree."

"Do you think it'll come to anything?" Malcot was interested. "My cousins made a handsome profit a few years back lending Duke Orlin of Parnilesse money to equip his militias."

"Did you hear how much the Silversmiths' Guild lost when they lent Duke Secaris of Draximal a chest of coin to pay his mercenaries?" Garvan countered. "When bandits stole it?"

Kierst shook his head belligerently. "I'll sell goods to any duke who pays me in Tormalin gold, but Lescar's no place to make money through speculation."

Tathrin did his best to keep his face expressionless. At least Parnilesse and Draximal were on the far side of Lescar, over towards the Tormalin Empire. Any fighting between those two dukedoms shouldn't come near his family in Carluse, which was closer to the Caladhrian border on the western side of Lescar. As long as Carluse's Duke Garnot didn't see some advantage to involving himself in the quarrel.

"It'll just be the same old nonsense over their claims to be High King," Kierst continued with loud contempt. "You might as well expect sense from hounds snapping over a mouldy bone."

Tathrin's jaw tightened with indignation. As he looked away, lest his expression betray his resentment to the other merchants' attendants, he noticed that the disgruntled furrier's loud voice was turning heads nearby.

"I wouldn't trust anything to the Great West Road. If you're looking to trade into Tormalin, Wyess, send your goods down the White River to Peorle. Have them carried across Caladhria by wagon, and then ship them down the Rel on sail-barges. The Relshazri will cut themselves a fat slice from your profits but it'll still be worth your while paying to get the goods onto a galley that can take them straight to Toremal."

What of the livelihoods of all those people, his own family included, who earned their bread by sheltering and supplying the travellers along the highway? Tathrin burned to ask Kierst that question.

"I don't think I'd send goods by that route," Garvan said thoughtfully. "If Parnilesse goes to war, mercenaries will flock to the ports all along the Lescari coast. The ones who can't find a captain to hire them often turn pirate."

Tathrin saw that one of the other merchants was listening intently. An older man, his bushy white brows were drawing together in a frown.

"Risk good furs on the road through Lescar and brigands will seize the lot." Kierst shook his head disdainfully. "Appeal to whichever duke supposedly rules the land where your goods were taken and he'll just throw up his hands, claiming it's nothing to do with him." He laughed without humour. "When the chances are better than even that the thieves were in his pay all along and he'll be selling your goods to line his own pockets."

"You can prove such accusations, Kierst?" The white-haired merchant strode over to poke a gnarled finger hard into the fur trader's chest. "You can introduce me to someone who's actually suffered such a loss and been scorned by a duke? Or is this merely one of your tales, some friend of a cousin's misfortune?"

"Everyone knows—" Kierst began feebly.

"No one knows," the white-haired merchant snapped before turning on Wyess. "You'll let him abuse our countrymen, will you? Not a word in defence of your Carluse blood?"

"Come now, Gruit." The philosophical cloth merchant raised placatory hands.

"Come now, Malcot," the white-haired merchant mocked. "You should be ashamed of yourself," he said with sudden savagery. "Is that all warfare in Lescar means to you? Opportunity to lend money for profit? Why not lend money to both Draximal and

Parnilesse and be certain of a good return, whoever wins? No need to concern yourself if the coin comes stained with blood. Innocent or guilty, water and lye will wash it off."

"No one wishes warfare on anyone," Garvan protested.

"No?" Incensed, Gruit rounded on him. "When half the Smiths' Guild keeps journeymen busy through the winter hammering out swords and spear-points? Selling wire to the mail-makers so they have a stock of hauberks ready and waiting? Don't you think there might be a year without fighting if you weren't so ready to sell blades and armour to whichever dukes Malcot and his cronies lend their coin to?"

The entire room fell silent as the last threads of other conversations died away. Everyone stared at the white-haired merchant.

"Have you nothing to say for yourselves?" Gruit challenged them all. "I hope you have some answer when Saedrin calls you to account at the doors to the Otherworld!"

"What's it to you if Draximal and Parnilesse go to war?" Kierst rallied. "You're from Marlier."

"What of it?" Gruit picked a stony-faced man out of the gathering with a jab of his forefinger. "You were born in Draximal. And you—' he fixed another individual with a ferocious glare "—how many brothers did you leave in Carluse?" His probing finger found another target, and another, and another. "Your wife's from Triolle, isn't she? As were your mother and father. You, you've one grandsire from Sharlac and the other from Parnilesse."

He turned his wrath on the whole gathering. "How many of you acknowledge the blood that runs through your heart or in the veins of the wife who tends your hearth, who bore your children? You wrap yourself in Vanam cloth and muffle your true voices. Have you no pride? Have you no honour? Our fine guests here joke about Lescari folly and Lescari thieves and you show your teeth in a meek little smile. You should be snarling!"

He waved at the waiting banquet, spitting with fury.

"Am I the only one sick to my stomach of festival gatherings where we sit on our fat arses and cuddle our fat purses? Have you no feeling for your kith and kin who can only fear the lengthening days as the year turns to Aft-Spring? Will For-Summer bring armies to plunder their crops again, militias to enlist their sons or mercenaries to despoil their daughters? Doesn't this fine white bread taste of bitter ashes when you know Caladhria's farmers will be giving thanks to Drianon this Spring Festival for last year's fine harvest? As they debate whether they'll earn more gold selling their wheat to the mercenary camps or to the dukes as they lure men to sign up for militia service to save their children from starvation."

Tathrin saw the whole gathering standing frozen, some faces appalled, more ashamed.

The old man continued before anyone could attempt a reply. "Whatever duke presumed to claim our allegiance when we were born, we all left such quarrels behind when we came to Vanam, to any of the cities across Ensaimin. For the love of whatever gods your beleaguered families cherish..." His voice cracked with anguish, tears standing in his faded eyes. "Can we not find a way to stop this strife that curses our unhappy homeland?"

The hall erupted. Anguished voices protested how often they sent coin to salve the worst hurts of warfare. Men and women insisted they offered friends and relatives a safe haven in times of trial, even securing apprenticeships for their sons and respectable marriages for their daughters.

His heart racing, Tathrin tried to pick out the most earnest faces. He did his utmost to find some distinguishing feature, some quirk of dress. An enamelled collar here, a fistful of diamond rings there—anything that might help him identify the men and women who seemed to be in fiercest agreement with the old man.

"Wyess, Garvan." The cloth merchant spread apologetic hands, colouring with embarrassment. "You know I hold you in the highest esteem—"

"Gruit's been drinking too much of his own wine," Kierst sneered. "Too much time on his hands since he buried his wife and married off his daughters."

To Tathrin's utter astonishment, Wyess spun around and knocked the long-nosed man clean off his feet with a single colossal punch.

Chapter Three

Karn

**Emirle Bridge, in the Dukedom of Draximal,
Spring Equinox Festival, Fourth Day, Morning**

"Why change horses here?" A thin-faced woman stepped down from her carriage with an angry flounce of her gown.

"This is the last town safely inside Draximal."

Karn didn't care if the harassed man with her was her steward or her husband. He was just pleased their argument was attracting everyone's attention. Chewing the last of his morning bread, he headed for the wide gate to leave the inn's stable yard unremarked.

"We must hire a team here to take us across the bridge," the hapless man explained. "Then we change horses in Tewhay."

He should just tell the shrew to shut up, Karn thought, and let him manage their journey.

"We're paying a day's hire for horses taking us three leagues?"

The woman's shrill outrage followed Karn into the road and he looked back over his shoulder. It was curious that someone should set out to travel between Draximal and Parnilesse and not know that the horse-masters at inns all along the highway refused to allow their beasts to cross the border. North and south, they condemned their counterparts as thieves and scoundrels with near-identical curses.

Perhaps he would wait until this coach arrived at the bridge before crossing on foot himself. Coaches attracted more attention from the guards. No one would waste time detaining him, with his ragged cloak and threadbare breeches, when they could be cozening money from someone richer. He felt discreetly inside his doublet to make sure his purse was safely hidden.

The high road through the town was deserted. Karn stepped around a fallen festival garland spattered with some incautious reveller's vomit. Broken earthenware was further evidence of the previous night's excesses. Karn smiled. The guards on the bridge would hardly wonder about him this early in the morning while Misaen's hammers were pummelling their heads.

Travelling over the five days of a festival weighed on both sides of the balance. With so few folk on the roads he could make much better speed. On the other hand, it was easier to go unnoticed just before the holiday actually started, while the world and his wife were hurrying home to make merry with family and friends.

He followed the curve of the road down towards the bridge, his thoughts returning to the inn yard. That old-fashioned coach had come a good distance. Karn's practiced eye told him that. Where were they going? The shrew hadn't been berating her escort for failing to reach their destination in time for the Spring Festival. Were they merchant stock or minor vassals of Duke Secaris of Draximal? The woman's dowdy dress meant nothing. Wealthy folk often travelled in such a disguise for fear of bandits on the wilder roads.

If he caught up with them again, he'd find some answers. Not from the woman. She looked like a hard, dry furrow to hoe, not the type to let secrets slip in pillow talk once a charming stranger had softened her up with skilled hands and practiced tongue. The man, though—he'd pour out his heart over a game of runes with a sympathetic stranger. Especially if that stranger made sure the poor fool cast the strongest runes more often than not. He probably hadn't seen Halcarion roll the bones in his favour since the day he'd met the shrew.

It would be good to have something to report to Master Hamare. All Karn had garnered on this journey so far was rumour and speculation, even if the self-appointed sages in Draximal Town were confident that Duke Secaris was going to enforce his claim to all the woodland and marshland of this oft-disputed region. They insisted his forces would push Duke Orlin's vassal lords back so far that Tewhay and Quirton would find their walls marking the border.

Sceptical, Karn had kept his eyes as well as his ears open as he'd travelled south. All around the stone-walled farmsteads, cows were being turned out to enjoy the new grass, sway-hipped heifers round-bellied with calves soon to come. Shepherds were cleaning out their huts in more remote pastures, ready for lambing. Cottagers were herding pigs into common fields left rough over the winter so that hungry snouts could begin breaking up the ground for pease planting.

He passed through the open gate in the town's wall and started down the slope to the river. The solid grey pillars of the fortified bridge cut the river into a skein of swirling silver threads. Each end was guarded by a squat tower and a taller fortification kept watch from the centre of the bridge. Two long, low boats heaped with sacks rode the flood towards the central span. Each was steered by a solitary figure with a stern oar and both were sunk deep in the water. Beyond, the high road continued along the embankment reaching out across the sprawling reed beds.

Common folk's lives depended on knowing which way the winds blew. If the same peaceable activity was evident in Parnilesse, it would take more than market-town gossip to convince Karn that either duke planned an attack. Would Master Hamare consider that good news or bad?

Galloping hooves scattered his thoughts as horses raced through the sleepy town. Karn sprang into the tangled grass by the side of the road and crouched low. He saw a company of armoured men reach the town gate. A militiaman, braver or more foolish than the rest, challenged them, waving his halberd. The first horseman swung his sword, cutting clean through the shaft to sever the man's head from his shoulders.

A maidservant standing close by screamed with horror as blood spattered her white apron. The first cries of alarm from whoever was keeping watch at the near end of the bridge down below were lost beneath the fearsome howls of the attackers. They spurred their horses fearlessly on down the sloping road. Bloody blades told Karn that more bodies lay behind them in the town.

He settled down to watch. Someone on the bridge managed to shut the gates. Men in Draximal livery were left outside to face this onslaught. Panicking, half of them turned to hammer on the wood instead of readying their weapons. Someone up on the battlements remembered his crossbow, but too late to kill more than one of the attackers' rearguard. He could only look down helplessly as his friends, inextricably mingled with the enemy, died with shrieks of pain and terror.

Was the town militia about to take on these brigands? Karn looked around for activity by the town gate or on the walls. There was no one to be seen. Who would have expected an attack in the middle of festival?

Turning back to the bridge, he saw that a second assault had been launched against the gatehouse on the far side. He suspected that the duke's men on that side of the bridge had managed to release their portcullis. Certainly the attackers hadn't broken through to the roadway. On this side, however, whoever had managed to shut the gate had failed to bar it. Between the guards seeking refuge and the attackers pursuing them, it was soon forced open.

What of the men holding the central tower that straddled the bridge, where the road passed through a wide archway? Thinking back to a previous journey along this road, Karn recalled the portcullises at either end of that passageway, ready to cut the bridge in half. If they could trap their foes between the gates' lethal confines, there were gratings in the roof. Defenders in the tower room above could drop murderous darts or pour boiling water onto whoever they trapped.

But he saw the fools rushing out of the tower onto the bridge. They deserved to die for such stupidity, he concluded.

Then he realised that quarrels from crossbows on the central tower's battlements were sending the militiamen sprawling across the hard-packed stones of the roadway. More were picking off the defenders atop either end tower rather than piercing the armoured assailants down below.

Downstream, there was no sign of the laden boats he'd seen passing beneath the bridge's central span. Karn laughed. He should have wondered who could send sacks of turnips to market at the end of a hungry winter. This armoured band must have hidden men beneath the sacking, and they'd snagged the underside of the bridge with grapnels. There must be some doorway down below by the waterline, some last escape for besieged defenders. It had been turned against them.

Now a crowd was gathering by the town gate. Demands that something be done were immediately challenged. Just what did they propose? Foolhardy exhortations that the townsfolk take up arms were swiftly scorned. A cry went up for the duke's reeve, heartily endorsed. The crowd stilled, expectant.

Karn settled himself more comfortably on the damp grass and waited to see what transpired. He'd definitely have something interesting to tell Master Hamare now.

The defenders on the far side of the bridge soon capitulated, only to be stripped and marched naked out onto the causeway. The militiamen captured on this side of the river suffered the same humiliation. The crowd shouted, urging them to run for the safety of the town walls. One bold man ran forward to offer the foremost a cloak. When he wasn't cut down by a crossbow bolt, others did the same.

Karn had no sympathy for the weeping youths who passed him, scarlet-faced and trying to hide their inadequate manhood with shaking hands. They were still alive.

Now the force who'd taken this tower began throwing the naked dead through the gate to lie tumbled on the muddy road. Wails went up from the crowd.

"Where's the reeve?" a militiaman bellowed, the hair on his chest and groin as grizzled as that on his head. "Where's Nuchel?"

"I'm here." A portly man, doublet unbuttoned over a stained shirt, forced his way through the crowd. His breeches flapped loose at the knee, yellow stockings drooping over his tarnished silver shoe-buckles.

"I have a message." The militiaman scowled. "Captain Arest of the Wyvern Hunters presents his compliments. Anyone who wishes to pass across the bridge is welcome to do so for the appropriate toll."

The reeve gaped. "What's the toll?"

The militiaman spat on the road. "Whatever they think you can pay."

"Mercenaries." The reeve trembled with fury. "Dastennin drown the filthy curs!"

Curses rose, lamentation and accusation. Karn ignored the clamour. Master Hamare would want to know who these mercenaries were and who was paying them.

How could he get close enough to pick up some hint? By crossing the bridge. He had to cross to get to Parnilesse anyway. Master Hamare would be most unimpressed if he turned tail and took the western route home to Triolle, through the hilly ground along Draximal's border.

He wasn't going to be the first offering himself up for the triumphant mercenaries to rob and abuse, though. Was there any sign of that battered coach with the two travellers from the inn? No. He'd bet good coin their horses were already being whipped back northwards.

Still, there would be local people trapped on the wrong side of the river. Labourers come to the town to revel with friends. Townsfolk who'd visited family farmsteads for more sober revelry now unable to return. Karn wrapped his tattered cloak around himself. He'd wait till sufficient folk gathered to get up the nerve to approach the bridge together. He could hide himself among their number.

While he waited, he watched the priest from the shrine to Dastennin lead a nervous gang of townsmen to pick up the dead. Once it was clear the mercenaries weren't going to retaliate, more men hurried to help drag the hurdles with their grisly burdens back up the slope. Women waited, sobbing piteously. Not such a fair festival for them, Karn thought distantly.

No mercenary came to retrieve their fallen comrade. The sentries on the tower didn't react when two townsmen, bolder than the rest, spat on the corpse and kicked it into the ditch. A man who'd had no true friends, Karn concluded, not even among the handful who'd shared a tent with him when they'd been tallied together on the muster roll. More fool him for riding with them.

The morning wore on. Karn ate some bread and leathery ham that he'd tucked in his cloak's pocket and began to contemplate other routes into Parnilesse. The ford at Reddock was half a day's walk upstream, but it would only take him to the high road running east. That was no good if he wanted to get back to Tri-olle as fast as possible.

Wheels rumbled on the cobbles. Karn turned his head. Was the dried-up woman so desperate to continue her journey that she'd ordered her downtrodden escort to face the mercenaries? No. The elegant carriage approaching was newly built in the latest Tormalin fashion and drawn by horses that would have cost more than the duke's reeve hereabouts took in dues every quarter day.

The coachman drew up and leaned down to talk to someone by the town gate. Karn watched him jump from his seat to explain the situation to whoever was travelling inside. Then the coachman climbed back up to his perch and reclaimed the reins from the lackey sitting with him. The throng withdrew respectfully. Instead of turning the carriage around, though, the coachman carefully directed his horses down the slope towards the bridge.

Seeing the coach forging ahead, a few men and women straggled after it. The bravest of those needing to cross the bridge, Karn guessed. Rising from his grassy seat, he tagged along, scuffing suitably reluctant feet.

Dawdling meant he got a good look at the fallen mercenary in the ditch. The dead man wore sturdy boots and buff breeches beneath a dull steel hauberk over a padded black jerkin. These mercenaries could afford to let valuable armour rust in a sodden drain.

Karn walked on towards the gate tower. The blue Draximal banner with its flaming fire-basket in red and gold had been hauled down. A creamy pennant replaced it, bearing a black wyvern hovering with clawed feet extended. The Wyvern Hunters. Karn hadn't heard the name before the captain's message had been repeated to the reeve.

They were a free company; that was the important thing. The screaming wyvern wasn't hovering above the Draximal brazier. Why would Duke Secaris send men to seize a bridge in his own territory, after all? But Karn wouldn't have been surprised to see the winged beast clutching the halberd or the long sword that crossed on Parnilesse's badge, or the oak garland that ringed them. Any one of those elements would have indicated that these mercenaries bent their necks to accept Duke Orlin's leash for the sake of the coin he paid to retain their services.

So this was nothing to do with Parnilesse. Karn unobtrusively quickened his pace as the elegant coach drew up to the gate tower.

"What toll do you propose to pay?" A solidly built mercenary stepped forward to talk to the coachman.

Karn didn't hear the man's reply. The mercenary frowned, snapping his fingers to summon someone else from inside the half-open gate. Along with everyone else, Karn watched with interest. Two yellow-headed men of less than common height emerged and he gasped with the rest. Such blond hair meant they were Mountain-born.

Uncommon, though not unheard of among mercenaries, he thought privately. Mountain Men were generally notable fighters and these two in particular carried themselves like practiced swordsmen. Anyone hoping to join this warband and choosing to prove their mettle against the shortest members would soon rue their mistake.

The two blond men approached the door of the coach. A neatly dressed maid opened it and the heavy-set mercenary gallantly offered his arm. She accepted it calmly and stepped down. There was someone else in the coach. The maid turned to say something and one of the Mountain Men laughed. Frustrated, Karn couldn't get close enough to hear.

The maidservant folded her hands demurely and placed a chaste kiss on the tallest Mountain Man's cheek. She almost had to stoop; he was barely her height.

The second Mountain Man stepped up smartly. Before the woman could object, he swept her into a close embrace, kissing her full on the lips.

"Trimon's teeth!" Outraged, the coachman rose to his feet and the carriage swayed alarmingly.

"Don't be a fool." The heavy-set mercenary half-drew his sword as a warning.

"Toll's paid." The first Mountain Man cuffed the second around the back of the head. "Drive on, with our compliments."

The second blond man released the girl, grinning widely. As soon as her hands were free, she slapped him as hard as she could. He just carried on smiling, despite the mark of her hand on his fair skin burning as red as her outraged blushes. Shaking his head, the heavy-set mercenary helped the girl back into the carriage. As soon as the gates to the bridge opened, the coachman whipped up the horses and drove on. Karn noted how perilously close the lash came to the shorter Mountain Man's head.

"They'd better not want kisses from me," a labourer beside him growled.

"Don't think you've got the looks for it," Karn commented.

These men might take a few liberties with pretty girls but everyone else would be paying with solid coin. If all they had was lead-weighted Lescari marks, they'd pay with whatever else they were carrying.

He had enough Tormalin silver in his everyday purse to satisfy them so that they wouldn't go looking for the gold hidden inside his shirt. As soon as he was safely in Parnilesse, he'd steal a swift horse and ride for home. Master Hamare would want to know all about this day's happenings.

CHAPTER FOUR

Tathrin

Master Wyess's Counting-House, in the City of Vanam, Spring Equinox Festival, Fourth Day, Morning

"MASTER WYESS PUNCHED Master Kierst?"

"In the Furriers' Hall last night?"

All the younger clerks in the airy ledger room abandoned their sloping desks to crowd around Tathrin.

"Yes, he hit him," Tathrin said shortly.

"Saedrin's stones!"

Tathrin clipped the excited boy round the ear. "Dishonour his name like that again and I'll wash your mouth out with vinegar."

"What happened after that?"

"Master Kierst went home and so did Master Gruit and everyone else ate their dinner."

Kierst had said nothing further, possibly because he feared his loosened teeth would fall out if he opened his mouth.

Tathrin looked sternly at the boys until they abandoned hope of learning more and returned to their desks.

"Conversation over the nuts and brandy must have been awkward." One of the older clerks leaned against the doorpost.

Tathrin took a moment to place him. Eclan, who'd warned him that Master Wyess would question him when he least expected it. "It was mostly speculation over which troupes of players have the prettiest dancing girls this festival." He couldn't help grinning at the recollection.

"Nothing of consequence, then." Eclan clapped his hands briskly. "If you lads want to stuff yourselves sick with cakes this afternoon, you had better see to your morning duties. If there's a set of sack-weights or corn-measures in this counting-house left uncertified by noon, I'll flog the lot of you!"

A few voices rose in protest, but the younger boys hurried towards the stairs regardless.

Tathrin thought Eclan was joking. Although he had seen the clerk wield the birch that hung by the door when one lad had stumbled into work stale-drunk on the first morning of the festival.

"Master Wyess said you're wanting to get your father's coin-weights certified?" Eclan crossed the room to unlock one of the cabinets. "I'm to take the counting-house sets. Give me a hand and the magistrate can assess yours at the same time."

"Thanks." Tathrin was relieved. He hadn't been sure of the correct procedure.

"No need to thank me." Eclan hauled out a heavy casket. "Let's just get there before the queue stretches all around the Excise Hall."

"Right."

Tathrin fetched the polished cherrywood case that he'd locked in his own desk over in a favoured spot lit by both the tall windows and the room's broad skylights. Tucking his father's weights securely under one arm, he took one of the chest's handles.

Eclan took the other. "So what were people really saying after Wyess flattened Kierst?"

"The next bells came and went before anyone did more than ask for the pickles." Tathrin grimaced as the weight of his burden pulled at his shoulders. "As soon as the libations to Raeponin were done, people started leaving."

"I wonder how he's feeling this morning." Eclan shifted his grip. Carrying the chest between them was awkward given that he was a head shorter than Tathrin. "Did you have to carry him home?"

"No," Tathrin said shortly.

Though Wyess had drunk a prodigious quantity of wine, silently seething, ignoring the sumptuous banquet, he had leaned heavily on Tathrin's arm all the way back to his own doorstep. At first Tathrin had worried that some footpad might mark them down as a pair of drunks ripe for rolling. Then he'd been more concerned that Master Wyess might welcome such a fight.

They reached the bottom of the stairs and went out into the counting-house yard. Tathrin helped Eclan lift the chest into a pony cart that a groom held ready.

"They must have discussed what Master Gruit had said." Eclan settled himself on the seat and gathered up the reins.

"Mostly they were reassuring each other that they already do all they can for Lescar." Tathrin couldn't help a heavy sigh as he climbed up. "Convincing themselves they cannot be held to account for such suffering." He'd made sure he remembered those for whom such consolation didn't seem to suffice. Now he just had to find out their names and businesses.

Eclan slapped the reins on the pony's dappled rump. "I've never really understood Lescar."

Tathrin looked ahead as they drove through the gate. If the streets were half-empty compared to the night before, they were still twice as busy as on any normal market day.

"Why is that man wearing four hats and three cloaks?" The breeze from the lake was refreshing, but it wasn't that cold in the bright sunlight.

"He's a second-hand clothes seller too miserly or too dishonest to pay half a mark for a stall in the cloth-market. If his customers are lucky, they won't feel the Watch's hand on their shoulder," Eclan added blithely, "because some festival visitor was robbed of that self-same cloak and hat while they were busy between some whore's dimpled knees."

"I see." Tathrin couldn't help a grin.

"So why are you Lescari always fighting each other?" Eclan curbed the pony with deft hands as the beast threatened to shy at a street sweeper. "You want to be a trader, don't you? I'll swap you answers for whatever you want to know about Vanam."

Tathrin chewed his lip as the cart carried them down to the wide road that skirted the lakeshore wharves and warehouses to link the city's myriad marketplaces.

"Ask me anything you want to know." Eclan wasn't about to give up. "I've lived here all my life."

So he probably knew where Master Gruit lived. Tathrin slid a glance sideways. Eclan could have been any of the boys he had grown up with: middling in height, well enough muscled, neither handsome nor ugly, until some misfortune left its mark. Though few of Tathrin's friends had had the blue eyes that were so common in Vanam, or the coppery glint that the sunshine found in Eclan's brown hair.

He drew a breath. "The days of antiquity saw the Tormalin Empire to the east and the Kingdom of Solura to the west divided by that region known as the land of many races, where neither king nor emperor's writ ran. In the old tongue, it was called Einar Sain Emin—"

Eclan interrupted. "Now known as Ensaimin, a region of independent demesnes and proud cities, the most prosperous and noble of which is Vanam. I learned that in dame-school. Why did the fall of the Old Empire leave the Lescari fighting like cats in a sack? The Caladhrians don't, nor yet the Dalasorians."

"Tormalin Emperors ruled over Dalasor in name only," Tathrin said tersely. "Those folk carried on tending their horses and cattle and moving their camps as they saw fit. There's little to quarrel over when five days' hard riding separates one herd and the next.

"When the Tormalin Emperor invaded Caladhria, the fighting was over in half a season. They're farmers. The Emperor granted local lords title to their traditional fiefdoms. As long as they paid tributes, they saw no more soldiers. Caladhria's a fertile land, so securing their peace by filling Tormalin bellies with grain was no great hardship." Tathrin paused to swallow the bitterness rising in his throat. "When the Empire fell, the wealthiest lords agreed they'd hold a parliament every Solstice and Equinox where new laws would be debated and agreed by all those attending."

"And Caladhria stagnates peacefully as a consequence," Eclan said with some impatience. "Didn't Lescar's dukes like that idea?"

"How can you not know this?" Tathrin demanded with sudden anger. "Every mentor insists new pupils attend the elementary history lectures."

"I was never admitted to the university," retorted Eclan. "I never applied. My father would have thrashed me for wasting my time and his money."

The pony cart rattled over the cobbles. Eclan turned the pony's head to take a left-hand fork and a right-hand turn after that. They reached a crossroads where a brewer's dray was unloading barrels into an inn's cellars. Wagons and carriages waited to pass by on the other side of the road. The pony snorted with a jingle of its brass harness ornaments.

Tathrin wasn't sure if anger or embarrassment coloured Eclan's angular cheekbones. "What's your father's trade?" he asked tentatively.

"Leather." Eclan flicked the cart whip idly at a wisp of straw blowing past. "He owns one of the biggest tanneries down by the lake. He shares business interests with harness-makers and shoemakers, glovers and such. The only time he ever left Vanam was to cross the lake to Wrede when my grandsire proposed a match with one of his trading partners' families. He had the pick of all their daughters and my mother suited him best. Happily they proved well matched." Eclan smiled with genuine affection for his parents.

"My older brothers will take over his interests here, so I've been set to learn all I can from Master Wyess about trading more widely." He snapped the braided lash over the pony's ears as a gap opened up ahead. "What does your father do, that he can spare the coin for you to study mathematics?"

"He's an innkeeper in Carluse," replied Tathrin.

Eclan jerked at the reins, surprised. "A tapster?"

"He owns a coaching inn on the Great West Road, just before Losand," Tathrin corrected him. "Merchants warehouse goods with us sometimes, for purchasers to collect. We help if they need to hire guards or trade horses. One of my sisters married a blacksmith who set up his forge there." And of course, there was the money-changing his father did in defiance of Duke Garnot's edict.

Eclan encouraged the pony into a brisker walk. "So there's plenty of coin to be made."

Tathrin shook his head. "I earned my board and lodging in the upper town as a servant for richer students."

That did surprise Eclan. "It was worth it? For a ring to seal your documents with the proof that you're a scholar?"

"It was," Tathrin said firmly.

His father would have paid ten times as much to see him safely away, after those dreadful days when Duke Moncan of Sharlac had sent his mercenaries into Carluse, carrying slaughter to the very walls of Losand. The carts had been loaded with all they could bear and Tathrin's family had made ready to flee, waiting for word of the battle's outcome. His father had paced the hall, spade in hand, ready to dig up the gold he had buried in the cellar.

Unable to stand not knowing, against all his father's wishes, Tathrin had saddled a horse and set out for Losand. Riding only as far as the nearest market town, he'd nearly blundered into a detachment of mercenaries who'd abandoned the main battle in search of easier prey. Seeing the slaughtered bodies of men and boys whom he'd known all his life, he'd realised how close he'd come to death through his own arrogant folly.

Not knowing might have been better than never forgetting. Tathrin looked down to see he was gripping his father's box of weights so tightly that his knuckles showed white beneath his skin.

"So why isn't Lescar as dull as Caladhria?" Eclan prompted as they turned uphill away from the lake.

Tathrin forced his thoughts back to ancient history. It might stop him recalling recent horrors. "You know the princes of Tormalin choose their Emperor from amongst their own number?"

"I've never understood that," Eclan said frankly.

"Tormalin's princes all rule vast holdings. Tens of thousands of men and women are sworn to each noble family. The yearly trade that any noble house controls could equal that of Vanam." Tathrin united the hills and buildings ahead with a sweep of his hand. "So any quarrel between two noble houses could soon turn into all-out warfare. They have the men and the coin to raise armies as quick as they like." He snapped his fingers.

"That's why the Princes' Convocation chooses an Emperor to preside over the law courts and the law-makers. Everyone is charged with protecting the greater good from individual ambition, and bound with sacred oaths. As long as whichever family holds the Imperial throne proposes talented successors, the other princes confirm them. If an Emperor stumbles too often, some other noble family will present their own candidate. Every so often the princes decide it's time for a change of dynasty."

"And all this ensures peace and harmony?" scoffed Eclan.

Tathrin grinned. "There are untimely deaths and convenient accidents and no end of negotiations over land and marriage settlements, but the princes know that cooperation serves their own best interests." His smile faded. "They still remember how their ancestors were fool enough to allow Nemith the Last to claim the throne because every wiser man was busy quarrelling with his rivals. Until Nemith brought the Old Empire crashing down into the Age of Chaos."

"And the Lescari liked chaos so much they've cherished it ever since?" Eclan teased.

"Ancient Tormalin rule over Lescar was different." Tathrin tried to stifle his irritation, but it still coloured his tone.

"I didn't mean to speak out of turn," Eclan said slowly. "I'm just curious."

They drew to a halt outside the imposing severity of the Excise Hall.

"Are you two going to sit chewing your cheeks all day?" A man in Excise Hall livery glared at them.

"We're here to get our weights certified." Jumping down from his seat, Eclan used his fingers to blow a piercing whistle. Three urchins idly picking through litter beside a public fountain came racing up the street.

Eclan held up a silver quarter-mark and each boy's eyes fixed on it. "Water the pony and keep your pals off the cart and there's one of these for each of you when we come back."

"Aye." The tallest of the three spat into a grimy palm and held out his hand.

Eclan spat and shook on it without flinching. Tathrin didn't think he could have done the same.

"Right, let's get these weights certified."

They carried the heavy chest through the arch into the Excise Hall's forecourt. There was already a long line of people waiting to be summoned before the assessors.

Tathrin saw a close knot of short, stocky men with flaxen hair and guarded expressions wearing high-collared tunics. "Mountain Men?" he queried.

"It's not just Lescari tapsters who value a properly certified set of weights." Eclan lowered his end of the chest. As Tathrin did the same, Eclan sat on it and looked up expectantly. "So what happened when the Tormalin legions of the Old Empire first invaded Lescar?"

"Move up." Eclan shifted and Tathrin sat beside him. "They conquered the local lords and divided Lescar into six provinces. Each province had a governor who answered to the Emperor. All revenues were sequestered for the use of the armies and the administration of justice wherever Imperial writ ran. So Lescari coin financed the conquest of Caladhria and Tormalin ventures into Dalasor and Gidesta. The governors all competed to earn Imperial favour by increasing revenues, and some say that's how the rivalries first started." He tried to keep his tone level.

"And when the Old Empire fell?" Eclan was watching the line moving slowly through the door to the assessors.

"Each of the governors did his best to hold his province together, assuming the Emperor's writ would soon be re-established. Different claimants to the

Tormalin throne offered them whatever coin they could scrape together to win their support. By the end of the Chaos the governors were calling themselves dukes and taking up arms against each other, claiming they had the Tormalin Emperor's sanction to rule the rest as High King. Each still believes his line has the truest claim to that throne. Each one bequeaths the insanity to his children." Tathrin couldn't hide his bitterness. "Since the Chaos, when the Tormalin princes whose lands run up to the River Asilor started thinking the grass looked greener on the opposite bank, other noble families didn't want them expanding their holdings. So they agreed that only the Emperors would wage any warfare outside ancestral Tormalin lands. Hence, the Lescari dukes have been left to their own disastrous devices ever since."

"No one's ever won?" Eclan stood up and they dragged the chest a few paces forward. "In twenty generations?"

"Kycir of Marlier, ten generations ago, he fought everyone else to a standstill." Tathrin sat down again with a sigh. "He ruled Lescar until he died in a duel defending his wife's honour. When they went to tell her, they found her in bed with his brother."

Eclan laughed. "I'm sorry, but it is funny."

"It's a fair example of the honour and insight of our noble rulers," Tathrin said sardonically.

"No wonder anyone who can get the gold together leaves," Eclan said dismissively. "Oh, look, they're waving us in."

Tathrin picked up his end of the chest and helped carry it into the hall. Eclan had clearly lost interest in Lescar's endless tragedy. Perhaps that wasn't surprising. Put so simply, it did sound trite.

The interior was deeply shadowed after the bright sunlight outside. As his eyes adjusted, Tathrin saw a long row of tables. An excise clerk sat at each one with a set of scales and precisely graded weights engraved with the ornate seal of the Excise Hall. Behind, officials walked to and fro, collecting any weights that failed to pass muster. Men in heavy leather aprons stood beside black anvils, and the hall rang with the strike of their hammers and chisels. Confiscated and defaced, unfit weights were tossed into baskets for melting down.

Raeponin, god of justice and balance, gazed down from the painted wall, robed in blue and hooded in white. Stern and implacable, he held up his scales with one hand, his bell ready in the other to ring out over the forsworn, the deceitful and all those irretrievably abandoned to self-indulgent vice. To his right, the virtuous were bathed in sunlight and surrounded by plenty. To the left, the dishonest and immoral grovelled beneath the shadow of the god's displeasure.

Tathrin held his father's box tight. Without the weights, no merchant would trust his father to change his coinage.

"We're from Master Wyess's counting-house." When their turn came, Eclan began taking out the leather bags holding each graduated set of weights.

"Copper penny, bronze penny, silver penny, silver mark, gold mark." The excise clerk counted each one off as he tested them with deft fingers. His eyes barely shifted from the central needle of his scales. "All true." He looked up as he swept the last ones back into their pouch. "Are those for certifying?"

"If you please." Tathrin handed over his father's box. He saw sweat from his fingers marring the glossy wood. Was it possible the weights could somehow have become unreliable?

The excise man examined each one. "An heirloom set?" He looked up, mildly curious. "I can't recall when I last saw weights so old."

"Handed down from my grandsire, and his sire before him," Tathrin explained.

"They're still weighing true." The man handed the box back. "Swear by Raeponin's bell and balance that all these weights will be used in fair and equitable trade, may the gods bring all deceivers to ruin."

"We swear. Talagrin take all oath-breakers." Eclan was gathering up all the counting-house weights.

"I swear," Tathrin echoed. "Raeponin rend me if I lie."

"Get all your certificates sealed over there."

The clerk was already looking past them as another merchant's apprentice unbuckled a leather-bound coffer. They joined the next line.

"I need to send these back to my father. Do we have any other duties today?" Tathrin asked.

"As soon as we get these safely back to the counting-house, our time's our own. Pay the extra and use the Imperial Tormalin courier," Eclan advised. "There isn't a bandit between the Great Forest and the Ocean who dares attack their coaches."

"I'm going to buy some ribbons and lace for my mother and sisters." Tathrin did his best to sound offhand. "I might buy some wine for my father. Where's Master Gruit's storehouse?"

"Halfway up the Ariborne, past the Mercers' Bridge." Eclan collected the freshly sealed certificates that the second clerk was shoving at him.

Eclan's confidence in the urchins hadn't been misplaced. Reclaiming the pony cart, they retraced their route. Though the day was considerably busier, the carts and carriages were all moving swiftly enough.

"Me and some of the others are heading for The Looking Glass this evening." Eclan pulled the pony up by Master Wyess's entrance. "There's a troupe of players come all the way from Toremal to give us *The Chatelaine's Folly*. They're bound to have pretty dancing girls showing plenty of leg."

"That sounds good." Tathrin had only managed a few visits to Vanam's acclaimed playhouse. Each time, he'd found imagined worlds of passion and challenge where he could forget his own trials and secrets, if only for a little while.

"We're meeting at the cheese market at the bottom of the Bairen at the second hour of the night." Eclan grinned. "If you're not there, I'll assume some lacemaker made you a better offer."

"You never know." Tathrin managed an embarrassed smile.

Eclan snapped his fingers at a gang of younger clerks who were playing an idle game of runes on the step. "Two of you, come and carry this inside! Shall I lock those up for you?" He held out a hand for Tathrin's father's weights. "No need to carry them around while you're... shopping."

"Thank you."

Tathrin started walking. It wasn't far to the thoroughfare that wound up the shallower face of the Ariborne. On this side of the hill, the recently built houses of the newly prosperous sought to leave the sprawl of the lower town behind them. On the far side, the long-established coveted their wealth in spacious mansions. Above, the upper town's ancient walls looked down from the heights where the Ariborne, Teravin and Dashire hills joined together.

He reached the Mercers' Bridge, which carried the road across a rocky cleft. On the far side, the shallow swell of the Pazarel stood guard over the high road to the west. Horns and shouts sounded from the scrub below. The hog hunters were still beating the bushes for the tusked fugitives that found sanctuary amid the wooded defiles threading through the city.

Gruit's name was boldly displayed above a storehouse's door beside a fine statue of Ostrin. The rotund and bearded god of hospitality smiled down, a flagon in one hand, a bunch of grapes in the other. It was the busiest of all the warehouses lining this stretch of the road. Liveried servants were directing storemen carefully carrying casks of fine spirits. The wax-sealed necks of bottles poked out of woven straw in tightly packed baskets.

Tathrin walked cautiously inside. Soberly dressed clerks were offering glasses of wine to prosperous men and women in silken gowns. No one paid any heed to him in his drab clerk's doublet. He saw a staircase leading to a half-open door at the back of the building. Steeling himself, he walked up.

Gruit was making notes in a ledger, a glass of wine and an open bottle to hand. "If you go back down, I'll send someone to wait on you."

He didn't look up as Tathrin hesitated on the threshold. Recalling Kierst's slander, Tathrin wondered if that was the first bottle of the merchant's day.

"Forgive the intrusion." He cleared his throat. "But I'm not here about wine."

Gruit looked up, his faded eyes narrowing. "I know your face." He thought for a moment. "You were with Wyess, last night." He startled Tathrin with a bark of laughter. "How are his knuckles? I should send him some mustard to poultice his hand, along with my thanks for knocking Kierst on his arse."

"I'm not here on my master's behalf." Tathrin's mouth was dry. "I was interested in what you had to say last night, about how all Lescari should take some responsibility for what happens at home."

Gruit considered him. "Where are you from, lad? Carluse, by your accent?"

Tathrin nodded. "I know someone who'd very much like to meet you. Someone who wants to improve the lot of all Lescari."

"I don't travel, not back to Lescar." Gruit shook his head regretfully.

"No, he's here, in the city—' Tathrin broke off, unable to think how to explain further.

Gruit laid his reed pen across a brass inkwell and looked at Tathrin. "I thought I knew all the exiles here who haven't turned their backs on their homeland."

"He keeps himself to himself—' Again, Tathrin couldn't go on.

Gruit rubbed a wrinkled hand across his grey jowls. "You think I should meet him?"

"Yes." Of that, Tathrin was certain.

Gruit smiled wryly. "Will your reclusive friend have heard about last night's events?"

Tathrin nodded. "But he'll want to have the truth of it from your own lips."

"What will he say?" challenged Gruit.

Tathrin wasn't about to hazard a guess. "You should find that out for yourself."

"Intriguing." Gruit shook fine sand across his page. "Of course, you could just be planning on luring me down some blind alley where your accomplices will knock me out and steal my rings and purse."

"Master, I swear, on whatever gods you cherish, I'm coming to you in all good faith." Tathrin was taken aback. He'd imagined Gruit would need some convincing to leave his business in mid-morning. He hadn't expected to be accused of plotting to rob him.

Gruit dismissed his words with a wave of his hand. "I hope you don't play the runes, my lad. You'll lose your shirt with a face that easy to read." Now that the ink was dry, he tipped the sand carefully into a little dish to be used again. "Besides, I don't suppose Master Wyess would have hired you without making very sure you could be trusted, and had assurances from your family sealed by a notary into the bargain." He locked the ledger in a drawer. "Saiger!"

A man ran up the stairs from the warehouse floor. "Master?"

"I'm going out for a while. If I'm not back for my appointment with Widow Quaine, rouse the Watch and send them to make enquiries about Master Wyess's new apprentice here."

So Master Gruit was both bold enough to go with him, and canny enough to make sure of such safeguards. Tathrin's spirits rose. Gruit really could be the man they'd been looking for.

Moving swiftly for a man of his years and bulk, the wine merchant crossed the room. He stowed his key chain safely inside the breast of his old-fashioned tunic, then took a brown mantle from a peg. As they walked out past the casks and baskets to the road, he bowed to his customers.

"My compliments. Fair festival."

Tathrin followed, trying to look unobtrusive.

Gruit turned downhill. "Where does this friend of yours hide himself away?"

"No, Master, it's this way." Tathrin pointed back towards the upper town and the austere battlements of the university's nearest gate.

Chapter Five

Aremil

**Beacon Lane, in Vanam's Upper Town,
Spring Equinox Festival, Fourth Day, Noon**

Soup slopped as the knock on the door startled
Lyrlen. Most of the spoonful landed back in the bowl,
but a few drops splashed onto the napkin tucked into
Aremil's collar.

"Are you expecting anyone?" Exasperated, the old
woman rose from her stool ready to ward off unwanted visitors.

"No." Aremil swallowed, acutely conscious of the
soup on his chin.

"Master Aremil, it's me, Tathrin."

Lyrlen clicked her tongue but set the bowl back on
the tray. "You must eat later, my lord."

He didn't reply as she cleaned his face with the napkin, her hands as deft as they had always been.
Though her step was becoming slower and her hair
was now as white as her linen cap.

Tathrin knocked again. "Mistress Lyrlen?"

"A moment, if you please." She straightened Aremil's collar. "Are you warm enough? Do you want a blanket?"

"No, thank you." He managed a smile to convince her. Truth be told, he was a little cold despite the fire in the hearth. But he was no more going to sit swaddled like an infant than wear some aged invalid's chamber robe. If doublet and breeches exposed his twisted frame, well, visitors' reactions gave him a useful measure of their character.

The smile was worth the effort. Lyrlen went out into the hall to open the door. "Tathrin, you're very welcome."

Aremil heard him introduce someone. "This is Master Gruit, a wine merchant."

"Come in and welcome," Aremil said as the two men appeared in the doorway. "Lyrlen, that will be all, thank you."

"As you wish." She took up the tray and curtseyed before withdrawing to her kitchen.

"Master Gruit, you are indeed welcome." Aremil hoped the man would step closer. At the moment he was a mere impression of a long brown mantle topped with white hair.

"You heard about last night?" the wine merchant asked wryly.

"Naturally. Tathrin, please serve some wine." Aremil tried to look as welcoming as he could without risking a smile that would distort his face. "Master Gruit, I hope the vintage meets with your approval. Please, sit."

Gruit took the nearer end of the settle where Aremil could see him clearly. A heavily built man, he was solid rather than fat, not overly tall. Past his prime, his jowls sagged and wrinkles were carved deep into his face. But he was clearly still vigorous, his expression both alert and astute.

"Am I supposed to have lost my wits or merely my temper?" Gruit asked.

"Opinion's divided."

Aremil watched him taking in every detail of this comfortable sitting room. What was Gruit making of the thick maroon carpet, the brocaded upholstery, the shelves of tightly packed books? Assuming this was a wealthy scholar's lodging? But he'd have noticed that no university hall's crest of books or quills or lanterns was carved into the door of the house. Private property was hardly unknown in the upper town; nevertheless, it was uncommon.

Tathrin handed Gruit a crystal goblet. The merchant raised it to his lips before hesitating, seeing Aremil had received no drink.

"Please, quench your thirst. I'm subject to weakness in my hands so I prefer not to drink in company." Aremil glanced at Tathrin. "Has our friend explained my infirmities?"

"He's said little about you, other than that you keep largely within your own doors." Gruit covered his embarrassment by taking a sip.

"As you see, my weakness extends to my legs." Aremil managed a casual tone. There was no point in pretending otherwise; even at rest, his scrawny legs were awkwardly flexed.

"Yet you have heard all about last night. You're plainly a man of resource as well as resources. My compliments—this is a fine vintage. Ferl River, some two or three years old?" Gruit drank his wine and nodded at the painting hung above the fireplace. "That's Ilasette Den Pallarie's work, isn't it?"

"It is," Aremil confirmed. "That's to say, you're quite correct about the wine, and yes, Madam Den Pallarie rendered the landscape for me."

"Pardon my frankness." Gruit set his goblet down carefully on the polished rosewood table where onyx and agate game pieces clustered beside the white raven board. "There's a curious quality to your voice that I assume stems from your infirmities. I would say you're Lescari, but I cannot quite identify which dukedom you're from."

"Draximal," Aremil said calmly. "Though I have lived in Vanam for many years now."

"While your friend here is only recently come from Carluse." Gruit glanced at Tathrin.

Aremil risked an attempt at a half-smile. "We've long since decided that our common heritage unites us more than our fathers'—" he caught himself and hoped Gruit would think the stumble of no consequence "—and forefathers' quarrels divide us."

"So your call for unity among those of us in exile struck me," Tathrin added quickly.

"Is that so?" Gruit glanced from Aremil to Tathrin. "How did the two of you become acquainted if Master Aremil spends his days by his own fireside?"

"My family aren't wealthy," Tathrin explained self-consciously. "While I studied I worked as a scholars' servant."

Aremil wondered what the merchant made of his ungainly awkwardness and hesitant speech when Tathrin was so tall, fresh-faced and straight-limbed. While he sat concealing the pains it cost him to stay motionless, lest any but the most trusted see the tremors that often shook him. Did Gruit realise Aremil was Tathrin's elder by barely five years? Between the trials of his condition and his inadequate eyesight, Aremil knew his own face was thin and lined. It would not have surprised him if the merchant took him for ten years older than Tathrin.

"Are you congratulating me for making our countrymen feel miserable and guilty?" Gruit castigated himself rather than challenging Aremil.

"Tathrin says a number appeared to agree with you." Tension worsened the pains in Aremil's back. "Only they could see no way forward. So I have a suggestion for you and your fellow merchants."

"Do you indeed?" Gruit raised bushy white brows, halfway between hope and scepticism.

"Our countrymen send money to their kith and kin, to enable them to pay the dues the dukes demand in lieu of taking their sons to serve in the militias." Aremil felt a bubble of saliva at the corner of his mouth and paused to swallow. "But these remittances merely throw fuel on the smouldering fires of Lescari strife. As soon as a duke can wring sufficient silver out of his subjects, he hires mercenaries to try to impose his rule over all the rest."

"If there was no money, there could be no warfare," Tathrin said bluntly.

Gruit shook his head. "The dukes would draft men from the villages into the militias at spearpoint. At least foreign blood stains the battlefields if such dishonourable men choose to risk their lives for silver."

"The dukes couldn't leave the fields untended," Aremil countered, "if they had no coin to buy Caladhrian grain to keep bread on their tables."

"The dukes and their families will be the last to go hungry," retorted Gruit. "Their hired swords would just seize what they wanted from the peasantry."

"If they're not being paid, there will be no mercenaries to do such plundering," Aremil insisted.

"If they're not being paid, mercenaries will go looting on their own behalf," Gruit said promptly. "Good coin is all that can buy peasants relief from such predation."

"You were calling on the merchants to stop selling them the arms and goods they need." Tathrin was annoyed. "How is denying them coin so different?"

"I lost my temper last night, lad. Once I went home, my blood cooled." Gruit's face sagged, discouraged. "I realised that if every Vanam merchant born or wed to Lescari blood refused to trade with the dukes, all that would happen is the smiths and clothiers and provender merchants in Peorle and Col and Selerima would grow richer."

"You don't think Vanam's example would unite the Lescari-born in all the towns of Ensaimin?" Tathrin asked.

"You think everyone would agree? That no one would break ranks to enrich themselves when prices offered in Lescar would rise with every passing market day?" Gruit shook his head. "Besides, if every Lescariborn merchant from the Ocean to the Great Forest spurned the dukes' gold, Caladhrians wouldn't turn their noses up at it, nor would Tormalin traders."

"If the flow of coin to the dukes is cut off, they could not pay those Caladhrians or Tormalin," Aremil said as swiftly as his recalcitrant tongue allowed.

"Only till the dukes go to Col's moneylenders," Gruit retorted, exasperated.

"Col's bankers baulk at lending to any man, common or noble, who can't show sufficient income to promise repayment of principal and interest," Aremil pointed out. "If the exiles stop sending money, the dukes' revenues will dry up like a winter stream in summer."

"It would be an impossible undertaking." Gruit ran a gnarled hand over his white head. "There would be no point starving one, two or even three dukedoms of funds. They would just be overrun by whichever other duke could still find the coin to pay for arms and mercenaries."

"Which is why we must persuade everyone to put the good of Lescar above any loyalty to their birthplace," Tathrin chipped in. "As you said last night."

"How could you find every exile in this patchwork quilt of a land?" Gruit sighed. "You'd have to do that before you could even try to convince them not to send their coin home."

"We might do that with magic," Aremil said boldly.

"Oh no." Gruit raised an open hand. "The Archmage's edicts are clear. No wizard is to involve himself in Lescar's warfare. Even assuming you could find one who wouldn't prefer comparing the merits of burning wood and coal or assessing the particular properties of water from assorted springs," he added sourly.

"I've heard there are scholars around the university studying the ancient system of aetheric magic," Aremil said carefully. "The Archmage has no dominion over them."

"Aetheric magic?" Gruit was startled into a laugh. "You'll be telling me you believe children's tales of the Eldritch Kin next."

"Haven't you heard what's happened in the east?" Tathrin scowled. "Tormalin mariners have made landfall on the far side of the Ocean. They found men and women from ancient times sleeping there, locked in aetheric enchantment."

"I'll believe that this new land has been discovered," Gruit said slowly. "The ripples of new trade across the Ocean are already reaching this far. But you ask me to believe there were Tormalin folk from the Old Empire living there, kept safe through the generations by some fanciful magic?" He shook his head. "Confusion, speculation and exaggeration have all been woven into a tissue of nonsense. The Tormalin Emperor has wrapped that around the truth to prevent anyone else laying claim to the place."

"You are ill informed, Master Gruit," Tathrin began hotly. "Master Aremil is acquainted with a mentor who has travelled there himself and spoken with these people."

Aremil silenced him with a gesture. "You must have heard, Master Gruit, that this ancient magic, this Artifice, is what held the Old Empire together, enabling those in Toremal to know exactly where their allies were and what they were doing."

"It didn't stop their Empire crashing down round their ears." Gruit was unimpressed. "Do you know how they did such things?"

Now Aremil's hesitation wasn't due to his infirmity. "Not as such. But I am confident I could persuade those who do to help us."

If Mentor Tonin, who'd travelled to these new lands overseas, could be persuaded to be a little less circumspect about his recent discoveries. But Aremil knew he would have to show the scholar a rising tide of determination to bring peace to Lescar to achieve that. So they had to persuade Master Gruit to continue his eloquent challenge to the exiles. He swallowed and pressed on as forcefully as he could.

"Even without the aid of enchantments, we could begin finding all those Lescari exiles living in Ensaimin. We could try to persuade them to withhold their coin. I have a breadth of contacts that would surprise you, for spreading such ideas as well as gathering news."

"You must have better contacts than half the Guilds in the city to have purchased all these books. I know scholars who'd sell their ancestors' ashes to the soap-makers for some of the titles here." Gruit surprised him with a grin. "And you not only have a painting by one of Toremal's most highly regarded artists, you talk of her painting it for you personally."

He stood and went to take a closer look at the dramatic clouds surging across a glittering wilderness of willow and water. "Was this a favourite view of yours? From your family's home? Just who are you, anyway? I've seldom come across a man of your age with your degree of self-assurance."

And in a cripple, it's truly astonishing. Aremil waited for Gruit to say something along those lines but the merchant merely scrutinised the painting.

"I was the Duke of Draximal's first-born son," he said stiffly.

"Were you indeed?" Gruit looked around the room.

Aremil sat patiently. The merchant could look all he liked for some sign of Draximal's fire-basket badge. He wouldn't find it.

Gruit's gaze came back to him, more intrigued than sceptical. "Why by all that's holy should I believe that?"

"My servant Lyrlen has been with me since birth." Aremil held his gaze without blinking. "I can call on her to vouch for me. She'll swear an oath to whichever god you cherish."

"So who are you now? Since Draximal's heir is undoubtedly the honourable Lord Cassat." Gruit found a kerchief in his mantle and wiped sweat from his brow. "I do recall something about an elder son besides the quiverful of daughters. But if anyone asked me, I'd guess he died an early death of some illness that was never quite agreed on."

"I don't believe my father has ever lied outright about my fate." Taut with emotion, Aremil couldn't help an awkward jerk of his shoulder. "He has allowed that tale to spread so that no one will be so crass as to enquire and cause my lady mother undue grief."

That was what Lyrlen said. Aremil kept his own counsel on the matter.

"You've been tucked out of sight here in Vanam since when?" asked Gruit.

"Since my eighth year. Since I was inconsiderate enough not to succumb to some childhood ailment." Aremil didn't like giving so much of himself away, but it was clear Gruit wasn't going to trust them without hearing all his history.

"As far as anyone knows, I am the crippled son of a minor nobleman." He grimaced with chilly amusement. "Since the people of Vanam are content to lump all Lescari together, no one is bothered who that noble might be. Not as long as my bills are settled."

"Your father makes you a generous allowance." Gruit's gesture took in the comfortable room. "How are your needs to be met if you bankrupt him?"

"I would live in a barrel on some street corner, begging for bread in rags, if that was the price of bringing peace to Lescar." Aremil shifted in his chair as cramp seized his wasted legs.

"Or the price of revenge upon your father, for discarding you," hazarded Gruit. "Or upon your brother for taking your rightful place as heir?"

"I did not bring you here to insult my friend." Tathrin was on his feet, indignant.

"No, it's a fair question." Aremil raised an unsteady hand. "Master Gruit, the mentors of Vanam's university halls teach rigorous logic that encourages a philosophical attitude. I could never have ruled Draximal. Even at peace, there's always the threat of warfare. A duke must be able to ride a horse and command an army. I could never have done either. As my father's heir, I could only have brought disaster on Draximal, as our neighbours of Sharlac or Parnilesse invaded to take advantage of my weakness. I'd rather the commonalty were spared such grief, just as I'm happy to be spared responsibility for their deaths."

"So why torment yourself with Lescar's tribulations?" Gruit wondered. "Live here in comfort and pay no heed."

"Wilful ignorance isn't so easy." Aremil swallowed. "The scholars of Vanam entertain themselves picking over the sorry history of our beleaguered land. Every summer brings broadsheets detailing the atrocities of warfare. The streets fill with beggars fleeing each new wave of fighting."

"You hear their pleas all the way up here in the upper town?" Gruit shook his head regretfully. "I don't mean to insult you, but you sit here with your books and games of strategy for which everyone knows and agrees the rules." He gestured at the white raven pieces. "In the confusion of the real world, this business of denying the dukes their funds could never work. Set aside the difficulties of finding every exile, you would never persuade them to stop sending coin. Their families scrimped and saved and lied to reeves and bailiffs to gather the coin that bought them their passage out of danger. These are not debts of silver but of honour."

But Gruit couldn't contain his frustration, pacing between the hearth and the window. "Even if you could cut off the flow of coin from every Lescari exile, it would make no difference. Some cabal of bankers or merchants, or even mercenary captains, would back one of our noble dukes, regardless of his impoverished state, on seeing that none of the other dukedoms could mount a challenge as long as their coffers remained empty." His voice thickened with contempt. "They would support whoever promised them first pick of the plunder once he was crowned High King."

He reached absently for the bottle of wine that Tathrin had left on the small sideboard. "How long would that peace last? Seeing their families with Sharlac boots on their necks would soon prompt your Draximal brethren to send coin home again. Your fellows would soon refill His Grace of Carluse's war chests." He gestured towards Tathrin and then realised he held nothing to pour the wine into.

At Aremil's nod, the younger man silently handed the merchant his glass. Gruit filled it.

"Forgive me. I honour your desire to do something for our unhappy countrymen. But these days, it takes too much wine to make me hope for peace in my lifetime."

"I refuse to believe that we are condemned to wretchedness," Tathrin said forcefully. "I will not accept the lies the Caladhrians tell of us, or our ridiculous reputation in Tormalin. I will not acknowledge the disdain of even our friends here in Vanam. I know every man of Lescar can be as true and as valiant as any born elsewhere."

"Saedrin make it so." Gruit raised his glass to the god and drained it. "With your determination, you may yet achieve something. Try something less ambitious. Found a new charitable fraternity at one of the shrines, something to help those unfortunates who will be caught in the fighting between Draximal and Parnilesse this summer, if those rumours are true."

Aremil shook his head. "Such charities are like cowardly doctors merely seeking to alleviate symptoms instead of addressing the cause of a sickness."

"You don't believe that some ailments cannot be cured but must simply be endured?" Gruit reddened and he set his glass down. "I beg your pardon. That was appallingly ill-mannered of me."

"But you are quite correct," Aremil retorted with biting politeness. "Nevertheless, I am certain Lescar's suffering can be eased, even if my own cannot."

"It has been a pleasure to meet you, but I think it's time I took my leave." Gruit bowed to Aremil and then to Tathrin. "Don't trouble your servant. I can see myself out."

Aremil saw the mortification in Tathrin's face as he closed the door behind the merchant.

"I'm sorry."

"You need not apologise." Aremil leaned back and didn't try to hide the tremors shaking his limbs. "It was an education meeting Master Gruit."

"As the mentors always tell us, no education is ever wasted." Tathrin poured himself another glass of the Ferl River vintage. "Is he right?"

Aremil sighed. "He argues a powerful case."

"So what can we do now?" Tathrin sat down on the settle, staring into the fire.

"First, if you'd be so kind, I'll take a glass of wine with a spoonful of the green tincture." Aremil winced as cramp bit deeply into his legs.

"I'm still making a list." Tathrin prepared the medicine and held the glass to Aremil's lips. "Of the men and women most deeply affected by Gruit's outburst."

"We had better ready some arguments to counter the objections that Gruit just raised before we approach anyone else." Aremil drank and turned his head to wipe a trickle of wine away on the shoulder of his doublet. "I will see if I can get Mentor Tonin to explain the specifics of aetheric magic to me, rather than the generality."

"It's like those logic puzzles they tested us with when we first came here." Tathrin put the glass down beside Aremil and looked out of the window towards the forbidding towers of the university's halls. "How can you have an egg without a bird? How can you have a bird without an egg?"

Aremil felt the insidious sweetness of the drug relax him. "How are you finding life in Master Wyess's employ?"

"Interesting." Tathrin turned away from the window. "Challenging. Confusing. Everything's turned upside down at the moment. I'll get a better feel for the intricacies of his trade once festival's over, and for the lower town, come to that."

"Good." Aremil hoped Tathrin saw that he truly was pleased for him. "Why don't you stay for dinner? Tell me about life in the lower town. Master Gruit was right to say my vision of wider issues is limited by these four walls."

Tathrin was sliding his scholar's ring around on his finger. "Thank you."

Aremil heard the reservation in his voice. "If you have some other engagement, don't let me detain you."

"I won't stay to dine. I do need to write a letter to my father and buy some presents for my mother and sisters." Tathrin sat across the game table from him. "We have time for a round of white raven, though. Do you want to play the raven or the forest birds?"

"The forest birds."

"Let me see if I can finally build a thicket to baffle you." Tathrin picked up the agate trees and considered their placement. His forehead creased.

Aremil hoped it was only concern for the game prompting that frown. He knew Tathrin's father had never approved of him serving a Draximal master. Even one who was apparently a noble of lowest rank and a cripple at that, never likely to play any part in the poisonous politics of the dukedoms. How would the innkeeper react if he discovered his son was really serving Duke Secaris's own son, even a son so comprehensively discarded and disinherited? Aremil didn't want to be the cause of any rift in Tathrin's family.

Someone with Tathrin's intelligence and integrity deserved a better future than dancing attendance on an invalid. Or a pointless death clutching a pike in Duke Garnot's militia. That was something Aremil and Tathrin's distant father must surely agree on.

Hopefully this apprenticeship with Master Wyess would lead to a secure and wealthy future for the younger man.

Tathrin looked up from the game board, a glint in his eye. "Where do you want these?" He took up the horned owl figurine and the pied crow.

"Put the owl by the holly tree and the crow behind the second oak from the right." Aremil focused his attention on the challenge of the game. Tathrin had clearly been thinking how to arrange the trees and shrubs to offer most shelter to the solitary white raven. Well, it was his task to see that the rest of the birds drove the mythical bird out of the forest, regardless. "Put the swordwing in front of the sour apple."

CHAPTER SIX

Tathrin

**Master Wyess's Counting-House, in the City of Vanam,
Spring Equinox Festival, Fifth Day, Morning**

"MASTER GRUIT IS in the courtyard." Eclan stuck his
head around the partition separating Tathrin's bed
from the next one. Senior clerks warranted a little
more privacy than the open dormitory the younger
boys shared. "He wants your seal on a letter he's sending to your father."

"Oh, right." Tathrin covered his confusion by gathering up the ribbons and lace spread across his
blanket.

"Master Wyess has no duties for us today. Will you
be coming to the hangings?" Eclan grinned. "Or are
those for one of last night's dancers? That red-headed
beauty was smiling at you and you know what they
say about Forest girls. The pick of those pretties
should win you a feel of her frills. This isn't your birth
festival, is it? Give yourself a proper treat if it is!"

"I was born in For-Winter, and these are for my sisters." Tathrin dragged his private chest out from under the bed and swept the fripperies into it. "No, I won't be at the hangings. I want to buy a book of maps."

Then he'd visit Aremil, to make up for leaving him alone last night while he enjoyed himself at the playhouse.

"We'll see a merry midwinter," Eclan mused as they walked down the stairs. "There's more than half the senior clerks born between the Autumn Equinox and the Solstice, and Master Wyess puts up a gold crown for every one of us celebrating at each festival." They reached the half-landing and continued down the next flight. "Anyway, that's three of us this time round, so we'll be drinking Master Wyess's health at the Star in the Thorn after the last villain swings and there'll be high-stakes rune games if that takes your fancy."

"Maybe," Tathrin temporised.

He had little enough coin he could afford to lose, and anyway, gambling for high or low stakes held no attraction for him. He'd grown up playing the usual childish rune games and when he'd begun fetching and carrying in his father's taproom, he'd seen how a single cast of three could throw gamblers into ecstasy or despair. One quiet evening he'd sat down with a set of the nine three-sided bone tokens and a slate and worked through some calculations.

The heavenly rune had the Sun, the Greater and the Lesser Moon on its three sides. All the rest were different, carved with three symbols taken from the traditional sets of four: plants, animals, earthly domains, instruments, winds and elements.

That was one of the first things Tathrin had wondered about. Granted, the Wolf, the Pine and the

Mountain went together naturally enough. So did the Deer, the Oak and the Forest. But the Drum, the Calm and Earth? The Harp, the South Wind and Water? Who had decided which three symbols should share a rune, why and when? Who had decreed that two runes from every set of four should be weak and two should be strong? That the Sun should be strong while both Greater and Lesser Moon were weak?

Nine bones and each gambler threw three. Each rune had three faces, one landing flat on the table, one face showing an upright rune, the other with its rune upside down. Tathrin began calculating the likelihood of each symbol turning up. He added in the uncertainty of the heaven symbols, since those had no up or down. Then he took account of the occasions when a strong upright rune would override a weak one.

By the time he had filled the slate with sums, wiped it clean, filled it again, cleaned it and filled it a third time, he had concluded that turning to rune games in hopes of making a fortune was as much folly as using the rune bones for telling fortunes, as the Forest Folk were supposed to do.

His father, seeing Tathrin working steadily, had come over to find out what was fascinating his son. He'd been relieved to learn that the boy wasn't succumbing to the lure of the bones. Then he'd paid a thoughtful visit to the shrine of Misaen on the Losand Road. The second son of Lord Camador, who had inherited that particular priesthood tied to the family's lands, had once studied at Vanam and earned the university's seal of scholarship. He had agreed with Tathrin's father that the lad's aptitude for calculation deserved more challenges than running an inn could provide.

They reached the ground floor and Eclan clapped Tathrin on the shoulder. "I'll see you later," he said cheerfully, disappearing into one of the strong-grooms.

Tathrin watched him go. The senior clerks spent a great deal of their leisure time together. His father had told him not to hold himself aloof. If he was going to make a success of this apprenticeship, he didn't want the other clerks thinking he scorned them for not being scholars. But if he was going to go drinking with Eclan and the rest, Tathrin wondered how he would visit Aremil as often as he might like without causing comment.

Emerging into the sunshine of the counting-house courtyard, he saw Master Gruit chatting to Wyess's wagonmaster.

"Good morning, Tathrin. Let's seal that deal on your father's wine." Gruit swept his mantle back, tucking his hands into his brown tunic's pockets.

Tathrin walked with him towards the gate. "I don't recall telling you anything about my father."

"Jerich Sayron, whose family has owned the Ring of Birches Inn on the Losand Road for five generations. The house has a sound reputation for good food and clean beds. It's a safe place to house goods, and they say any guard your father recommends can almost always be trusted." Gruit slid him a grin. "You satisfied the mentors of your scholarship inside two years when the talented sons of Vanam's rich and idle usually take three or four years to earn the university's seal ring. Your friend Master Aremil isn't the only one who can find things out."

Tathrin wasn't about to be flattered. "What do you want with me this morning?"

"I want you to meet a couple of people." Gruit lengthened his stride. "You may also care to know that no one is particularly interested in the pitiable Lord Aremil for whom you fetched and carried while you studied."

"Master Aremil," Tathrin corrected him. "He sees no merit in unearned titles."

Gruit waved an airy hand. "Quiet as a dormouse and twice as dull, apparently. There's some curiosity over what will become of his house when he dies, since he's hardly likely to have an heir of his own body. He has no testament of bequests deposited at Raeponin's shrine, so it's assumed it'll be a simple sale." He looked more sharply at Tathrin. "How robust is his health? If he sinks into a decline, someone might go looking for his relatives, in hopes of making a pre-emptive bid on the property. If he doesn't want his birth to be discovered, he should think on that."

"Drianon be thanked, he is usually quite well." Tathrin tried not to scowl. Master Gruit clearly had excellent sources of information.

"Though often in pain," Gruit observed. "What befell him? Childhood illness or accident?" The merchant took the road leading up the spreading flanks of the Grastan Hill, where the pig hunters had caused such chaos the evening before last.

Tathrin hesitated. Was this his tale to tell? Doing so would save Aremil the awkward task. He knew how much his friend disliked discussing his infirmity.

"His mother laboured in childbed so long that they were both despaired of. Though they survived, he remained a weakly baby. As the duchess did her duty and bore more children, it became apparent that Aremil was not learning to crawl or to use his hands like any other infant. Fortunately, before he could be condemned as an imbecile, he was babbling and then talking."

Gruit glanced at him. "His noble birth presumably saved him from being dumped in some shrine to Ostrin?"

"He lived secluded with his nurse in a remote manor house," Tathrin said briefly. "Never mentioned, to avoid embarrassing his lady mother, and to deny his noble father's enemies the opportunity of arguing that his firstborn's afflictions were proof of the gods' displeasure with Draximal." He grinned despite himself. "Only no one thought to tell Lyrlen her nurseling was supposed to waste quietly away and oblige everyone by dying. She cherished him and taught him to read and write."

"So Duke Secaris found he had a crippled scholar on his hands and decided Vanam was the best place for him." Gruit looked thoughtful. "My opinion of His Grace has gone up somewhat."

They passed the house front where Tathrin had been crushed by the crowd. At the top of the street, the angular façade of the shrine to Misaen dominated a square crowded with booths and stalls piled high with books, new and old. The weathered bronze figure of the smith-god looked sternly down, the sun in one hand, the hammer he'd used to make it in the other.

"Almanac, Master?" A huckster waved a smudgily printed booklet at him. "Know the turn of every season, in every city from Selerima to Toremal?"

Tathrin ignored him. The calendar bequeathed by the Old Tormalin Empire had always irritated him. Why did almanacs printed in different cities give different dates for the turn from season to season? Worse still, when the calendar slid out of phase with the sun's year, each city's priests decided for themselves where extra days would be added to summer or winter festivals. Since coming to Vanam and learning how simple calculations could avoid all such confusion, the outdated system infuriated him still more.

"Master Gruit, I need a book of maps." He wondered if he had enough money with him.

"Later." Gruit pushed through the crowd to a stall where a narrow-eyed merchant stood guard over gold-embossed books bound in gleaming leather.

"I'll take this." A tall woman in a crimson gown handed one to the merchant.

Her hair was dressed tight to her head in a style that did nothing to soften her severe features. Tathrin knew his sisters would condemn her dress as hopelessly outdated and he was surprised to see someone of his mother's generation out without a shawl for modesty's sake, never mind the cold wind coming up off the lake.

"Lady Derenna." Gruit tapped her familiarly on one shoulder.

A noblewoman. Which explained the Tormalin cut of her gown, for all that her accent was clearly Lescari. Though Tathrin would never have expected to see a noblewoman shopping without any attendants.

"Master Gruit, a moment." She turned back to the bookseller. "With the Kaddisoke Alchemy and that Aldabreshin treatise on higher calculus, I'll pay you fifteen silver marks."

Her manner reminded Tathrin of the inn's least welcome visitors. But nobility could hardly be turned away and his father always said arrogance didn't stick to the coin.

"Lescari silver?" The bookseller was sucking his teeth dubiously.

"Do I look like a lead merchant?" the woman asked acidly. "Caladhrian marks."

"Eighteen marks and you have a deal, my lady." The bookseller began wrapping the books in a ragged woollen cloth. "You're at the same address as before?"

She nodded. "I'll have the coin waiting for your man. Make sure you send me word as soon as any of those other titles come into your hands," she warned.

Tathrin wondered how she could spend such a sum with only the merest pretence at hard bargaining.

"Master Gruit, fair festival." Lady Derenna turned to grant him her full attention.

He smiled. "My lady, I have just received a consignment of fortified wines from Dusgate."

"Good." She accepted Gruit's courteous offer of his arm.

As she did so, the wind coming up from the lake ruffled the fall of lace at her elbow. Tathrin saw that her forearm was pitted and blotched with ugly white scars.

"Who is your young companion?" She turned intense dark eyes on him.

"Tathrin, Carluse-born but no friend to Duke Garnot." Gruit cleared a path through the crowd with his free hand. "A scholar of the university who hopes to see an equitable peace in Lescar for all ranks, from highest to lowest."

Tathrin made the best bow he could amid the crush of people and offered his ringed hand as proof.

"A scholar?" Lady Derenna ignored such ceremony. "Of what discipline? Under whom?"

"I studied mathematics, my lady," Tathrin said politely, "under Mentor Peirrose."

"A sound man," she allowed, "if too much inclined to relish theory over practical application."

"You know him?" Tathrin was surprised.

"Are you one of those who cannot conceive of female scholars?" she challenged. "Asserting that the highest intellectual calling a woman can hope for is merely playing the whetstone to sharpen superior male minds?"

"No, not at all," Tathrin assured her.

"You're a rational man?" Unmistakable meaning weighted her words.

"A rational thinker, my lady," he said carefully, "but no Rationalist."

"A wise answer." Gruit laughed. "Let's get some refreshment."

They had reached a space in front of the shrine where an alewife was dispensing her brew from barrels carried by a patient donkey.

"You may come to a fuller understanding of Rationalist philosophy in time." Lady Derenna regarded Tathrin. "My own interests are alchemical, as are my husband's. We work together as equals, agreeing that a finer understanding of natural philosophy must surely lead to a better life for all, from highest to lowest."

"Will I have the honour of meeting your lord?" Tathrin asked politely.

"No." Derenna accepted a coarse pottery tankard from Gruit and drank without concern for such unladylike behaviour. "Duke Moncan of Sharlac has decreed he cannot leave our residence. A detachment of His Grace's personal guard sees to it."

"Why?" Realising that was an impertinent question, Tathrin hastily drank his own ale.

"My husband spoke out against a decree that Duke Moncan announced to his noble vassals last Winter Solstice," Lady Derenna said crisply. "If anyone, of whatever rank, cannot pay their land dues over the course of this year, Duke Moncan will transfer title to the property in question to anyone who comes forward to pay those arrears."

"That's monstrous." Tathrin had often heard his father call the Duke of Sharlac "Jackal Moncan". It appeared the epithet was well deserved.

"Saedrin save those who don't have friends or family abroad to send them coin," Gruit said with a pointed glance at Tathrin.

"My husband wasn't the only one to speak out. Many born to higher rank are as eager as anyone else to see an equitable rule of law established across Lescar." Lady Derenna held Tathrin's gaze. "But Duke Moncan has been looking for an excuse to punish my husband ever since he failed to show sufficient grief at Lord Jaras's death."

Tathrin wondered if the duke ever spared a thought for all the other fathers' sons who'd died in that awful battle at Losand where the heir to Sharlac had been slain. "Can you not return home, my lady?"

"I could return, but I doubt I could leave again." Lady Derenna smiled thinly. "So I travel in hopes of persuading influential men and women to write to Jackal Moncan and protest his actions until he's shamed into freeing my husband and repealing the property decree."

"While Reniack stirs up the common folk for you." Gruit grinned at Tathrin. "Do you reckon Lescari lordlings will risk telling their duke all these things he doesn't want to hear if enough disgruntled peasants are hammering on their gates?"

"Hush!" Derenna looked around crossly. "If Duke Moncan learns I have any connection with that man, my husband will pay dearly for it."

"I won't say anything," Tathrin assured her. Anyway, the name Reniack meant nothing to him.

"Thank you." Derenna handed him her empty tankard as if he were still the pot-boy in his father's taproom. She looked up as the loud bell in the shrine's tower rang out the third hour of the day. "I must return to my lodgings. Gruit, I'll call on you later today to sample those wines. I'm sure my husband will welcome a cask."

Tathrin watched her walk away. "Why did you want me to meet her?"

"To show you that not every Lescari noble is your enemy," said Gruit. "Come on, you should meet Reniack. Listen to what he has to say about the sufferings of the common folk of Lescar before you beggar them further." He went to give the alewife back her crocks.

That noblewoman might not be his enemy, Tathrin thought, but she still treated him like a servant. That was no more welcome than Gruit ordering him around. All the same, he was curious about this man Reniack. He knew Aremil would want to know of someone who could stir up the common folk of Lescar. "Where are we going?"

"The temple of Saedrin." The wine merchant turned with a slight frown. "Come on, lad."

Tathrin slowed. "I've no wish to see men hanged."

After the battle at Losand where Lord Jaras had been slain, the mercenaries who'd fought for Sharlac had turned brigand. Duke Garnot had sent the war-band he'd paid to defend Carluse after them. Every last bandit had been hanged in chains along the high road.

"They won't start decorating the gallows till noon." Gruit began walking.

Tathrin followed reluctantly, promising himself he'd be long gone by then. He tried not to think about the two thieves who'd choked and writhed and soiled themselves as they swung from the gibbet by his father's inn. They'd been no older than he was, and he'd overheard his father telling his sister's husband that the duke's mercenaries had raped the girl before they strung her up.

It wasn't far to the temple to Saedrin up on the summit of the Grastan Hill, but the streets were choked with hawkers.

"Discover the secrets of Aldabreshin soothsaying." A girl with the dark skin of the distant southern islands tried to hand him a crudely carved circle of wood. "Read your future in the passage of the stars."

"A contest of dancing bears! In the Mercers' Market at noon tomorrow!" The burly man jangling a length of sturdy chain looked half-cousin to a bear himself with his bushy beard and long black hair.

"Come and see the two-faced pig! Two snouts, three eyes." A smaller man was approaching from the other direction. "A marvel of nature!"

The bear-ward rattled his chain violently. "Dancing bears, noon tomorrow in the Mercers' Market!" he roared.

"The two-faced pig and more freaks besides," the smaller man bellowed. "At the horse-market outside the Selerima Gate!"

"Dancing bears!" The bear man scowled ferociously and pulled the chain taut between his fists. "From the mountains of Gidesta!"

"A two-faced pig and a six-legged calf!" The pig's herald squared up to him, bold as a cockerel. "From the wildlands of Solura!"

The two men stood motionless in the middle of the street, gazes locked. Then the bear-ward threw back his head and laughed. The pig's herald grinned and offered the bigger man his hand. Relief rippled briefly through the crowd as people who'd slowed to see if there was going to be a fight began moving again. Tathrin wondered if the whole encounter had been deliberately planned.

"The wizards of Hadrumal keep you in ignorance while the dead can speak through those who can weave necromancy's spells!" A skinny man in a garish purple cloak shouted into the momentary lull. "The keys to Saedrin's door no longer lock away the secrets of the Otherworld!"

Tathrin saw a priest in yellow robes belted with an orange rope come out onto the steps of Saedrin's temple. He pointed the blasphemer out to three solidly built men also liveried in the god's colours.

"Want to know all the shields and blazons of Lescar's dukes and their vassals?"

Tathrin was about to brush the man aside when he saw Gruit accept the grubby sheet of paper.

The pamphleteer bowed to the merchant. "My congratulations on castigating the worthies of Vanam so eloquently, my friend."

He was a man of medium height and solid build, blunt-featured with brown hair and beard, both close-cropped and fading to grey. He wore a ragged blue doublet and grimy buff breeches, his lower legs bare and his shoes tied up with twine. Tathrin would have taken him for a beggar.

"If you can remember exactly what you said, I'll print it up." The man clapped Gruit on the shoulder. "It's time someone challenged Lescar's exiles to decide if they are sheep or goats."

What had happened to the man's ears? Tathrin wondered. Both lobes were raggedly torn, and not so long healed, judging by the red of the scars.

"I don't recall saying anything about sheep or goats." Gruit was amused.

"You may as well have done." The pamphleteer reached inside his doublet. "Do they want to be sheep, penned and fleeced? Or goats, roaming free, answerable to no man?" He showed them both a sketch of remarkably stupid-looking sheep looking through a wooden fence as fearsomely horned goats put a mangy pack of hounds to flight. "When goats could chase off those dogs of mercenaries."

A gap-toothed woman came up to nudge the fellow's elbow, her hands full of scraps of dirty linen. "I can't find no more. Not without getting a beating from the local rag-pickers."

The pamphleteer pulled a canvas sack from a pocket and shoved the linen into it. "Wait by the gallows and see what you can get when they cut the bodies down." Seeing Tathrin looking askance, he grinned. "You know the price of paper, apprentice? There's ways around that. Keep papermakers in rag and they pay in offcuts."

"I admire your resourcefulness," Tathrin said politely.

"This is Reniack—" Gruit began.

"A whore's bastard from the free enclave of Carif on the southern coast of Parnilesse." The pamphleteer bowed again, elegant as any lord. "I call no man father and I call no man master. My only allegiance is to the truth, which I spread as far and wide as I possibly can. What can words do, you ask me? What can one rock slipping down a hillside do? Scant damage. But send another after it and then another? A landslide can change the course of a river. What do you say to that, apprentice?"

"I think your imagery still needs a little polishing," Gruit said dryly.

"What if every Lescari exile lent a hand to bringing change?" Reniack wasn't deterred. "I know your history, Master Gruit."

A brazen clangour interrupted him. Gleeful, Reniack spun around. "Your pardon, good sirs. I must make a note of every name and accusation. Every honest man in Vanam will buy my broadsheet to learn exactly who has been defrauding them."

As Reniack shoved through the crowd, Tathrin saw shivering men wearing no more than their shirts led out in front of Saedrin's temple. Each one's head had been roughly shaved, tufts of hair that the razor had missed clotted with blood from deeper scrapes. The yellow-robed priest had been joined by another in the blue and white colours of Raeponin, while a third in the dour black of Poldrion carried the pole that symbolised the ferryman of the dead.

The priest of Raeponin rang his handbell and an acolyte read out the charges in the silence that followed. "Histen Soway pays this penalty for unpaid debts in the amount of six hundred and thirty-two gold crowns. Those with a claim on his goods should present their case to the Saddlers' Guild at the close of festival."

A heavy-set man in blue and white livery forced the offender to his knees. Another placed a clapperless bell on his head and beat it with an oak club. The noise was deafening. Tathrin hated to think what it must be like to suffer such punishment. As the man with the club lifted the bell, which was still ringing faintly, the unfortunate fell forward to lie half-stunned on the cobbles, bleeding from his nose. Two shamefaced men scurried forward to drag him away.

Tathrin didn't want to see any more. "If you'll excuse me, Master Gruit, I want to buy a book of maps."

"I'll walk with you." The merchant thrust his hands in his tunic pockets again. "So, I've been thinking. This notion of cutting off the flow of silver to Lescar's dukes is still folly. But if you and Aremil could come up with a better idea, Lady Derenna and her husband could spread the word among the nobles in all the dukedoms who share their fascination with alchemy and mechanics and such. Scholars don't let trifles like the quarrels and alliances of their overlords interfere with the free exchange of ideas and discoveries."

Tathrin frowned. "If her husband's under house arrest, surely his letters are read by Duke Moncan's spies?"

"Not the ones I smuggle in with the shipments of wine that I send for her, or the ones that come out the same way." Gruit smiled. "Now Reniack, he can send a scandal east and west quicker than the Imperial Tormalin couriers. He'd be the man to spread some scheme among as many exiles as possible in Ensaimin, as well as explaining it to the ordinary folk of Lescar."

He pursed his lips. "You should read his broadsheets. For every tale you can tell of greedy dukes and unjust levies and mercenary crimes, he can tell ten without pausing for breath and some will turn your stomach. He sees it as his duty to make sure those who've escaped Lescar's torments don't forget those they've left behind. But he won't be party to beggaring those who are already paupers," he warned, "so don't suggest this business of withholding coin to him."

"I see," Tathrin said uncertainly.

"Do you?" Gruit was sceptical. "Lescar's wars have been a weeping sore for generations. We won't come up with a cure. But if you and Aremil think you can concoct some salve, call on me. I'll see if I can make you think better of it. If I can't, we'll let Derenna and Reniack try their luck. If none of us can show up your next notion for the nonsense that last one was, perhaps there might be something we can do."

"Thank you." Tathrin grinned despite himself.

"Go and buy your maps, lad." They reached the turn that would take Tathrin back to the bookstalls by Misaen's shrine. "Enjoy your festival." Gruit walked away without further ado.

Tathrin made his way slowly back to the booksellers and managed to agree a fair price for a book charting all the major roads. It wasn't new, but it didn't look too out of date and he could make his own amendments. He walked slowly back to Master Wyess's counting-house, deep in thought.

"I thought you weren't going to the hangings." Eclan caught up with him, cheerful and flushed. Tathrin smelled liquor on his breath. "I saw you, when the debtors were having Raeponin's bell rung over them. What were you doing with Master Gruit?"

"Talking about wine," Tathrin said carefully.

Eclan shook his head. "My father says he's lost all real interest in the trade since he buried his wife and married off his daughters."

Tathrin recalled the unpleasant furrier Kierst saying the same. But Master Gruit didn't strike him as a man who'd given up on life.

"He was a wild one in his youth." Eclan laughed. "My grandma told me he tried to raise a mounted troop to go and drive the mercenaries out of Marlier when some warband took the old duchess hostage on account of not being paid. The old duke, he just said they could keep her and welcome." He rubbed his hands together. "Anyway, there's going to be cockfighting at the Golden Spur. Coming?"

Tathrin hesitated. He'd been about to go and see Aremil. He had no real taste for cockfighting, but how much more might Eclan tell him about Gruit with his tongue loosened by drink? He held up the book of maps. "I should put this safely away first."

"Till later, then." Eclan broke into a run.

Tathrin turned into the courtyard gate. As he climbed the stairs to the dormitory floor, a thought struck him. Sitting on his bed, he opened his book and leafed through the maps until he came to one depicting all of Lescar.

Aremil had long lamented the impossibility of getting news from all the dukedoms. The two of them had scant understanding of the quarrels between Sharlac and Marlier. But Lady Derenna was from Sharlac and Gruit was from Marlier. Whatever Reniack might say about a free enclave, the Duke of Parnilesse ruled the port of Carif. Aremil was born of Draximal blood and he was from Carluse himself. Between them, they represented all the dukedoms of Lescar, except Triolle. That would interest Aremil.

Putting the book in the chest under his bed, he walked thoughtfully back down the stairs. Might Gruit know some trustworthy exile from Triolle? A meagre place, it was still part of Lescar. He'd see what Aremil thought about asking the wine merchant such a question, once he'd learned all he could about him from Eclan.

CHAPTER SEVEN

Litasse

**Triolle Castle, in the Kingdom of Lescar,
2nd of Aft-Spring**

WAS IT ONLY eight days since she'd last had a chance
to walk the battlements? It felt like half a season.
Litasse stood motionless, gazing at the distant horizon, league after league away; reminding herself that
there was a world outside these grey castle walls. The
bracing wind carried a welcome breath of spring,
albeit a damp and marshy one in this bog of a dukedom. It was all so unlike the high wolds of home.

"Your Grace." Valesti's voice was sharp with disapproval.

"A few moments won't leave me irredeemably
weather-beaten." Litasse shot the woman a sharp look
to remind her who was maid and who was mistress.
Then she offered an apologetic smile. With so few
allies in the castle, she'd be a fool to alienate any of
them. Especially one who kept her secrets. This was

her home now. She mustn't forget it. "Forgive me—
I've been shut indoors too long."

The spring festivities had been tiresome enough, as
she spent endless hours in tedious conversation with
Triolle's vassals' ladies. Still, there had been dancing
and banquets and musicians and travelling players.
She'd had new gowns and gifts and been paid countless compliments. Even Iruvain had been pleased with
everything she had arranged, from the festival garlands for the great hall to the dishes she had chosen for
each table.

But now the entertainments were over and the guests
had gone and even the minor celebrations when the
season turned from Aft-Spring to For-Summer were
forty-two long days away. She was ticking each
morning off in her almanac. Meantime, every day
dragged as long and joyless as the whole of Aft-Winter.
The most exciting thing the stewards had reported
today was moths infesting a remote linen closet.

"His Grace your husband will be expecting you." As
Valesti spoke, the clock housed in the tower opposite
chimed and the brass arrowhead marking the daytime
hours slid downwards to the fourth sunburst on the
sloping scale.

Litasse heard quacking floating across the wide
mere that flanked this side of the castle. Peering over
the parapet, she saw wind stirring dense clumps of
reeds, waterfowl dabbling around them. A dog
barked, racing towards a huddle of birds on the
steeply sloping bank. A man in a maroon doublet
shouted a reprimand, the wind snatching his words
away. The birds were already taking wing to soar
across the water. Green grebes, Triolle's emblem, so
much more elegant in life than in the carvings of the

castle and on the pale yellow flags flapping above the gatehouse.

"Iruvain's still exercising his new hound." As Litasse pointed, the sun struck fire from her gold and garnet rings. "We can take the long way round."

She began walking, careful where she put her slippered feet. Winter's rains had left a treacherous film of green scumming the uneven stones.

"Tell the castellan I want this walkway scoured clean," she said with sudden decisiveness. "I wish to be able to take the air up here without needing hobnailed boots."

"The gardens below satisfied the late duchess, Your Grace."

"I am not the late duchess," Litasse said tartly.

"Indeed, Your Grace." Valesti's tone was unreadable.

Litasse looked down into the broad bailey ringed by this massive curtain wall. From the outside, the castle appeared unchanged for generations. A ten-towered fortress of rugged stone, it had the mere on one side and a rock-cut ditch on the other. The only entrance was defended by a murderous bastion manned by the best troops Triolle's dukes could afford.

Within the walls, though, Triolle's successive duchesses had insisted on some comfort. The towers around the curtain wall originally had just one room on each level, lit only by arrow slits. Now they had all been rebuilt to offer separate bedchambers and private parlours, and their inner faces had been refashioned with wide diamond-paned windows.

Looking outward, the cautious narrow slits were untouched. Duchess or not, Litasse had to don hood and cloak on stormy days to cross from her own apartments to her husband's tower, even to reach the dining hall. The lofty wall walk remained the only way to move between each turret without crossing the open bailey. If invaders ever conquered the bastion, Triolle's defenders could still make them fight for every room and every stair of each and every tower.

If that should happen, Litasse decided, enemy soldiers trampling the garden that her husband's mother had laid out would have her blessing, so that no future bride would be expected to walk in pointless circles following the geometric paths of coloured gravel curling between knee-high hedges. Fragrant shrubs and clusters of herbs dotted the dark earth, waiting for the first spring flowers. At least the former duchess had left her mark on the castle. What would Litasse's legacy be?

"How diligently do the townsfolk remember Duke Gerone and Duchess Casatia now?" Litasse looked across the mere to the walls of Triolle Town. Beyond the ramparts, shingled roofs huddled close. One building stood out amid the twisted streets. Circular, it was tiled in vibrant blue and yellow, the pattern of Drianon's wheat sheaves glowing in the thin sunshine.

"There are always fresh garlands laid before their funerary urns, Your Grace," Valesti confirmed.

Hammering echoed across the glassy green water and Litasse noticed figures moving between the crenellations of the town walls. The militia must be repairing the wooden hoardings after the winter storms, lest spring and summer bring man-made destruction. She had better go and hear what tidings the freshening winds had brought Master Hamare.

Movement caught her eye. Duke Iruvain was striding across the bailey, the young dog wayward at his heels. His duties always seemed to leave him time to indulge his own pleasures, she thought resentfully. Everyone excused him, saying he was so young to be shouldering the rule of the dukedom. He had seen twenty-three summers to her twenty-two, and yet everyone said she was lucky their mothers had made this marriage before she grew too old to be a bride.

Seeing Iruvain enter a doorway below, she walked more quickly.

"Your Grace." The man-at-arms eating a meat pasty on the top of the Messenger Tower choked. His coughing startled the dozing pigeons into petulant fluttering against the bars of their cages.

"The door, if you please." Litasse favoured him with her sweetest smile as she discreetly twitched up her poppy-red gown to keep her lace-trimmed underskirts out of the muck.

"Of course." He sprang forward.

"Your Grace." The men on the floor below were as startled as the sentry. One of them swept the rune bones they'd been gambling with under a chair.

"Good morning." Perfectly poised, Litasse swept through to the stairs beyond.

Valesti followed, demure in brown gown and linen cap. When they reached the landing below, her manner was anything but meek. "Your Grace! Your hair!"

Litasse stood still while the maid's deft fingers subdued whatever wisps the wind had teased out of her crown of black plaits. "Well?" She arched one finely plucked brow, her blue eyes challenging.

Valesti nodded with limited approval. "Fresh air has improved Your Grace's complexion."

"Let's hope my lord and husband appreciates that." Whatever Iruvain might think, Litasse was pleased.

The reflection in her looking glass that morning had been pale as whey. She moderated her smile as they reached the foot of the next flight of stairs.

"Your Grace." The man-at-arms on duty stiffened in salute and opened the door. "Master Hamare, Her Grace Duchess Litasse requires you."

Hamare bowed low, nevertheless continuing his conversation with a lean young man with light hair. "Did you ever find out who they were?"

The youth shrugged. "A governess and a tutor who'd been turned out when Lord Berneth's children outgrew their schoolroom. They were on their way to beg charity from some half-Tormalin cousins in Solland."

"We may yet find a use for them. Well done, Karn." Master Hamare, a slender man of no great height, leaned across the paper-strewn table to find a pen and make a note. "There's no sign as yet that this business with the bridge is anything but an opportunist attack by mercenaries?"

"None," the young man assured him.

Litasse was untying the ribbon securing her short cloak. She handed it to Valesti. "You may return to your duties in my chambers."

"As you wish, Your Grace."

To Litasse's surprise, the maidservant smiled and hurried to the door, slipping through it just as the youth, Karn, was about to close it behind him.

"Hamare." Before Litasse could say anything more, boots thudded on the boards outside. "I hope he hasn't brought that half-trained pest of a dog," she muttered.

"Let's hope." Hamare's quick smile was gone by the time the man-at-arms opened the door for Duke Iruvain.

"Thank you. See that we are not disturbed." As the door closed, the duke brushed a kiss against Litasse's rose-petal cheek. "My lady wife, good day to you."

Leaving Litasse to seat herself by the round table, Iruvain walked over to study the tapestry map hanging on the far wall. "Hamare, what's this new quarrel between Draximal and Parnilesse?" he demanded as he bent to look more closely at the embroidered border dividing the two easternmost dukedoms.

"The Duchess of Draximal visited several Tormalin noble houses during the course of Aft-Winter and For-Spring, all of which are well placed to lend support if Dalasorian horsemen resume their raids on Draximal once the weather clears." Hamare sounded sceptical. "However, Her Grace was also accompanied by all her daughters."

"She can't marry off the rest until she has the eldest settled." Iruvain considered this. "What's she planning that's put Parnilesse's nose so far out of joint?"

"Duke Orlin of Parnilesse has learned that Duke Secaris of Draximal proposes to wed his eldest daughter to a Tormalin prince, the Sieur Den Breche, handing over a sizeable portion of Draximal's flax harvest as her dowry," Hamare explained. "Which leaves Orlin of Parnilesse standing at the castle gate, empty cap in hand, with his own flax and linen unsold."

"My heart bleeds for him." Iruvain's scorn was withering. "Duke Secaris of Draximal should be more concerned with Duke Moncan of Sharlac's displeasure. Have we had any answer to our letter conveying Spring Festival greetings to the old Jackal?"

"Not as yet, Your Grace," Hamare said slowly. "But the recent wet weather hasn't favoured our couriers."

Iruvain shot a glance over his shoulder at Litasse. "How do you think your father will take this news?"

"Lord Jaras has been dead for more than two years." She swallowed the dull ache of sorrow that still tightened her throat at the thought of her lost brother. "His tie to Draximal's eldest daughter was still informal as no actual betrothal had been blessed by a priest. My father is a pragmatist."

"Write to your mother and find out," Iruvain ordered her, "and ask again why your father's been lying as low as a whipped cur for so long," he added with some irritation. "Did she say nothing of interest when she wrote to you at festival?"

"She sent me a mother's love and an aunt's blessing for you." Litasse's smile covered her hurt. She had never imagined she would be so cut off by her family, even when her mother had said that marriage meant she must forget Sharlac, turning all her attention to Triolle's concerns.

"I imagine Duke Moncan is determined to avoid offering either Duke Garnot of Carluse or Duke Secaris of Draximal any pretext for attack," Hamare suggested, "until Lord Kerlin is old enough to take Jaras's place both as heir and captain-general of Sharlac's militias."

It never seemed to occur to Iruvain that Litasse might still be mourning Jaras. She wondered how he could dismiss such grievous losses so easily. It wasn't even a year since he had fulfilled an heir's most painful duty by lighting his own parents' funeral pyre.

Iruvain went back to studying the tapestry map. "Is Draximal set on stealing trade with Tormalin from Parnilesse?"

Hamare nodded. "I hear rumour of a new agreement between Draximal and the border lords on tariffs along the Great West Road."

"More of your innkeepers' tattling?" Iruvain queried with faint distaste.

"Intelligence is intelligence, whatever its source." Hamare shrugged.

Litasse looked through her lashes at the spymaster and then at her husband. Hamare had pleasing, regular features, but no one would call him handsome, not while Iruvain was in the same room. The duke's clean-shaven jaw was firm and square, his lips full and sensual, high cheekbones lending distinction to his countenance. Where Hamare's hazel eyes were deceptively mild, Iruvain's dark gaze was compelling.

Hamare wore a black doublet and breeches of indifferent tailoring. Richly clothed, the duke was half a head taller, with broad shoulders and muscular legs. Hamare still wore his mouse-coloured hair and beard as close-cropped as any scholar. A touch of grey at his temples and around his mouth indicated the ten years' advantage he had over his lord. Iruvain's dark-brown curls gleamed with scented pomade.

"Parnilesse has another quarrel with Draximal," the spymaster said with a thin smile. "Hostile letters are being nailed to shrine doors at night."

"Again?" Iruvain shook his head with mild disbelief.

"What are they saying this time?" Litasse demanded.

"As before, that the dowager duchess poisoned her late husband to speed Duke Orlin's accession to his father's honours," Hamare said carefully. "And now, that she did so with all her sons' full knowledge, not just Orlin's as heir-apparent."

Iruvain whistled. "That's bold. Duke Orlin believes Duke Secaris is behind these rumours?"

There was no doubt about the marsh fever that had killed Iruvain's mother and father. Litasse was grateful for that.

"Many drops make a puddle," Hamare observed. "Many puddles make a flood. If enough Tormalin nobles suspect Duke Orlin of Parnilesse of having some hand in his father's unexpected and untimely death, they'll prefer to trade with Duke Secaris and Draximal."

Iruvain surveyed the whole map. "Do we know what Duke Garnot of Carluse makes of this?"

The dukedom of Triolle sat at the centre of the tapestry. To the right lay Parnilesse, with the borderlands of Tormalin beyond it. Marlier was on Triolle's left-hand side, with the Caladhrian marches stretching out beyond the wide blue course of the River Rel. Across the upper half of the map, Draximal sat above Parnilesse, and above Marlier, Carluse reached out along the Great West Road dividing Triolle from the northernmost dukedom of Sharlac. Tufts of green wool sketched in the untamed grasslands of Dalasor still further north.

However skilfully the long-dead weavers had ornamented the tapestry with gold thread and marked its towns with garlands of enamelled silver, there was no disguising the unwelcome truth that Triolle was the smallest of Lescar's provinces and the only one without a border to a neighbouring country. Leaving without crossing some other duke's territory meant taking ship from the paltry stretch of coastline to the south, running the gauntlet of privateers' ships when storms weren't lashing the Gulf of Lescar.

"Duchess Tadira of Carluse will always support Parnilesse," Litasse asserted.

Hamare nodded. "She sees any suggestion that her brother was involved in poisoning their father as a personal insult."

Though it was probably true, and who knew, Tadira might even have been involved herself. Litasse could believe anything of a woman wed to that murderous villain Duke Garnot. How could Iruvain be so blind to the man's duplicity, so taken in by his compliments?

"As long as Parnilesse and Draximal keep their squabbles within their own borders, I don't see that they need concern us. As long as Duke Ferdain of Marlier keeps out of it?" Iruvain looked at Hamare, brows raised.

Litasse looked at the map apprehensively. The dukedom of Marlier was half as big again as Triolle. The quickest way for Duke Ferdain to attack Parnilesse would be to send an army straight across Iruvain's dominion. It wouldn't be the first time a Duke of Marlier had ridden roughshod over Triolle.

"Duke Ferdain is wholly concerned with improving Marlier's trade with the Caladhrians and the Relshazri," Hamare assured Iruvain.

"He hasn't acquired enough gold to satisfy him yet?" The duke scowled.

"Your Grace, we could always consider improving our own rivers, thereby offering the northern dukedoms an alternative trade route to the sea." Hamare's hand went unerring to a map of the rivers that marked out Triolle's borders to east and west. "If we were to strengthen some embankments here on the River Anock—" his finger moved across from the right-hand border to the left "—and renew these bridges here and here on the river Dyal."

"No." Iruvain shook his head. "Those swamps and floodplains have been Triolle's defence too often. We cannot sacrifice them."

Irritated, Litasse spoke up. "There have been grievous floods along the upper reaches of both rivers this spring. The planting season has been sorely disrupted. If we have another poor harvest, we will have to buy in wheat from Caladhria again."

Iruvain waved her away with an impatient hand. "Then we buy in wheat. I take it our mines are still producing ore?"

Hamare nodded. "But the proportion of silver to lead has decreased sharply over the past year."

"Again?" Iruvain sighed. "Oh well. It all looks the same when it's stamped into coin." He turned his back on the map. "Is there anything else to discuss?"

"There's the question of your brother's betrothal," Hamare said slowly.

Iruvain hesitated before shaking his head. "Our mother may have wanted to see him wed one of Duke Garnot's daughters, but that's all ashes along with her funeral pyre. He weds within Triolle's nobility or not at all, like our sisters."

Litasse breathed more easily. Iruvain might flatter himself that Duke Garnot of Carluse was his friend, but he still wasn't going to let any other dukedom establish a claim on Triolle through a mingled bloodline. Not for the first time, she suspected Iruvain would have repudiated their own betrothal if the tragedy of his parents' death had befallen Triolle before their marriage.

"Anything else?" Iruvain went to the window and squinted up at the clouds scudding across the sky.

"The weather hasn't been kind to my poor pigeons." Hamare began tying up sheaves of paper with black ribbon. "I have had several reports of a merchant in Vanam disrupting some Guild celebration with an appeal for Lescari unity, but it will take time to decipher all the dispatches."

"I have no interest in exiles." Iruvain glowered. "Cowards and sons of cowards who abandoned their birthright rather than fight for it."

"As you say, Your Grace." Hamare concentrated on securing a troublesome knot.

"I'm going to the mews," Iruvain decided. "Perhaps we can go hawking tomorrow, my lady, if the wind drops."

"That would be lovely, my lord." Litasse let him see how much the prospect of a morning on horseback delighted her.

"What will you be doing with your day?" he asked politely.

"I must beg some of Master Hamare's time. I'm still having difficulty with the cipher in my mother's letters." Litasse could feel a blush colouring her cheeks and cursed inwardly.

Iruvain smiled with faint derision. "I'm sure you'll get the hang of it eventually. Until dinner, my lady."

"Your Grace." Hamare opened the door and bowed as the duke departed.

"The man outside?" Litasse asked as soon as the door closed.

"Mine," he confirmed. "Utterly loyal."

Crossing the room in a few swift strides, he took Litasse in his arms.

She breathed in the lavender scenting the shirt beneath his black doublet. "He doesn't mean you, when he talks of cowardly exiles. He knows you're as loyal to him as you were to his father."

"I only wish he'd listen half as intently as his late Grace did." Hamare pressed a forceful kiss against her hair. "He cannot ignore everything and everyone beyond Lescar's borders."

Litasse sighed. "He promised me, before we wed, that we'd travel to Tormalin and to Relshaz. But my dressmakers have journeyed further than I have."

"His father was determined he should travel before he inherited the title." Now Hamare sighed. "But it wasn't to be."

"He'll be asking me to fill his nursery soon, as a good duchess should." Litasse grimaced. "I'll be wracked with childbed fever and hemmed in by cradles. Drianon save me."

"He's no more eager than you." Hamare's arms tightened around her. "As soon as he's a father, not even escaping to his hawks and his hounds will let him make-believe he's still neither duke nor husband."

Litasse hoped he was right. Iruvain hadn't spoken of children yet and besides they'd only been married a little more than a year. Everyone knew children came later in a marriage between cousins. During the festival, no one had been looking to see if her waist was thickening, whispering behind their hands that it wasn't.

"Do you miss Col?" she asked suddenly. "Are you never tempted to go back?"

"I'm grateful my father sent me there to study but I could never make a life there, no matter how much he might have wished me to." Hamare held her shoulders so he could look her in the eye. "I am Triolle-born and this is where all my loyalties lie."

"Just your loyalties?" she asked coquettishly.

"Where all my passions are irrevocably committed." He ducked his head to kiss her neck.

Why didn't the touch of Iruvain's lips arouse such heat in her? She shivered with delicious anticipation. She fought the urge to kiss Hamare back as hard as she could, to smear her rouged lips, to redden her cheeks with the scrape of his bristles. But she couldn't leave this room looking fresh from a tumbling for all to see.

As he nuzzled the hollow of her collarbone, she felt him loosening the laces of her gown with practised fingers. She let the merest suggestion of a moan escape her. So unlike the nights when Iruvain came to her bed. She made sure to delight him with ecstatic cries and loud encouragement. No maid or manservant within earshot could doubt their connubial bliss. No servant passing a door closed on her private conversations with Hamare would suspect their duchess was deceiving her husband so quietly.

"Do you love me?" She closed her eyes the better to concentrate on the exquisite sensations teasing her.

"With every beat of my heart." He eased the red velvet off her milky shoulders. "With every breath I take." His kisses followed as he slid her lace-frilled shift down to expose her breasts. "Can we?"

"Valesti found a festival peddler to replenish my store of raspberry leaves and maidsgirdle. She agrees it's only sensible for a bride of my youth to regulate her monthly courses before thinking of childbearing." She opened her eyes. "I wish Pelletria was still my lady-in-waiting. We could both trust her."

"Forgive me, my love. I needed Pelletria on other business." Hamare lifted Litasse to sit her on the edge of the table.

"Did Iruvain know?" Litasse pushed him away for a moment. "That she was your spy? Did he ask you to find out if I could be trusted?"

"No." Hamare twisted around to kiss her pale shoulder. "That was the old duke's last order."

"Can we trust Valesti?" Litasse glanced involuntarily at the door. "She was one of the old duchess's women."

"She barely knew Her Grace." Hamare began sliding Litasse's skirts up over her knees. "According to Karn, she's no more than she seems: a maidservant with a sour disposition."

Karn, that was the spy who'd been talking to Hamare when she arrived, Litasse recalled. One of his most trusted enquiry agents, along with Pelletria whom she still missed. Quite apart from anything else, the old woman had been an excellent personal maid. "What has Karn to do with Valesti?"

"He's a good-looking boy." Hamare's searching fingers traced the line of Litasse's garters. "He has a winning way with women whatever their mood. He tells me she's lusty enough under all that starched linen. If Valesti ever thinks she can let your secrets slip, you should inform her that her reputation will suffer so badly that few will believe anything she says."

Litasse stiffened. "Don't play the puppet-master. Just the lover." She gasped as his deft touch melted her indignation.

"As you command, Your Grace." Hamare ducked his head to kiss her breast as he began unbuttoning his breeches.

CHAPTER EIGHT

Aremil

**Beacon Lane, in Vanam's Upper Town,
3rd of Aft-Spring**

"Can I help?" Tathrin hovered anxiously.

"You can bring these people here," snapped Lyrlen, "to suit my lord's convenience."

"You can both be quiet, please." Aremil concentrated on placing his crutches securely and sharing the burden of his weight as best he could between his legs and hands. His feet twisted awkwardly and he struggled to grip the crutches. But letting them dig into his armpits hurt even worse and caused worrying numbness in his hands.

Lyrlen plucked at her apron. "Master Tathrin—"

"No." Aremil would crawl across the flagstones before he'd let anyone carry him to the waiting carriage.

"You'd best sit with your back to the horses, to make the downhill stretches easier." Tathrin was opening the door, unfolding the coach's step, doubtless a duty he'd performed countless times at his father's inn.

Aremil nodded. "Very well. Lyrlen, if you please?"

She took his crutches as he rested one hand on the arm Tathrin was offering and gripped the doorframe with the other. Unasked, the taller youth lifted him bodily up into the coach. Aremil's balance deserted him and he fell backwards onto the padded seat. He stifled his annoyance. At least it was a relief to be sitting down again.

"We must remember to thank Master Gruit." Aremil managed a half-smile for Tathrin. "For the use of his carriage."

Tathrin took the crutches from Lyrlen and tossed them onto the floor of the coach. "I am sorry to put you to this trouble." He folded up the step and pulled the door closed as he sat opposite. "But it's best if this man Reniack doesn't know where you live."

"If he's half the man you say, I imagine he'll find out soon enough," Aremil observed.

At the snap of the coachman's whip, the carriage moved off.

"Perhaps." Tathrin didn't look too pleased at the prospect.

"You think he'd use my parentage against me?" Aremil wedged himself into the cushions as the coach rumbled over an uneven patch of road.

"You've read his broadsheets. He'd use anything he discovered for his own purposes." Tathrin frowned out of the window.

"He sounds like a perilous ally, but he could be useful," Aremil said cautiously.

"Master Gruit seems to think so," Tathrin agreed. "And if Reniack has no love for nobles in general, he's honest enough to judge individuals on their merits. Otherwise he wouldn't be working with Lady Derenna."

"I have learned more about her husband." Since Tathrin had told him about Master Gruit's unexpected introductions, Aremil had been making his own enquiries.

"Oh?" Tathrin looked torn between curiosity and his stubborn dislike for the woman.

"Lord Rousharn was the second son and so his father agreed he could study in Col." Aremil allowed himself a wry grin at Tathrin's grimace. "Don't hold his choice of university against him. He studied alchemy and became fascinated by the properties of rare minerals. Soon he discovered that volatile airs could be released by heating them or mixing them with vitriol and such." He swallowed. "The mentors of Col have archived several of his studies."

Tathrin was impressed despite himself. "And then?"

"Once he had won his seal ring, he travelled to Vanam and throughout Tormalin. He made a great many friends among the more intellectually inclined princes. He also met various Lescari lords with a taste for scholarship who were making similar visits." Aremil broke off as the coach rounded a corner with a rattle that sent a spasm up his leg.

"Gruit was right. There's a sizeable web of correspondence linking like-minded lords across all the dukedoms. They exchange books and opinions and recommend further reading to each other. A good many favour Rationalist philosophies, notably the writings of Niamen of Meche." He stopped to catch his breath.

Tathrin looked thoughtful. "Niamen argues that demonstrable merit is the most important measure of a man."

"He has also written extensively on the responsibilities of the high-born to use their wealth and position to improve the lot of the less fortunate." Aremil tried to ignore the strain the coach ride was putting on his back. "Just as those with practical expertise are morally obliged to build things like better drains and roads for the good of all."

"Has his lordship put any of these theories into practice?" Tathrin asked sardonically.

"He's spent time and coin making all manner of improvements to his estates." Aremil saw that surprised Tathrin. "He's held in high regard by all his people, down to the swineherds and road-menders."

"How did he come to inherit?" asked Tathrin.

Aremil took a breath. He didn't relish repeating this tale.

"Twelve years ago, his elder brother was killed in a border skirmish with Draximal troops. My uncle Lord Dacoun, my father's second brother, was hunting brigands who'd raided a merchant's mule-train on the Great West Road. He followed the trail into Sharlac." He shook his head awkwardly. "According to Dacoun's account, Lord Rousharn's elder brother was hand in glove with the raiders. He was caught with some share of the spoils and strung up from the nearest tree."

Tathrin wrinkled his nose. "I doubt Lady Derenna has heard the story quite like that."

"Let's not put her principles to the test by announcing my parentage," Aremil agreed.

Tathrin nodded. "How did they come to marry?"

"Lyrlen tells me she was born third child and eldest daughter to Lord Raitlen of Kerowth. Her tastes were always for study rather than embroidery, so her mother despaired of seeing her wed. Especially after she concocted some volatile mixture that exploded and scarred her arms so badly."

Tathrin grinned. "I wondered about that."

"It seems Derenna happened upon Lord Rousharn reading an alchemical tome when they were both guests at some Winter Solstice celebration. Her lady mother had Rousharn's signature on a betrothal contract before the day was out. They live together quite happily, boiling up concoctions that seldom explode. Scarred arms or not, she has done her duty and borne him five children—" Aremil broke off, hearing incautious bitterness in his own words.

Tathrin looked out of the window as the rumble of the coach's wheels deepened and the shadows of the upper town's gate cloaked them. Aremil slipped awkwardly on the seat as the slope of the road grew steeper. Tathrin took hold of a leather strap nailed by the door.

"Where are we going?" Aremil managed to force himself upright.

"Master Gruit owns property all across the city." Tathrin kicked Aremil's sliding crutches aside. "He's letting Reniack use an unlet house."

They heard the coachman shouting as they left the comparative quiet of the upper town. The lower streets were far busier and noisier. As their progress slowed to erratic fits and starts, Tathrin kept watch out of the window. Aremil was relieved not to have to talk any more. It was tiring and he felt ominous cramps threatening his legs. Finally, at long last, the coachman reined in the horses.

"Where are we?" Relieved, Aremil looked out through the window.

"On the northern slope of the Pazarel Hill." Tathrin threw open the door and jumped down.

Aremil used the doorframe to haul himself upright and tried to work out how to exit the carriage. He didn't trust his chances of negotiating the folding step safely.

A rough-haired mongrel ran up barking, startling the horses.

"Saedrin's stones!" the coachman swore, and cracked his whip at the dog.

Aremil fell through the open door when the unsettled horses jerked the coach forward. Tathrin's strong hands saved him, setting him down safely on the flagstones.

"This is a harness-makers' district." Tathrin remarked as he tucked Aremil's crutches securely under his arms.

"Indeed." Aremil surveyed the workshops and storehouses interspersed with rooming houses and narrow-fronted dwellings. He felt the flush of humiliation fading from his cheeks. If Tathrin saw no need to refer to his near-mishap, he need not embarrass either of them by thanking his friend.

"Good day to you." Gruit appeared from a doorway. "Thank you, Draig." He nodded to the coachman. "Back here at the seventh hour, if you please."

"As you wish." The coachman whipped up the horses and departed.

"This way." Gruit held the door open.

Aremil looked carefully for slippery filth that might betray his crutches. "Who's here?"

Gruit coughed. "Let me introduce you."

He opened the single door and ushered Aremil through the narrow hallway into a sparsely furnished sitting room. "Lady Derenna, may I introduce Aremil, a scholar of Vanam."

That was nicely done. Assuming Derenna was a stickler for etiquette, she wouldn't suspect Aremil was a duke's son. Those of higher rank were always addressed first when formal introductions were made.

She didn't look to be a perfectionist where her appearance was concerned. Sitting straight-backed in an upright chair beside a scuffed table, her dusty black gown was frayed around the hem and her lace wrap yellowed from careless storage. The silver combs securing her hair were polished but mismatched.

"A scholar." She frowned at his ringless hands. "Unsealed?"

"My infirmities..." Much as he hated to, Aremil let the excuse hang in the air, limp as his body between his crutches.

"Please, sit here." Tathrin ushered him to a cushioned settle by the empty fireplace.

Tathrin often argued that Aremil should present himself to the mentors and satisfy them that he was worthy of their accolade. But that would mean registering his name and parentage with the University Archivists. Aremil wasn't prepared to lie, and telling the truth was no option.

"Wine?" Master Gruit busied himself with a crystal ewer and glasses. "Kalavere white, all the way from Tormalin." He handed a glassful to Tathrin.

"I'm Reniack." The burly man who'd been lounging against the back wall stepped forward to take one of the fluted goblets. He looked at Aremil with frank curiosity.

Aremil met him stare for stare. "What happened to your ears?"

Reniack laughed, startlingly loud in the confined space. "I was pilloried, before the shrine of Drianon in the centre of Parnilesse town on the middle day of the last Winter Solstice." He tucked his ragged grey hair behind his ears to show everyone their tattered lobes. "To make sure I stayed put to suffer my punishment, Duke Orlin's man nailed me to the wood."

"You tore your own ears to free yourself?" Aremil was willing to provide the man with the audience he so obviously craved. Then he wouldn't be the centre of attention himself. "To escape the sticks and stones?"

"The mob brought mistletoe, ivy and smooth-leaved holly to throw, till I was up to my ankles in berries." Reniack smiled broadly. "I still fought to free myself. Freedom is the natural condition all men are born to, whatever might befall them after they've taken their first breath."

Aremil suspected the man couldn't call for a refill in an alehouse without indulging in such rhetoric. "Are you a Rationalist, sir?"

"Of the radical persuasion." Derenna looked severely at Reniack as she sipped her wine.

"What had you done to outrage Orlin of Parnilesse?" Tathrin asked.

"A broadsheet circulated details of his father's last banquet." Reniack shrugged. "We listed who was there, what food was served and precisely who partook of which dishes. As I recall, we wondered whether his late Grace's face most closely matched the green or the black of his servants' liveries when he was taken ill, since that would give some indication of what might have made him so unwell." He shook his head with mocking concern.

A knock at the door interrupted him.

"Excuse me." Gruit slipped out into the hallway.

Aremil looked at the glasses still on the table. Gruit had half-emptied his own, and there was the one that the wine merchant had belatedly remembered not to offer to him. And one other.

Gruit came back into the room, bright-eyed. "I have the honour to introduce Mistress Larch."

Tathrin straightened and then bowed low. Aremil found himself wishing he was able-bodied and could do the same.

The woman was a true beauty. Every feature was a painter's dream, from her oval face, broad, high forehead and elegant nose to her irresistibly sensuous lips. Her skin was flawless, her coiled hair burnished chestnut. The silk shawl draped around her shoulders was the exact same shade of violet as her wide, wise eyes.

"Mistress Larch?" Reniack looked askance at her. "When Orlin of Parnilesse was entertaining the Tormalin Emperor's cousin, I'll swear to Saedrin you were Lady Alaric."

"Doubtless I was." She took an empty chair by the table with fluid grace. "You may have heard of Lady Rochiel?" She favoured Lady Derenna with a charming smile.

The two women were about the same age, Aremil decided. Though the newcomer's black gown looked fresh from the seamstress, impeccably cut to flatter a figure perfectly balanced between slenderness and seductive curves.

Derenna narrowed her eyes. "I believe so."

"Mistress Larch?" Gruit was quite at a loss.

"It'll be easiest if you all call me Charoleia." She accepted the glass of wine he offered and drank. "An excellent choice. From Kalavere?"

"You have a remarkable number of names." Aremil edged sideways to get a clearer view past Reniack.

"I have a great many pairs of shoes." She smiled at him, quite at her ease. "So I don't wear holes in any particular favourites."

"While a change of name means you never wear out your welcome." Admiration coloured Reniack's laugh as he raised his own glass in salute.

The pamphleteer was blocking Aremil's view again. He shifted along the cushions. "Master Gruit invited you here?"

Charoleia rose and came to sit on the other end of the settle. "He hoped I might be able to contribute some ideas, if you're discussing the best way to bring peace and prosperity to Lescar."

"Are you Lescari?" Reniack sounded uncharacteristically uncertain.

"I can be. When it suits me better, I am Tormalin born and bred. If we met in some other city, you might swear I'd never set foot east of the White River." As she spoke, her words slid seamlessly from Imperial silkiness to the sharper accents of western Ensaimin.

"Lady... Charoleia—" Gruit stumbled over the name as he took the empty chair beside Derenna "—is an information broker."

"I should be able to find out whatever you might need to know, once you have a plan to resolve Lescar's confusions." She smiled at them all.

"Is that what we're doing here?" Derenna looked uncertain.

"Can it hurt to discuss some options?" Gruit challenged her.

Aremil wondered if anyone else had noticed how deftly Charoleia had brought them all into a circle. Now Reniack was standing between her and Gruit while Tathrin filled the gap between himself and Lady Derenna. "Why would you help us?"

"I'm assuming I'll be handsomely paid."

Her violet eyes were even more remarkable close to. Aremil couldn't see any deception clouding them. Though, he reflected, any woman living under however many names this beauty had was doubtless a skilled dissembler. He tried not to let the subtle allure of her perfume distract him.

Charoleia sipped her wine again. "Gruit tells me you all believe that the common folk of Lescar would seize peace, if only it came within their reach?"

"I am convinced of it," the merchant said instantly. "Every tradesman and merchant with Lescari blood tells me of friends and family desperate to live free of apprehension and suffering."

Tathrin spoke a breath ahead of Reniack. "My father says the talk in hostelries all along the road always comes round to how much better life could be if there was no more fighting."

"It's time the common folk were masters of their own destiny." Reniack wasn't to be denied any longer. "We in Parnilesse see our fields and forests plundered to suit the whim of Tormalin's lords, all for the sake of the fat purses they offer Duke Orlin. They cart away our timber and lime while we live in hovels with leaky roofs and crumbling walls. His Grace sells the flax and the hides that are the fruits of our labours, while our women dress in rags and our children go barefoot.

Tormalin merchants demand thrice the price they paid us when we need to buy linen and shoes."

"Only Parnilesse suffers?" Charoleia raised her perfectly shaped brows.

Gruit scowled. "Every dukedom's resources are sold to fund the same foolish ambition."

"Will the people of Parnilesse believe that?" Charoleia looked intently at Reniack. "Could they find common cause with Draximal's peasants? When they've been told so long and loud that all their sufferings are their neighbour's fault? That Draximal's lust to rule over them means rape and plunder unless they fight back? Could they ever believe that Draximal's folk go in just as much fear of Parnilesse's fell purpose threatening their lives and livelihoods?"

"I believe so." Reniack looked steadily at her. "If they were told long and loud how suffering unites the common folk of Lescar far more than lordly quarrels divide them."

"If every Lescari living in exile told them the same," Aremil realised, "and that no Caladhrian, nor anyone in Vanam or Col, pays any heed to whether we're Marlier-born or Draximal. All we are is Lescari."

"Best not say that's such a term of contempt," Reniack commented sourly.

"A byword for folly," Derenna agreed. "As pointless as brother fighting brother and trampling their inheritance into the mud between them."

"That galls you?" Charoleia challenged them all. "Then use it to goad the common folk of Parnilesse and Sharlac to make common cause with those of Triolle and throw the lie back in everyone's teeth."

"It's not just the common folk who are tired of warfare," Lady Derenna said, nettled. "Those of elevated rank see the suffering more clearly than anyone. We have the education to truly understand such improvidence, but we're caught in a cruel vice. Our tenants cry out for relief while our overlords demand ever more burdensome levies and tithes of meat and grain."

"Why not refuse such demands?" Charoleia wondered.

Derenna stared at her. "We would have armed mercenaries breaking down our gates to take whatever they could find of value."

Aremil was beginning to see that this newcomer was as astute as she was beautiful. One of his most respected mentors always drew his students towards the conclusion he desired with questions, so they believed they had discovered it for themselves.

"Mercenaries." Reniack spat into the empty fireplace. "They have no interest in peace, no stake in Parnilesse's prosperity. They are parasites. Everyone hates them."

"A loathing that unites common folk and nobility," Charoleia said lightly.

"The common folk cannot stand against mercenaries." Gruit shook his white head as he refilled his wine glass. "The militias are so poorly armed and seldom trained."

"You do your people disservice," Reniack asserted. "Militiamen have fought to the death in courageous defence of their hearths and homes. Mercenaries flee the field of battle as soon as their own skins are threatened."

"Which is one reason why so few battles are ever conclusive," Aremil pointed out.

"The dukes dare not put decent weapons into skilled hands." Derenna shook her head. "If they did, honest men and women could demand more rational rule."

Frustrated silence filled the room. Charoleia broke it.

"So are you all convinced it's only the dukes who want this warfare?"

Aremil met Tathrin's glance and saw his friend's agreement. "I believe that's so."

"Then Lescar could indeed have peace, if everyone else refused to involve themselves in the dukes' quarrels?" Charoleia asked.

Now the silence was stunned.

"The wind's already blowing in that direction in Carluse," Charoleia assured them. "Isn't it, Tathrin?"

Aremil looked at him. Astonished, he saw that the tall scholar looked as guilty as a schoolboy caught putting a snail in someone's boots.

"Yes," Tathrin said reluctantly.

"What's afoot in Carluse?" demanded Gruit.

Tathrin rubbed a hand over his mouth, looking uncomfortably at Aremil. "I would have told you, but it wasn't my secret. I was sworn not to tell. I shouldn't tell now."

"I understand." Aremil swallowed.

"I don't," Reniack said robustly. "Come on, don't keep us guessing! Or are you afraid Raeponin's going to ring his bell over you for telling?"

"I don't see why he should be mocked for keeping his word." Derenna looked crossly at the pamphleteer. "I can assure you, Master Tathrin, and I'll swear whatever oaths you may choose, that I'll not breathe a word of whatever you may say."

"That goes for all of us," Gruit assured Tathrin.

"It does." Reniack looked intently at the young scholar. "I'll spill no secrets that would get you hanged, just as I'll trust you with knowledge that could send me to the gallows."

Tathrin nodded, making up his mind.

"In our inn, there's a basement room. Young men, young women, too, they come to stay for a night or so. They talk to no one, keeping out of sight. We're told never to mention them. Then they move on, some with the wagon trains and a few of the muleteers, always the same ones. My father says they're going to Caladhria or to Ensaimin, wherever they have kin. Guildmasters send them, and sometimes the priests, so they're not hauled off to serve in a militia. Sometimes their families just can't bear the burden of feeding them, if fighting has ruined their harvest or mercenaries have plundered their stores."

"Carluse's guildsmen have allies all along the highways." Charoleia smiled. "They're sick of seeing the youth and hope of their crafts and families dying in pointless battles. They tell Duke Garnot's reeves that the apprentices have run off or died of some pox, that the girls have married a distant cousin or died of an unwanted baby." She looked at Gruit. "Wouldn't the guildmasters of Marlier agree that's a stratagem they could usefully copy?"

"I believe so," he said with slow incredulity.

Reniack's loud laugh filled the room. "How do you celebrate festival if no one turns up to dance?"

"Could we really persuade everyone to refuse to fight?" Aremil found the notion intoxicating. "Across all six dukedoms?"

"I could persuade more than half. Just let me write the pamphlets. If Gruit's fellow merchants can carry them into Lescar, I can get them into every alehouse and market square." Reniack began pacing back and forth. "My sympathisers will nail them on every shrine door!"

Derenna was torn between shock and hope. "But the dukes will still have their mercenaries to call on."

"Mercenaries fight for whoever is paying them." Aremil was struck with sudden inspiration. "What if the coin that so many exiles send home paid the curs not to fight instead?"

"If the common folk were left alone to tend their crops and herds, they wouldn't need that coin to save themselves from starving." Tathrin looked at Gruit.

"No militia answering their summons and no mercenaries to call on." Reniack's expression grew distant. "Why, our noble dukes would have to settle their arguments man to man. Let's put the six of them in a field with swords and maces to fight it out. The last one standing could call himself High King. No one need pay more heed than they would to a cockerel crowing on a dung hill."

Derenna looked astonished. "It cannot be so simple, surely?"

"It wouldn't be nearly so simple," Charoleia said calmly. "But it's an idea, the beginnings of a plan. Isn't that what you wanted?"

She had come to this meeting having already thought all this through, Aremil was convinced of it. Was there more to come from her? Though this was no time to raise the notion of using aetheric magic, he decided reluctantly. Not until he had more certain knowledge than the vague explanation he'd offered to Gruit. Besides, he'd want to be sure Reniack wouldn't look to use such a thing for his own unscrupulous ends. And Derenna would surely dismiss the notion with true Rationalist scorn. Aremil found he had no wish to look a credulous fool in Charoleia's violet eyes.

"Do we have anything to lose by trying?" Gruit looked around the room.

"We can do a lot between us, and through the men and women we know, to spread this idea." Reniack had no doubts. "If it takes root, who knows what the result might be?"

"Lady Derenna's right about the mercenaries. They'll fight as long as the dukes give them gold." Tathrin frowned. "Who could negotiate with them, to take them out of the balance?"

"I know resourceful swordsmen who've fought with the finest mercenary bands," Charoleia remarked. "They could help persuade such men to stay safely encamped for the sake of a share in the coin you're offering. It's a better deal than risking their necks for some duke who'll only pay those still alive at the end of the day. Provided you pay them well for their trouble."

"Naturally," Gruit said wryly. "Where might these resourceful men be found?"

"At present, they're seeing what the squabbles between my lords of Draximal and Parnilesse might offer by way of pickings." She smiled. "I can write a letter of introduction for someone to carry to them."

Reniack shook his head. "I cannot be seen in Parnilesse. Duke Orlin's spies are hunting me and I'm too easily recognised now," he said with some disgust. "I couldn't open my mouth in a mercenary camp before someone cut off my head to collect the price on it."

"If you're sending a letter, you must write everything in cipher." Derenna set her jaw. "None of this evening's discussion must leave this room. If Duke Moncan of Sharlac gets wind of such a conspiracy, my husband's as good as dead."

"Everything must be kept secret," Tathrin agreed instantly. "No one must know what I've told you about the Carluse guildsmen."

"I'd travel to Draximal or Parnilesse or anywhere else." Gruit scowled. "But I'd be missed. Too many people would be asking where I was and what I was doing."

Aremil caught Tathrin's eye. "I doubt these bold swordsmen would find a cripple a convincing envoy. That leaves you, my friend."

"You had better leave as soon as possible," Reniack said promptly.

Chapter Nine

Tathrin

The Road to Emirle Bridge, in the Dukedom of Draximal, 22nd of Aft-Spring

"You don't want to go no further." A disgruntled packman trudging along the verge shouted up to the laden cart.

"Says who?" the carter replied belligerently. He threw back the torn sack he was wearing as a makeshift hood, pulling on the reins to halt his shaggy-legged pony.

Sitting on the cart's tail, Tathrin twisted around. He hunched his shoulders, the upturned collar of his cloak half-hiding his face. Even here in Draximal, he couldn't stop worrying that he might run into someone who'd once stopped at his father's inn. The last thing he wanted was word that he'd left Vanam to get back to his family. Besides, turning up his collar helped stop the insidious drizzle from seeping down his neck.

"Some gang of bastards have seized the Emirle Bridge." The wiry packman shifted his burden to ease his shoulders. "The only way you'll pass is by giving them the pick of your goods."

"Parnilesse scum?" The thick-set carter gripped his whip like a weapon.

The packman shook his head wearily. "Brigands, from the north."

"Drianon's tits," the carter cursed. "Where are you heading?"

"Reddock Ford." The packman began walking. "Unless some other flock of shitcrows have got there first."

"Piss and pox." The carter climbed stiffly down from his seat and went to the pony's head. "That's going to be half a day out of my way. You'll think better of going to Emirle Bridge, boy, if you've any sense."

"I have business there." Tathrin was already pulling his leather travelling bag from under some wicker baskets that had been added to the cart in the last village.

The carter shook his head. "You'll walk over hot coals for a cut coin, you Carluse men."

Tathrin gritted his teeth as he shoved at sacking bundles to stop them sliding off the cart. All across Draximal, whenever he'd opened his mouth, someone had made a snide remark about Carluse miserliness.

Which was rich, after he'd seen one innkeeper charge a local traveller three-quarters of a penny when he'd taken two whole pence off Tathrin for a bowl of mutton broth and turnips. Another had given an empty room to a local after swearing to Tathrin there was nothing free beyond a half-share in a bed whose mattress hadn't seen fresh straw inside a year.

"You mind them goose eggs," the carter shouted, seeing Tathrin touching a straw-filled box. He hauled on the pony's head to turn the cart around.

"No harm done." Tathrin ducked his head through his bag's strap and slung it across his body.

"Book learning won't buy passage over the bridge," the carter said with spiteful satisfaction. "Can't be one in ten of those scum can read." He clambered back onto his seat and roused the pony with a shrill whistle. The shaggy beast began ambling back the way they had just come.

Tathrin watched the cart go without much regret. He'd travel at least as fast on his own two feet. To his intense frustration, he had travelled fewer leagues on each successive day of this journey. The sailing barge on which Master Gruit had bought him a berth had carried him down the White River to Peorle in a handful of days. Then the merchant's gold had got him a seat on the courier's coach that galloped along the northern edge of Caladhria. He'd made Abray, where the Great West Road crossed the River Rel on the Lescari border, by the fourteenth day of Aft-Spring. But all across the southernmost edge of Carluse, and through Draximal, his progress had been painfully slow. It was already halfway through Aft-Spring. When Master Wyess had given him leave to go home for a sister's supposed wedding, he surely hadn't expected his apprentice to be gone till the turn of For-Summer. Tathrin hated to think of the lies he'd have to tell when he got back.

He began walking. Even if he didn't miss the bandy-legged carter's sour attitudes or the reek of his unwashed linen, he did feel uncomfortably alone. In Carluse, he'd been safe enough as his local accent was invariably taken as proof of trustworthiness. Once he'd crossed into Draximal, however, a constant chill of apprehension nagged at him like a draught on the back of his neck. Why should these people be any more generous to him than Carluse folk had been to the bloodied man who'd stumbled into an inn on the Tyrle Road, where Tathrin had stopped for the night?

As soon as the unfortunate had opened his mouth, his Triolle accent was obvious, even mangled by his broken teeth. All those who'd initially clustered round in concern had walked away. The badly beaten man had even had to pay for hot water and rags to clean and bind his grazes. Tathrin had struggled to finish his dish of pottage, silently mortified by his countrymen's callousness.

But he hadn't dared to draw attention to himself by going to the man's aid. He knew Aremil would have said he was doing the right thing, that the letter he carried was too important to risk like that. It didn't make him feel any less ashamed.

So he'd cadged a ride on the pony cart. Like the carriers carts winding their circuitous routes through the villages back home, intermittent passengers came and went for the price of a copper coin. Men and women bringing their packages for transport or collecting something sent from some other village took no notice of him or anyone else.

Well, Emirle Bridge wasn't far now and if he was walking alone, at least he didn't hail from Parnilesse. If Draximal tavern-keepers thought Carluse men were skinflints, they condemned everyone from Parnilesse as whoremongers, thieves and worse. When the carrier hadn't been abusing his pony as a lazy lump of dog meat, he'd regaled Tathrin with endless tales of

Parnilesse duplicity witnessed by some friend's cousin's brother by marriage. Or he'd detailed some brutality suffered by the sister of a man who'd once sold a wagonload of charcoal to his neighbour.

Tathrin picked up his pace. Those trees on the horizon marked the beginning of the forest that ran all the way from the hills of northern Triolle just visible in the distant mist to the River Asilor, marking Tormalin's border two hundred and fifty leagues away. He knew that from the map in the book he'd left safely under his bed back at Master Wyess's. Exactly where the boundary between Draximal and Parnilesse ran through those trees was anyone's guess. Naturally, each duke was accustomed to claiming all the woodland for himself. According to the carter, so many battles had been fought under those trees that lichen-stained bones lay thicker than winter-fallen branches.

Mercenaries wouldn't care where he came from, surely? Tathrin found his lips were dry despite the drizzling rain. He reached inside his doublet to reassure himself that he still had Charoleia's double-folded and thrice-sealed letter safe. What would he do if her signet meant nothing to whoever was holding this bridge? Would the names of these mercenaries she was sending him to find prove to be the talismans she'd promised? This plan had sounded all very well in Vanam, but his confidence had been ebbing away with every league of this journey.

At least the mercenaries were still holding the bridge, if that peddler could be believed. All the while he'd been on the road, Tathrin had been worrying about what might have happened without him knowing. What if he arrived to find that Duke Secaris's men had recaptured the bridge for Draximal? If he turned up asking for these two mercenaries by name, only for someone there to hang him for a bandit like them, just to be on the safe side?

The sooner he covered this last stretch of his journey, the better. He lengthened his stride again. The road followed a shallow ridge of higher ground rising above the water meadows and he could see the glint of the river in the distance. Countless streams ran down from the hills behind him to meet here and swell the headwaters of the Anock.

It wasn't long before he saw the walls of Emirle Town ahead. He slowed. Inside his bag, his fingers found the long dagger that Master Gruit had given him. Should he hang it from his belt? His eating knife would be scant use in a fight. But Gruit and Reniack had both told him not to show a weapon. If he looked as if he could defend himself, he was all the more likely to be attacked in a mercenary camp. Then why had Gruit given him the dagger?

"Hold up, there." A heavy-set bearded man stepped out from behind an unkempt hedge and planted himself in Tathrin's path. Much like a Carluse militiaman, he wore iron-bound boots, thick black breeches and a heavy leather jerkin.

Tathrin would have liked to ignore him and walk straight past, but the man was holding a long and brutal-looking sword. Even beneath the overcast sky, the steel gleamed with dull menace.

He wasn't to be some tavern-song hero, Aremil had said very explicitly. He was to deliver Charoleia's letter. If he didn't look like a threat, she had assured him, as long as there didn't look to be any profit in it, any mercenaries he met along the way were unlikely to kill him.

At that moment, the word "unlikely" struck Tathrin as a flaw in this plan big enough to drive the carrier's pony cart through. He let go of the dagger and slowly withdrew his hand from his travelling bag. "Good day to you," he said breathlessly.

"Polite, ain't he?" a voice behind him mocked.

Heart pounding, Tathrin looked around. Taller and thinner than the first man, this second was wearing the same gear. But both men's clothing was far better made than the crude uniforms thrown at Duke Garnot's unwilling recruits. And neither man wore anything resembling Duke Secaris of Draximal's colours of red and gold or the burning beacon-basket that was his badge.

"We can be just as polite." The bearded man smiled unnervingly.

"We can't be that tall, though, not unless some bastard racks us. Long drink of water, ain't he?"

Tathrin saw that another man had joined the first, squinting up at him. Two more were coming out of hiding on his left-hand side. All had long swords, though at least their weapons were still sheathed. None looked overly concerned that he had half a head's advantage on the tallest of them. Why should they, when all of them were broader in the shoulder and thicker in the thigh than him?

"On your way to town?" the man with the drawn sword asked genially.

"Yes," Tathrin said cautiously.

"Looking to cross the bridge?" The swordsman smiled. "You'll be paying the new toll."

Tathrin wasn't inclined to argue the point.

"We'll take it amiss if you turn back now," the second to speak pointed out. "We're getting a bit tired of folk doing that."

Tathrin didn't doubt it. "I'm looking for someone, for two men." He was pleased he managed to keep his tone calm and level. Then he realised he had no idea if these men would see the word "mercenary" as an insult. Better not to risk it. "A man called Sorgrad, and his brother. I have a message from a friend of theirs." His voice rose as apprehension tightened his throat.

"Sorgrad, you say?" The bearded swordsman looked blank. "Don't mean nothing to me, pal."

"The message is from Lady Alaric." That was the name Charoleia had told him to use to anyone but Sorgrad himself.

"Never heard of her," the one behind him said dismissively.

A sinking feeling in his stomach, Tathrin looked around the circle closing in on him. Every man's face was as unhelpful as the first.

He managed a weak smile. "I'll go and ask in Emirle, if you'll let me pass."

"So you're not looking to cross the bridge?" The speaker behind him was a man of fixed ideas.

"That depends on whether I find the men I'm looking for in the town," Tathrin said slowly.

"Don't bandy words with a scholar, Jik." The gang's leader grinned through his black beard. "You ain't got the wits for it."

Tathrin saw every man's eyes fix on his silver seal ring. He clenched his fists.

"We won't rob you of that." The bearded leader sounded truly shocked. "We're not bandits."

"We'll take a look in your bag, mind." The second speaker came up close behind him, drawing his sword. He was a thin man, but looked as tough as whipcord and leather.

Sweat mingling with the drizzle on his brow, Tathrin lifted the strap of his bag over his head and offered it up.

"Good lad," the man called Jik approved. He stepped back to let one of his nameless associates take it.

"Here's a nice piece." The man handed Jik the dagger Gruit had given Tathrin. He threw Tathrin's battered purse to another. "Salo, see how much is in there."

Tathrin tried to look suitably concerned, as if that purse held all the coin he carried. The rest of Gruit's gold was only safe as long as these men didn't search him too closely, so he really didn't want to give them reason to do that.

"Change of linen, some maps, a book." The nameless man was sorting through the rest. He flicked briefly through the small leather-bound volume. "Aldabreshin mathematics."

"Lescari marks, soft as shit." Salo was testing the coin from Tathrin's purse with stained teeth. He scowled. "A man could die of lead poisoning in this cursed country."

"Nice dagger," Jik observed grudgingly. "Gidestan steel, hilt and finishing by an Inglis craftsman."

"So where's this message you were talking about, pal?" The man who'd been searching his bag threw it back at him.

"I have it safe," Tathrin managed to say.

The man shot the gang's leader a look but Tathrin couldn't read it.

"Let's see it." The bearded man held out a commanding hand, his sword still ready.

Tathrin reached slowly into his doublet to retrieve it. He held it out, but when the bearded man went to take it, he twitched it out of his reach. "You can see the seals and read the direction but I'm not letting you open it."

Charoleia had been very clear with her instructions. Which was all very well since she wasn't the one risking a sliced throat. Tathrin clenched his jaw. If this man was set on reading the letter, he was hardly in a position to stop him.

The bearded man grinned. "I do like to see a lad taking pride in his work." He bent forward to peer at the impressions in the wax and Charoleia's flowing script. "Fair enough. Best be on your way."

At the bearded man's nod, the others all stepped backwards.

"Thank you." Tathrin tucked the letter back inside his doublet and slung his bag over one shoulder. He hesitated.

The man holding his purse chewed his lip before pouring half the contents into one grimy hand. He tossed the lightened pouch back to Tathrin. "That'll get you a bed for the night in town and pay your way across the bridge."

Jik, the man who had taken Gruit's dagger, just grinned as he tucked the weapon through his own belt. "Better hope you find your friend."

"Shut your mouth." The bearded man smiled pleasantly at Tathrin. "Best be on your way."

"Thank you." Tathrin squared his shoulders and began walking. He didn't dare look back until the next curve in the road offered a chance to sneak a quick glance over his shoulder. There was no sign of the men who'd accosted him. Presumably they were hiding in the hedgerows again, waiting for the next pigeon to step into their trap for the plucking.

He swapped his bag to the other shoulder and kept on walking, his pounding heart gradually slowing. He still had the letter and he still had Gruit's gold, thanks to Reniack's advice. Even if walking with the purse inside his linen drawers wasn't exactly comfortable.

Emirle's walls soon rose up before him. Common grazing stretched out towards the streams on either side. Horses were tethered here and there and he could see small knots of cows ostensibly being herded by youths who seemed more interested in huddling together for purposes of their own. The town gate was open and Tathrin could see men and women milling around. What was he going to say to them?

Heavy boots ran up behind him. Black cloth enveloped his head, a cord wrapping around his neck. He struck out wildly but rope snared his arms, quickly drawn tight. He was choking, golden flashes fracturing his vision in the musty darkness. Someone kicked his feet out from under him, hobnails brutal on his ankle bone. He fell heavily, unable to save himself. Hands grabbed him by the shoulders, waist and knees. He writhed and kicked as best he could but the choking tether tightened and his head swam. Was that a faint laugh he heard?

He was slung over someone's shoulder, carried like a bundle of hides in Master Wyess's storehouse. The noose around his neck slackened just enough for the strangling sensation to fade. He hung limply as he was jolted along, struggling to draw breath through the muffling cloth, fighting not to lose his senses. If they knew he was conscious, would they choke him again? The thought of dying like that was terrifying.

Where were they taking him? Into the depths of the woods to be robbed and murdered and worse? Fear and uncertainty were as much of a torment as the man's shoulder digging into his stomach. Hanging head down like this was making him feel sick and the breath was knocked out of him time and again. He tried to tuck his chin onto his chest to save his neck from the worst of the jolts but the noose threatened to throttle him.

After what felt like half a lifetime, the pounding boots slowed and stopped. Tathrin clenched bowels and bladder, his breath coming faster, harsh with dread. He was trembling, he couldn't help it. Poldrion grant him a quick death at least. He tried to think of a suitable prayer to the god of the dead. All he could recall were the tales of torture and mutilation that the pony-cart man had related.

A despairing moan escaped him despite all his efforts. His family would never learn his fate. All they'd know was that he'd fled from his apprenticeship after repaying Master Wyess's generosity with a pack of lies.

Chapter Ten

Tathrin

Emirle Bridge, in the Dukedom of Draximal,
22nd of Aft-Spring

"You bide still, lad." Whoever was carrying him slung over one broad shoulder patted his thigh.

Before he could wonder at that unexpected courtesy, he was abruptly set down onto his feet. Still hooded and bound, he swayed, dizzy. Someone laughed and shoved him sideways. As he staggered, his feet found a slick slope. Toppling forward with a shocked yelp, he tried to curl up to break his fall. Something dug agonisingly into his side as he landed on a hard, rocking surface.

"You'll answer for any broken ribs, Macra," a menacing tone said.

Belatedly Tathrin recognised the bearded ruffian's voice. That was who had been carrying him.

Something splashed as he was hauled upright. Dampness seeped through his breeches and he felt wood beneath his hands. Everything swayed; that wasn't just dizziness. He was sitting in a boat. He coughed.

"Best not choke him on his own spew."

Tathrin couldn't tell who'd made that laconic observation. Rough hands loosened the cloak swaddling him. Blinking in the daylight, he gasped with relief as cold, damp air filled his lungs.

He was in a rowing boat with the gang who'd accosted him on the road. They were heading into the middle of the fast-flowing river. The bearded man was sitting on a thwart behind him. That must have been what he'd landed on. Tathrin took a cautious breath. He was bruised but thank Saedrin he didn't think he'd cracked a rib.

"Where are you taking me?" he asked, hoarse with apprehension.

"To deliver your letter." The bearded man's smile wasn't in the least reassuring.

"Thank you." Tathrin drew up his knees and hugged his bag, shaking with cold, damp and dread.

The bridge blocked their way, gatehouses at both ends and a tall tower rising in the centre. A pale flag was flying from the topmost turret but Tathrin couldn't make out the blazon. He was more concerned with what lay directly ahead. Each pillar supporting the bridge's seven spans was faced with angled stones that cut the foaming waters. The arches closest to either bank were each blocked by something anchored, but Tathrin couldn't make out what. Debris pressed up against the other pillars. Amid the drowned branches of some uprooted tree, he could see the unmistakable oval of a wrecked boat.

"Head for the middle steps," the bearded man advised.

The rowers facing Tathrin didn't answer, grimacing as they hauled on their mismatched oars. He heard shouts rising above the tumult of the river and saw men looking down from the parapet, waving and cheering. Over on the town bank, there was more shouting, harsher, outraged. Something cut a white streak through the boiling brown waters.

"Shit for brains, the lot of them." Sitting in the prow, Jik laughed. "Don't they know they can't reach us?"

"Let them waste their arrows if they want," the bearded man said equably.

Tathrin couldn't look away from the central pillar. They were hurtling towards it, the boat bucking like an ill-tempered horse. Far too late for his peace of mind, one of the mercenaries was handing out extra oars. Soon all of them were digging deep into the water, muscles bulging. Was drowning as quick and painless as it was supposed to be? Tathrin didn't think being pounded against the bridge's pillars was going to be an easy death.

The rowing boat glanced off the angled face of the central pillar and scraped along it.

"Catch hold!"

Tathrin realised there was a door in the broad base of the pillar, wide enough for two men to stand in. A rope slapped his arm. He grabbed at it without thinking, feeling it sear his palm before he got a firmer grip. He let out a hiss of pain. More ropes followed, the mercenaries dropping their oars to catch them. The boat slowed, pulled tight against the stonework.

The bearded man climbed up onto the weed-strewn stair leading up to the doorway. "Come on, lad."

Tathrin tried to follow but his legs were too weak for him to manage the first long step out of the boat.

"Shift yourself!" Jik shoved him in the small of the back.

Tathrin grabbed at the slimy stones and the ropes and hauled himself up. Jik followed close behind.

"Who's this?" A swordsman in black and buff garb was twisting a loop of rope around an iron hook.

"He's got a letter for Sorgrad."

"Has he, by Talagrin?" The stair guard looked at him with interest.

"This way, lad." The bearded man went on upwards.

Still hesitating, Tathrin was astonished to see that the rest of the gang were still in the rowing boat. They let go of their ropes, whooping and cheering as the flow snatched the boat away.

"Shift." The thin man shoved him again, not nearly as genial as his captain.

Tathrin made haste, hoping his knees would soon stop shaking.

The spiral stair was dark and dank but thankfully short. It emerged into a narrow room with slit windows in the three outer walls. The door in the fourth side opened onto an arched passage and Tathrin realised that the bridge's roadway cut through the ground floor of the tower. At the moment, the arch was serving as a stable for some horses and this guard-room was piled high with newly cut forage.

"Where's Sorgrad?" the bearded man asked a man sharpening a scythe with leisurely strokes of a whet-stone.

"Upstairs." The man nodded toward a ladder.

"Up you go." The bearded man jerked his head.

Glad to feel some strength returning to his arms and legs, Tathrin climbed up to find a room filling the whole width of the tower. It was crowded with armed men and, he realised belatedly, a small number of equally dangerous-looking women. Most of the mercenaries were little different from the common folk of Lescar, though quite a number had the burnished copper hair of the Forest Folk. There were even a few with the thickly curled black hair and rich brown skin of the Aldabreshin Archipelago. All wore the same uniform of black breeches and tunics.

Some were drinking, others crouched around lively games of runes. There was a wide hearth on the upstream face of the tower and several men and women tended cooking pots wedged into the ruddy embers. A few were watching a game of white raven being played out in front of the portcullis rising up from the floor on the western side. Stepping into the room so the bearded man could follow him up the ladder, Tathrin tried to look as unthreatening as possible.

"Sorgrad?" As he climbed up, the bearded man looked around.

"Who wants me?" A man of no great height stood watching the white raven players. He looked at Tathrin and raised pale yellow brows. "Not who you were expecting?"

Tathrin certainly hadn't been expecting a Mountain Man. He just wished his surprise hadn't shown on his face. "I have a letter for you, from Lady Alaric."

"Have you, now?" A second Mountain Man stood up from a huddle throwing trios of runes.

That must be Gren, Tathrin realised, Sorgrad's brother. Charoleia had said they looked remarkably alike.

The whole room fell silent, everyone turning to look at him with unwelcome interest.

"Where did you find him, Zeil?" Sorgrad asked the bearded man.

He shrugged. "On the road heading for the town. So we snatched him and hooded him and brought him along."

"Do you think he's a spy?" Gren looked at Tathrin with sharp suspicion. "Is that why you hooded him?"

Zeil shrugged again. "I just thought we'd see what he's made of."

"Was it brown?" Someone on the far side of the room chuckled.

Sorgrad laughed with the rest before shaking his head. "You just thought you'd amuse yourselves at his expense, because you're a nasty bastard."

"There's that, too," Zeil agreed easily, "and Jik was getting bored of sitting in a ditch."

"Strip him." A massively built man sitting on an upturned half-barrel looked up from the game of white raven. "Check for tattoos. Zeil, any word from either duke? I'm getting bored eating pickled fish and biscuits."

"No word yet," the bearded man replied.

The heavily built man grunted, forearms as thick as Tathrin's thighs resting on legs like tree-trunks. "Let the millers in the town know that I want their best offer by the full of the Greater Moon or we'll cut the mills loose and they can pick up the wreckage downstream."

That was what was anchored under the arches, Tathrin realised. Floating mills, protected by the bridge and easier to move than permanent ones when fighting threatened this border region. What would the people hereabouts do for bread if they lost the means to grind their flour?

"You can strip yourself," Sorgrad offered, coming over, "or I'm sure Zeil will oblige."

"I prefer my meat more tender." The bearded man grinned as the rest of the room laughed. "And willing." He glared pointedly at someone behind Tathrin.

"No, that's all right. I've no tattoos." At least Charoleia had warned him about this. Tathrin let his bag fall to the floor and unbuttoned his doublet. "Your letter." He handed it to the golden-haired man and, refusing to cower, shrugged his doublet off and pulled his shirt over his head.

"And your breeches." The enormous man was concentrating on his next move. "And your boots."

"There's nothing in his breeches there shouldn't be," Zeil said easily. "You can keep those on, lad."

That provoked another roar of laughter and ribald comments. Hoping he wasn't blushing, Tathrin sat down to unbuckle his boots. He began to feel more hopeful about escaping from this with a whole skin. Zeil wasn't giving him away even though he must have felt the solid lump of the purse hidden in his breeches when he was slung over his shoulder. He tried to convey his gratitude with a look as he handed his boots over for inspection.

"No hidden blades." Impassive, Zeil tossed his footwear back.

Sorgrad was studying the seals on the letter. "Can I take him up top, Arest?"

The massively built man didn't look up from his game. "Just give anyone down below a shout if you're planning to throw him off."

Tathrin realised he wasn't joking.

"Get dressed." Slightly shorter and a little less stocky than Sorgrad, the second Mountain Man was already halfway up a flight of open steps running up one wall. He threw open a trapdoor, prompting protests as a draught followed the daylight and sent smoke from the hearth swirling around the room.

Grabbing his clothes and boots, Tathrin followed, Sorgrad close behind him.

"Slide off down below," Gren said cheerfully to the sentry on the roof of the tower. "You can shake hands with your best friend later."

"Go piss up a rope," the swordsman said amiably as he went down the stairs. "We're not all panting for a whore."

The raw cold on the exposed roof raised gooseflesh on Tathrin's arms and chest. He dressed hurriedly.

Sorgrad was studying the letter. "Gren, shut the trap." He looked up as the wooden door crashed home. "Who did you say sent this?" His eyes were piercing sapphire blue.

Tathrin met his stern gaze. "Charoleia."

"Excellent." Gren's happy grin lit up his face. "What does she want us for?"

His blue eyes were a little lighter than his brother's, Tathrin noted, and he wore his straw-blond hair longer, roughly tied with a scrap of leather thong. Sorgrad's hair was as neatly trimmed as if he'd just stepped out of a Vanam barber's.

"A handful of Lescari-born in Vanam have come up with the cunning notion of paying mercenaries not to fight."

"That's a heap of horseshit," Gren said with disgust.

Tathrin realised Sorgrad had just read an intricately ciphered letter straight through without needing any recourse to paper or ink.

"Charoleia says you reckon buying us all off will put an end to the warfare tormenting Lescar. Would you like me to point out the flaw in your reasoning?" Sorgrad asked mildly.

"If you'd be so kind." Tathrin could see no scholar's ring on the Mountain Man's pale fingers, but he was clearly astute.

"Most mercenaries do fight for the coin, that's true. Arest and his Wyvern Hunters, for instance." Sorgrad gestured towards the pale banner fluttering in the breeze and Tathrin saw the black wyvern on it. "As soon as either Draximal or Parnilesse comes up with a decent bid, they'll take their money and be on their way. But there's plenty who won't be bought so easily."

"A lot just fight for the fun of it," Gren explained.

Tathrin didn't like the keenness in his expression. "For fun?"

Sorgrad looked grimmer. "There are always men with a taste for cruelty, and a few women, come to that. Stay at home and beat your wife to death or bugger your neighbour's son and you'll dangle from the nearest tall tree. If your mind's set on killing, you can dabble in guts up to your elbows in Lescar."

Nauseated, Tathrin couldn't think what to say.

"Or revenge." Gren was still musing on motives. "Half the men fighting with Arkady the Red just want another hack at Kairal's Minstrels, after the last time they got their arses kicked. Then there's the ones out for fame and fortune, and beardless boys running away from home who think killing for coin's easier than an honest trade."

"They're generally dead by the end of their first season." Sorgrad looked down, as if he could see through the roof tiles into the room below. "Then there's the ones with nowhere else to go."

"Men like Zeil. Even if you paid him off, he's no home to go back to," Gren explained.

"Your grandfather fought to defend Carluse's borders, and your father, I'm guessing?" Sorgrad looked at Tathrin. "You'll find men with just as many generations of mercenary blood. They spend their whole lives going from fight to fight."

"Didn't Charoleia say all this when you and your pals cooked up this porridge?" Gren chuckled.

"No," Tathrin said with a spark of anger.

"Did you ask her?" Sorgrad queried.

Tathrin remembered. "She did say it wouldn't be simple, or easy."

"So she sent you to ask our advice, which is the best thing you could have done." Sorgrad looked thoughtfully at the letter. "My advice is, don't pay mercenaries not to fight."

"You want them fighting for you, driving off the ones who can't be bought out." Gren smiled with happy anticipation.

"Plenty of honest mercenaries would take your coin for that," Sorgrad assured him, "and prefer it to hacking down peasants."

"There's no challenge killing someone who can't hardly find the pointy end of a pike." Gren shook his head.

"Perhaps," Tathrin began cautiously. "But I would have to put all this to Master—" He remembered Charoleia's lecture on secrecy. "To my colleagues."

"All of you scholars, are you?" Gren asked with interest.

"Never mind that." Sorgrad walked over to the trapdoor and hauled it open. "Does anyone know where Arkady is these days?" he shouted down.

"Kellarin," someone bellowed back.

"Sheepshit," Sorgrad swore with economy. "Bald Juris?"

"Dead," another voice called. "His wife slit his throat."

That raised a cheer that made the tiles under Tathrin's feet tremble.

"Kerroy?"

"Dead of spotted fever over the winter. Him, Orlat and Shoddy Nair."

Tathrin recognised the big man Arest's voice, harsh with scorn.

That came as unwelcome news to more than Sorgrad, judging by the lamentation.

"Do you think we could get Halice to come home for this?" Gren asked hopefully.

Sorgrad shook his head briefly. "She's pregnant."

"No?" Gren was enthralled. "Who—"

"Does anyone know where Markasir is?" Sorgrad called as the noise below died down.

There was uncertain conferring.

"Carluse?" someone suggested, but several shouts instantly disagreed.

Sorgrad's brow creased. "What about Lerris the Mason?"

"Heading for Carluse," a gruff voice announced confidently.

"Definitely," another seconded.

Sorgrad let the trapdoor fall closed. "If you want someone to recruit mercenaries for you, Lerris or Markasir would be good men to talk to."

"Duke Garnot already has mercenaries in his pay. They call themselves Wynald's Warband." Tathrin sat upright. "Is he thinking of war this summer? Is that why those mercenaries are heading for Carluse?"

"Who knows?" Sorgrad folded Charoleia's letter carefully along its creases and tucked it inside his leather jerkin. "How much do you know about hiring mercenaries, lad?"

"Do you even know the difference between a hound and a cur?" asked Gren.

Tathrin didn't think he was talking about dogs. "How do you mean?"

"Wynald's Warband—they're using the Carluse boar's head on their badge now?" queried Sorgrad.

"Yes." Tathrin had seen a few of the uniformed mercenaries on the road when he had last visited his family.

"That means Duke Garnot is paying them year round, whether or not he's fighting a campaign," Sorgrad explained.

"Keeping them close to do his dirty work," added Gren.

Tathrin recalled the corpses hanging on the gibbet by the inn. "Yes, they do that."

"Among ourselves, we'd call them house hounds, taking the duke's coin in exchange for his leash around their necks." Sorgrad gestured at the flapping wyvern banner. "You won't ever see Arest add some piece of a duke's badge to his blazon."

"That makes him a cur," Gren said with relish. "A dusty dog, leading a free company of mucky pups, hunting wherever he wants."

"I see," Tathrin said cautiously. "What does that mean for us?"

"Dukes like to leash the better mercenary bands," Sorgrad said frankly, "and you won't buy them off. Once their captain-general's taken that gold, the company won't betray their word."

"No?" Tathrin tried not to sound too sceptical.

"Not often." Sorgrad grinned. "More importantly, Charoleia says you want to keep all this as secret as possible until you're ready to strike. You won't manage that if you approach any mercenary captain with ties to a duke."

"So we must hire some of these... curs?" Tathrin asked dubiously. "The ones who are a match for the dukes' hounds?"

"The scholar knows how five beans make a handful," Gren said with sarcastic admiration.

"What about these men who are heading for Carluse?" Tathrin was seized with urgent apprehension. "Are they free companies? Could we persuade them not to fight for Duke Garnot but to join us instead?"

Then he could hope warfare wouldn't be threatening his family before the summer's barley ripened.

"We'd need to know what Duke Garnot of Carluse is offering so we can come up with a better bid." Sorgrad's blue gaze challenged Tathrin again. "Charoleia says your father drinks with some guildmasters who like to get their apprentices clear of militia levies?"

"What's that to you?" Tathrin wondered what else she'd written in that coded letter.

"Thinking back on the last time Duke Garnot of Carluse sent men into battle against Duke Moncan of Sharlac, someone knew exactly where the fighting was going to happen, well aware Duke Garnot was wanting to lure Sharlac forces across the border into Carluse lands before he struck. Word got to Losand in time for the guildmasters there to make ready and close the gates to save the town from Sharlac's men and Wynald's mercenaries both. That information didn't come from Duke Garnot's men. One of Wynald's lieutenants got a flogging for it, but I know none of that company would send a warning. Why should they? Losand's fate was no concern of theirs and besides, if they came on the town all unawares, they could loot it themselves and blame some Sharlac dogs." Sorgrad shrugged but his eyes didn't leave Tathrin's. "I reckon those guildmasters have someone inside Duke Garnot's castle in Carluse Town. If that person could tell you and me what the duke is planning, we'd know how best to buy off Lerris or Markasir."

"Buy them both off," Gren advised, "to make sure whichever company loses out doesn't go off to fight for Marlier or Triolle or whoever Carluse is thinking of kicking."

"We won't get anywhere going into this blind," Sorgrad told Tathrin bluntly. "I won't even try, not even for Charoleia."

"Not for all your friends' gold," Gren agreed.

Tathrin had no doubt both men mean what they said. "There's someone close to Duke Garnot's mistress," he said reluctantly.

Gren chuckled. "Friend, do you like to play the runes?"

"You've got an honest face, Tathrin." Sorgrad's laugh wasn't unfriendly. "So it's the mistress?"

"I think so." A horrid qualm twisted Tathrin's innards, and not just because his father would be furious with him for betraying such a secret. "But if Duke Garnot suspects, she's as good as dead, and I don't know for certain." He'd only overheard his father speculating as he shared a late-night glass of white brandy with his brother-in-law.

"No one will learn it from us," Sorgrad assured him.

"If it isn't her, the chances are she knows enough to be useful regardless," Gren said comfortably.

"I could see if I can get a letter to my father," Tathrin said slowly. "I think he knows someone who sometimes carries word to a friend of a man who lives in Carluse Town."

"Piss on that for a partner-dance," Gren said robustly.

"It does sound like one." Sorgrad grinned momentarily. "No, I'm not following a chain like that. Any link could be weak or false and we'd have Carluse's fetters snapped round our wrists quick as you like."

Gren cracked his knuckles with keen anticipation. "Simplest thing is to snatch her."

"She never goes anywhere without an escort." Tathrin didn't like the sound of this at all. "Besides, if it is her, how are the guildmasters to manage without her?"

"If she has an escort, whoever's left standing can take word back to Duke Garnot." Sorgrad was unperturbed. "If we do this right, she can always go back to spy for your father's friends."

Gren nodded. "As long as the ransom's paid."

"Ransom?" Tathrin protested.

"You think Duke Garnot would be convinced she was innocent if he didn't have to pay to get her back?" Sorgrad raised his blond brows.

"You do understand we're mercenaries?" Gren sounded genuinely concerned. "This game of yours and Charoleia's sounds like more fun than sitting on this bridge with our thumbs up our arses, but we'll still want a fat purse at the end of the day."

"So we'll kidnap Garnot's doxy and see what we can get out of her, and for her." Sorgrad clearly didn't expect further debate. "We'll call that a payment on account."

"If you haven't got the stones for it, lad, we'll meet you back in Vanam with the lass all tied up with a ribbon," Gren offered. "Charoleia will understand."

Tathrin couldn't think what to say. Kidnapping? Demanding a ransom? That's what mercenaries did. He'd been sent here to recruit mercenaries to their cause. If he didn't go along with this, he'd have to go back to Vanam and tell everyone how he'd failed.

If he didn't go along with them, it was a gold mark to a mushroom that these two Mountain Men would seize the girl anyway. How would they treat her? What would happen if she fled screaming from such an assault? If he was there, at least he could explain who they were.

He walked over to the parapet and looked both ways along the bridge. Around the gate to the town and on the other side along the causeway, men were camped wearing Draximal's red and gold and flying banners with the beacon-basket on them.

"How do we get off this bridge?" That was his most immediate question.

"Same way you got here." Gren came to make an obscene gesture at militiamen too far away to see it. "It's a wild ride with the river this high."

Tathrin's stomach lurched at the prospect. Going along with these two and their new plan would be just as hair-raising, wouldn't it?

Sorgrad opened the trapdoor and shouted down into the noisy gloom. "Jik, you thieving louse, give the lad his fancy dagger back. We're leaving."

Chapter Eleven

Failla

**Carluse Castle, in the Kingdom of Lescar,
31st of Aft-Spring**

THE SUN WOKE her early. The duke's formal bed-chamber boasted heavy velvet curtains and wooden shutters, but this dressing room where he actually slept had only a muslin drape to soften the window. Duke Garnot slept on, untroubled by sunlight striking the silver amid his dark wiry hair. He always claimed that summer campaigns in his youth had taught him to sleep in any conditions.

She was pinned between him and the wall. The bed was comfortably wide for one, inconveniently small for two. She eased herself out, tucking the sheet and quilt down so no chill draught might rouse him. Reaching the foot of the bed, Failla took care not to trip over his boots and breeches. She hurried to the door, her stomach tight with appre-hension. As she eased the door handle, no treacherous squeak from the hinges betrayed her. The pork fat had done its work.

It had been worth ruining her silken reticule for the sake of stealing a scrap of rind from the suckling pig served last night. But she must burn the ribbon-tied purse before some maid wondered at the grease stains. She didn't want someone carrying even such inconsequential gossip to the duchess's women.

There was scant chance Duke Garnot would notice his gift's absence. If he did, would he imagine she'd sold it for the few silver pennies it would bring her? He never showed any sign of knowing that she turned as many of his favours as she could into coin. But he had always made it clear that she need not expect him to support her once their dalliance was done. Duchess Tadira begrudged the lifelong pensions paid to respectable retainers. She wouldn't countenance the grant of a copper cut-piece to keep her husband's discarded whore from beggary.

Failla closed the door carefully and let the tapestry hiding the dressing room fall across it. Moving more purposefully, no longer feeling as if she were walking on eggshells, she hurried to the second room opening discreetly off the grand chamber. Once she'd used the chamber pot tucked beneath the washstand, she had her excuse for leaving Duke Garnot's bed.

Returning to the high-ceilinged chamber dominated by the canopied bed where dukes were begotten and born, she began reading the documents discarded on top of the map chest. Duke Garnot wouldn't recall exactly how he'd left them. Not after she'd answered his summons wearing only a flimsy bodice and lace petticoats beneath her cloak, complaining prettily that she'd just been undressing, assuming he'd talk late into the night with his advisors. All the same, she replaced each sheet as precisely as she could.

Some letters were in the duke's angular hand, others in less well-tutored script. This mercenary captain was boasting that he could bring enough individual bands together to field a company of three hundred mounted hand-tallies. In any such group of five, Failla knew, one or two would be more servant and squire to the experienced warriors. Those youths would be grooming horses and polishing armour rather than killing men. So in practice that probably meant somewhere between a thousand and twelve hundred fighting men. She set the letter down and found another from some warmonger offering to broker deals with archers and crossbowmen, promising contingents one hundred strong. There was no indication that Garnot was planning to reply to him, but Failla committed every detail to memory regardless.

A sketch map of the countryside around the market town of Ashgil offered notes beside each manor house within three days' walk. She recognised the handwriting of Duke Garnot's reeve. So those noble lords who'd failed to pay their shield levy at Spring Equinox would find themselves housing and feeding whatever mercenaries Duke Garnot hired this summer.

What was he planning? Ashgil was well inside Carluse, thirty leagues from the closest border, so there was no clue there. Duke Garnot's most enduring quarrels were with Duke Ferdain of Marlier away to the south and with Duke Moncan of Sharlac northwards beyond the Great West Road. But Duke Ferdain had concentrated on making all the coin he could out of the river trade down the Rel this past year.

Duke Moncan hadn't set foot outside Sharlac castle since his army's incursion into Carluse the year before last. After that campaign had ended in the bloody battle outside Losand where the Duke of Sharlac's son and heir Jaras had died, Garnot had been content to let the old Jackal lick his wounds in peace.

If only Veblen were still here. Failla clenched her bare toes in the thick wool of the Dalasorian carpet. Duke Garnot had always discussed his plans with his bastard son. Neither ever realised how much she learned, lingering to pick up her music from the harpsichord or gathering up her shoes before she slipped away. It hadn't occurred to them that she might still be listening outside the doors she closed behind her.

Veblen had seen her stripped to chemise and stockings often enough to discreetly desire her. Encouraging his humble hopes with artless charm, Failla had often discovered still more details of Duke Garnot's plans. Besides, she'd been looking ahead to the inevitable day when Garnot discarded her. It would have been no great hardship to let Veblen love her then.

But Veblen had died in the battle before Losand. Tears prickled Failla's eyes. Duke Garnot had told Duchess Tadira he'd got the better of that exchange. A man would sacrifice a swordwing for the sake of moving a marsh hawk nearer to the white raven, all the closer to winning the game. Duchess Tadira agreed that a bastard son was no loss, even one as loyal and able as Veblen. Not compared with the firstborn of the Sharlac ducal blood.

Failla drew a deep breath to curb her threatening tears. Duke Garnot disliked seeing her with reddened eyes. Unless he was the one making her weep, relieving his frustrations with cutting words and cruel lovemaking.

She looked down, smoothing her gossamer shift. If her hips were rounder, ripeness came to all women. Her waist was still slender, her breasts beneath the translucent silk full but not yet sagging. She had put so much effort into making sure of that, made so many sacrifices. But she had barely been out of girlhood when Garnot's gaze had found her. How long before his eye strayed towards some younger harlot?

She'd used to dread that day. Now it couldn't come soon enough. As long as she had hoarded enough gold and silver to get far away from Carluse. Just as long as no one discovered her secret before she had a chance to run.

She resolutely turned her thoughts to more immediate concerns. Could she slip upstairs before the duke woke? Would her cousin Vrist be working in the stable yard, to see the curtain in one of the empty rooms twisted around as if by some careless maid? Could she find time to write down her latest discoveries?

"Failla?" Duke Garnot's deep voice carried clearly through the closed door and the muffling tapestry covering it.

She set down the paper with trembling hands and hurried back.

"My lord?" She smiled, coquettish, expecting him to throw aside the quilt to hitch up his nightshirt and lie back against the pillows. Would he want her to ride his morning readiness or kneel between his feet to take him in her mouth?

Garnot sat up instead, a crease between his heavy brows as he swung his feet to the floor. "Duchess Tadira arrives before noon."

He was clearly none too pleased, but Failla knew better than to agree.

"The town will rejoice to see her."

Garnot grunted. "You're ready to travel, sweetness?"

"Of course." She ducked her head biddably before glancing up through her long lashes. "Though I will miss you."

"I'll miss you, poppet." He laughed, lazily pleased. "Give me a kiss."

Sitting on his knee, she teased his lips with her tongue. As his arm tightened around her waist, his other hand cupped her breast, his thumb teasing her nipple. Faintly on the far side of the castle, the clock struck the second hour of the day.

"It's later than I thought." Duke Garnot stood up, more than a head and a half taller than Failla even in his bare feet. "I want you out of here by midmorning."

"Of course, my lord—" A knock on the door interrupted Failla's answer.

It was Lenter, the duke's valet. As always, he took no more notice of Failla than he did of the chair by the window. "Your Grace, I'm ready to shave you."

"Do we know when they're arriving?" Duke Garnot left the room. "Will everything be ready?"

"The maids are busy with the final preparations," Lenter assured him.

The closing door and the fall of the tapestry cut off whatever else the valet said. Failla bit her lip. Who was coming? Duchess Tadira had her own wing of the castle, and the servants there who scorned Failla so would have everything arranged as their mistress liked. Duke Garnot wouldn't concern himself with that.

Failla looked up at the painted ceiling where Halcarion, goddess of love and luck, bathed with her maidens. It was long past time the moon maiden granted her some good fortune. She'd have no chance to slip upstairs to the duke's guest apartments if the maids of all work were already sweeping and dusting and making up the beds with fresh linens. Come to that, if Garnot wanted her gone by mid-morning, she had better hurry back to her own room.

She stepped into her petticoats and tied them loosely at her waist before donning her cloak over her chemise. Anyone who saw her would ignore her just as Lenter had. As soon as Duchess Tadira was expected, Failla became as invisible as a shadow from some children's tale of the Eldritch Kin. That suited her. Slipping bare feet into kidskin shoes, she stuffed her stockings into the silken reticule and folded that inside the bodice that Duke Garnot had so enjoyed unlacing last night.

If she found a chance to write a message, could she slip it to someone she trusted once she was outside the castle gates? That would depend who Horsemaster Corrad chose to escort her.

Leaving the ducal chamber, she ignored the grand central staircase in favour of the servants' stairs. No one could tell Duchess Tadira that the duke's whore didn't know her place. There was no one around to see her crossing the inner ward's lawns and she slipped through a side door into the range of buildings that divided the main castle bailey. Everyone would be hurrying to get everything just right, so they could change into clean livery before the duchess arrived. Saedrin save anyone whom Tadira saw with dust on the black quartering of their surcoat or a dirty smudge on the white.

As she ran up the back stairs to the empty garrets, she could hear the scrape of tables and benches being shifted in the great hall below.

Someone had brought hot water to the washstand in her small room this morning. Failla was surprised into a smile. Tepid now, it still meant she could wash. Whoever had done her that kindness had also left a plate of buttered bread and a glass of milk. She ate and drank and made a rapid but thorough toilette, brushing out her long dark hair before plaiting it into a practical braid. Refreshed, she found a clean chemise of stout linen rather than seductive silk and drew on woollen stockings. Buttoning a cornflower-blue riding dress over thick flannel petticoats, she pulled on black boots.

There was still no sound of anyone else in the attics. She glanced at the hearth. No one had lit a fire, so she would have no way of burning a letter if someone surprised her with it still half-written. But if Duke Garnot was recruiting mercenaries for some summer campaign, she must send a warning to her uncle. Once she was riding with her escort outside the castle, she wouldn't have a chance to exchange more than a few words with anyone. It might be days before she could get a letter safely away from wherever she was being sent.

Before her doubts got the better of her, she opened the drawer of her modest dressing table and took out paper, pen and ink. Hesitating over the cipher that her priestly uncle had drilled into her when she'd last visited the shrine in the town, she blotted the page several times. There was nothing she could do about that. She folded the paper hastily and tucked it inside her bodice. It would be safe there. Duke Garnot would have dismissed her from his thoughts as soon as he'd dismissed her from his presence and no one else would dare lay a finger on their duke's doxy.

Picking up her gloves, she took a heavy cloak from a peg and was about to leave the room when she remembered the reticule. She tucked the beribboned trifle into her cloak's inner pocket. Ignoring the bustle in the great hall, she walked briskly across the cobbled outer ward to the stable yard, where she looked around for Horsemaster Corrad. He wouldn't incur the duchess's wrath if he was seen talking to her. Tadira had no interest in Garnot's prized and pure-bred horses beyond the gold and silver they brought into the ducal coffers.

"You'll be riding Ash, and young Parlin's going with you." Corrad walked out of the harness room. He didn't look pleased. "You're going to Thymir Manor. Go easy, and Parlin is to rest the horses overnight before he comes back. Greater Moon's dark and Lesser Moon's all but gone, so I don't want him riding after sunset."

Failla nodded. "Of course."

As Parlin led out the horses, she stepped onto the mounting block. Once astride, she took her time settling her skirts and petticoats comfortably. No one could wonder at that, if she was going to be in the saddle all day. She looked discreetly around the yard but to her frustration, there was no sign of her young cousin Vrist.

Parlin scrambled gracelessly into his own saddle and Corrad handed him the leading rein of the mule loaded with Failla's leather-bound chests.

"Go easy," he warned Parlin sternly.

Failla gathered up her reins. Corrad wasn't just fussing about his precious horses. Thymir Manor was too far for anyone to visit and return to the castle inside a single day, so she need not worry about Duke Garnot turning up unexpectedly. If he wanted her within easy reach, there were several other closer houses he could have sent her to. Did that mean the duke expected to be spending all his time with these mysterious visitors? Who were they and what did they want?

Her uncle would want to know. He needed to know. She bit her lip as the grey mare's hooves drummed on the wooden bridge spanning the ditch that separated the castle from Carluse Town. Did Duke Garnot suspect that his secrets were slipping through his fingers? Was that why she was being sent so far away?

Or did he just want to be certain that no one else could leave the castle and visit her without a noticeable absence? Could Duchess Tadira have persuaded Duke Garnot that his pampered mistress would just lie back and open her knees to his own son? When he had seen for himself how Failla dealt with the youth's puppyish infatuation?

She had made very sure that Duke Garnot's men had seen her swiftly make her excuses and withdraw when Lord Ricart had contrived an unexpected visit to find her walking in the gardens between the outer walls and the sheer cliff of the crag the castle stood on. When the boy had sent her a handsomely bound book of Tormalin poems, she had taken it straight to Duke Garnot, carefully torn between amusement at such a ridiculous gesture and faint indignation that the callow youth imagined any man could ever usurp the duke's place in her heart.

No, it would be Lord Ricart whom Duke Garnot trusted least. After all, he was the one who had always taught his son that his rank entitled him to take whatever he wanted from those who owed him their fealty, body and breath. Meanwhile, Duchess Tadira would be determined that no shadow of scandal should come anywhere near the youth before she had safely negotiated a marriage to advance Lord Ricart's chances of being crowned High King.

Failla glanced idly from side to side as she let Parlin and the mule go ahead of her. They rode slowly down the long slope of Carluse Town's main street, windows here and there hung with black and white pennants to show their loyalty when Duchess Tadira passed by.

Most of the townsfolk were too busy with their own concerns to look at her. A few men indulged themselves, their expressions as lustful as if she rode clad in nothing more than her own hair. A couple of women leaving the alley that led to Saedrin's shrine spared her a glance of scathing condemnation.

She couldn't see anyone she could trust. Should she stop and tell Parlin she wanted to leave some token nailed to the door of the shrine? Not without everyone pausing to watch and wonder what favour she might be beseeching Saedrin to send her. There'd be more than one who'd carry the tale to the castle, to Duchess Tadira, for the sake of a few coppers.

Even if she did such an unexpected thing, there was scant chance she'd be able to talk to her uncle. Priest or not, he'd be in his house at this hour of the morning, teaching the sons of those merchants who hoped to see a university ring sealing their letters one day. Failla wouldn't dare interrupt him, not least in case someone found him teaching less than absolute loyalty to Duke Garnot. If Uncle Ernout fell under suspicion, what would become of the gold and silver he kept hidden for her among the dusty rows of funeral urns lining the rear of the shrine?

Failla rode on, her expression serene, showing none of the frustration twisting her stomach. She felt the letter she'd written crackle beneath her stays. How long would it be before the news that she'd left Carluse Castle reached someone like Master Findrin or Master Mausel? And it would be longer still before they found out where she'd been sent. The blacksmith and the baker were both resourceful men, though. One of them would find an excuse to send someone to her, to discover what she had learned since she'd last communicated with them.

She studied Parlin's back as they rode out through the town gate and onto the high road. He should be long gone from Thymir Manor before anyone she could give the letter to might arrive. Failla smiled as she settled comfortably in her saddle. A night to herself was a treat she intended to savour. It was only a shame Thymir Manor was so far from the farm near Dromin.

But with Duchess Tadira returning to the castle, if Duke Garnot was busy with these mysterious guests, it could be days before he sent someone to reclaim her for his bed. Could she risk the journey? No, she decided, regretful tears momentarily blurring her vision. If she wasn't found at Thymir, she'd be punished. If she was discovered anywhere near Dromin, how could she possibly keep her secret?

She would use the tedium of the journey to go over everything she had read that morning, she decided resolutely, to be quite certain she had every detail fixed in her mind. If she couldn't send that letter safely onwards, she would burn it at the manor. Along with the grease-stained purse.

The road from Carluse towards Thymir wasn't one of the dukedom's better highways, but heavy rain after the Spring Festival had been followed by bright days and strong winds, so the mud had dried to a decent enough footing for their horses. As the morning wore on, Parlin exchanged brief greetings with folk labouring in the fields, glad of an excuse for a moment's pause. Farmwives bustling around their vegetable gardens dismissed him with a curt farewell. The villages were quiet, everyone occupied within doors barring the occasional maid sweeping dust across a threshold, much to the mule's indignation.

Parlin tried striking up a conversation a few times. Failla answered politely enough but gave him scant encouragement. The groom soon fell silent and turned his attention to the road ahead. The sun rose high in the sky until it hung above them, marking noon.

They were walking the horses through a stretch of woodland sorely in need of coppicing. Failla was wondering how far it might be to an inn where they'd find decent food for themselves and water for the horses when three riders appeared ahead, coming towards them.

Parlin turned in his saddle. "Shall we stop for a luncheon, my lady? These travellers might recommend somewhere?"

"Perhaps." Failla shaded her eyes with one gloved hand. The riders looked to be in a hurry. The first two rode into a shaft of sunlight falling through the leaves. Their golden hair shone. Would Mountain Men know anything about taverns? She'd heard they shunned all company but their own kind.

Chapter Twelve

Failla

The Thymir Road, in the Lescari Dukedom of Carluse, 31st of Aft-Spring

THE THREE MEN heading towards them were urging their horses to a faster trot. Parlin hauled on the leading rein to draw the mule aside and Failla followed his lead towards the verge. The first two riders passed the groom with a brief nod.

As the third came close behind, he sent his horse veering into Parlin's mount. The groom cursed as the indignant mule brayed and threw its head back, the rein yanking Parlin's arm.

The man rose up in his stirrups, startlingly tall, and punched the groom hard in the face. The youth fell heavily to the road. The mule reared and tried to flee, soon defeated by the weight of the chests on its back and Parlin's senseless body dragging at its bridle.

Failla realised that the blond riders were intent on her, one reaching for Ash's bridle. The mare proved just as quick-witted. Rearing and turning on her haunches, she galloped away. Failla gripped the saddle tightly with her knees and wound a twist of pale mane around one gloved hand. She drew breath to scream if she saw anyone who could come to her aid.

The bandits' horses were fresher. They came up on either flank. Failla dug her boots into the mare's ribs, lashing Ash's neck with a loop of rein. It was no use. The bandits forged ahead, driving their unwilling mounts towards each other to force Ash to a stop.

The mare stumbled on a rut. Failla kicked her feet free of her stirrups lest she fall. One of the bandits was reaching for her. She slapped at his grasping hands, screaming as loudly as she could. Someone might hear. The man caught her elbows, dragging her from her horse, horribly strong. She writhed and squirmed. Better to fall than to be carried off. Ash neighed and reared away and Failla was indeed falling. Strong arms caught her; the second man had jumped down from his horse. As the first man let go of her arms, she twisted around to punch this second assailant as hard as she could. Her leather-clad knuckles split his lip.

"Maewelin's tits!"

He dropped her. She landed on her tailbone with a shock hard enough to take her breath away. Before she could recover, the man bent to lift her up, strong hands around her waist. She would have punched him again but he transferred his grip to her upper arms, forcing her hands down. She couldn't hope to fight back. He was so much stronger, even though he was scarcely taller than she was.

He grinned at her and she smelled cloves and salt on his breath and expensive scent on his linen. He was older than she had first thought, she realised inconsequentially. Fine wrinkles made crow's feet around his piercing blue eyes. What was a Mountain Man doing on Carluse's back roads?

"Help me get him roped!" The tall man was throwing Parlin across his own saddle.

"Knocked him cold? Good lad." The second Mountain Man tested a length of cord between his hands, flaxen hair bright in the sun. "Sorgrad, are we taking him with us?" He drew a dagger and wound his hand in Parlin's dark hair to lift the youth's head. "It's no trouble to cut his throat."

"No!" Failla screamed.

The man holding her winced. "You're louder than Maewelin's crows, girl. No, Gren. Leave him be."

"You said we needed him." The third man, so much taller than the other two, spoke hurriedly. "To take word back to the duke."

The blood froze in Failla's veins. These men were working for Garnot? Why would he send men to seize her like this? Because he knew she had betrayed him?

"Dump a body and sure as Misaen made the mountains, someone's nosy dog will find it before we're half a league away," the man holding her pointed out. "We don't want a hue and cry too soon."

"True enough." Shrugging, the second man sheathed his blade and passed the cord under the horse's belly to tie the groom's feet to his wrists.

The man holding Failla looked sternly at her. "Will you behave, to keep your man there alive?"

She nodded mutely.

"Good." The blond man released her upper arms, only to fasten one hand around her wrist. He led her, unresisting, to stand beside the horse now burdened with Parlin's unconscious body. The tall one went to gather up the loose horses while her captor's partner fetched the mule, which had taken its chance to go browsing on a hedge.

Behind her woeful expression, Failla thought furiously. Something must have happened since she'd left the castle. There had been no hint of trouble that morning. Or was that why Vrist hadn't been in the stable yard? Had Uncle Ernout been taken? Or one of the guildsmen? She tried not to let fear numb her wits.

Whoever Duke Garnot's men had seized, they couldn't know for certain that she'd been betraying his secrets from inside the castle. Otherwise she'd already have been tied to a horse's tail to be dragged back to Carluse so she could be whipped through the town by Duke Garnot's executioner, to be hanged, naked and bloody, on the gallows outside the gates. At most, surely, he could only suspect her.

Or did Duke Garnot think his castle's guards would let her escape rather than take her back to face such a fate? She was one of their own, after all, born in Carluse Town. Was that why he had sent these men to catch her? Mountain Men in Lescar could only be mercenaries. If Duke Garnot already believed she had betrayed him, had he sent these brigands to get the whole truth from her? Would she suffer rape or torture or both before she betrayed her cousin, her uncle, the guildmasters?

Failla knew she would talk in the end. Duke Garnot had told her captives always did. She began weeping.

"No need for that." The man holding her captive wiped her tears away with gentle fingers.

She snatched at the dagger in his belt. He was too cursed quick though, catching her wrist as her fingers fastened on the hilt. She fought all the same, desperate to draw the blade, to turn it against herself. Better to die quickly than betray the honest men and women she had lied and schemed to help.

The second Mountain Man came up and broke her inadequate grip on the dagger. Failla's knees gave way and she sank to the muddy ground, wracked with genuine despair.

"Don't cry, sweetness." The second Mountain Man knelt with her, comforting her like a distraught child. "You'll make your pretty nose all red."

Was he going to try seducing the truth out of her? Her fear receded a little. As long as she wasn't being beaten, there must be some hope.

"Tathrin, have you got those cursed horses in hand?" The first Mountain Man, the one with the sapphire eyes, walked away, all business.

"Promise you'll behave and you can ride comfortably." The man holding her raised Failla to her feet. He was easily as strong as the other one. "Break your promise and we'll tie your ankles beneath your mare's belly."

She could tell he wasn't joking. Failla wiped her cheeks with the edge of her cloak. "I'll be good." Her voice broke treacherously.

"Please, don't be afraid." The tall man was doing his best to control the restive horses. He sounded almost as upset as she was.

His Lescari accent—Carluse, no less!—spurred Failla to sudden wrath. "Don't be afraid?"

"Don't blame the lad," the first Mountain Man said calmly. "Now, where were you heading?"

"Thymir Manor." The truth was out before she thought to lie. "Where we will be missed," she added quickly.

"Not before nightfall." He grinned. "We'll be leagues away by then."

"Who are you?" Failla clung to the anger that was holding her fear at bay. "What do you want?"

The first man bowed elegantly. "I'm Sorgrad and this is my brother Gren."

"Pleased to meet you." The second Mountain Man's bow wasn't as polished, though his smile was more engaging.

"I'm Tathrin." The tall man was still struggling with the horses and now the mule was being awkward.

"There are Woodsmen in these coppices. They don't take kindly to bandits hunting on their roads." Failla tried to sound convincing.

"Is that so?" The less polished Mountain Man, Gren, looked around with happy anticipation. "Will they put up a better fight than that sack of shit?"

Slung over his own saddle, Parlin stirred and moaned.

"Let's be on our way." Sorgrad took Ash's reins from the tall man, Tathrin. "Give the lady a hand up, lad."

Failla noted that the tall one was wringing his hand as if he had hurt it punching Parlin. Ostrin said he had broken a knuckle and serve him right, she thought vindictively. He bent nevertheless, so she could use his linked fingers as a step and mount.

"Why's the duke sending you all the way to Thymir?" Sorgrad took hold of Ash's bridle to lead the mare beside his own horse. "That's a long way to come from Carluse to chase you round the bedposts."

Failla looked at him, suspicious. Was this false friendliness to tempt her into indiscretion?

"I'm leaving for a few days while Lord Ricart visits."

Let him pick the truth out of that and carry it back to Duke Garnot.

"The young cat's sniffing around the old tom's quean?" Riding by her other stirrup, Gren laughed. "Can't blame the lad, mind you." He leaned forward, not menacing, more confiding. "So what would a man have to do to get a pretty puss like you purring? Can anyone less than a duke tickle your belly?"

"Gren!" The Carluse man, Tathrin, was scandalised.

Following on behind, he was leading the mule and Parlin's horse. Failla saw him looking at the groom's hanging head with concern.

Failla returned her attention to Gren. His eyes were paler than his brother's. "Your rank is irrelevant," she said calmly. "I may be a duke's doxy but I am no whore."

"Good." By her mare's head, Sorgrad was smiling with more approval than she would have expected.

Had Duke Garnot sent them to test her loyalty to him? Was that what this was all about?

She held herself ready to answer their questions with measured defiance that would prove her devotion. Only there were no more questions. Sorgrad led them down a narrow lane cutting between the coppices and on through a spread of fields where the first spring wheat showed frail green shoots.

They finally reached a larger stand of trees that Failla guessed was the edge of the hunting forest separating Thymir Manor from the next demesne. "Where are we going?"

"For the moment, this'll do." Sorgrad led her mare into a green hollow amid the trees.

"My lady." Dismounting, Gren spread his cloak carefully over a log. "You don't want the moss to stain your skirts," he explained reasonably, "otherwise someone might think you'd had a tumble in the long grass." His grin told her he didn't mean a fall from her horse.

"We have bread, cheese and chicken." Tathrin was busy with a saddlebag. "And wine."

"Come on, girl, you must be hungry." Mouth full of bread, Sorgrad jerked his head. "Sit down."

"What about him, hanging there with his ears flapping?" Gren scowled at Parlin.

Failla wondered if the groom was still unconscious or merely, wisely, pretending to be.

"Fetch him another clout and he might not wake up." Sorgrad bit into a lump of cheese. "Hood him."

Failla dismounted as Gren dragged Parlin's cloak down over his head and tied it tight. What part did the groom have to play in all of this? They'd said he was to carry the tale back to Duke Garnot. Was Parlin the one under suspicion? Did the duke want to compare whatever the youth told him with the report these mercenaries made? Did he want to see if Parlin told anyone else what had befallen her? She breathed a little easier. Parlin was most assuredly innocent of any involvement in her uncle's schemes.

"Chicken?" Tathrin offered her a nicely browned leg.

"Who are you?" She glared up at him. "Why's a Carluse man riding with mercenaries within his lord's own borders?"

"I'm no mercenary," Tathrin protested.

Gren took a hunk of bread from him. "Not so's you'd notice."

"We are, though," Sorgrad said calmly, "and we need to know what Duke Garnot plans for the summer—which mercenary captains he's corresponding with and where he plans to fight."

"So you can make your fortunes out of Carluse misery?" She spat on the ground at his feet.

"So we can put a stop to it," Tathrin said forcefully.

Startled, she saw he was wholly serious. "How?" she challenged.

Sorgrad answered. "We know you pass word of Duke Garnot's plans to some of the guildmasters so they can get innocent folk out of harm's way. We want to save you the bother. There are folk, Lescari folk, far beyond your borders who want to buy off the mercenaries before the fighting starts."

"And not just in Carluse."

As Tathrin told her a halting, complex tale of people meeting and talking in distant places, Failla listened with growing incredulity. Finally concluding, he looked at her with eager expectation.

"Have you run completely mad?" She didn't know whether to be appalled or bleakly amused. "Have you and all these merchants forgotten the truth of life in Lescar, living in exile for so long?"

"What's your point?" Sorgrad asked mildly.

"You think Duke Garnot will simply give up his plans just because he can't hire mercenaries to fight at his bidding for a season?" She rounded on him. "That he'll renounce all he desires for himself and his son and his son's sons? The High King's crown isn't just the spur for this year's fighting. It's his life's central ambition, like his father and his grandfather before him. It's the one aim that unites him and Duchess Tadira."

"They will be forced to see reason," Tathrin said obstinately.

"Reason has nothing to do with it," she retorted. "I read their letters and I hear Duke Garnot and Duchess Tadira talking. I see all their calculations as they weave their carefully contrived marriages and alliances. Come Solstice and Equinox, I see whichever dukes might be visiting Carluse doing exactly the same, them and their duchesses. They don't just plot and scheme because they have nothing better to do with their time. It's what they learned as life and duty with their mother's milk. It's what they breathe with every waking moment. Every duke dreams of uniting Lescar as a kingdom under his rule!"

"If they have no mercenaries to fight their battles, all they can do is dream," Tathrin insisted.

"Until they call up the militias. Do you think the vassal lords will refuse to fight when their liege-lord calls them to defend their own by attacking his enemies? They'll whip their tenants into line if they have to," Failla cried. "Duke Garnot's successes offer his vassal lords wealth and honour. They will carry on fighting just as they always have." She shook her head. "Folk say scholars are next to fools. I never thought so till now."

"If the dukes have no coin to finance their wars—" Tathrin began stubbornly.

"They'll sell their peasants' children into Aldabreshin slavery to raise it," Failla interrupted him mercilessly. "Garnot of Carluse has done it before and so has Ferdain of Marlier. The other dukes would do the same."

That finally silenced Tathrin. Failla looked down to find she was still holding the chicken leg. Absurdly, she realised she was hungry and began to eat.

"It always comes back to these dukes." Gren chewed a crust, contemplative.

"So, Tathrin, don't have your friends in Vanam pay mercenaries to fight each other." Sorgrad went to a saddlebag and found a wineskin. "Pay them to get rid of the dukes."

"What?" Tathrin stared at him.

"That's not a bad notion." Gren produced a horn cup from a pocket. "Lescari militiamen are weak as wet wheat at the best of times. Even before your man Reniack starts convincing them not to fight with his night letters nailed to shrine doors." He paused to let Sorgrad pour him some wine. "If we brought all the best warbands together, we could throw down these dukes and whatever lords are fool enough to stick with them."

"Why not see if that wins you some peace?" Sorgrad produced a silver cup from his belt pouch and filled it.

"Who would rule over the wasteland you'd make?" Failla demanded.

"Aren't you already living in a wasteland? You soon will be once this summer's fighting starts." Sorgrad drank his wine. "All because of these dukes of yours. All your country's ills can be laid at their door. Ever seen a man lying sick with a rotting foot, Tathrin? Cut off all that dead flesh and pus, right back to healthy blood and bone, and he might just live."

"Is this some other notion of Charoleia's that she didn't think to share?"

Failla saw that Tathrin was angrier than ever, but not with her.

"Read her letter for yourself. Then see if you can apologise before I slap you senseless."

Sorgrad smiled at Tathrin and Failla felt a chill.

The younger man subsided, red-faced. "I beg your pardon."

"Let's get moving." Gren threw the dregs of his wine into the grass. "You don't get to kill this idea, lad, not without your friends having their say first."

"You're going back to Vanam?" Failla made a swift decision. "I'm coming, too. If there's any conspiracy to set mercenary bands fighting each other or fighting the dukes or anyone else, your people need to hear what I can tell you. Then I can warn the guildmasters. You won't get anywhere without their help and they won't believe anyone but me."

"Indeed." Sorgrad refilled his silver cup with wine and handed it to her. "Welcome to the dance, my dear."

"Excellent." Gren beamed. "Now, what kind of ransom would Garnot be willing to pay for you, sweetheart? Where's a good place to have him send it between here and the Caladhrian border? Tathrin, dig out your pen and ink and unwrap the pudding from his cloth so he can play courier." He gestured towards Parlin.

"A ransom?" Failla looked at Sorgrad, horrified. "No, I won't go back. Not now."

Not now she had the chance to get as far away as Vanam. If that meant leaving family, hoarded coin and secrets behind, it need only be for a little while. The odds were good that these people, whoever they were, would soon provoke enough turmoil to occupy Duke Garnot. Then she could come back and retrieve everything precious to her, after which she would flee as far and as fast as she could, a thousand leagues if need be. They were welcome to their victory or to ignominious defeat. She didn't care either way.

"We need to give Garnot a reason for your disappearance." Sorgrad smiled reassuringly. "We'll take the ransom and we'll take you, too, never fear."

Gren angled his blond head, mildly exasperated. "You Carluse folk, you do understand what mercenaries do, don't you?"

"If Duke Garnot thinks you're dead," Tathrin said reluctantly, "he won't go looking for you and discover something he shouldn't."

What did he mean by that? How could he know? No, he couldn't possibly. Failla's hand trembled and she drank the wine hastily before she spilled it.

CHAPTER THIRTEEN

Litasse

**Triolle Castle, in the Kingdom of Lescar,
1st of For-Summer**

"I CAN'T BE long." Litasse slipped through Hamare's door. "Iruvain and I must welcome For-Summer at Ostrin's altar at noon."

They would lead the prayers and pour libations of last year's wine in hopes that the god would grant a fruitful season. There would be revels in the market square for the townsfolk and Iruvain had promised they would show the commonalty that Triolle's youthful duke and duchess didn't scorn their humble entertainments. Then there would be dancing and feasting with the vassal lords who lived close enough to spend the day in fawning attendance. While Iruvain listened to the vassals' inevitable complaints, Litasse had high hopes of interesting gossip from their ladies, along with flattering admiration for her beauty, her gowns and her jewels.

Even though she had little time to spare, her skin tingled at the thought of Hamare's touch. For the first time in a handful of days, his man Karn was guarding the door, so they wouldn't be disturbed.

"What?" Hamare looked up from the letter he was studying, his eyes unfocused. He wore no doublet, his creased shirt ink-stained.

Had he been working all night? Even with the sunlight flooding through the windows, Litasse saw a couple of candles still lit. Burned down to a finger-length, they were clotted with wax.

"I needed to catch you before you left." He shot her a weary smile. "I take it you and Duke Iruvain will be sending your salutations to the other dukedoms as soon as you return from the ceremonies at the shrine?"

"Indeed. That's to say, Iruvain will walk round the room throwing out ideas. Then he'll take himself off to the stables or the kennels tomorrow morning while I spend my time stringing fine words together." Curiosity replaced Litasse's idle desire for her lover. "What do you want me to say?"

"We need to know if Draximal and Parnilesse are truly preparing for war." Hamare looked grim. "These mercenaries who seized Emirle Bridge have offered it up to the highest bidder. If Duke Orlin of Parnilesse has a mind to, he can buy himself a foothold half a day's march inside Duke Secaris of Draximal's borders."

"Why does this concern us?" Litasse took a chair, mindful of her pink gown's golden lace.

"Beyond making it advisable for Triolle to raise a militia contingent in every town along our side of the river, with all the expense and disruption that will cause?" Hamare grimaced. "If it's just Parnilesse and

Draximal fighting, that's one thing. But Duke Garnot of Carluse is negotiating with mercenary bands. At the moment, I've no notion what he's planning."

"Do you think Carluse would attack Draximal's eastern border in support of Parnilesse?" Litasse saw where Hamare's thoughts were leading. "For Duchess Tadira's sake?"

"She has a long history of arguing how Carluse's best interests are served by helping her brother of Parnilesse." Hamare rested his elbows on the table, steepling his fingers.

"What would that mean for Triolle?" Litasse looked at the tapestry map hanging behind Hamare. "Iruvain would seek a treaty, wouldn't he?"

With Carluse to the north-west and Parnilesse to the east, Triolle would have the choice of enemies on both flanks or being the linchpin in an alliance that could dominate Lescar. Duke Ferdain of Marlier would be isolated in the south-west. Duke Moncan of Sharlac and Duke Secaris of Draximal could be menaced separately in the north.

"He's always admired Duke Garnot of Carluse, too much for my peace of mind," Hamare admitted. "We need some clue as to Sharlac's likely reaction if Carluse attacks Draximal. Please, do all you can to convince your mother that Duke Moncan must write to Duke Iruvain. We must know what's going on in the north. If Duke Garnot of Carluse is recruiting mercenaries because he's planning a strike against Sharlac, that's a whole different fistful of runes."

"I'll try." Would this be enough to make her father break his silence? Or would her mother merely remind her again that Triolle's affairs and not Sharlac's were now her proper concern?

"There's something else." A faint smile lightened Hamare's weary face. "Duke Garnot of Carluse has mislaid his doxy."

"He's set her aside?" Litasse was puzzled. "Why does that concern us?"

"She has completely disappeared." Hamare laid a hand on a pile of letters. "She was sent away from Carluse Town when Duchess Tadira was expected and no one has seen or heard from her since."

"She must be pregnant." Litasse saw no mystery. "Duchess Tadira tolerated the bastards Duke Garnot spawned before their marriage, but she's always let it be known she won't stand for him acknowledging any more baseborn children."

"She's made full use of those bastards." Hamare was sceptical. "She saved Carluse a pretty penny last year by marrying off the red-headed daughter to the captain of those mercenaries he has on his leash." He paused. "Duke Garnot must be planning on putting that man in charge of the dukedom's militia. Carluse lost its most able captain-general when Veblen was killed at Losand. That's all that's curbed Duke Garnot's ambitions this past year—" He broke off and made a note.

Had her brother Lord Jaras deliberately set out to kill Duke Garnot's bastard son? Is that why he risked and lost his life for the sake of defending Sharlac? Did her father and mother truly appreciate his sacrifice? When whatever wounds he had taken had been so devastating that she hadn't even been allowed to see his body, only to weep as his corpse was set on its pyre shrouded in Sharlac's russet and grass-green, the ducal colours that should have become his own by right of succession.

Litasse knew she must not be distracted by the old bruise of that grief. She frowned and felt the pull of her hair at her temples. Valesti had woven her tresses into a painfully tight confection of curls threaded through with silken roses.

"If that's all, I had better go. The carriage will be waiting to take me to the shrine."

"Of course." Hamare put down his pen. "Please let me see any letter you get from Duchess Tadira. Pelletria is working inside Carluse Castle now and she'll be sending her own messages on those letters."

"How?" Litasse was intrigued.

Hamare smiled. "There are ways of writing something that can't be seen unless you know what to do with the paper."

"I'll expect you to show me how that's done," she warned Hamare.

"Gladly, Your Grace." He nodded.

"Is Pelletria likely to learn what Duke Garnot is planning?" If Litasse couldn't have the shrewd old woman serving her, she was happy enough to know she was inside Carluse. Pelletria knew Duke Garnot wasn't to be trusted, nor Duchess Tadira. She and Litasse had talked long and often about Carluse treachery. Pelletria's first concern would be Triolle, Litasse knew that, but Sharlac's interests would also be served.

"Possibly, but I really want to know what's happened to this whore." Hamare frowned.

"Why?" Litasse stared at him. "When it's all but certain she's merely pregnant?"

"Pelletria says there was no sign and the girl takes great care to avoid such a thing." Hamare looked at Litasse for a long moment before continuing, "Even if she were, that's of little concern. She's part of a conspiracy in Carluse linking guildmasters, priests, merchants and more. They send their sons and apprentices away to sympathisers in Tormalin and Ensaimin and Saedrin only knows where else, rather than see them recruited into Duke Garnot's militias. They send their daughters and maids away so they're not bedded by mercenaries or widowed before they've been wives half a season."

"You don't think she was discovered? That she's lying in some ditch with her throat cut?" Though surely that was no more than the harlot deserved.

"Pelletria says there's no whisper of that." Hamare shrugged. "I still want to find out what's befallen her."

Litasse narrowed her eyes. "Iruvain knows nothing of this conspiracy?"

Hamare looked at her with a wry smile. "I haven't had occasion to tell him."

"Don't tell him," Litasse said swiftly, "or he'll suspect the same plots here, like some child seeing Eldritch Kin in the chimney-corner shadows. He'll say or do something that shows our own guildmasters that he doesn't trust them."

"I've been thinking the same," Hamare admitted. "We cannot afford that, not while the craftsmen and merchants remain so uncertain as to how he will rule. They're still mourning the late duke and his duchess."

"It serves Triolle's purposes that this conspiracy weakens Carluse, even if only a little," Litasse said thoughtfully. "We're agreed on that?"

"We are." Hamare nodded. "More to the point, Duke Iruvain would give up this information to Duke Garnot simply to win his goodwill. I'd prefer to keep it until we want something more tangible from Carluse."

"Does Iruvain have any bastards?" The question was out before Litasse could reconsider it. She'd speculated. How could she not? She'd even asked him, in the scented privacy of their curtained marriage bed. He swore there were none. Had he told her the truth?

"No." Hamare looked at her, surprised.

"None?" she persisted.

"There was one serving maid who claimed she got her big belly by warming his sheets." Hamare leaned back in his chair with a grin. "It was easy enough to prove she'd been tumbled by some stable-boy."

"Did he have any mistresses before he wed me?" Litasse wasn't smiling. "Or since?"

"There were dalliances, not mistresses." Hamare gave her his full attention, quite serious. "One of his mother's dressmakers relieved him of his virginity, at the late duchess's request. Once he'd got his confidence, he set about seducing a dancer from a troupe of travelling players who stopped here a few times. They won't be coming here again," he assured her. "I've seen to that. Though the girl could no more outshine your beauty than a candle could outshine the sun."

Litasse coloured. "I was beginning to wonder if Iruvain's tastes run more to pestles than mortars." Her husband's lovemaking always seemed so perfunctory and hurried compared to Hamare's intoxicating, lingering ardour.

"He has no inclination to match his steps to his dancing master's." Hamare tried to curb a smile. "Karn would have found out, believe me."

Litasse was shocked. "You said Karn and Valesti were lovers!"

"Bedmates," Hamare corrected her. "I don't think Karn loves anyone. Did your nurse ever tell you that tale of a prince who was stabbed by a maid of the Eldritch Kin?"

"Because they were lovers and he was abandoning her to go back to his betrothed?" Hamare really must be tired to be indulging in such fanciful notions. Litasse noticed that his darkly shadowed eyes were webbed with red.

"A splinter from her shadow-knife lodged in his heart and he could never love again. That's Karn—" Hamare broke off as a yawn took him unawares.

"You sent him to seduce Iruvain?" Karn was a handsome youth in an understated way. Were his lean, wiry frame and long-jawed face as attractive to men as they were to women? Litasse wondered.

"The late duke thought it was as well to know for certain how Iruvain's tastes were fixed before he consented to your marriage." Hamare rubbed a hand over his face. "Keep this to yourself, my love. Karn's too useful to me to have anyone whispering and watching to see who he fondles next."

Litasse heard voices in the stairs. "I had better go." She rose with some relief.

"Pour your libations and say a prayer on my behalf." Hamare picked up a ragged sheet of paper and held one corner in a pallid candle flame. "Asking that we're all spared blood in the water and fire in the night skies this summer."

"Iruvain will come to my chamber tonight." Litasse paused, her hand on the door. "If I'm not the woman he'd have chosen for his bed, the wine will make him amorous. It always does."

"Indeed." Hamare let the burning paper fall onto a pewter plate of crusts and apple cores. "But he'll be making plans for a trip along our side of the River

Anock soon enough, to persuade his vassal lords to open their coffers and to rally their militias. Then you and I will naturally be spending more time together. There'll be dispatches to discuss and letters to write." He smiled at her. "So we'll put our heads together in Triolle's best interests."

"I suppose we'll have to." Litasse smiled and went on her way with a lighter step, never mind the ominous prospects for the summer ahead.

Chapter Fourteen

Aremil

**Beacon Lane, in Vanam's Upper Town,
6th of For-Summer**

Aremil braced his hands on the arms of his chair, set
his feet on the floor as solidly as he could and raised himself up. He teetered on the edge of sinking back down as
his arms began to tremble. Then he heard voices.

"Duke Moncan of Sharlac hasn't travelled anywhere
for well over a year?"

That was Tathrin, keen to learn all he could of
recent Lescari affairs.

"He hasn't left the castle. Not to visit his vassal
lords, not even those with holdings he could reach
inside a day. Not even to hunt."

That was Failla. Why was she here?

Aremil forced himself onwards and reached for his
crutches. There was no question of having Failla see
Tathrin lift him to his feet like some baby encouraged
to take its first steps.

"They say he's grieving." Failla entered as Tathrin courteously opened the door for her. "He keeps Lord Jaras's urn in his own chamber and refuses to have the ashes dedicated to Poldrion in the castle shrine."

As usual, Aremil saw that her demeanour was as modest as her high-necked grey dress and the cream lace shawl around her shoulders. So why didn't he trust her?

Tathrin was about to say something when he realised Aremil was already on his feet. "Are we late?"

"We don't want to be." Aremil realised he sounded unpleasantly peevish and fell silent.

"I'm nervous." Failla favoured Aremil with a charming smile.

"You're probably still a little tired." He tried to sound encouraging. "You had a long journey."

"No, I mean, yes, I did." As Failla smiled at him, a dimple came and went by her enchanting mouth. "I'm perfectly rested, though. You've been very kind."

Her gaze slid to Tathrin. Was it his imagination, Aremil wondered, or did his friend's eyes brighten whenever he looked at her?

"Master Tathrin's hired you a carrying chair." Lyrlen came into the room, smoothing her apron with satisfaction.

Aremil stood motionless. A carrying chair. As if he were some decayed relict bent with joint evil or an aging profligate paying for a lifetime's gluttony with Ostrin's curse of gout.

"It's too short a distance to warrant asking Master Gruit for the use of his carriage." Tathrin was looking at him anxiously.

"A good notion." Aremil was thankful for the mask that a lifetime had made of his face. At least he could walk out through his own front door on his crutches. That salved his pride somewhat.

Outside, the carrying chair proved to be one of the simple, open design rather than some cumbersome closed affair. That was a minor mercy. He lowered himself down and tucked his crutches beside his knee.

"Good day to you, sir." The man at the front gave some signal to his counterpart and they lifted him without a jolt.

Tathrin courteously offered Failla his arm. "I was wondering," he said as they began walking, "do you know a maltster, Master Arlet? He travels between Losand and Ashgil."

"I met him once." Failla looked up at him with that smile Aremil considered so unreasonably seductive. "At an inn called the Duck Roost, on the Ashgil Road."

"I know it." Tathrin nodded. "You met him on your uncle's business?"

This was one reason why Aremil didn't like carrying chairs. Being seated meant conversation invariably went back and forth over his head. As the other two talked about places and people Aremil didn't know, he tried once again to work out why it bothered him so to see Tathrin paying the girl such attention. She had risked her life, spying on Duke Garnot of Carluse to help the guildmasters save countless Lescari youth from peril.

They had so much in common, Tathrin and Failla, both Carluse-born and tied into this conspiracy that the guildsmen had woven. They'd had twenty or so days' travelling to become friends, the latter half of the journey cooped up in a coach, courtesy of Master Gruit's generous purse. Had they become more than friends overnight at some coaching inn? Though Mountain Men were reputed to guard their own women's virtue with jealous knives. Had they proved effective chaperones for a duke's whore?

Aremil looked down the street past the muscular shoulders of the chair-man. Did he mistrust her because she was a whore? She was very unlike those whores who had been paid to attend to his twisted body, on those rare occasions when Lyrlen could be persuaded to spend an evening visiting her few friends elsewhere in the city. Aremil never asked Tathrin where he found such women, just grateful that his friend found nothing remarkable in him confessing to the same desires as able-bodied men. Everyone else assumed he was as sexless as some hapless slave castrated by the Aldabreshin savages.

So Tathrin knew how to deal with whores. He should be proof against whatever blandishments Failla had up her ostensibly demure sleeves.

"We turn right there." Tathrin pointed for the chair-carriers' benefit before smiling at Failla. "Have you ever seen the bridges at Palastrine?"

"No." Failla's wide-eyed gaze invited him to continue.

Was she an actress as talented as any gracing the stage at The Looking Glass Playhouse? On the other side of the balance, why shouldn't she find Tathrin attractive? He was tall, handsome and straight-limbed, and shared her passion for righting the wrongs of their homeland.

Was his mistrust of her simple jealousy? A moment's rational thought reminded Aremil that he had absolutely nothing to recommend him to such a beauty. Who would ever imagine that he might desire

Failla? Not even Lyrlen thought there was any impropriety in her staying as his guest. After all, there was no way he could negotiate the staircase to the guest bedrooms even if he had a mind to.

No, he reflected, he wasn't jealous. Tathrin could bed the wench, if not with Aremil's goodwill, then at least with his understanding. He was more envious of the time Failla had spent with Tathrin over the last half-season. He really didn't want to hear about their journey and their long conversations lamenting the harsh reality of life in Lescar and their speculations as to Duke Garnot of Carluse's plans. Aremil wanted to tell Tathrin about his own discussions with Charoleia and Gruit, with Reniack and Lady Derenna, as they had pooled their knowledge and ideas. He wanted to hear Tathrin's opinions on the tales of aetheric enchantment that he'd been assiduously gathering.

Quite apart from all that, he just wanted to spend some time with Tathrin, to play white raven and talk about whatever inconsequentialities occurred to them. After being so used to having a friend, he hadn't enjoyed returning to his old isolation.

"It's the house with the green door." Tathrin pointed ahead.

The chair-men set him down gently in front of it. Aremil waved Tathrin away and managed to get to his feet on his own. "I have dined here several times while you've been away."

"Good day, gentlemen." Charoleia's maid opened the door.

A serene Relshazri woman, Charoleia had certainly not found her among the girls lingering in the portico of Drianon's temple in hopes of a profitable hire. Aremil wondered how long she had served her mistress and just how much she knew about the mysterious Lady Alaric and all her other guises.

"Failla!" A stocky blond man with an engaging grin followed the maid out onto the steps. "We've missed you!"

With his unkempt hair, sturdy boots and plain brown doublet and breeches, he looked as rough-hewn as any of the Mountain Men who visited Vanam from time to time. But his accent had nothing of the uplands about it.

"Hello, Gren." Her smile was polite but not encouraging.

"Master Aremil," Gruit said in welcome.

Aremil noticed the wine merchant watching him apprehensively as he followed the others into the parlour on slow crutches.

"Let me." Tathrin held the door open for him.

This sitting room was refreshingly clear of clutter, which made it all the easier to notice the expensive furniture, and the elegant statuettes of the gods on the marble mantel. Paintings of Vanam's hills in the days before the upper town had spread beyond its walls quietly suggested that this wealth had deep foundations in the city.

Reniack was pacing back and forth across the wide bay window, keeping a watch on the street. A second blond man was sitting opposite Derenna, a small table with a half-played game of white raven between them, the pieces all enamelled bronze on a patterned marble board.

This must be Sorgrad, Aremil decided, the other blond man's brother. The one whom Tathrin seemed to think was more dangerous. Contemplating the game pieces with quiet intensity, he was dressed in dark-blue broadcloth tailored with all the understated elegance of Vanam's wealthiest residents.

Derenna wore the same shabby black dress Aremil had last seen her in, with the same lack of concern.

"Who's winning?" Gruit went to look at the game while Aremil lowered himself carefully into a chair.

"We don't know as yet." Derenna shot her opponent a sharp look of reluctant admiration.

"For the moment, honours are even." Sorgrad's expression was amiable and unreadable.

"Anyone want to roll some runes?" Gren asked hopefully.

"Are we all here?" Trailing a scent of summer flowers, Charoleia arrived in a gown of amethyst silk. Her maid followed with a tray of glasses and a bottle of Master Gruit's finest Tormalin red wine.

"You two think you can improve on our plans?" Reniack turned around. He wore a dark tunic and breeches with stockings and polished shoes, all clerkly neatness, but his manner was as combative as ever.

"Yes." Gren raised his glass with cheery smile.

"We can." Sorgrad was quietly confident.

"Please explain." Charoleia sat, gesturing with a silver-ringed hand.

Aremil waved the maid's offer of a glass away. After the door closed behind her, he watched Derenna and Reniack as Sorgrad outlined the case for overthrowing all of Lescar's dukes. Tathrin had already set out their reasoning to Aremil, summarising the long debates he'd had with Sorgrad and Failla as they had travelled together.

Was it possible? Aremil wondered. Could they do this? He'd spent most of the previous night staring at the ceiling of his darkened bedroom, his usual pains a minor consideration as he turned this astonishing proposal over and over in his mind. He asked himself time and again what this stranger could possibly gain by persuading them all down a road to ruin. What profit could there be for a mercenary in that?

"You want to kill the dukes?" Reniack said with disbelief.

"Overthrow," Tathrin corrected him.

"You won't overthrow Duke Orlin of Parnilesse," Reniack told him roundly. "He'll take death before defeat."

"His choice." Sorgrad shrugged. "This is still Lescar's best road to peace. You've been talking about attacking the dukes' ability to fight by cutting off their funds and depriving them of fighting men. That's fine as far as it goes, but you've already realised that weakening one dukedom will only leave the others in a stronger position. If you really want to put an end to this strife, you have to rid Lescar of them all."

"Could we?" Gruit breathed.

Aremil saw that the idea had caught the old man's imagination.

"With the right mercenary companies fighting for you." Gren lounged against the marble fireplace. "As long as you have enough coin to keep them sweet."

"You also need the right captain-general for those mercenary forces." Sorgrad moved an enamelled swordwing and smiled at Derenna. "Your move, my lady."

"Do you know the right man?" Gruit demanded.

Derenna spared the game a cursory glance and moved the white raven behind a gorse brake.

"Evord Fal Breven." Sorgrad studied the board.

"He would be my first choice," Charoleia agreed.

"Never heard of him," Reniack said dismissively.

"He'll be very glad to know it." Sorgrad didn't look up from the game. "That doesn't alter the facts. Fourteen years ago, he commanded one of the most successful mercenary companies that Lescar's seen in a generation."

"Captain-General Evord is a Soluran," Charoleia said calmly. "He earned his spurs fighting in their western provinces. Mercenaries in the pay of the border barons keep beasts and wild men from crossing the Solfall River and make sure the Mandarkin don't come south through the mountains."

"What brought him to Lescar?" Gruit asked curiously.

Gren shrugged. "Easier fighting for better money."

"Where is he now?" Tathrin wanted to know.

"He went back to Solura." Sorgrad moved a pied crow. "He got sick of never being allowed to win a victory that would actually solve anything. He would accept a commission from a duke, come up with a plan and carry it through. Before he could force a decisive conclusion, he'd be whistled back like a recalcitrant hound when some duchess's petticoat plotting or a realignment of the dukes' alliances made it all moot."

"You would set a Soluran to rule over us?" Derenna moved the white raven, snapping the alabaster figurine down with unnecessary force. "How long would that peace last? Nobles and commoners alike would refuse to bow to a foreign usurper."

Aremil shifted so he could get a better view of the game board. The Mountain Man was a very skilled player.

"Evord would have no interest in Lescar's so-called throne." Sorgrad shifted an owl. "Which is another reason why you want him in charge of this army. He'll do what he's paid to do and then retire to his own lands in Solura."

"As long as you pay him with gold coin," Gren pointed out, "not Lescar's lead-laced excuse for silver."

"You would leave us with anarchy." Derenna shook her head, exasperated.

"There are a great many systems of government, real and imagined." Sorgrad's cold blue gaze challenged her. "Scholars and philosophers debate them endlessly by their comfortable firesides. Are you saying that all you educated and scholarly Lescari wouldn't be able to come up with a way forward between you?"

"Whatever's decided, it won't be the nobles laying down the laws," Reniack asserted. "The poorest folk can finally have a voice if we can get rid of the dukes."

"All shouting at once," Derenna scoffed.

"You'd deny them their right to speak?" Reniack's chin jutted belligerently.

"That would hardly be rational." Sorgrad smiled.

"This whole notion is irrational," Derenna said stubbornly. "If mercenaries attack one duke, or even two, as soon as the rest realise that the same threat extends to them, they'll unite to fight out of simple self-preservation. Quite rationally," she said acidly.

"So we attack them all." Gren clearly didn't see the problem.

Sorgrad smiled. "Get everyone in the right places before the first blood's spilled and it could be a very short campaign."

"How?" Derenna demanded. "How could you possibly bring everyone you needed into such a plot and hope to keep it a secret? How could you send word to all the people you needed to act without being discovered?"

Something on the game board caught her eye and she frowned before swiftly moving the white raven again.

Reniack laughed with harsh amusement. "How do you think I've escaped Duke Orlin's hangman with no more than torn ears? There are plenty of ways of spreading news as well as gathering it. I don't suppose you have much to do with men in the travelling trades, my lady, but thatchers and chimney sweeps, ox-handlers and slaughtermen, candlemakers and charcoal burners—they all carry bundles of my pamphlets and broadsheets around Parnilesse without anyone being the wiser." He looked from Tathrin to Gruit. "You have all those same trades in Carluse and Marlier?"

"Quite so." Gruit smiled slowly. "And I know any number of merchants who carry discreet letters from place to place. You know that yourself, my lady."

"Tavern musicians carry letters for the guildmasters in Carluse," Failla volunteered.

"Troupes of players and musicians travel between vassal lords' manor houses." Charoleia smiled. "As do tutors and painters and map-makers and doctors. Many such people are well known to me, and most owe me favours."

Aremil had wondered just how she came about the information she traded. He'd guessed she must buy it from servants and the like. He hadn't thought about the humbler trades who cooperated with Reniack, though. The pamphleteer's words were more coin tipping the balance in favour of this plan.

"Every one of these unknown people becomes another link to us," Derenna cried with exasperation. "How long do you think it will be before we're loaded down with chains?"

"Stay out of Lescar and no duke can seize you." Gren shrugged.

"Then our families will pay the penalty," she said bitingly.

Sorgrad was unconcerned. "Mostly folk will just need to know one thing, one place to be at a certain time. If no one but ourselves knows the whole story, any thread a duke's spy pulls on will snap before it leads to us."

He moved a pied crow that had been shielding a trio of mistle thrushes clustered round an oak tree. Derenna instantly shifted the white raven and put them to flight off the edge of the board.

"I must go back to Parnilesse." Reniack looked grim. "The people we'll need there have felt the lash of Duke Orlin's whip too often to trust anyone but me."

"I'll be going back to Carluse," Failla said quickly. "I'm the only one the guildmasters will believe, and as far as Duke Garnot is concerned, I'm dead anyway."

"How in Poldrion's name did you manage that?" Gruit asked with misgiving.

"It would be a cursed sight easier if you people buried your ancestors like decent folk instead of throwing them on bonfires," Gren said cheerfully, "but there's always some unclaimed dead on a Lescari battlefield. So we found the site of some old fighting and dug around a bit."

Aremil saw Failla pale at the recollection while Tathrin looked anxious.

"Duke Garnot got her clothes and some bones back, half-burned but still recognisable enough to convince him." Sorgrad moved a russet owl figurine with a soft click.

The Mountain Men had played that trick before, Aremil was convinced of it.

"So we're to achieve all this when we have to send letters all the way from Vanam to Reniack in Parnilesse and to her while she's skulking around Carluse's back roads?" Derenna flung a hand towards Failla. "It took the boy nearly a whole season to get to Draximal and back. How can you hope to manage this business with such delays? How long before something unexpected makes a mockery of whatever you have planned?"

Aremil decided it was time for him to speak. "We won't send letters. We will use magic to communicate with each other."

"Of all the follies I've heard today, that's quite the most ludicrous." Derenna looked scornfully at him.

"Please hear Master Aremil out," Tathrin said tightly.

"If you think for one moment we could get away with involving wizards in this madness, you should send that scholar's ring back to your mentor," Derenna retorted with rising anger.

"Don't bite the lad's head off."

Aremil was slightly alarmed to see Gren take a step away from the fireplace, his face hardening.

"I don't mean magecraft," Aremil said hastily. "You must have heard of aetheric magic?"

"Tricks and charlatanry." Derenna's lips narrowed.

Charoleia looked at her with mild surprise. "You must be aware that Vanam's university leads the study of such ancient enchantments?"

"You lowlanders forgot all about the old magics when your empires fell into ruin." Sorgrad took up his untouched glass of wine and studied it. "Then you found you had mageborn among you who could manipulate earth and stone, fire and water, even the wind and rain. Wizardry became the only magic that mattered. You've never paid much attention to what goes on in the uplands, not beyond convincing yourselves there's no harm in stealing our land to graze your sheep on. If you had, you'd know that what you call 'aetheric magic' had never been lost."

He paused, contemplative. "There are learned men and women in the remote mountain valleys well versed in more than sharing their thoughts. They can pluck the very memories out of your head if they see fit, or see your innermost intent, and you'll never know they've done it. They travel from settlement to settlement to give judgement and counsel, to heal the sick, to greet the newly born, to comfort the dying. No one sees them on the road. They come and go as suits their own purposes. They spread news and carry appeals for aid or alliance from one settlement to another. As long as they believe those in need deserve help," he qualified. "If they don't, one lone traveller becomes ten or twenty stepping out of the shadows. No one will enter a valley the *sheltya* have declared closed. They also do whatever's needed to curb a pestilence or to find the truth of some crime against innocent blood."

"And then?" Tathrin broke the uncertain silence.

"Sometimes the settlements are found empty, all their people gone."

Even Gren's cheerful demeanour was subdued, Aremil noticed.

"Or the folk still there have had their minds emptied of any recollection of what's gone on," Sorgrad concluded.

"I don't know about the remote mountains, nor Vanam's scholars, come to that," Reniack said with uncharacteristic caution, "but I've heard rumours coming out of Tormalin. Whatever you make of these tales of lost lands rediscovered across the Eastern Ocean, the Emperor and all the princes are searching their archives and libraries for hints and fragments of the lore that underpinned the Old Empire. Artifice, they call it. They say it's a magic that can get inside a man's head, to find out all his secrets or convince him some illusion is solid reality."

"It's all the same magic," Gren agreed. "But if Artifice gets inside your head, you can always—"

Sorgrad silenced him with a word of what Aremil assumed was the Mountain tongue.

Wondering just what had been said, Aremil continued, "My lady Derenna, I am acquainted with a mentor of unimpeachable reputation among the university's scholars who's travelled extensively in search of such lore. He has told me that those adept in the more complex enchantments can communicate with each other over hundreds of leagues, if not thousands."

"But none of us are adept," Derenna countered, "nor likely to become so any time soon."

"These Mountain adepts, would they help us?" Gruit asked, hope and apprehension following each other across his face.

"No." Sorgrad was still studying his glass of wine. "They haven't involved themselves in the scholarship here, though thanks to curious scholars like Master

Aremil's friend, they know all about it. So with luck, they won't step out of some shadow to chastise us if we communicate through aetheric magic instead of letters."

Gruit's brow creased in thought. "Do adepts of Artifice have to be born to this magic, like wizards?"

"I'm told Artifice can be learned by anyone with sufficient self-discipline and application," Charoleia remarked. "Musicians find it easier than most, apparently."

"I will write to Mentor Tonin, the scholar I'm acquainted with. I shall ask him to introduce me to those of his pupils who are Lescari born or have Lescari blood." Aremil felt nothing was to be gained by saying he'd already sent such a letter and had been waiting for a reply since before the Spring Festival. "We need only find a handful we can trust. If one such adept travels with Reniack, and another with Failla, we can send them whatever instructions we need to and learn all that they have discovered without anyone setting pen to paper."

"There'd be no delay, nor any risk that some duke's spy might intercept a letter," Tathrin said confidently.

"Might there be some way to use these enchantments to rid ourselves of the dukes without any bloodshed at all?" Failla looked at him hopefully.

All Tathrin could do was look at Aremil.

"I have no way of knowing," he had to admit. "Not yet."

"Aetheric enchantment is still magic, though, isn't it?" Derenna objected reluctantly. "Won't the Archmage be watching whoever uses it as closely as he watches his wizards?"

"He's made no objection to the Tormalin Emperor's men and women using the enchantments they have discovered," Charoleia assured her. "Though I suspect he might, if aetheric magic were used for open violence," she added.

"People seem to think Archmage Planir's omniscient and omnipotent." Sorgrad twirled his glass around. The sunlight struck ruby glints deep in the wine. "He isn't. I've met him, and played white raven against him, which I have to say he plays remarkably well." He glanced down at the board. "As do you, my lady, although—my apologies—you've lost this game."

Derenna stared at the board. "That's not—"

She bit down on the word but everyone in the room knew she'd been about to say "fair".

"I was distracted." Spots of furious colour blossomed on her cheekbones.

"You kept playing," Sorgrad pointed out.

He looked around the room. "If we're going to try winning this particular game instead of just talking about it, we should start by finding Captain-General Evord in Solura and rounding up an army for him. Gren and I can work on that. The rest of you should start thinking about getting all the other pieces we'll need into play so we can win the game before the dukes even realise they're playing."

"You say this mercenary captain Evord lives in Solura?" Derenna snapped. "Clear across Ensaimin and all the way on the other side of the Great Forest besides? We're already into For-Summer. By the time you've travelled all that way, even assuming you can persuade him, and brought back an army ready to fight, Winter Solstice will have come and gone!"

"I don't know about that, but we'll be lucky to see you back before Aft-Autumn." Gruit's enthusiasm wilted.

"I can get me, Gren and the long lad there to Evord's doorstep before nightfall." Sorgrad smiled as the wine in his glass boiled into a pink mist, filling the room with its fragrant bouquet. "Though leaving tomorrow morning would suit me better. I have a dinner engagement this evening."

Aremil saw that Tathrin was as dumbfounded as he was, along with everyone else. No, not everyone. Gren was just grinning. Of course he'd know. Charoleia also looked entirely composed. She would also have known something as momentous as that.

"You're a wizard?" he finally managed to say.

"Not a wizard." Sorgrad pulled at the glass, as malleable as soft wax in his hands. It sparkled with the unmistakable crimson of magelight. "Mageborn, if you like, but I've never studied in Hadrumal's halls. I've sworn no loyalty to Archmage Planir the Black. Which is how I know he has no secret means of keeping track of everyone using elemental magic."

"They say a wizard can only use magic to travel somewhere he's already been," Aremil said slowly. "Then you've visited Solura before?"

"Obviously." Sorgrad rolled the glistening glass into a ball and set it carefully on the table, where the vivid red at its heart slowly faded. "It'll take us rather longer to get back, of course." He looked around the room with a brisk smile. "Regardless, you should be starting your war before Aft-Summer sees its second brace of full moons. As long as you really want to do this. Do you? All of you?"

"Yes."

Reniack's determined assertion was followed a breath later by Gruit.

"We do."

Failla just nodded. Tathrin looked at Aremil.

"Yes, we do." For the moment, Aremil refused to contemplate all the things that could hamstring them. Not least his failure to deliver the promised aetheric adepts.

"Yes." Tathrin nodded.

"Madam?" Sorgrad turned to Derenna.

She pushed at the ball of glass with a curious fingertip. "I'm beginning to think we should at least try."

Chapter Fifteen

Tathrin

Master Wyess's Counting-House, in Vanam's Lower Town, 7th of For-Summer

"Tathrin? Two Mountain Men want to see you." His face dubious, Eclan came down the stone stairs.

Tathrin had been sitting in the clerks' dining hall since before the pearly dawn light had reached the half-basement's barred windows.

Everyone had been so astounded by the realisation that Sorgrad was mageborn that no one had objected to the Mountain Man including him in this trip to Solura. Even Tathrin hadn't thought to challenge it until too late, when everything seemed agreed.

He'd sat silently as the others had discussed how soon Reniack might reach Parnilesse. They had debated how Failla could travel discreetly back to Carluse. Even Lady Derenna had agreed to write to her fellow noble scholars across Sharlac. Charoleia had assured everyone she had contacts travelling throughout

Lescar who could safely act as couriers until they had secured communication through aetheric enchantments. Aremil had looked as confident as ever, promising he would deliver this capability as soon as possible.

Succulent ham lay untouched on Tathrin's plate. He'd thought he would choke on the single mouthful of bread he'd eaten. He hadn't dared try a second bite.

How could he refuse now? He'd be letting Aremil down horribly. He'd look like a coward. What would Failla think of that?

But he didn't want to go. It was as simple as that. He didn't want to ask leave of Master Wyess a second time and risk all his prospects here. He didn't want to travel to some unknown land with those unnerving brothers. Why was it so essential he went with them to serve the cause of peace in Lescar?

How were they going to travel? He hadn't dared ask. Having Aremil find people willing to use this Artifice, this old-fashioned magic that had the historical scholars so fascinated, that was one thing. But what might an outraged Archmage do to those implicated in unsanctioned magecraft?

"Tathrin, what's going on?" Eclan asked in an urgent undertone.

"Never mind." Tathrin pushed away from the table and headed for the courtyard. He wasn't ready for this. He had to talk everything through with Aremil. There had to be an alternative.

Sorgrad and Gren were sharing the seat of a two-wheeled gig, looking idly around. Both wore travelling cloaks and sturdy boots.

"Hop up." Gren gathered his reins.

"Where's your gear?" Sorgrad frowned.

"I can't come, not just yet," Tathrin said quickly. "I have duties here. I've already been away too long."

"This was all agreed yesterday." Sorgrad looked sternly at him.

"No one asked me." Tathrin shook his head. "I want to talk to Aremil. He'll understand."

Gren pursed his lips. "Will Failla?"

Tathrin didn't want to think about that. "You can't make me come with you."

"He can."

"Believe it, long lad."

Tathrin didn't know which was more unnerving: Gren's cheerful conviction or the cold certainty in Sorgrad's blue eyes. Just what could wizards do? All he knew about magic was culled from highly coloured tavern tales.

"You don't need me in Solura." He hesitated. This conversation was attracting unwelcome attention from everyone else in the courtyard.

"Yes, we do." Sorgrad looked at him, unblinking. "Our friend will want more convincing arguments than we can offer him. We're Mountain-born and mercenaries besides. What's Lescar to us but a means of making money?"

"Tathrin?" It was Eclan again.

He spun around. "It's nothing."

"Master Wyess wants to see you." Eclan looked apprehensive.

"That's not necessary." Tathrin shook his head. "These men are just leaving."

"Not till Master Wyess says so." Eclan waved a hand.

Wood and iron slammed against stone as the heavy gates to the courtyard closed. Burly men stood in front of them, arms folded.

"This raises the stakes," Gren observed with interest.

Unwillingly, Tathrin looked at Sorgrad. "Wait."

Wyess was in the hallway. "In here," he said curtly.

Tathrin followed him into the antechamber. Empty chairs lined the walls, ready for callers waiting on Master Wyess's convenience. Strip maps ran around the walls, detailing the routes leaving each of the city's gates.

"What's going on, lad?" Wyess wasn't angry, just concerned.

Tathrin felt as if that lump of obstinate bread was still lodged in his gullet. "May I have another leave of absence, Master?"

Faint hope teased him. If Wyess refused to let him go, that would at least win him some delay, till he could find the reasoning to counter Sorgrad's arguments. Surely he could serve Aremil and the cause of peace in some different way?

"Another sister's wedding?" The furrier sounded sceptical. "My counting-house will be left half-empty if I let you come and go as you please. How can I deny the other clerks if I allow you such liberty?"

Tathrin could feel himself colouring. "This is urgent business for my father."

"He's entitled to some call on your time." Wyess nodded slowly. "But he sent you here to learn from me. Must I write to him, to remind him you cannot serve two masters?"

Tathrin could only shake his head.

"A merchant needs to know how to tell a convincing lie and how to tell when someone else is lying." Wyess studied the closest map, intent on every crossroads, inn and watering place on the highway between the Pazarel Gate and Leverda on the Selerima Road. "I spend all my days balancing the dross in a man's words against the gold. Don't try to deceive me. What's really going on?" he asked more urgently. "Mountain Men? Have you been gambling? Raeponin knows, uplanders play their runes seriously and take their losses hard. Do you have debts you can't honour? I'll lend you the coin before I let them take you to some back alley and beat you senseless!"

"No, it's nothing like that," Tathrin protested, stricken.

"You've been spending time with Master Gruit and he drinks like a man with a five-day fever." Anxiety furrowed Wyess's weather-beaten brow. "Have you tripped into some mischief when you were too drunk to find your feet? Insulted one of their women? I can have a handful of wagoners give those yellow-headed short-measures a kicking if that's what's needed."

Tathrin felt sick despite his empty stomach. How would he explain that to Aremil or to Charoleia? Or, more likely, how would they explain to the Vanam judiciary what lay behind Sorgrad and Gren killing a yardful of innocent men? If the pair weren't wearing the swords they had routinely carried on the road, Tathrin had no doubt they were both still armed with the remarkable number of daggers they seemed to find necessary.

He had no choice. It was as simple as that.

"I'm sorry. I have to go." He looked Master Wyess in the eye. "There are people, honest Lescari, trying to bring some peace to our benighted homeland. I've agreed to help them."

"You're caught up in Gruit's madness? He's raising some troop of Lescari lads to go and fight again?" The furrier seized him by the shoulders, shaking him in his exasperation. "Don't be a fool, boy! When have you ever held a sword, never mind used one against another man?"

"It's nothing like that." Tathrin resisted the urge to push the older man away, but it was a close-run thing. He couldn't back down. If he hadn't wanted to go, he should have spoken up earlier. Realising he had only himself to blame, he felt oddly calm.

"No." Exasperated, Wyess shook his head. "These ideas come around every few years like the sweating sickness off the lake. The only thing to be done is grit your teeth and stay home till the fever fades, then thank Saedrin you'll never suffer the same way again when you hear how the boys who succumbed can't even be found and brought home for decent burning."

"Boys I grew up with died beneath the walls of Losand and in the towns and villages all around that were pillaged by mercenaries in the pay of both Sharlac and Carluse. Their own mothers couldn't put names to some of the dead's faces to claim them, so every shrine has anonymous funeral urns." Now that he'd opted for honesty, Tathrin found the words coming easier.

"I've been here two years now, Master. Seeing Vanam's justice at festival time only reminds me of the hangings and the floggings that Duke Garnot thinks will keep us loyal, or cowed—he doesn't care which. Every cripple I see on Vanam's streets reminds me of the men who'd come to my father's inn begging for bread because they'd lost an arm or a leg or an eye to the fighting and couldn't work at their trade any longer or in the fields. I see them all in my nightmares."

"Then take yourself off to Arrimelin's shrine," Wyess said angrily. "Talk the moons down from the sky with her priestesses until the horrors fade."

"The gods help those who help themselves." Tathrin squared his shoulders. "I can't stand idly by, Master, not any more."

He'd been talking in hopes of convincing the merchant. Now he realised he'd convinced himself.

"You're not the man I thought you were," Wyess said bitterly. "Get your gear and go. Don't show your face here again." He strode from the room, shoulders hunched and head bowed. Crossing the hall to his private office, he slammed the door hard behind him.

Tathrin walked slowly out of the antechamber.

Eclan was still by the front door. "Tathrin, what's going on?" he asked in a strangled whisper.

"Nothing. Everything." Tathrin ran up the stairs to his sleeping quarters.

It was the work of moments to throw his modest possessions into his leather-bound chest. He was only grateful there was no one around to see the angry tears he couldn't hold back. When he found the book of maps he'd bought so recently, he nearly threw it down on the floor. Why not leave it behind, along with all his hopes of a merchant's life?

Had he ever really wanted to be a merchant, though? If he had, wouldn't he have spent his leisure in the lower town during these past few years? Wouldn't he be glad to go out carousing with Eclan and the other clerks and learning all he could about their lives? Instead of sitting with Aremil and endlessly debating how someone, someday, might somehow bring peace to Lescar. Until someday was now and someone was him.

There was no point thinking about that. He drew a shaking breath and scrubbed at his eyes with his sleeve. Thrusting the book into the chest, he buckled the straps. There was no point thinking about anything apart from getting through the next few moments.

Hoisting the chest on his broad shoulders, he made his way carefully back down the stairs. Falling and breaking his legs probably wouldn't get him out of this obligation anyway. Not by Sorgrad's reckoning.

The dapper Mountain Man was waiting patiently, holding the horse's head and talking quietly to the beast in his own tongue. Gren was up on the gig seat, whistling the same casual snatch from a ballad over and over again.

He raised his pale brows when he saw Tathrin's burden. "You need travelling gear, not your whole inheritance."

"I'm not coming back." Tathrin threw the chest into the gig and climbed up to sit beside it.

The courtyard was still full of men waiting for Master Wyess's instructions. Tathrin fixed his gaze on his boots to avoid catching anyone's eye.

"Open up." Eclan appeared in the doorway, his face sorely troubled.

The gates were so well balanced and oiled that there was no squeal from the hinges or scrape along the flagstones. The louder sounds of the street told Tathrin they were free to go. That he was leaving for the last time.

"That's that." Sorgrad climbed up next to Gren, took the reins and set the horse trotting briskly through the archway.

They had gone along several streets, taking turns to right and left, before Tathrin looked up again. "Why did you come with a vehicle?"

Sorgrad glanced at him. "You thought we'd disappear from the steps of Master Wyess's counting-house in a haze of magelight?"

"No." Tathrin hadn't thought much beyond refusing to go.

"This way, you've gone off on a journey just like anyone else. No one will be spreading tales in the taverns about anything else." Sorgrad concentrated on the busy road. "Only about your breach with Master Wyess, and I don't suppose that could be helped. We're playing a long game here. The winnings should outweigh the losses."

"Indeed." Tathrin said curtly. He didn't want the Mountain Man's sympathy.

"Evord's no fool," Sorgrad continued. "If Gren and I put this proposal to him, he'll have no end of questions. Is Master Gruit setting up all this commotion to make a little fortune for himself? Reniack's some firebrand son of a whore. Would you trust him? Either of the women in this coil could just be out to make trouble, curdled by love and revenge: Lady Derenna's intent on getting her husband out from under Duke Moncan of Sharlac's boot heel, while Failla was Duke Garnot of Carluse's doxy. Who's to say she left him, when it could just as easily have been him throwing her out on her pretty arse?"

"Don't talk like that about Failla," Tathrin snapped.

Sorgrad shrugged. "After travelling back to Vanam with the pair of you, I could tell Evord more about her than the rest of your friends. I can tell him I asked you all the awkward questions I could think of on that journey. That still wouldn't be enough. You know Aremil, you know Master Gruit. Lescar's your home. You're the one who needs to come and explain everything."

"So I'm coming," Tathrin growled. "Happy?"

"Happy enough." Sorgrad carefully guided the carriage horse through a narrow gap. "Though I suggest you mend your manners before you meet Evord. It's your case you'll be arguing, not mine. If he turns you down, we can find some other way to make a coin or two, me, Gren and Charoleia. You won't find a better hope of bringing peace to Lescar."

Tathrin bit back a pointless retort and sat in resentful silence. Assured with whip and reins, Sorgrad drove the gig towards the far slopes of the Pazarel and a district where once-fine houses were sliding into decay. He turned the horse between stone gateposts stained with rust from hinges holding desultory remnants of wood.

"Gruit does have his finger in a lot of pies." Gren was studying the derelict house ahead.

Tathrin looked warily at a man emerging from the depths of the overgrown garden before recognising him as Gruit's coachman. "Draig?"

"You don't want to be hefting all that around Solura." Sorgrad nodded at Tathrin's chest as he pulled two sturdy drawstring sacks out from under the seat. The pommels of short swords stuck out from both. "Take what you need. Draig will ferry the rest to Aremil for safe keeping." He looked at the coachman for a nod of confirmation.

Tathrin quickly stowed necessities in the same leather bag he'd carried on the road to Draximal. After a moment's thought, he added the finely made dagger that Sorgrad had retrieved for him. "All done."

Draig grunted an acknowledgement and drove the gig away. The wheels left dark lines on the crushed weeds and the scent of bruised tansy in the air.

"Gren!"

As Sorgrad called with some exasperation, Tathrin looked up to see that the younger Mountain Man was climbing up the cornice carved above the empty house's wide front door. He acknowledged his brother with a wave before coming down, the boards nailed across the window frames as good as any ladder to him.

"Empty." He brushed dust from his hands. "It's always worth making certain."

"What now?" Tathrin looked nervously at Sorgrad.

"This." Sorgrad reached for his left hand and Gren took his right.

Intense white light bleached Tathrin's view of the shabby garden to nothingness. Could magic blind him? Apprehension rising, he screwed his watering eyes tight shut. A faint aroma teased him. What was it? Recollection of his mother making sure the maids finished up the laundry came to him. He could smell the subtle scorching that hung around freshly ironed cloth. That made no sense.

Colour played across his inner vision, but not as it did after a long day's study, when he tried to ease his tired eyes with gentle fingertips. This wasn't shifting darkness laced with ruddy gold. Vivid coils of scarlet and blue threaded through creamy pallor.

Now a breeze was wrapping round him, warm and dry like the breath of summer noon. He realised he couldn't feel his feet. Or rather, he couldn't feel the ground beneath his feet. Or the weight of his leather bag on his shoulder. He still didn't dare open his eyes. Was this really a breeze he could feel? Or was he being blown through the air, tumbled like some helpless leaf?

Dizziness crept up on him. First it was unease, like he'd felt for the first day or so aboard the sailed barge he'd travelled down the river on. The sensation worsened and he swallowed apprehensively. Now he was recalling the day when he and some friends had stolen a bottle of white brandy from his father's cellar. He hadn't drunk himself to puking but the world had swirled around, his hands clumsy, his feet numb. Which way was up? As he wondered, he felt violently nauseous. For the first time that morning he was grateful for his empty stomach.

Then his feet found the ground with a thump that ran right up his spine to jar his neck.

"Welcome to Solura," Gren said without enthusiasm.

Chapter Sixteen

Tathrin

Castle Breven Demesne, in the Kingdom of Solura, 7th of For-Summer

As THE MAGICAL glare dissolved, he felt the two Mountain Men release his hands. Tathrin cautiously opened his eyes. Purplish smudges blurred his vision and he had the beginnings of a sickening headache. It was like the time he'd spent too long in the harvest sunshine without a hat. He blinked as he clutched at his travelling bag, its bulk some reassurance, but things didn't improve much.

"Solurans don't like wizards." Sorgrad looked meaningfully at Tathrin as he pulled a sword-belt out of his own baggage. "At least, not ones like me who refuse to be apprenticed to a mage who's already sworn his life away in obedience to an elder wizard's circle. That's how they work magic hereabouts."

"So keep your mouth shut about whatever you think he can do." Gren buckled his own weapons on.

"In general, keep your mouth shut," Sorgrad advised.

Tathrin nodded mutely as he looked around.

This was very different from the countryside where he'd grown up, and it wasn't like any of the places he'd seen travelling between Lescar and Vanam. Wherever he'd been between the White Mountains and the Southern Sea, he was used to broad sweeps of land with long vistas reaching to the horizon. Where there was high ground, like the fells to the north of Carluse, the ground rose steadily towards it, the hills visible from a good distance.

Here the land was rumpled with hillocks and gullies like the blanket on an unmade bed. There was no neat delineation between field and forest, no regular pattern of villagers' strip-fields and common grazing. Haphazard stands of scrubby woodland were separated by stretches of cropped grass. Here and there, erratic stone walls enclosed small patches of land. Tathrin couldn't see crops being protected or any stock confined. Apart from the walls, the whole landscape looked untouched by man and beast.

He swallowed, his throat unaccountably dry. "What do we do now?"

Gren handed him a leather-bound water bottle. "Evord's the lord of Castle Breven."

"A castle?" Tathrin didn't know whether to be impressed or overawed. It was some recommendation if this mercenary captain had earned enough coin to retire in such style. On the other hand, how was he supposed to coax the man out of peace and comfort to take up arms again?

"I don't suppose it would impress a Lescari duke, but it's never fallen to an enemy." Quenching his own thirst from a silver flask, Sorgrad was already walking towards a scar running across the turf.

The Lescari wouldn't dignify this with the title of track, Tathrin thought, never mind call it a road. Though it wasn't too long before he saw that there must be people living somewhere around here. Once they left the dell, handfuls of coarse-coated black cattle picked their way through rough pasture. Several already had calves trotting at their heels and the rest looked ripe for giving birth.

Without anyone to tend them? Who milked them? Tathrin looked around. A land as wild as this must surely have wolves? He didn't fear attack, not in daylight, but what losses must the cattle suffer? This Captain-General Evord was no herdsman, however fine a mercenary he might be.

He still couldn't see anything like tillage for crops. The only sign of anyone taking a spade to the land was some way further on. The road, such as it was, continued on a narrow embankment across a stretch of rank bog. Tathrin tried to make sense of black lumps stacked beside a moist hole dug into the sod. "What's that?"

"Peat." Gren looked at it incuriously. "For fires."

How could anyone burn earth? Tathrin wondered. Wizardry? He didn't ask.

A little further on, the road took them around a rocky outcrop scarred with stonecutting.

"Castle Breven." Sorgrad paused. "Evord's ancestral home."

Gren chuckled. "You can see why he went looking for a more comfortable life."

"Where he could earn some solid coin," Sorgrad agreed.

A small lake shimmered at the far end of the shallow valley. Sharp-edged against the bright water, a tall, narrow tower stood defiant. A stone wall protected lesser buildings clustered around it, their tidy thatched roofs and smoking chimneys just visible. Tathrin had only seen Carluse Castle, but he'd heard tales of Sharlac Castle and Draximal, too. A Lescari duke wouldn't think this was fit for a hunting lodge.

"You don't see villages here, not like in Lescar." Sorgrad was striding onwards. "There are steadings scattered across the land. When there's trouble, everyone comes running for their lord's protection."

"How far does his writ run?" While the tower was solid, it wasn't very big. Tathrin counted four tiers of windows beneath the steeply pitched slate roof.

"As far as his reputation in times of strife." Gren chuckled. "So for Evord, that's pretty much all the way to the Solfall River and the border with the wildlands."

"He exaggerates." Sorgrad spared his brother a glance. "We're a good long way from the wildlands here. Thirty days' hard march, maybe more."

"Anyone between here and there would be happy to swear fealty to Evord," Gren protested.

"He won't let them." Sorgrad glanced at Tathrin this time. "I told you, he has no such ambitions. He won't want to conquer Lescar and hold it for himself."

Tathrin frowned. "Where's the gate?" The wall presented an unbroken barrier on this side.

"Facing the lake." Gren was walking alongside Tathrin. "Some of the small castles right by the border, they don't have any gates at all. Everyone goes in and out by ladder."

Tathrin suspected he was being teased. "Even the horses?"

"They're stabled outside in compounds tucked away in defensible places," Gren allowed. "But when they need to get wagons into the castle precinct, they just take down a section of wall and then build it back up again." He sounded perfectly serious. "Misaen blind me if I lie."

Sorgrad smiled at Tathrin's scepticism. "That way the wild men can't launch a strike on a permanent gate."

"Wild men?" Tathrin realised Vanam's obligatory lectures on Tormalin history had told him almost nothing about Solura.

"You know all those tales your grandmother told you about shadow-blue men stepping through rainbows from the Otherworld, armed with flints struck from moonbeams, lying in wait for lost travellers and naughty boys?"

"Yes," Tathrin said slowly.

Gren's smile broadened. "The Eldritch Kin would run screaming from the beast men who roam the wildlands across the Solfall."

If that was so, Tathrin found it all the more remarkable that cattle were left wandering the landscape.

A pair of riders appeared, coming from the castle. Tathrin guessed there were sentries in the slim turrets rising from the encircling wall.

As soon as the horsemen came within hailing distance, Sorgrad cupped his hands to his mouth and shouted, "We're here to see the captain-general."

Raising a hand in acknowledgement, the riders wheeled away to carry this news back.

As the three of them walked around the outer wall, Tathrin heard the clash of blades within and the solid drumming of hooves amid the general bustle. When they reached the gate, he saw nothing akin to a village but rather an armed camp that wouldn't have disgraced a Lescari duke's standing guard. Over to one side a farrier was shoeing horses, the smithies flanking him echoing with the strike of sword-makers' hammers. In front of lean-to sheds lining the wall, men sat making chain mail, taking advantage of the sunlight.

In the open space, youths about Tathrin's own age practised sword-strokes against imaginary foes in repetitious drills. Older men circled in wary two and threes, broadswords ready to test each other to the edge of injury. Quarterstaffs clashed and pole-arms were swung with lethal grace.

The sentry said something Tathrin couldn't understand and Sorgrad answered in the same language.

"Don't they speak Tormalin here?" Tathrin quietly asked Gren.

"Why should they?" He looked puzzled. "This is Solura."

As they were allowed through the arched entrance, hooves pounded on the hard-packed earth. Tathrin saw a mounted warrior run a lance right through a figure made from sacking and straw. Its canvas head was a snarling mask of teeth and glaring eyes, sewn with rank strips of animal fur for hair and beard. At least, Tathrin hoped it was animal fur.

"Sorgrad." A grey-haired man half a head shorter than Tathrin and slightly built turned away from a fiercely fought wrestling match. Like everyone else, he wore sturdy boots and buckskin breeches, with a chainmail hauberk over his homespun tunic.

Whatever he said next was presumably in the Soluran language. Sorgrad replied, as fluent as the old man. Tathrin reflected that whatever entrenched evils the Old Tormalin Empire had bequeathed to Lescar, at least all the countries that had fallen within its reach still shared the benefits of a common tongue.

"Gren." The old man nodded cordially.

"Captain-General." A wicked smile teased Sorgrad's lips as he continued in smoothly accented Tormalin. "This is Tathrin Sayron, scholar of Ensaimin's finest university and son of Carluse's finest ale-seller."

"You studied at Col?" The man, who Tathrin now saw was not so much old as prematurely grey, extended a courteous hand. He might be slightly built but Tathrin was willing to bet he was as tough as whipcord and leather.

"I studied at Vanam, my lord." He refused to look at Sorgrad.

"I won't hold that against you." Evord turned his hand to show Tathrin the silver seal ring on his own middle finger.

Well worn, the engraving was still clearly the shield and blazon of the city of Col. Evord's tone was as cultured and his formal Tormalin as fluent as any of the senior mentors who governed Vanam's university. So Tathrin bowed as he would to any master scholar.

As he straightened, he saw a smile crack Evord's solemnity. "I gather you three have an interesting proposal for me. While Sorgrad makes his case, Gren, take the lad to meet Ludrys."

"Captain." Gren snapped his head up and down in the briefest of bows. He led Tathrin over to some men armed with a miscellany of swords, long knives and small studded shields. "Got that pretty dagger on you, long lad?"

"Yes," Tathrin said apprehensively.

"Best have a sword." Gren offered his own.

"I don't know how to fight with that," Tathrin protested.

"No," agreed Gren.

Before Tathrin could argue any further, a leanly muscled man with ragged hair and whiskers that weren't so much a beard as a dislike of shaving came towards them. He spoke in Soluran and whatever Gren said in reply made him laugh out loud as he studied Tathrin.

"What's going on?" Tathrin took Gren's sword. It was that or let the blade fall to the dry earth.

"You want to start a war, you'll need to fight." Gren was backing away. "Ludrys is going to see how much you've got to learn. Take your doublet off."

Tathrin jumped, startled, as the bearded man threw a dagger at him. Just as he realised it wasn't aimed at him, it fell into the dust an arm's span away. The onlookers laughed.

"Pick it up," Gren advised. "Two blades against his one and you'll be the one attacking. You'll have all the advantage."

Tathrin very much doubted that. "I don't know what to do."

Ludrys said something and someone tossed him a small round shield. He picked it out of the air.

"Try not to die." Gren wasn't smiling any more. "Ludrys isn't out to kill you, just to test you. Start by proving that Lescari men aren't the cowards everyone says they are."

Tathrin reluctantly unbuttoned his doublet and handed the garment to Gren. Ludrys said something. Tathrin hoped the bearded man's smile was supposed to be encouraging.

He bent and picked up the long dagger, keeping his eyes on Ludrys all the while. The Soluran stood with his weight on his back foot, the little shield defending his midriff while he held his own sword out wide.

"Do the same," Gren instructed.

As he took the same stance, still unwilling, Tathrin didn't need the Mountain Man to translate the shouts from the other men. They wanted him to attack. Ludrys stood patiently waiting.

There was no point attacking the man's sword. Tathrin swung his own blade at Ludrys's head, vainly hoping his greater height and reach might carry the strike over the small shield. But what would happen if he did hit the warrior? That sudden thought robbed his blow of any real strength.

Ludrys stepped inwards, easily deflecting Tathrin's sword with a swing of his shield. In the same movement, he brought his own blade down to rest on Tathrin's cuff.

Tathrin looked down. He could all too easily visualise the bleeding stump of his forearm, his severed hand on the ground clutching uselessly at Gren's sword hilt.

"Try again." Gren didn't sound amused.

Tathrin licked his dry lips as he copied Ludrys's ready stance a second time. So the Soluran's shield was as much a weapon as a defence. This time he stepped in himself and tried to cut at the bearded man's sword-arm with his own long blade. Ludrys swept his shield across to block the stroke, his body turning. Tathrin was half-expecting that, so as soon as his blade was knocked down, he dropped his sword's point to thrust at Ludrys's knee.

Fluid as quicksilver, the warrior angled his own weapon downwards to bar Tathrin's blade. Inside a breath, he twisted the point back up to prod his belt buckle. Tathrin looked down and imagined his innards spilling out like unruly sausages on a butcher's slab.

What was the point of this? As Ludrys took up his ready stance again, Tathrin just stood still, weapons hanging loose by his sides. Ludrys grinned and looked away as if to speak to Gren.

As Tathrin relaxed, Ludrys suddenly attacked, driving the shield straight at his face. All Tathrin could do was flinch and close his eyes. He felt the studs press lightly against his cheek as Ludrys said something.

"He says you must remember it only takes one man to make a fight."

Tathrin opened his eyes to see Gren looking exasperatedly at him.

"I might remind you that you have two blades, Misaen curse you."

Ludrys stepped back, briefly holding sword and shield in one hand so he could raise a single finger at Tathrin.

"One more time," Gren told him. "Even if he already has won the best of three."

Tathrin took a breath, adopted the stance and thought rapidly. If he attacked Ludrys's shield side, the blow would be turned aside. So he'd be ready for that. He moved, and as soon as his sword was knocked away, he stepped closer in still. Bringing his dagger up, he tried to stab at Ludrys's sword-hand. He was so close that the Soluran's heavy blade was swinging round behind Tathrin, useless.

Ludrys laughed and let his sword-arm fall back, as if he had indeed been wounded. Then he drove the metal rim of his shield uncomfortably hard into the angle between Tathrin's neck and shoulder. He felt a shiver of numbness run down his whole arm.

Ludrys stepped away, nodding with approval all the same.

"That last try wasn't so bad," Gren allowed as he reclaimed his sword.

"Thank you." Tathrin realised he was sweating. His hands shaking slightly, he offered the dagger back to Ludrys with a polite bow.

"Water? Ale?" One of the onlookers offered him a choice of two horn cups.

"Ale?" Tathrin took the one with the foaming top. "You speak Tormalin."

The man's grin stretched an old pale scar on one cheek. "Enough for eat, drink and whore."

"All a man really needs." Gren had already secured a cup of ale. He was watching Sorgrad's conversation with the captain-general. "Evord's not the only one here who's spent time fighting in Lescar."

As Tathrin quenched his thirst, the older man cut Sorgrad off with a curt hand and walked over to join them.

"I see you're no mercenary masquerading as an honest Lescari potboy," he commented. "Come, walk with me. Tell me what you people really want me to do."

"Didn't Sorgrad say?" Tathrin looked at the Mountain Man, who just shrugged.

"I want to hear it from you." Evord spared the brothers a minatory glance. "Amuse yourselves without injuring anyone who doesn't deserve it while I talk to my guest." He began walking towards the lofty tower.

Gren tossed Tathrin his doublet. "Go on."

"There are a great many of us who long for peace." Tathrin hurried to catch up with the older man. He shrugged himself into his doublet, swapping the horn cup awkwardly from hand to hand.

Evord took it off him. "So you want to start a war to get it. Don't they teach logic in Vanam's halls any more? Have you any idea of the costs of war? Are you prepared to commit innocent men and women to all that pain and misery without even giving them a choice in the matter?"

They stopped at the foot of the stairs leading up to the tower's formidable door and Evord fixed him with a pale stare, his eyes more grey than blue.

"Are you willing to risk your own life? Because on that showing against Ludrys, you'll soon be dead if you go into battle. Are you willing to stand before your gods and explain where you got the authority to put countless strangers to the torment of fire and sword and pillage?"

"Sorgrad and Gren said—"

Evord silenced him with a curt hand. "Gren says some fortune-teller back in the mountains swore he was born to be hanged, so he doesn't think a blade can ever kill him. I don't know why Sorgrad left the mountains but he gets by with a quick tongue, faster reflexes and a talent for breaking heads when all else fails. They won't suffer, even if all of Lescar goes up in flames from the River Rel to the Tormalin border."

Tathrin found his voice. "Honest men and women suffer regardless, year in, year out. We want to bring an end to their trials, once and for all."

Evord pursed his lips. "What will you do, lad, when your duke gets to hear you're working against him? What if he sends his men to burn your home and rape your mother and sisters? Do you think he'll drown your brothers to poison your family's well before or after your father's been hanged from his own door-post?"

Tathrin stood for a moment, paralysed with dread at such a prospect. "I can't think like that," he said slowly. "This isn't just about me. It's about everyone in Carluse, everyone in Lescar. As long as I think like a scholar, I can tell you why this undertaking is our best hope of peace."

"Then come and do so." Evord began walking up the stone stairs. "Then I'll tell you exactly what your proposal will cost in lives and deaths and destruction. Believe me, that bill will be a steep one. Then you can tell me if this particular dance is worth the price of the candles."

Tathrin followed. Why, he wondered bleakly, did everything rest on his inadequate shoulders?

"Then you can explain this business of using some magic dredged up from the collapse of the Old Empire. Sorgrad seems to think that's going to keep everyone in step." Amused, Evord opened the door.

"I can assure you that Artifice is quite real." Tathrin felt momentarily on surer ground. As long as Aremil could make good on his promises.

"I hope so." Evord went into the gloom, his tone severe again. "Because at the moment, that's the only thing I can think of that could save this campaign from being arrant folly."

CHAPTER SEVENTEEN

Aremil

Beacon Lane, in Vanam's Upper Town,
22nd of For-Summer

"MASTER AREMIL." LYRLEN entered the sitting room
with a dour expression. "You have a visitor. Another
one." She handed him an unsealed fold of paper.

*May I introduce Branca Flavisse. I believe she can
assist you most ably with this new project.*
With all good wishes,

The signature was an illegible scrawl, but Aremil
recognised Mentor Tonin's handwriting with profound relief. Finally, the scholar was back from his
travels. Without him, Aremil found it impossible to
trace rumour and conjecture to someone who was
actually studying ancient aetheric magic.

"Please, show her in."

Aremil tucked the note beneath the latest of Master Gruit's daily queries. How soon would they have some magical means to contact Tathrin? If this Soluran captain-general was refusing to help, did Charoleia know someone who could contact Failla, Lady Derenna and Reniack? They would have to recall them, to make new plans. Master Gruit had never seen the sense in sending them off on the road to Carluse and beyond when everything was still so uncertain. Had Charoleia learned anything more of Duke Garnot of Carluse's plans?

Aremil set such anxieties aside. He was more concerned to know if this girl could truly reveal the mysteries of speaking to someone so far away. She looked like a milkmaid in her brown linen gown, a plain cotton wrap around her shoulders.

"Master Aremil? Good day to you." She extended a broad hand with roughened knuckles. Milkmaid or scullery maid?

He shook it as best he could and saw her silver seal ring. "Good day, Madam Scholar. Can I offer you refreshment?"

It was a bright sunny day outside his window and he could see sweat moistening the band of her linen cap. A tendril of mousy hair stuck damply to her plump cheek. She was a well-fed milkmaid, somewhere between Tathrin's age and his own. Still, she had her scholar's ring and she hadn't won that in a tavern game of runes.

"Thank you." She took a seat, quite composed.

Aremil looked at Lyrlen, who was waiting by the door, stony-faced. "Wine for our guest, if you please."

Branca raised her unladylike hand. "Small beer would be more welcome."

"Of course." His nurse reluctantly withdrew.

Aremil gestured towards the note he'd just read. "Mentor Tonin doesn't tell me your particular field of study."

"In the beginning, I studied the history recorded in the University Annals. Latterly I've been seeing how those records tie up with more informal history." Branca studied the books on the shelf closest to her. "By which I mean those tales told by the fireside and retold in ballads. Mentor Tonin tells me you are a scholar, though not as yet sealed by the university."

"My infirmities prevent it." Aremil was surprised Tonin hadn't forewarned her of his crippled state.

"So you've gone from discipline to discipline, comfortable in the knowledge that your income is sufficient for you to indulge yourself." She turned dark, sceptical eyes on him. "There are a great many books here on all manner of subjects."

"As you see, I'm unable to do much besides read," Aremil said with mild exasperation.

"Now you're interested in studying aetheric magic?" Branca angled her head. "Why?"

Aremil hadn't expected to have to justify himself to this bluntly spoken, blunt-featured young woman. Though Master Tonin couldn't have told her much. Given Charoleia's insistence on secrecy, Aremil hadn't told the mentor anything beyond claiming an interest in learning more about Artifice.

Which was true enough. The more he had read of such lore since the Spring Festival, the more Aremil was resolved to master this arcane art himself. He wasn't merely going to find those versed in aetheric enchantments. If he couldn't travel the highways and byways like Tathrin or Failla, or wield influence and coin like Charoleia and Gruit, he could at least make this contribution to their undertaking.

"You're of Lescari blood?" If she wasn't, there was no point in continuing this conversation. He could only hear the lifelong accents of Vanam's lower town in her words.

"My father was born in Triolle. My mother's people came from Marlier." She raised her dark brows. "What of it?"

At that moment, Lyrlen returned with one of the kitchen tankards incongruous on a polished silver tray.

"Thank you." Branca took it with a pleased smile. "You're not having something, Master Aremil?"

"Not just at present."

"On account of your infirmities?" As she drank, her dark eyes teased him over the pottery rim.

"Because I dislike ale." He looked at his nurse, who was bridling at such impertinence. "Thank you, Lyrlen."

She withdrew with a disapproving sniff.

Branca set the tankard down on the table. "To return to my first question, why do you want to study aetheric magic?"

"I have a good friend who is travelling in Solura. Given how erratically letters make their way through the Great Forest, I'd like to be able to know how he's progressing." He tried to sound casual, though after fifteen days' silence, he was just as impatient for news as Gruit. "Mages can only bespeak other mages, so wizardry's no use to me. Then I recalled Mentor Tonin saying that these older enchantments enable him to contact fellow adepts over unimaginable distances."

Branca looked thoughtfully at him. "How good a friend is he? Are you lovers?"

"What?" Aremil was startled. "No."

The unmistakable sound of Lyrlen choking on her outrage on the other side of the door was hastily followed by the patter of her shoes on the kitchen tiles.

Branca rose. "It's a lovely day. Shall we take some air?"

Aremil stared up at her. "I am hardly accustomed to casual strolls."

"My father has half an arm and barely a quarter of one leg. He's never let that hold him back." Branca fetched his crutches from the corner where Lyrlen had stowed them. "Ask your mother mastiff for permission if you must, but if we're to continue this conversation, we'll do it outdoors."

Aremil could tell she would leave without a backward glance if he refused.

"Bear with me," he said through gritted teeth.

He managed to get to his feet and Branca calmly handed him first one crutch, then the other. "Where shall we go?"

"My lord!" Lyrlen was in the doorway.

Now that Branca had planted the image in his mind's eye, Aremil could see how his nurse might resemble a watchdog. "We're just going to take some air." He tried to hide his own qualms.

"I'll bring him back safe." Branca's eyes were teasing him again.

"Lyrlen, if you please." He held the old woman's gaze until she yielded and opened the front door.

"Do you like the physic garden in Hellebore Lane?" Branca tucked the stray wisp of hair under her linen cap.

"I don't know it." Aremil squinted as he negotiated the doorsill. Outside the sun was surprisingly bright.

At least the flagstoned path was smooth and dry after a run of fine days.

"You should get out more." Branca curbed her pace to his slower progress. "You're very pale."

"You're very pink," he retorted.

"I often am." She nodded.

Aremil concentrated on getting to the end of the short street. He wondered who was watching his ungainly progress from the shadows of their windows, amused by his clumsiness. When they reached the junction, he had to stop to get his breath back. "Is this some kind of trial?"

"Of sorts." She was unabashed. "You really should get out more. Exercise might ease your aches and it'll keep your breathing clearer. But we can find you a chair for the rest of the way."

Aremil stiffened as she plucked a silver penny from the leather purse belted at her waist. "I came out without any coin."

"You can pay me back." Unconcerned, Branca waved the penny at a boy leaning on his broom until someone wanted to pay him to sweep a crossing free of horse muck. He came running.

"We need a carrying chair." She held the coin out of his eager reach. "Quick as you like."

"Quick as spitting, Mistress." The urchin darted away.

Branca studied Aremil as he rested on his crutches. "I take it your condition stems from birth?"

"It does." Aremil decided to turn the conversation on her. "I take it an accident crippled your father?"

"A bolting team of brewer's horses." Branca grimaced. "The dray's wheels crushed both limbs on his right side. The surgeon had no choice but to amputate."

Aremil winced. "He must have been a strong man to survive. I imagine you despaired of him."

"He was only in his nineteenth summer." Branca slid him a sideways glance. "Long before he met my mother, and I am the second of seven children. He's never seen any reason not to lead a vigorous life."

Aremil coloured and cast around for a less awkward topic. "So what can you tell me about ancient enchantments?"

"What do you know of aetheric magic?" Branca countered.

"Let's assume I know nothing." Aremil saw the youth approaching with two chair-men hurrying behind him.

"You know something of elemental magic, I take it?" Branca paused as the open carrying chair arrived.

"Wizardry stems from an inborn ability to perceive and to influence the four basic elements of air, earth, fire and water." Aremil didn't want her thinking he was a complete fool. The crossing-boy tried to help Aremil take his seat. He waved him away peevishly. "The mageborn have a particular affinity with one such element. Through study and training, a wizard learns to wield magic involving them all."

"In rare cases a mage might have a double affinity." Branca handed the boy his penny and smiled at the chair-men. "We're going to the physic garden in Hellebore Lane, if you please."

As the men took Aremil up, she walked beside the chair, quite relaxed. "Magecraft requires magebirth and it's a magic of the physical world. Artifice is a magic of the mind. In some instances, of many minds. Aetheric enchantments depend on the adept's mental resilience first and foremost, but an advanced practitioner can draw on the strength of those close by, sometimes irrespective of their willingness. Ancient scholars concluded that something must link us all, some medium that an adept can use to take thoughts from another's mind, to see through another's eyes, to hear with their ears. They called this 'aether'."

"You can do such things?" Aremil wondered what the chair-men were making of all this. Their pace hadn't missed a step. Were they even listening?

"An advanced adept can. In theory, anyone can learn the secrets of Artifice, but doing so requires rigorous mental discipline. Crucially, only a certain amount can be achieved by reading enchantments aloud. Those who cannot memorise incantations reach a point where they simply cannot progress further. Other things can hinder proficiency. Emotion for one."

Aremil nodded. "Wizards risk losing control of their affinity if they're angry or grief-stricken, or in raptures." Everyone knew how mageborn youths and maidens were shipped off to Hadrumal after they'd set a chimney on fire or brought down a hailstorm on a hay crop.

Branca smiled. "It's hard to wreak inadvertent havoc with aetheric enchantments." She looked at him more seriously. "You may be a worthy scholar but this may be beyond you. Extremes of emotion and sensation, pain, or even the mildest fever make Artifice impossible. An adept must rise above all physical discomfort."

Aremil refused to be deterred. "I have spent my life doing that."

Branca acknowledged that with a nod. "There are other hindrances. Those deaf to music are incapable of

Artifice, since even the most minor charms must be spoken with precise timbre and rhythm."

"I like music a great deal," Aremil assured her.

"Good. So do I. But however fine your feeling for pitch and melody may be, the hesitation in your speech may present problems," she mused.

"Let's not assume that before I've made some attempt," Aremil said curtly.

"Indeed." Branca nodded. "Do you play runes?"

"Seldom." The triangular bones were too cursed difficult for him to pick up. "I prefer white raven." Aremil wondered at the change of subject.

"I should have guessed that." A half-smile lifted the corner of Branca's generous mouth. "Can you at least tell me the set of runes that symbolise weather?"

So now he was being treated as a student. Did that mean she was going to teach him? Aremil cleared his throat. "The Storm; the Calm; the North Wind from the mountains; the South Wind from the sea."

"Good. The runes are an ancient collection of symbols," she continued. "The Forest Folk have used them for divination since time out of mind and the Mountain Men believe they were devised by their own gods, Maewelin and Misaen."

She could treat him like a student but not like the dullest pencil in the box. "The Mountain Men still have practitioners of aetheric magic among them."

"Who told you that?" Branca's eyes betrayed the intensity of her interest.

"A Mountain Man." Aremil permitted himself a carefully controlled smile. "Who's travelling with my friend. I can let him know you'd welcome an introduction. What have runes to do with any of this?"

Branca looked thoughtfully at him before continuing. "Those for wind and weather also symbolise the four aspects of aetheric magic. We find such images woven into many incantations and they consistently relate to the different uses of Artifice. We also find the runes for music cropping up—the Horn, the Drum, the Chime and the Harp—but those relationships are less clear cut. Let's stay with the weather runes for the moment.

"Much aetheric magic is concerned with the power of the mind as it relates to the physical world. Imagine stormy gusts, all unseen, nevertheless shaking trees, raising waves, stirring fires. Aetheric enchantments can be used to move things, to break them, to affect them in all manner of ways. By contrast, the Calm symbolises the adept's ability to remain unaffected by physical forces—to stay warm in the depths of winter, for example." She looked up at the clear blue sky wryly. "Or to stay cool, however hot the sun."

"And the North and South Winds?" Uncomfortably hot, Aremil wouldn't have minded a cooling breeze. "What enchantments do they relate to?"

"The other half of Artifice pertains to the influence an adept can have on another person's mind. Someone need have no understanding or even knowledge of aetheric magic to be susceptible to it. Though it seems that a common background or some other shared understanding makes it easier to work enchantments on another person," Branca observed. "The harsher these magics are, the more obvious, the more they're tied to the North Wind."

Aremil saw how this might be so. "The cold, dry winds that roll down from the mountains can be most destructive."

"While the South Wind is seen as benevolent, bringing rain and good harvests." Branca was looking serious again. "All the enchantments woven around that rune are subtle and not necessarily benign. The ability to read another's thoughts, to sift through their memories and desires, even to plant ideas in their mind? Such enchantments could be horribly abused without the victim even knowing what had happened."

Before Aremil could think how to respond to that, Branca halted. "And here we are."

"All the way to the gate, Madam Scholar?" the foremost chair-carrier asked.

Aremil saw a gravelled path leading away between two buildings newly built in the most severe and Rationalist architectural style. The dark granite that made Vanam so forbidding on a dull day sparkled in the bright sunshine.

"This will be fine, thank you." As the men set the chair down, Branca reached into her purse.

"Up you come, Master." The rearmost man lifted Aremil to his feet with impersonal efficiency. As soon as he tucked Branca's coin into an inside pocket, his forward counterpart offered his crutches.

"Thank you." Aremil was excruciatingly embarrassed. How could he have been so foolish as to come out without money? He settled himself on his crutches and attempted a casual manner. "So, madam, shall we proceed?"

Branca waited until the chair-men were out of earshot. "Are you interested in learning how to influence others without them even realising it?" she asked bluntly.

"No, and besides, wouldn't the mentors have something to say about that?" Aremil replied. "I cannot see Mentor Tonin allowing such things."

"Who's to tell him?" Branca countered. "If the victim's left all unawares."

"The Archmage is content to leave such powerful magic undisciplined?" Regardless of what Charoleia had said, Aremil still wondered about that.

"He has little choice, given that wizards are the only people besides the musically deaf who seem quite incapable of working any Artifice." Branca laughed without much humour. "Which isn't to say he's ignorant of what's been discovered about Artifice. You may not have heard, but a group of mages closely tied to the Archmage have founded a new scholarly hall."

"Yes, I have heard," Aremil said crisply. "On the islands of Suthyfer in the midst of the Eastern Ocean."

"Quite so." Branca wasn't bothered by his tart answer. "Mentor Tonin has spent much of this last year there, working closely with those adepts from the Old Empire who were found sleeping in the rediscovered lands. They have taught us so much. That's as may be. I imagine the wizards in Suthyfer keep the Archmage very well informed of all such developments," she concluded wryly.

"I imagine so." Aremil wondered what that might mean for his plans, and those of his co-conspirators.

Branca looked at him and folded her arms. "Mentor Tonin has been good enough to recommend me to the mage-masters and adepts in Suthyfer's new hall. I am not about to pass up the opportunity of travelling there in favour of teaching you. Not unless you tell me exactly what secret you're hiding." Her brown eyes challenged him.

Chapter Eighteen

Aremil

**The Physic Garden, in Vanam's Upper Town,
22nd of For-Summer**

"It's extremely hot." Aremil looked up at the cloudless sky. "If there's somewhere we could sit to continue this conversation, I'd be grateful."

"There are plenty of cool corners in the physic garden." Branca indicated the gravelled path.

Aremil began making his way cautiously along the potentially treacherous surface. "What are these splendid buildings?"

"That's the new Apothecaries' Hall." Branca waved to the right. "Naturally, the School of Physicians wasn't going to be outdone by mere poultice-makers, so they've been rebuilding. Thankfully everyone saw sense and left the gardens untouched."

At the far end of the path, Aremil saw a wrought-iron fence protecting an expanse of trees and plants, some flowering, some merely leafy. People were walking to and fro, some dawdling at their ease in twos and threes, others striding with single-minded purpose.

"I've never been here." As far as Aremil was concerned, doctors and apothecaries came to his door. Only paupers risked the attentions of their half-trained pupils at the university's back doors.

"You're not denying that you have a secret," Branca observed.

Aremil was looking at the kissing gate at the end of the path. He had no hope of negotiating that on crutches.

"A moment, Master." A liveried porter appeared and bent to find a latch.

Aremil saw how a hinged section made a cunningly concealed gate in the fence. A metallic squeal from the hinges turned heads all across the lawn and Aremil braced himself for incautious expressions of revulsion and hastily turned shoulders.

To his surprise, few people gave him more than a cursory glance. Only a youthful maiden halted, eyes wide with shock, the back of her hand pressed to her lips.

"Do you suppose she's stupid enough to think your condition is catching?" Branca asked conversationally as she went through the kissing gate. "It's not as if you're covered in sores."

Her laugh, like her question, was loud enough to be heard by the girl, who blushed furiously and hurried away.

"I wouldn't care to guess." Angry humiliation knotted Aremil's stomach regardless.

"This way."

Branca indicated a path running along the side of the garden and Aremil advanced carefully, his shoulders aching. The tall trees cast welcome shade and thankfully it wasn't far to an empty seat beneath a bower thick with honeysuckle.

"It is hot." The five bells of noon rang out across the upper town as Branca pulled off her linen cap and shook out her hair. It was lighter than Aremil had expected, touched with hints of blonde as it fell to her shoulders. She undid the plain pin securing her cotton wrap and fanned herself with one corner.

Aremil lowered himself carefully down and wished he could unbutton his doublet or at least loosen his shirt collar. He propped his crutches against the bench and noticed that the honeysuckle spread up a tall stone wall enclosing a separate space within the wider confines of the physic garden. "What's in there?"

"Poisonous plants." Branca left her wrap loose around her shoulders. "Some apothecaries' preparations require minute amounts of herbs that are deadly in any quantity." She grinned at Aremil's astonishment. "The poisons garden is always locked and there's broken glass embedded in the top of that wall. There are always doctors' pupils and apothecaries' apprentices around, never mind the gardeners."

"Even in the middle of the night?" Aremil drew a deep breath and found the scented air unexpectedly invigorating.

"I assume there's a watch kept since Vanam doesn't suffer epidemics of poisoning." Branca shifted to look directly at him. "So, what is this secret of yours? Why is it so important that you study Artifice under someone of Lescari blood?"

Aremil had been thinking how best to answer her as they had made their way to the seat. "Do you know why so many Lescari become apothecaries rather than physicians?"

Branca folded her hands in her lap. "I can guess, but why don't you tell me?"

"Money," Aremil said bluntly. "Studying medicine requires funds for several years of dedicated scholarship. While an apothecary learns, he earns his room and board as a condition of his apprenticeship. Lescari are always poorer than the people of Ensaimin. Even those who've lived in Vanam for generations struggle to lift themselves out of poverty because the misery of their kith and kin back in Lescar constantly leeches away their coin."

"Not mine," she assured him. "I see enough suffering in Vanam's gutters. If I ever have coin to spare, that's where I spend it."

"Then you are an exception," Aremil said. "Most Lescari-born in Vanam constantly try to salve the suffering of those they've left behind. They don't begrudge the coin, but they'd certainly welcome peace in Lescar and an end to such a drain on their purses. So some of us living here in exile have decided it's time to put an end to the senseless waste of lives and livelihoods, and every selfish duke be cursed."

"You expect aetheric enchantment to mend a situation that's gone unresolved for twenty generations?" Branca stared at him, astonished. Then she looked more suspicious. "You want to convince the dukes to abandon their hopes of the High King's crown by means of Artifice?"

"Could we?" Aremil looked levelly at her.

"No." She narrowed her eyes at him. "I don't believe there's an adept alive who could unpick an ambition so deeply woven into someone's life. To do that to all the dukes and all their families, with lasting effect?" She shook her head. "It couldn't be done."

That might dash Failla and Lady Derenna's hopes of a bloodless triumph, but Aremil wasn't surprised.

"Then it's just as well we have a different scheme. One which will be a great deal easier if we can use Artifice to contact each other rather than ciphered letters and courier pigeons."

"If Mentor Tonin hadn't assured me your wits are as sharp as your legs are weak, I'd say you were mad." Branca ran a hand through her hair.

Aremil ignored that remark. "If you have no interest in helping, can you introduce me to some adept whose Lescari blood still runs hot in his veins?"

"You really should get out more." She shook her tousled head. "You may move in circles where Lescari blood and Lescari rank still count for something. I don't. As for those still suffering in Carluse or Parnilesse or wherever else, if they find their lives so wretched, why don't they just leave to look for a better life elsewhere?"

"That's hardly so easy for the elderly or infirm." Aremil felt his anger twisting his face. He didn't care. "What of those burdened with children?"

"My father managed." Branca's tone hardened. "On crutches, with half an arm and still less of a leg. My mother's mother walked barefoot from Marlier, her husband murdered and her belly swelling with some rapist's child. She put all that behind her and made a new life, a new marriage and raised all her children as equals. None of my family cares a tinker's curse about my uncle's blood. None of my friends give a pennyweight's consideration to whether it's my mother or father who's Marlier- or Triolle-born.

Down in the lower town, we're Lescari only in name. What of it?"

"What of it?" demanded Aremil. "When 'Lescari' is a byword for stupidity, for treachery and theft? However much you achieve, isn't 'Lescari' always hung around your neck like a brick to drown a puppy? Don't your friends have to be twice as good as any Vanam-born, just to stop such shackles holding them back? Wouldn't you all rather be free of such associations?"

"Your oratory is getting away from you." Branca's colour was rising, and not merely from the heat.

Aremil realised spittle was slipping from the corner of his mouth. He tried to swallow. "Peace in Lescar would prove we're not all such fools."

"You don't think offering hope is the greatest folly of all?" Branca looked away for a moment.

"You're refusing to help me?" Aremil wondered why Mentor Tonin had sent him this exasperating girl.

"We'll see." She looked down at her hands. "Let me try to find your travelling friend for you. That's the least I can do after bringing you all the way here."

Aremil was tempted to refuse her offer. But Tathrin had been away for fifteen days. If his quest in Solura wasn't prospering, they had to know. Master Gruit was right. They would have to send word through some contact of Charoleia's to recall Failla, Reniack and Lady Derenna. "Thank you," he said curtly.

"You must understand that contacting someone by means of Artifice is not like talking to them face to face. It's not even like a wizard's bespeaking that deals in sounds and images reflected through some magical mirror. There's an intimacy that cannot be avoided. I will see more deeply into your friend's thoughts than he might wish. I wouldn't normally seek to find someone who hadn't given me their permission first." She looked searchingly at Aremil. "Are you a good enough friend that you're willing to give me leave on his behalf? And I will need to see him through your recollections since I don't know him myself."

"What else might you see if I allowed that?" Aremil asked suspiciously.

"More of your reasons for wanting to study Artifice," she said frankly. "More of whatever it is that drives you to try to heal twenty generations of Lescari pain when everyone else I know is content to let the dukes go hang along with anyone fool enough to bow down to them."

"Is that the price of your assistance?" Aremil knew his scowl must be making a gargoyle of him. "Will you give me your word that's all you will go looking for in my thoughts?"

"If you want to know how your friend's faring, this is the only way." She didn't blink.

He held out his hand wordlessly. What choice did he have if he wanted to know what Tathrin was doing? None, not until he could write to Mentor Tonin and ask for an introduction to a more congenial aetheric adept.

Branca took his thin fingers in her sturdy hand and murmured something under her breath.

Aremil didn't understand the words but heard swift poetry in the cadences. He tensed. It felt as if a hand were stroking his brow. A shiver ran down his spine as if a finger had been traced along his bare skin. Branca was looking at him. He couldn't break free from her dark eyes.

He knew he was still sitting in the physic garden in Vanam. He could feel the sun's heat and smell the flowers. At one and the same time, he was sitting in a chair in the centre of a vast empty hall. Cool light reflected back from the pale stone walls. The high vaulted roof was full of echoes that he couldn't quite hear. Shadows he couldn't quite make out flitted behind distant pillars. He wanted to look at them, to see what they were, but he couldn't look at anything but Branca's eyes. Even though she wasn't there.

He wanted to shout, to make his presence known to whoever was hiding in this strange place. Then he realised he was mute, as if he'd never learned to speak. As if he had never known that speech was even possible. Most peculiarly of all, none of this was the least bit frightening. That realisation intrigued him more than anything else.

"Thank you." Branca's voice was inside his mind, soft and unimaginably remote.

At the same time, his ears were hearing her say the same thing an arm's length away. Aremil snatched his hand back, shaken but consumed with curiosity. "Well?"

"I won't be able to talk to your friend. I don't know him and he's no adept. But I should be able to see what he's doing." Branca stared fixedly ahead. Her eyes grew distant and unfocused as she whispered something lyrical in its urgency.

Aremil sat motionless, feeling tension threaten him with cramp in his legs. It occurred to him to wonder what some passer-by might make of the two of them sitting here, him watching while Branca muttered to herself. Would some interfering apothecary come bustling up with a potion to calm such a sadly deranged girl? Half-amused, half-concerned, he was relieved to see Branca smile a few moments later.

She tried to curb her amusement, intent on the charm she was repeating. For a few moments, she didn't falter. Then she stumbled over a syllable and half-laughed, half-gasped. The vagueness in her eyes vanishing, she shook her head ruefully.

"Your friend is well, I can tell you that much. He's travelling with three other men," she said with calm certainty. "Sorgrad and Gren and Evord."

Proof if any was needed of Artifice's potential. Aremil hadn't told her about any of those men. He looked forward to challenging Master Gruit's scepticism with that.

"They're all in excellent spirits," she went on, "which is no bad thing, because Tathrin is trying to learn how not to be killed in a battle. He is quite determined to improve his skills with a sword." She looked quizzically at Aremil. "But he thinks Sorgrad suspects he has no aptitude for it. Sorgrad is the Mountain Man you mentioned earlier?"

"He is." Aremil nodded. "Where are they?"

"In the pine forests in the northern reaches of Solura," Branca said thoughtfully, "heading into the foothills. They're going to skirt the northern fringes of the Great Forest and come back to Ensaimin by way of the lakes and the Ferring Gap."

That was hardly a well-travelled route. Aremil could only hope this man Evord or Sorgrad knew what they were about. The uplands should be safe enough at this time of year, shouldn't they? He reached for his crutches. "Thank you for that reassurance. If you'd be so good as to help me to find a chair, I should go home."

"Not so fast." Branca twisted her hair into a coil, tucking it up as she put her linen cap back on. "Who are Failla, Derenna and Reniack?"

"Why do you want to know?" Aremil asked with suspicion. Just how much had she seen in Tathrin's mind? Or his own? "What do you already know?"

"I know that they're travelling and Tathrin is concerned that you have no easy way of contacting them." She re-pinned her wrap decorously across her shapely chest. "So you need at least three Artificers, don't you? Besides yourself."

"You think I could learn these enchantments?" Aremil asked before he could restrain himself. He quickly set that aside. "So you are going to help us? To find more adepts willing to help us? They must be utterly trustworthy."

Branca held up a hand to silence him. "I know that." She frowned, though not at Aremil. "I can think of a few scholars we could approach, but don't get your hopes up."

"No." He tried to curb the eagerness rising within him. "Please, do you think I could use Artifice?"

"I think it's worth making the attempt to teach you." She leaned back, looking at him with new interest. "Why don't we hire a gig and go to the lower town? I can cover the cost, and buy us lunch, as long as you can pay me back. I take it your mother-mastiff keeps some coin in the house for daily bread and firewood?"

"I believe so." There was no way he would eat or drink with her but Aremil didn't want to risk her newfound cooperation by refusing. It would undoubtedly cost him aches and pains, but he had tinctures for those.

Branca smiled. "There's a tavern where many of us who see our Lescari blood as an irrelevance gather. You should talk to them before you go trying to convince them otherwise."

"Very well, then." Aremil nodded, even though he knew full well Reniack had addressed himself to this question. The rabble-rouser had left a stock of broadsheets with Master Gruit before setting out on the road to Lescar.

Branca tilted her head. "Now, are you going to ask me to loosen your collar for you or do you want to stay stewing in your own juices?"

Aremil caught his breath. "I thought you weren't going to intrude into my thoughts any deeper than you had to."

"I can see you're sweating like a cheese without using Artifice." Branca shook her head. "If you learned to accept help with what you cannot manage, and set your mind to making the most of what you can do, you'd find your life a great deal fuller."

"Did your father tell you that?" Aremil asked crossly.

"No, I worked it out for myself." She was quite relaxed. "Just as I realised I'd make precious little of myself if I allowed myself to be beaten down by the fact that my sisters and I had to share a single pair of shoes some winters. If I let threadbare pride stop me from accepting the charity that meant I could learn to read and write. So I sat at the feet of Maewelin's statue with orphans and paupers and practised my letters on my slate. I scrubbed the university's dining halls in the evenings so I could spend my days in the libraries and didn't let myself notice there were laundry maids there with better gowns than my own."

If she hadn't noticed, why did she mention it? Aremil thought. "Tathrin worked as a scholars' servant so he could study."

Branca nodded. "I look forward to meeting him." She made no move to rise from the seat. "So, are you going to bend that stiff neck of yours so you can be more comfortable?"

"Very well. Thank you," Aremil managed to say with distant courtesy as she unbuttoned his collar with deft fingers.

This was not a price he'd imagined paying when he'd wondered what inducements might secure an aetheric adept's assistance.

CHAPTER NINETEEN

Failla

Viscot Crossroads, in the Lescari Dukedom of Carluse, Summer Solstice Festival, Day One, Night

"YOU CAN SEE the stars so clearly." Reniack gazed upwards.

"Get off the road before someone sees you." As Derenna snapped, her horse flattened its ears.

"There are plenty of people still travelling home for festival." Failla soothed her own mount, stroking its neck. She was heartily sick of trying to keep the peace between Reniack and the noblewoman.

"Precious few will be lurking round gibbets at midnight," Derenna said waspishly.

Reniack was unconcerned. "What do you suppose that poor bastard's crime was?"

Failla had been trying not to look at the gruesome shape hanging from the post by the mile-marker. Fortunately there was scarcely any wind to set the chain squeaking as the body swung. Better yet, the dead man, felon or merely unfortunate, had been dipped in pitch before a smith encased his corpse in the iron lattice, so they were spared the reek of decomposing flesh.

She could sympathise with Derenna's weary ill-humour. Thirty days' travelling, near enough, and only two spent on mundane matters such as washing their linen and brushing dust from their skirts and cloaks. At least Reniack rinsed out his own shirts and drawers, even if the two women were masquerading as his wife and daughter.

How safe were they now? On Charoleia's advice they had shunned the high road since Duryea, still five days' journey inside Caladhria, because there just might be some boot-boy or maidservant who'd fled the uncertainties of Lescar for safer servitude at a Caladhrian inn, and who just might recall seeing Duke Garnot's whore.

Failla's gaze was drawn to the hanged felon. Would this be her fate, if Duke Garnot caught her? Forbidden a funeral pyre and the sanctity of a shrine for her ashes? Her body left to rot as her spirit lingered amid the torment of Poldrion's demons? When long-delayed dissolution of her remains freed her to cross the river of the dead, would Saedrin grant her rebirth into the Otherworld?

"The Aldabreshi read all manner of prophecies in the skies." Reniack made no effort to move his horse from the crossroads. "Foretelling births and deaths and charting the fates of their children."

"Does anything up there suggest when these friends of Charoleia's might arrive?" Derenna asked tartly.

Failla shivered despite the balmy summer night. Catching the draught of Poldrion's cloak, that's what her mother called it. According to her grandam, one of the Eldritch Kin in the Otherworld had stepped on the spot where your shadow lay in this world. She looked down to see her shady outline cast on the beaten earth by the unclouded light of the Lesser Moon. Then she heard hoofbeats.

"Reniack?" Derenna stiffened.

"I know." He wheeled his horse around, drawing his newly donned sword, too incongruous to be worn by a meek tutor travelling in Caladhria. No one looked twice at an armed man in Lescar.

Failla encouraged her darkly dappled horse into the shadow of a holly thicket and saw Derenna edge her mount behind a flourishing birch tree. If these men proved to be mercenaries or worse, Derenna would break for the north while Failla fled to the west. On their way to this rendezvous, Reniack had indicated a deserted farmstead that would serve as a refuge in such a crisis.

Failla watched, tense, as he waited in the road, sword hanging loosely, hidden from the riders approaching on his other side.

"Fair festival and Saedrin's blessings on you and yours." The younger man rode a grey horse so pale it shone in the moonlight.

"It's late to be travelling, friend," his older companion observed.

Reniack shrugged. "I'd rather have two moons to guide me, but the Lesser's sufficient on its own at the full."

The second man nodded. "As long as there are no clouds."

"So Charoleia says." Reniack sheathed his sword, gleaming steel vanishing into the dark scabbard. "I'll have your names, friends, just to be sure."

"I'm Welgren, and he's Nath." The second man encouraged his horse towards the gibbet. "You're Reniack, I assume. Who's our friend here?"

"Are you talking about the felon or me?" Derenna emerged from hiding.

The man made a graceful half-bow, sweeping off his hat to show a balding crown surrounded by sparse white hair. "My lady."

"Derenna will suffice." She walked her horse out into the moonlight.

"You haven't got time to cut him down and cut him up." The younger man sounded apprehensive.

Reniack turned his head to stare at the older man. "I thought you were an apothecary."

"I am," the older man confirmed, "but one of the nicer things about Lescar is that no one asks to see your Physicians' Guild credentials before you anatomise a corpse. Don't worry, Nath. He's been tarred to keep the crows off, so he's no use to me."

"You're the map-maker?" Reniack turned to the younger man. "You sound like a man of Tormalin."

"I'm Tormalin born and bred but my father was a weaver born in Draximal," Nath said firmly. "That blood is all that counts as far as Tormalin's princes are concerned. If we can have peace in Lescar, I'll bring my sons and daughter home to a land where they won't be so unjustly despised."

"You escaped being tied to a weaver's loom. Who do you make maps for?" Derenna asked bluntly.

"In Tormalin, I work for merchants who have won themselves a fortune without being beholden to any noble family. They like to buy land and build grand houses, so I chart streams and measure hills and advise on clearing trees and digging lakes." Nath smiled engagingly. "In Lescar, I survey boundaries to make sure no one is claiming a finger's width more land than they're entitled to. I look for ores or quarrying stone, and if a vassal lord pays me enough, I won't tell whichever duke would claim the greater share for himself. As I travel, I chart the roads and I sell those maps to whichever printer pays best for accurate maps in his almanac."

"And you sell Charoleia whatever secrets you glean on the way?" Derenna was unmoved by his charm.

Nath's face hardened "I have children to feed, a wife and a widowed mother to support. I have no claim on any Tormalin noble family; no such fealty will save me and mine from starving by the roadside."

Reniack broke in before Derenna could respond. "What about you, Master Welgren?"

"Why do I correspond with Charoleia?" The older man looked mildly at him. "Or why do I want to see peace in Lescar?" He answered his own questions briskly. "I correspond with Charoleia because that's the price of her sending me news of advances in physic and surgery that I'd never hear about otherwise. I don't go out of my way to ferret out secrets. I just tell her things I've observed."

He shook his head slowly. "I have always longed to understand the mysteries of anatomy and of all the marvellous processes of vitality. But if Saedrin himself were to offer to explain it all, as a boon, I'd ask him to end this wicked waste of life in Lescar instead. In return for such a gift, I'd lay my scalpels and potions on his altar and never probe another wound or visit a sickbed again."

Failla rode out onto the road. She was less concerned with their motives. "You both travel from dukedom to dukedom without anyone hindering you? You've never come under any suspicion?"

"As far as anyone's concerned, I'm Tormalin," Nath said wryly.

Welgren shrugged. "The sick are more concerned with a doctor's effectiveness than his origins. Anyone stopping me on the road generally lets me pass when I explain they risk Ostrin's vengeance if the desperately ill patient I'm hurrying to dies."

Derenna looked dubious. "Have you never been robbed or detained?"

"I carry little enough coin and my books and instruments are of no value to anyone else. Most of my medicines can be replaced straightforwardly enough, and when I explain how easily they might accidentally poison themselves, would-be thieves tend to lose interest." Welgren smiled a little. "The price of my freedom has been treating some mercenary band's wounded a few times. That's no great trial. I can test new treatments and they don't hold the deaths of men already written off their muster against me."

"Charoleia trusts them." Reniack looked at Failla and Derenna.

Derenna nodded. "Then let's make haste before we miss our next meeting."

"Follow me." Failla headed past the gibbet.

Uncle Ernout had insisted, in his ciphered letter replying to the one she'd written at Charoleia's dictation, that she was to be the only one who knew where to find him tonight. What would his answer be, she wondered, to the astonishing proposal that had come from the conspirators in Vanam? Would he join with them or send them away? If he rejected this scheme of theirs, what would she do?

"What do we call you?" Nath the map-maker brought his horse up beside her.

Derenna followed, flanked by Reniack and the apothecary Welgren.

"Failla." It was a common enough name and Charoleia had advised against trying to use something unfamiliar. She'd said few things attracted attention like someone failing to answer when they were supposedly addressed.

"Where are we going?" asked Nath.

"This way."

The sprawling blackness of the ducal hunting forest lay ahead.

There was a rattle and Failla saw Nath making sure his own sword was ready to hand.

"Runaways and bandits lurk along forest tracks," he said defensively.

"We should be safe enough." Failla smiled. "From the Woodsmen anyway."

Behind her, Derenna was immediately curious. "The Woodsmen?"

Welgren chuckled. "According to tavern tales, they're the ones the peasants have to thank when a fresh-killed deer is laid on their doorstep the very day after some mercenary band has stolen their only pig. Or when some despairing goodwife measuring out her last barley to brew ale for selling finds a bag of coin in her grain bin to pay the ducal levy."

"How often does that happen?" Derenna asked acerbically. "Outside tavern tales?"

"We can turn tavern tales to our purpose, whether they're true or not." Reniack dismissed her cynicism. "As long as they show how woefully Duke Garnot fails his people."

Failla kept her mouth shut. She'd already said too much. She didn't want Reniack's broadsheets linking her Uncle Ernout and the guildsmen to such charity. As long as Duke Garnot sent his mercenaries hunting the mythical Woodsmen, they stayed safe.

As Welgren regaled Reniack and Derenna with more stories, Nath was searching the darkened coppices flanking the road ahead. "Charoleia tells me you and I will be travelling together. As brother and sister," he added hastily. "I have a wife and three young children."

"My felicitations." Failla looked for the waymarks Uncle Ernout had described. The first was a lightning-struck tree.

"Do you have a steady hand and a good eye for drafting?" he asked diffidently. "If so, you could act as my assistant."

"I believe so." She needn't explain how she'd honed such skills copying Duke Garnot's private papers.

Seeing a leafless skeleton amid the summer's lush growth, she urged her horse on.

"Will her ladyship be able to play the part of Welgren's nurse?" Nath sounded doubtful.

"After five children, a sickroom shouldn't come as any great shock to her."

To her relief, Nath took the hint and fell silent. Failla turned down a track that forced them into single file. As the trees grew taller, the boughs overhead hid the spangled night sky. Leaf litter muffled their mounts' hooves as they all slowed to let the horses pick their own way safely through the darkness.

Nath spoke up behind her. "I can smell burning."

"Solstice bonfires." Through the black branches, Failla saw moonlight striking pale rock.

As they emerged into a clearing around a rocky crag, Nath looked dubiously at scorched patches of turf ringed with stones. A few half-burned logs were still smoking. "You'd think they'd quench them more thoroughly when the forest is so dry."

"And risk the god's displeasure?" An old man, cloaked and hooded, sat in a niche carved into the rock.

"Saedrin's stones." Reniack was startled. "I took you for a statue."

"Uncle!" Failla slid from her horse and embraced him with relief.

"Drianon's blessings on your birth festival, child." He held her, strong despite his scrawny frame and snowy hair. "Until I got your letter, we all feared the worst."

"I'm sorry." Failla pressed her face to his woollen weskit.

"Be careful." Her uncle's arms tightened around her. "Your aunts tell me too many folk are still curious as to what's become of you. The duchess's women are forever debating the latest gossip."

Failla pulled away reluctantly, aware that everyone else was waiting. "Can we talk here?"

Nath had caught up her horse's reins. The animal whinnied at the scent of fresh water. A spring flowed from the rock to fill a pool carved at its foot. Long ago, the crag above had been shaped into a sternly bearded visage surrounded by billowing clouds. Pious hands had scoured it clean ready for the Solstice rites.

"This shrine is dedicated to Dastennin?" Derenna looked at Ernout. "You're its priest?"

"No." He shook his head. "Lord Hanriss inherited that honour from his father, as his father had done before him."

"Does he know we're meeting here?" Reniack asked suspiciously.

"Only that I have come to supervise the Solstice rites in Saedrin's honour." Ernout shook his head. "Lord Hanriss is too frail to leave his home and he has no sons left to inherit the priesthood. They all died fighting for Duke Garnot's father. He feels no obligation to Duke Garnot's quarrels, nor to any hopes of greatness for His Grace's son and heir."

Failla remembered hearing about the reclusive old lord from one of her cousins. He wanted revenge above all else, on Duke Garnot and his long-dead father, for the sake of his slaughtered sons. Would hatred that he'd already cherished through two generations keep him alive to see all the dukes brought low?

"I know too many families who feel the same." Derenna accepted Welgren's help and dismounted. "I take it his death means his estates will fall into Duke Garnot's hands to be laid waste by His Grace's folly?"

"Or used to bribe some favourite." Ernout waved a hand at the pool as several horses strained towards the water. "Let your mounts drink. I don't imagine Dastennin will take offence."

"I believe you represent the Guilds of Carluse?" Reniack dismounted and led his horse forward. It joined the others already drinking noisily, bits and bridles jingling.

"A Parnilesse accent," Ernout remarked. "Yet you're committed to the cause of peace in Carluse?"

"To the cause of peace in Lescar," Reniack said firmly. "I leave for Parnilesse tonight, where friends will hide me from Duke Orlin as we spread new hope among all who despise his rule. Lady Derenna—" he spared her a nod "—will travel with Welgren through Sharlac and Draximal, telling those whom they trust to expect a new dawn. If you will spread our word through Carluse, Failla and Nath will head for Marlier, to find men and women of equal goodwill to support our endeavour."

Ernout was unmoved by Reniack's oratory. "Goodwill is all very well, but Failla's letter said you were bringing an army to force Duke Garnot to his knees and to terms thereafter. Where are these fighting men now?"

"We have been travelling too far and too fast for news to catch up with us—" Reniack began.

"I have a letter from Charoleia." Nath reached into the breast of his jerkin. "She says your associates are recruiting in the hunting and mining camps of northernmost Ensaimin. They'll muster their forces in Dalasor by the middle of Aft-Summer."

Derenna looked at Ernout. "Can you convince your guildsmen and townsfolk not to fight? If they cannot escape service in a militia, they must flee the battlefields at the last moment."

"When did you get that letter, Nath?" Welgren was rummaging in a leather wallet belted beneath his cloak. "I have one from Charoleia here. They want to recruit mercenaries who've been wintering in Marlier, according to… Tathrin, is it?" He looked up enquiringly.

"Tathrin, yes, that's his name." Failla felt a pang. She'd much rather be travelling with him again. How was he coping with the hazards of his journey? She wasn't at all convinced those Mountain Men could be trusted, not if they faced a choice between saving his neck or their own.

"When exactly did you get this?" Welgren took Nath's letter and compared them.

The map-maker thought for a moment. "The morning of the forty-first day of For-Summer."

"But it's dated on the twenty-fourth day of the season." Welgren gave Nath his letter back. "I had this on the thirty-seventh, written on the twenty-ninth."

"So the plan has changed in some particulars." Reniack waved both letters away impatiently.

"This doesn't inspire confidence." Ernout looked severe. "If the right hand doesn't know what the left is doing, how is anything to be achieved? How secure are those ciphers? Letters can be intercepted and copied, no matter how secret you think your courier chains might be."

"We will soon have far faster and more secure means of communication," Reniack assured him.

"I don't think we should promise that just yet," Derenna interrupted.

"How so?" Nath demanded simultaneously.

"I wouldn't want to get your hopes up," the older woman said tersely.

Ernout looked at Failla and raised his brows in silent question.

"I can't tell you, exactly." Charoleia had insisted they tell no one outside the Vanam conspiracy that they hoped to use aetheric magic. Besides, Failla was still unclear as to how it was supposed to work. "But I trust those who say it can be done."

If Aremil's twisted body and intense manner unnerved her, Failla knew Tathrin believed in him absolutely. Whatever the circumstances of their first meeting, Failla had found she trusted Tathrin and not just because of his resolute defence of her on their journey to Vanam. The Mountain Men had questioned her closely, as if they knew she was concealing something. Tathrin had accepted what she told him. More, he'd shown no sign of contempt for her trading her body for Duke Garnot's favours. He'd just let her see his admiration for all she had done to help the guildsmen and their undertakings.

"This plan of yours will only work as long as no whisper of it reaches Duke Garnot's ears." Ernout looked stern. "I have discussed your letter with my allies among the Guilds and shrines of Carluse. We are not prepared to identify ourselves or share our plans with you. If one of you lets something slip to compromise us, whether by accident or folly, all that we have achieved over these past few years will go for nothing."

"Don't you want peace?" Reniack demanded, pugnacious.

"Can we trust all those you've told about us?" challenged Derenna.

"I can," Ernout assured her, "and I trust Failla."

Well he might. She smiled tremulously. He knew all her secrets. She would never be able to keep them without him. By way of repayment, doing his bidding had seemed so obvious when she'd lived at Duke Garnot's beck and call, of no more account than some caged songbird.

"We will help you." Ernout raised his hand to silence Reniack's triumphant gratitude "But not without conditions. Failla and Nath can spread your ideas through Carluse with our blessing. We will make sure they have food and shelter and that any talk of their presence is curbed. But we have our own undertakings to carry through and we will not involve you in those. The only point of contact between our people and yours will be Failla. If that's not agreeable, I'm sorry." He shook his head slowly. "We will go our way and you may go yours."

Even in the half-light, Failla could see Reniack's face darken. "That's—"

"Acceptable," Derenna said briskly. "Thank you."

To Failla's intense relief, the rabble-rouser heaved a grudging sigh. "Very well."

She couldn't blame Uncle Ernout for doubting these people and their conspiracy to bring down all the dukes. Far away in Vanam, she had been so easily seduced into believing them. It wasn't nearly so easy now, standing beneath the Solstice night sky in the midst of the forest.

She had thought she'd feel safer once she knew this plot was being folded into the guildsmen's intrigues. On the other hand, all along the road through Caladhria, fear had gnawed at her. If the Vanam conspiracy was discovered, then all the guildsmen and priests working for the common good in Carluse would be at risk. If their plots were uncovered, how could she hope that her own private secrets would remain hidden?

"It's very late." Welgren looked up to assess the Lesser Moon's passage across the night sky. "We should all get some distance away from here before dawn."

"Indeed." Ernout stepped forward to embrace Failla once more. "Saedrin watch over you, my dear." He continued more softly, for her ears alone, "Be careful.

If you need to, you can always come to me. But only you."

She nodded, mute with the effort of holding back unexpected tears. The thought of leaving her uncle's comforting presence to travel with yet another stranger tore at her.

Reniack was already mounted. "Dastennin grant us safe haven. May his storms bring confusion to our foes!" He departed with a wave of his hand.

"Saedrin send us all peace and prosperity." Welgren looked grave as he courteously offered Derenna his cupped hands so she could remount. "Even if it must be at the cost of a final year of warfare."

"Indeed," she agreed gravely as she gathered up her reins.

Failla watched them ride into the trees, soon swallowed up by the darkness.

"Shall we be on our way?" Nath was looking uncertainly at her.

He was afraid she was going to start sobbing in earnest. Failla tucked away that realisation for some future use. Drawing a resolute breath, she waited until she felt the threat of tears recede. "Indeed."

"Master Priest." Nath turned warily to Ernout. "Can we escort you?"

He shook his head as he wrapped his cloak around himself and sat in the carved niche once again. "I will keep vigil here till dawn. My vows demand it."

"Then we'll wish you fair festival, sir, and Dastennin's blessings." Nath inclined his head respectfully before looking at Failla. "So where do we go now?"

Ernout answered him anyway. "To the White Hound Inn, on the Ashgil Road out of Viscot."

"That's an inn used to keeping the guildsmen's secrets," Failla explained to Nath as she climbed into her dappled horse's saddle.

As they reached the trees, she looked back once, to see her uncle still seated beside the carved face looking out from the rocky outcrop.

It was time to take stock of her own situation. She was back in Carluse, but no one knew she was here besides her uncle and this man Nath. Did the mapmaker even know who she was, or rather, what she had been? She would have to take care to find out without letting him know, if he was indeed ignorant of her time spent pleasuring Duke Garnot.

She was back in Carluse. If she could reach her uncle's shrine in Carluse Town unnoticed, he would hand over her hoarded gold without questions. That was a relief, because she had never lied to him and would hate to have to start doing so. Besides, he had an uncanny talent for knowing when someone was telling him less than the truth.

If Aremil and Charoleia, back in Vanam, could find aetheric adepts to help them, all well and good. If this conspiracy could bring down the dukes and secure the peace that her uncle and all his fellow plotters yearned for, that would be better still. If all that the Vanam conspirators brought was more of the usual fighting, as long as Uncle Ernout stayed out of it, that would suffice. She would lose herself in the confusion and finally put her own desires first instead of serving so many other people's needs.

Failla looked covertly at Nath. He rode beside her, oblivious to her scrutiny. It should be easy enough to give him the slip, when it came to it. The only question was, how devoted was he to his faraway wife? Would her absence leave him willing to seek comfort in Failla's bed? Would it serve her purposes to seduce him? Time would doubtless tell.

Chapter Twenty

Litasse

Triolle Castle Demesne, in the Kingdom of Lescar, Summer Solstice Festival, Third Day, Noon

"What do you think, my love?"

Litasse smiled with genuine delight. "She's beautiful."

"A most generous Solstice gift." Iruvain whistled through his fingers like a stable-boy. On the far side of the grassy expanse, the groom persuading the chestnut mare to show her paces raised an obedient hand.

"Such generosity costs Duke Garnot of Carluse little enough, given he breeds the animals." Litasse fanned herself with a silver-mounted spray of black feathers. It was a hot day to be wearing a riding dress of emerald wool and she had been standing waiting while Iruvain looked over every new horse his loyal vassals had sent him.

This mare was the last, Duke Garnot's gift to her since this was her birth festival. Well, she wouldn't

hold the stable where it was foaled against the innocent animal. Litasse looked forward to riding into the
cool shade beneath the trees of the ducal hunting park
that stretched out before them. Even if the tended trees
and streams merely feigned the freedom of Sharlac's
wild woods.

Iruvain ran a hand around his neck, loosening his
sweaty shirt collar. No one thought less of him for
shedding his doublet in the heat, Litasse thought,
whereas any hint of such informality would be scandalous in their duchess.

"You must write and thank Duke Garnot, and find
some suitable gift for Duchess Tadira," he announced.

"Naturally, my lord."

Could she find some appropriate jewel in the coffers of Triolle bequests? If she did, Litasse suspected
Duchess Tadira's keen eyes would immediately
recognise it. Perhaps she could find some outdated
piece whose stones could be reset? In silver, by way
of tacit declaration that the mines were still enrich-
ing Triolle.

The groom brought the mare towards them at a
smart trot. How long could she escape for? Litasse
wondered. She had done her duty planning every
detail of the five days of festival. Surely the castellan
could cope with whatever minor crises arose among
the kitchen and household servants while she rode out
for an hour? She would be back before the entertainments planned for the most favoured vassal lords and
their ladies, who had been invited to spend this most
auspicious day of festival with their duke. When the
lords would laugh and applaud with Iruvain as the
tumblers and mummers pranced to the minstrels'
music. While their whey-faced ladies confided their

fears, as if she could avert the warfare that threatened their sons and husbands.

One of them was bound to enquire about news from Sharlac. All she'd had was a brief letter of blessing from her mother. Her father hadn't written a word to her for three full seasons now, but she had thought he'd remember her birth festival. Iruvain hadn't noticed, with his thoughts full of Carluse horses.

"I'm sure Duchess Tadira would welcome a string of Aldabreshin pearls," Iruvain said suddenly.

He proposed giving pearls to the woman who'd helped encompass her brother Jaras's death? Litasse had no doubt that Duchess Tadira had known all about whatever trap Duke Garnot's bastard had sprung on Sharlac's forces at Losand. Pearls, when he'd merely given her topazes that morning.

Litasse looked around. There was no one to over-hear them. Valesti stood stony-faced beneath the light pavilion erected fifty paces away. Grooms tended the other horses in the shade of the trees framing the gate at this end of the bridge crossing the rock-cut ditch. The tower-crowned wall of the castle rose up behind them, blocking any sight of Triolle Town.

"My lord, such a gift would be ruinously expensive. According to the Solstice accounts from our reeves, we're owed more in levies than they have managed to collect."

Iruvain looked sharply at her. "All the more reason why we should show Duke Garnot of Carluse and everyone else that we still have all the coin we might wish to spend."

"It will do nothing for Triolle's reputation if some Relshazri merchant presents his bill and we have to ask for time to pay." Litasse shook her head. "The price of pearls has risen beyond all reason with all these improbable tales of dragons and other calamities throwing trade with the Southern Seas into chaos."

"Not pearls, then." Iruvain coloured. "But a handsome gift all the same. See to it." His glare warned Litasse to say no more as the groom approached with the mare.

"Your Grace, I believe you're wanted." The boy was looking over their heads towards the gate.

Litasse turned to see newcomers talking to the grooms.

"It's Hamare." Iruvain smiled unpleasantly. "He can wait while I try her paces. You, boy, down."

The youth slid quickly from the saddle and Iruvain mounted. Swiftly adjusting the stirrups for his longer legs, he rode away before Hamare reached them.

"Your Grace."

As the spymaster bowed to her, Litasse heard the irritation in his voice.

"You." She looked sharply at the groom. "Be off."

Hamare watched the lad go before turning his attention to Iruvain. The duke was urging the mare to a canter across the grass. "This is the third time he's summoned me, only to keep me waiting on his whim like some lackey. Have I done something to offend him?"

Litasse felt suddenly cold despite the midsummer sun. "You don't think he suspects, do you?"

"No," Hamare said shortly.

Litasse searched his face for any hint that he was lying. All she saw was that he was hot and exasperated, in his black breeches and tightly buttoned doublet. "Do you want some wine and water?"

"No." He was still watching Iruvain. "Thank you."

The grooms by the gate whistled and clapped their approval as the duke schooled the horse through the elegant paces for which Carluse saddle horses were famous.

It struck Litasse for the first time that Iruvain hadn't come to her bedchamber even once since his return from his lengthy progress along the dukedom's eastern border. Did he suspect she was dallying with Hamare? He couldn't know, not for certain. Was he about to accuse her regardless?

The duke was riding towards them now, his expression clearly darkening.

Surely Iruvain wouldn't denounce her in the midst of the festival? Litasse felt sick. Could she pretend to faint and blame the heat? Though the fuss would only delay a confrontation. And if she swooned, every vassal lord's lady would spread the rumour that she was pregnant. That wouldn't help matters.

"Duke Garnot of Carluse is most generous to his friends, is he not?" As Iruvain rode up, he ignored her, all his attention on Hamare.

"He made Solstice gifts of saddle horses to every duke." The spymaster had to shade his eyes with his hand as he looked up. The sun was right behind the duke's head.

Iruvain made no move to dismount. "Even Duke Ferdain of Marlier?" He scowled.

"Even Marlier," Hamare confirmed.

"What's to do with Marlier?" Litasse looked from her husband to Hamare. She was used to Iruvain not telling her things, but she'd trusted Hamare to keep her informed.

"You don't think Duke Ferdain would seize Duke Garnot's whore?" Iruvain challenged the spymaster. "Their present truce be cursed, Marlier and Carluse have been at daggers drawn for generations."

"If the doxy fell into his lap, I imagine he'd see what he could shake out of her petticoats," Hamare answered Iruvain with some irritation. "I cannot believe he would send mercenaries to kidnap her." He spared Litasse a quick glance. "This is the latest rumour. I give it little credence."

"I find it wholly believable. Ferdain of Marlier has long been Secaris of Draximal's ally." Iruvain jabbed an emphatic finger at Hamare. "If Draximal is about to march openly into Parnilesse, Duke Secaris will want Duke Garnot of Carluse distracted, not massing his forces on their common border ready to come to his wife's brother's aid. If this whore has told Ferdain of Marlier where he might strike at some Carluse weakness, Duke Orlin will be left whistling for Duke Garnot's aid when Draximal marches south."

"Are Draximal and Parnilesse truly preparing for outright war?" Litasse asked doubtfully.

Hamare shook his head. "There's no indication of anything more serious afoot than For-Summer's customary skirmishing."

"No indication bar the warnings of every vassal lord with lands along the banks of the Anock," Iruvain retorted.

"Those lords must talk long and loud about such dangers if they don't want the militias they have mustered deserting to go back to their hayfields and harvests." Hamare wiped sweat from his forehead.

"I find their foreboding quite credible." Iruvain's lips tightened. "If Marlier attacks Carluse, and

Parnilesse attacks Draximal, we will be surrounded by warfare. Before summer's done, we'll see starving wretches overrunning our borders followed by the bandits who prey on them." He shook his head, grim-faced. "We may have no choice but alliance with Carluse and Parnilesse. Our three dukedoms share common borders and that would leave Marlier, Draximal and Sharlac all isolated. None of them will be able to act alone." His expression lightened a little.

So much for Sharlac's alliance with Triolle, sealed with the bloodstains on her wedding sheets. Litasse bit her lip. So why should she feel guilty because Hamare's breath on her skin and the pulse of his blood inside her was the only consolation she found in a marriage even lonelier than her rank had led her to expect?

"What if Duke Garnot of Carluse isn't interested in attacking Draximal on Parnilesse's behalf?" Hamare demanded. "He may be sending Duke Ferdain Solstice gifts, but I still believe Duke Garnot has every intention of attacking Marlier in the autumn. That's why he has been recruiting mercenaries. He'll plunder the gold that Duke Ferdain has amassed from the increased trade down the Rel. Then Duke Garnot will secure the river trade for himself."

"Don't expect me to weep for Duke Ferdain's losses," Iruvain said coldly. "He's never been a friend to Triolle."

"Never, Your Grace, but consider the hardship for Triolle when those fleeing the fighting in Marlier seek sanctuary here." Hamare visibly curbed his frustration. "To return to the question at hand. Neither Duke Secaris of Draximal nor Duke Orlin of Parnilesse has been able to raise the mercenary forces they would need to invade the other. I really don't believe they are ready to go to war. Come to that, Duke Garnot of Carluse hasn't been able to hire all the men he might want." Hamare let his frustration slip. "That, Your Grace, is only one of several puzzles we should be unravelling as a matter of urgency, instead of listening to the fearful imaginings of your vassal lords."

"You're talking about Vanam again."

Hamare ignored the warning note in Iruvain's voice. "There is trouble brewing among the exiles there."

"I ordered you to ignore such nonsense," Iruvain said ominously.

Hamare was standing with his hands laced behind his back. Litasse saw him clench his fists as he looked up at the duke.

"Orlin of Parnilesse is no longer so hot for war because he's not being goaded by pestilential night letters nailed to shrine doors. I've discovered that the scoundrel behind that was a man called Reniack, who fled to Vanam. The woman I have searching for Duke Garnot's whore tells me she's certain that's where the doxy went, too. Now there are persistent rumours that merchants of Lescari blood are urging exiles' sons to form an armed brigade."

"We hear this same prattle every handful of years and I've yet to see a single man set foot on Lescari soil. If exiles had any honour or courage they'd never have fled their homes and fealty in the first place." Contemptuous, Iruvain looked down at Hamare. "Don't waste my time. We must be fully prepared, because Draximal and Parnilesse will join battle as soon as they see an opening. We must be ready to do all we can to curb Marlier's aggression against Carluse. If you cannot, or will not, supply the intelligence I need, I'll find someone more willing and able to take your place."

Litasse stood aghast. Was he truly threatening to dismiss Hamare? She managed a hasty smile as Iruvain turned to her.

"You have a beautiful new horse, my love, and bear in mind, Duke Garnot could just have sent you a gelding, given how closely he guards his stock's bloodlines. I'm sure he's looking for an alliance with Triolle. Why else would he offer us the chance to put a Carluse mare to our own stallions?"

"You want to breed her?" Litasse looked at the dainty mare. "I thought she was to be my saddle horse."

"Until she comes into season." Iruvain nodded decisively. "Now, you should go and change your gown, my lady, before our guests arrive."

The mare pricked her ears, her head questing forward. Litasse stroked her soft nose.

So much for Duke Garnot of Carluse sending me a gift, she thought. *You'll just take her away, my lord husband, to grow fat and ponderous dropping a foal a year to strengthen your bloodlines and those of whichever lords you favour.* Disillusion dulled her day as surely as clouds covering the sun.

"I want to ride her now."

Iruvain shook his head. "I can't spare a groom to accompany you." He moved to lead the mare towards the stable-men waiting by the gate.

Litasse took hold of the reins. "I will ride by myself, then."

"That's hardly seemly, my lady." Iruvain stared at her, more surprised than angry.

"My man Karn is over there," Hamare said quickly. "He could accompany Her Grace."

Litasse held her ground. "Just for a short ride."

"Make sure you're fit to be seen before our guests arrive." Iruvain yielded the reins to Litasse with ill grace and strode away.

Hamare watched him go with hooded eyes.

"Can't you ride with me?" Litasse asked in an undertone.

She longed for the chance to indulge in a little spite about their Solstice guests, swapping wry observations on this vassal lord's loutish manners or that lady's unfortunate choice of gown.

He shook his head. "I need to think how best to prove to my noble lord that Draximal and Parnilesse really aren't about to go to war."

He waved and Litasse saw Karn detach himself from the men at the gate. The lean youth's long stride soon closed the distance between them. Litasse watched, but he didn't spare Valesti the briefest of glances. Were they still lovers?

"Find yourself a horse and accompany Her Grace on her ride," Hamare ordered.

"And then?" Karn looked keenly at him.

"Then you ride for Vanam. Though as far as anyone else is concerned, you are taking Solstice greetings from Her Grace to her lady mother in Sharlac." Hamare spared Litasse an apologetic smile.

"What am I looking for in Vanam?"

Litasse found Karn's hungry expression unsettling.

"I want to know what that shit-stirrer Reniack is doing." Savage frustration prompted Hamare's uncharacteristic coarseness. "If he's not sticking thorns in Orlin of Parnilesse's arse it's because he's found some riper mischief. The last rumour was that some Sharlac noblewoman whose husband's fallen foul of Duke Moncan was looking for him. See if you can pick up his scent trailing through the affairs of this Lord Rousharn. The wife is called Lady Derenna and she was definitely in Vanam for Spring Equinox. Then find out what lies behind these rumours of exiles making ready to fight."

"I take it I'm asking the usual sources?" Karn narrowed his pale eyes.

"They're cursed useless," Hamare growled. "Find out if that's because they know nothing or because they're choosing not to tell. If that's the case, find out who's buying their silence. Ask Lady Alaric."

"If she's in Vanam, there's definitely something afoot." Karn had no doubt.

"Perhaps, perhaps not, but she has her finger on the pulse of every rumour running from Toremal to Solura." The spymaster rubbed a hand over his bearded chin and looked at Litasse, embarrassment warring with the determination in his eyes. "This woman's information is always gold but she demands the highest price for it. His Grace is hardly about to give me a fat purse to spend on investigating something he considers nonsense."

Litasse hesitated, but only for a moment. "I can give you some jewels that won't be missed."

Iruvain seldom paid heed to her choices of rings and brooches. *If he ever asks after a particular piece*, she thought rebelliously, *I'll tell him I sold it to pay for Duchess Tadira's precious gift.*

"Offer Lady Alaric every consideration you think appropriate." Hamare gave Karn a meaningful look.

Did he mean for Karn to seduce the woman? Litasse felt a chill for the second time. Her lover was so very good at using people for his own ends. Was he just using her, too? Were his fervent whispers of devotion worth any more than his apparent loyalty to Iruvain, when he was going against Iruvain's express orders by sending Karn to Vanam?

"I'll give you those jewels on one condition."

Both men looked at her, astonished.

"Your Grace?" Hamare recovered first.

"Find out all you can about Duke Garnot of Carluse's plans to attack Duke Ferdain of Marlier. We'll send everything we learn to my father. He won't pass up an opportunity to threaten Carluse's northern border if all Duke Garnot's attention is focused to the south." Litasse spoke with more confidence than she felt. But surely this would be enough to draw her father out of his seclusion? He would have to answer a letter bringing such crucial news.

Hamare nodded thoughtfully. "If Carluse feels threatened by Sharlac, he won't expose his flank by attacking Draximal. If Parnilesse cannot be sure of support from Carluse, he won't march north."

Karn grinned. "On the other hand, Duke Secaris of Draximal won't march south as long as he fears Duke Garnot has mercenaries sitting idle who could be loosed against him."

"Then we will have peace this summer and Iruvain need make alliances with no one, least of all Duke Garnot of Carluse," Litasse said bitterly.

Who knew how the runes might roll after that? Sharlac forces harrying the border might get the chance to make Carluse pay a fitting penalty for her brother Lord Jaras's death. Duke Garnot deserved to lose more than one of his bastards.

Tears prickled her eyes and she turned to the mare's side to hide them, looping the reins around one hand. "I'm going to ride. Karn, find a mount and catch me up. I'm not waiting for you."

"Your Grace." Karn offered his cupped hands to help her mount.

"Thank you." She settled her skirts and belatedly found the stirrups too long.

"Let me." A trace of concern creasing his brow, Hamare adjusted the leathers while Karn ran for the gate.

The mare must have sensed Litasse's urgency to be gone for the horse sprang away at the first touch of her boots. The grooms by the gate raised a hearty cheer for their duchess as she galloped across the grass towards the illusion of freedom among the trees.

Chapter Twenty-One

Aremil

Beacon Lane, in Vanam's Upper Town,
9th of Aft-Summer

HEARING THE KNOCK at the door, Aremil hastily set his book aside and reached for his crutches. "Is that the carrying chair?" He heard the door being answered and brief conversation on the step. "Lyrlen!"

"You shouldn't be going out, my lord." Entering the sitting room, his nurse set her hands on her hips. "Let me send for Master Sempel."

Aremil managed a rueful smile. "He's an excellent doctor, but he cannot cure what ails me."

"He can make you more comfortable, my lord." Anxiety furrowed Lyrlen's brow. "Don't tell me you're not in pain. You're not eating and you're not sleeping."

He shouldn't have tried getting out of bed in the night. He'd underestimated just how tired his limbs were and thus more than usually recalcitrant. Though Lyrlen must have been lying awake herself to hear the noise of him losing his grip on the bedpost and falling to the floor.

"I ate my breakfast," he reminded her.

"Little enough of it," she retorted.

"Because I agreed to that dose of poppy tincture when you helped me back to bed," he said with some asperity. "You know it kills my appetite."

"You need to rest, my lord." Lyrlen was twisting her apron between her hands, always a sign she was unhappy. "Gallivanting up and down to the lower town has left you at a standstill."

Despite his irritation, Aremil had to laugh. "Lyrlen, I couldn't go gallivanting if I wished to."

Lyrlen smoothed her apron with angry hands. "That girl has no notion what you can and cannot do without harming yourself."

Aremil's smile vanished. "Branca has no more say over what I do than you have, Lyrlen. Please don't blame her. Now, I am already late, thanks to that cursed poppy tincture making me oversleep. Kindly pass me my crutches and help me out to the chair."

"Very well, my lord." Lyrlen escorted him over the threshold, as anxious as a black-feathered hen cherishing one precious chick. "When shall I expect you back?"

"No later than noon." He settled himself in the chair. None of the muslin drapes at his neighbours' windows twitched. The sight of his ungainly progress on his crutches was evidently no longer a novelty. "I'm only going to Mistress Charoleia's house."

Lyrlen looked somewhat mollified. "Very good, my lord."

The chair-men picked him up. This particular pair didn't need directions any longer, they were getting so used to carrying him the few streets to Charoleia's door.

Aremil listened in vain for bells. What time was it now? How long had it taken him to get up and dressed and send Lyrlen to find some urchin to summon the carrying chair? He shifted uncomfortably. Last night's dose of poppy tincture had long since worn off.

Lyrlen was right, not that he was about admit it to her. He was nowhere near recovered from his exertions over the Solstice Festival. His shoulders, back and legs all ached. Cramps had wracked him for at least a day after his visits to the lower town. But such visits were essential, if this undertaking was to prosper. It was the only way he could meet Lescari exiles without inviting them to the upper town, and that would attract unwelcome notice.

Regardless, he wasn't going to take any more poppy wine than he absolutely had to. It did his precarious digestion no good at all. More than that, its lingering effects made it impossible for him to work even the simplest of the aetheric enchantments he'd persuaded Branca to show him. He was determined to master them. If that meant mastering his pain through sheer effort of will, so be it.

"Here we are, my lord." The carriers set the chair down outside Charoleia's green door. "What time shall we call for you?"

"Noon. Thank you." Aremil accepted the foremost chair-carrier's strong arm and struggled to his feet.

The door opened as he settled himself on his crutches. Charoleia's maid was vigilant, as always.

"Are they here?" he asked without preamble.

"Madam Branca and the mistress are with them in the drawing room." As soon as she'd seen him manoeuvre safely though the entrance, she hurried to open the inner door. "Master Aremil, my lady."

"Please forgive my tardiness." Aremil did his best to sound offhand. "Some business arose that I had to deal with this morning."

"As it so often does." Charoleia smiled.

Settling himself in a chair, Aremil stole a swift look at the other people already in the room. Did they believe him or were they pitying his pathetic excuses? He fancied he saw a measuring look in Branca's dark eyes. The two men in the room barely spared him a glance, both clearly deep in thought.

"I take it you've explained our proposal to Master Kerith and Master Jettin?" Aremil propped his crutches at the side of his chair.

"I have," Charoleia confirmed.

Aremil nodded. He would find out from Branca exactly what had been said. He trusted Charoleia, more or less, but he wanted to know how she had shaded her words. What arguments had she used to persuade these two that their adeptness with aetheric enchantments would serve the cause of peace in Lescar?

"It is certainly a remarkable notion." Kerith, the older man, looked as impassive as ever, forbidding in his long black scholarly tunic. Aremil was beginning to wonder if he ever showed any emotion.

"It's a noble ambition," Jettin said fervently. Young, slightly built, he was the most intense of all the exiles whom Branca had introduced to Aremil, even if his accent showed no trace of his father's Triolle blood.

"Most assuredly," Kerith agreed.

If he wasn't as ready as Jettin to challenge taproom experts talking nonsense about Lescar, Aremil had seen the older scholar comprehensively demolish a mentor's ill-founded arguments at a university Solstice reception. The mentor had blithely favoured letting Lescar's warfare run its course until an undisputed High King emerged. What evidence could the man produce, Kerith had demanded, in the Carluse accents he made no effort to shed, that argued such an approach would ever yield results? It never had done in the past.

"So, are you willing to help our unfortunate folk?" Charoleia asked, her accent just coloured with a Marlier intonation.

Aremil admired her calmness. He and Branca had little enough to show for the hours they had spent mingling with exiles over those exhausting days of festival. There weren't many Lescari men and women studying the ancient enchantments of Artifice and still fewer were able to work enchantments with any degree of consistent success. They needed to find adepts sympathetic to their cause and bold enough to risk all the hazards of this clandestine undertaking. Most difficult of all, they had to find people they could trust to keep such a dangerous secret.

Running a hand through his black curls, Jettin didn't hesitate. "Of course."

Aremil was glad his impassive face would betray none of his misgivings about Jettin. The youth had broken off their first conversation to rush to defend a Lescari man accused of rolling weighted runes in the crowded tavern where Branca had found him. Jettin hadn't even known the man. But Charoleia had made her own enquiries and said the youth kept his father's

spice-trading secrets as close as his own skin. Judging
by Jettin's fine clothes, that spice business was certainly prospering. And Aremil had convinced Jettin to play
a game of white raven with him one evening. He had
been favourably impressed by the young merchant's
shrewd tactics.

The scholar Kerith was still frowning. "I'll give you
my answer in a day or so, if that's agreeable."

"Of course," Charoleia assured him. "If you have
any concerns, or any more questions, don't hesitate to
call upon me."

As she spoke, the elegant timepiece on the wall
struck the third hour of the day.

"If you'll excuse me, my lady, Madam Scholar,
Master Aremil—" Kerith rose and favoured them all
with a brief bow "—I am expected at the Mordaunt
Hall."

"And I'd better be about my father's errands." Jettin
sprang to his feet.

"Let me show you out." Charoleia favoured both
men with her most charming smile.

Aremil looked at Branca as the door closed behind
them. "Are you sure Jettin can keep his mouth shut?"

She nodded. "He's nowhere near the reveller he
looks. He won his legal advocate's ring inside three
years, still working for his father all the while."

Aremil jerked one shoulder in a non-committal
shrug. "Do you think Kerith will help us?"

Branca smiled. "Before you arrived, Charoleia was
telling him how extraordinary times have always led
to extraordinary advances in natural philosophy and
alchemy."

"Warfare generally leads to progress." Aremil considered this. "Kerith is very keen to see how well

Artifice works outside the halls and libraries, in more testing conditions."

"And to try some of the enchantments that the mentors have no interest in," Branca pointed out. "Are you all right, Aremil? You don't look well."

It was impossible to take offence at her matter-of-fact observation. "I'm tired."

"Do you want to leave off trying your own Artifice till tomorrow?"

From the outset, she'd been content for him to choose his own pace.

"I'll try and we'll see how we fare."

Whether he tried and succeeded or tried and failed, she would neither praise him for prevailing despite his handicaps nor chastise him, however kindly, for overtaxing his strength. She'd merely assess his progress and discuss his understanding of the relevant aspects of the enchantments.

Charoleia came back into the room looking pleased. "I think they will do very well."

"You think they'll join us?" Aremil hoped she was right.

"I do." She nodded. "We should send Jettin to join Reniack. He'll appreciate the boy's enthusiasm and know how to channel it effectively, and how to curb it when need be."

"And Kerith?" Branca enquired.

"He'll do best in Carluse," Charoleia said with conviction. "He's committed to the common Lescari cause as far as his reasoning goes, but Carluse's fate is still what holds his heart."

Aremil nodded. "So we still need to find someone to join Lady Derenna and someone to join Tathrin, Sorgrad and Gren."

"I think I would prefer to keep contact with Tathrin between ourselves." A crease appeared between Charoleia's perfectly shaped brows. "I'm confident neither Kerith nor Jettin would betray us deliberately, but there's always the chance they'll let something slip by mistake. Halcarion forfend, but if they're ever questioned, we want to be certain there'll be little they can say about anyone else's part in this business. The same goes for Failla and Nath, Lady Derenna and Welgren. Having our efforts in any one dukedom discovered will be bad enough. If the dukes get wind of Captain-General Evord's army, that'll be a whole different roll of the runes."

"I can continue to communicate with Tathrin," Branca said calmly. "It won't be long till Aremil can do the same."

Her confidence heartened him. She never flattered him, after all. He resolutely set aside his doubts in the despairing watches of the night, when he'd feared he'd never manage the enchantment. That was why he'd tried to get out of bed to retrieve the book of ancient lore, convinced that the light of the Greater Moon, riding unchallenged at its full in the cloudless dark, would be bright enough to read by.

"Have you spoken to Tathrin today?" Charoleia might have been asking if Branca had met him on the street rather than wielded enchantment reaching hundreds of leagues.

Branca nodded. "He says they're travelling at a good pace. There's only a small group with Evord, but a good many people have come and gone and Sorgrad's confident they will find a sizeable force mustering at the time and place Evord has appointed."

"When is that?" Aremil asked. "And where?"

"Tathrin didn't say." Branca surprised him with a grin. "He doesn't know. Evord won't tell him, nor Sorgrad."

"They both know the value of silence." Charoleia was unperturbed. "Is Sorgrad confident no word is trickling down to the lowlands?"

"He is," Branca confirmed.

Hearing news at second and third hand was intensely frustrating. Aremil clenched his feeble fingers. The sooner he could contact Tathrin for himself, the better. Then he realised Branca was looking slightly troubled.

"Tathrin says Evord and Sorgrad agree they need a banner, something with a bold blazon."

Charoleia was far from being surprised. "Of course."

"Why 'of course'?" Aremil looked curiously at her.

"They're raising an army," the composed beauty pointed out. "When they go into battle, they'll need a standard for Evord's personal company, so that the rest of the bands can see where he is. The lesser captains will need to send runners to his position or rally to him in case of retreat. They need a blazon that the other companies can add to their own standards. Evord will need to see how his own forces are faring across the battlefields."

Battlefields where men and women would fight and fall injured, some of them dying. Tathrin could so easily be among the wounded or—Poldrion forfend—the dead.

Aremil looked at Branca and saw his own misgivings reflected in her dark eyes.

"Foolish, isn't it?" she said frankly. "We've been talking about raising an army and overthrowing the Lescari dukes, but I've never really thought about the bloodshed."

"We're none of us warriors," Charoleia pointed out, "which is why we are leaving such things to Sorgrad and Evord. We must trust them while we play our part here." She paused. "We don't merely need to devise a standard. We need to see banners sewn and dispatched."

"Without anyone knowing what they're for," Aremil warned.

"Whatever we choose, it had better not be anything that could be confused with the dukes' badges," Branca said after a moment.

Aremil saw what she was thinking. "We don't want anyone to assume that this undertaking is just some feint to put a particular duke on the High King's throne."

"We don't want anything that could be mistaken for some Tormalin prince's insignia, either," Charoleia agreed.

"What manner of badges do they use?" Branca asked uncertainly.

"A great many animals." Aremil searched his recollections. "The swan for the House of Tor Kanselin, the lynx for D'Olbriot."

Branca sighed. "With Carluse's boar's head, Sharlac's stag and Triolle's green grebe, we had better avoid beasts and birds altogether."

"And weapons," Aremil agreed, "given Marlier's swords and Parnilesse's halberd and long sword."

Charoleia was still thinking about Tormalin badges. "D'Alsennin uses the holm oak and Den Dalderin the honeysuckle. Tormalin princes use at least as many trees and flowers as they do birds and animals, so we had best shun all such motifs."

"What does that leave?" Aremil looked at Branca and saw she was as bereft of inspiration as him.

"We need a design that mercenary companies can easily blend with their own."

Charoleia looked for Aremil's agreement but he could only look blankly at her.

"Why so?"

"A mercenary company that's sworn fealty to a duke or a Tormalin prince adopts some element of their paymaster's insignia alongside their own." She raised her brows. "Did you not know that?"

"I left Draximal as a child," he reminded her, "discarded as unfit to lead men into battle. No one explained the intricacies of hiring mercenaries to me."

"Master Reniack will want something that's easily drawn and copied, if he's to include it in his broadsheets and night letters," Branca observed.

Aremil nodded. "A blazon to identify our common purpose could serve more ends than just rallying men on the battlefield."

"So it must symbolise all aspects of our common endeavour." Charoleia frowned.

The faint sound of wheels on the cobbles outside emphasised the silence in the room.

"Perhaps Master Gruit can lend us a helping hand," Charoleia said at length. "He'll need to send the banners along with everything else we will need him to buy to supply Evord's army. We can ask him where we might buy the necessary cloth, and have the pennants made up by seamstresses who can keep their mouths shut."

"We want everyone in Lescar lending a helping hand to our common purpose," Branca said suddenly. "Let's show that on this standard."

Aremil looked at her. "I don't understand."

"Linked hands would show cooperation." Branca crossed her own chapped hands in demonstration.

"Six hands, to show the six dukedoms united?" Aremil mused.

"Hands holding something other than weapons," Branca said with feeling, "to show that we're concerned with common folk's lives, not dukes' and nobles' warfare."

"Ordinary folk from highest to lowest. A broom and a pitchfork for goodwives and farmers, or a sheaf of wheat?" he suggested.

Branca smiled. "A handbell for priests and a quill for scholars?"

"A hand holding a halberd like those the militiamen use would show that these common folk are ready to raise arms in their own defence." A sudden smile lightened Charoleia's expression. "If you'll pardon the jest."

"Does anyone already use a similar blazon?" Aremil couldn't think of any such.

"Some of the lesser Tormalin families use a single hand or arm, and some of the mercenaries show gauntlets and the like, but that doesn't signify." Charoleia looked at Branca. "How would you arrange six hands without this badge looking like the leavings on some battle surgeon's floor?" She softened her words with a smile. "Since Gren's not here, I feel I should play the mocker. Believe me, mercenaries are most inventive when it comes to pouring scorn on a rival warband's insignia."

"I'm sure the dukes will be just as eager to diminish our challenge with ridicule," Aremil allowed.

"I'm no artist." Branca shook her head.

"Nor me," Charoleia admitted ruefully. "But I know some talented painters. Shall I see if one of them can make something of these ideas?"

"As long as you can think up some convincing excuse for offering such a curious commission." Aremil was beginning to wonder just how long they could keep all their planning a secret. More and more people were being drawn into this plot, even if they didn't know it.

Chapter Twenty-Two

Karn

**Ronde Street, in Vanam's Upper Town,
20th of Aft-Summer**

THE SULTRY NIGHT didn't need blazing torches adding to the stultifying heat. Karn didn't need their yellow glare making it impossible to find concealment closer to the house he was watching.

But the Greater Moon was fading past its last quarter and the Lesser was barely waxing to its half. Poldrion forfend the rich and privileged stub their toes on an uneven cobble.

At least the upper town's alleys were swept clean of filth and vagrants. Karn could wait comfortably enough while watching to see who was coming and going to buy information from or sell it to Lady Alaric.

He was curious. A day or so gathering gossip suggested Lady Alaric was spending most of her time within her own doors. Her visits to Vanam usually saw her spending her evenings at dances and gambling parties or as an honoured guest in one of the upper town's sedate drawing rooms, where incautious scholars would find their tongues loosened by wine and a beautiful woman's flattering attention.

Karn had played that game himself, and on the one occasion he had seen Lady Alaric before, she had been strumming on the vanity of the Tormalin Emperor's master of music with all the skill of a celebrated lutenist. Karn hadn't spoken to her then, passing unnoticed through the throng in a lackey's livery.

When would he get the chance to introduce himself tonight? How many guests was she entertaining? Like most of the other houses along the street, the shutters and casements above the ground floor stood open in a vain attempt to entice a breeze inside. To his intense frustration, he couldn't get close enough to distinguish between the shadows crossing and recrossing her lamp-lit windows. Every shape might be a different man, or some restless individual might simply be pacing back and forth.

He yawned. He was still feeling the effects of his punishing journey here, though steaming himself in a bathhouse on the Ariborne that afternoon had gone a long way to easing his aches. And encountering an amiably corpulent glovemaker there had gone a fair way to replenishing his purse. Such men were usually happy to reward an agreeably anonymous lad with firm, deft hands. Karn always liked to show Master Hamare how little of Triolle's silver he needed to spend.

A clock struck somewhere, four chimes echoing around the granite buildings. Karn shifted. Not long till midnight. The summer darkness this far north of

Triolle was short enough before it was divided into the night's ten hours. Lady Alaric's party would soon be ending. Scholars went early to their solitary beds and those who might wish for more frivolity showed due consideration for the university's customs. The university's mentors were generally their landlords, after all.

He pursed his lips. Who was renting this discreetly prestigious address to Lady Alaric?

A heavy hand landed on his shoulder "I'll have your name and business, lad."

"I have a message but I don't want to interrupt her ladyship." Ducking his head, he made sure his voice broke nervously upwards.

"Let's have a look at you." The Watchman shoved him towards the golden light of the closest torch. Despite the heat, the broad-shouldered man wore a voluminous cloak.

Karn noted the line of a weapon hidden beneath it to supplement his official stave. A club or a sword? No matter. It didn't suit his purpose to get into a fight tonight.

"My name is Karn Mellar." He folded his hands, hunching his shoulders as he met the Watchman's gaze, meek but not afraid. Fear would imply he knew he had no right to be here.

"Who's your message for?"

Karn knew the Watchman was taking in his clean-shaven face, his expensively tailored doublet and the sheen on his boots. Upper-town Watchmen were no fools. They were the ones with the experience and influence that won them the right to walk quieter streets through the darkness. Stupid recruits didn't last the course. The attractions of petty power and a bell to ring over erstwhile friends and rivals lost their lustre after the fourth or fifth taste of having the cockiness kicked out of them in some tavern courtyard.

"My Lady Alaric Verlayenne." Karn assessed the Watchman's interest. No, the man's face betrayed no hint of unsavoury lusts driving him to walk the darkened streets instead of sitting by his own fireside with a wife and child.

"Lady Alaric? Let me take you to her door." The firm hand behind his elbow brooked no argument.

Karn offered none. Lady Alaric was doubtless buying the allegiance of the local Watchmen, which was why the man was prowling the back alleys instead of keeping to the middle of the streets on his prescribed route.

The Watchman rapped smartly on Lady Alaric's polished door with the brass-bound end of his stave.

Karn heard the scurry of slippered feet on tiles and a maid opened the door to them. No slip of a girl, she was old enough to have been Karn's mother. Had his mother lived.

"Compliments to your mistress." The Watchman tipped his stave to his temple in brief salute. "Lad says he's got a message."

"You can give it to me." The maid held out a smooth hand showing little sign of days spent scrubbing or polishing.

"I beg your pardon, but it's not a letter," Karn said respectfully. "My master told me to speak only to her ladyship."

"Did he, indeed?" The maid looked at him, her expression unreadable though her Relshaz accent was plain. "You had better come in and wait until it suits my lady to see you."

"Thank you." Karn ducked his head. There was something faintly familiar about the woman. What was it?

The Watchman slapped the end of his stave into a leathery palm. "I'll bid you goodnight, then."

"Thank you for your vigilance." The maid favoured him with a pert smile before she beckoned Karn inside with a peremptory gesture.

Lady Alaric would be paying the Watchman well enough to guarantee he wouldn't go far while she had a strange man in her house. He'd come running if her servants shouted an alarm, ready to use whatever weapon he carried under that cloak.

"In here." The maid lit a spill from the candle in the closest mirrored sconce and opened a door across the panelled hall.

"Thank you." Karn surprised her with a cheeky grin.

Her expression didn't change. "If you please."

Karn followed her into the shadowy room.

The maid lit the silver branch of candles waiting on the marble mantelshelf. "Please, refresh yourself while you wait."

She crossed to a rosewood table with spindly legs where a tray of crystal glasses stood between a squat bottle of white brandy and a decanter of plum-coloured liquor.

"Thank you." Karn wouldn't give offence by declining but he wasn't about to cloud his wits, not after so long a day.

The maid smiled at him. "My lady will see you soon."

As she walked to the door, the soft metallic melody of a music box filled the room. As the door closed,

Karn went to look at the marquetry casket she'd opened. The brass drum revolved steadily, its pattern of fine bristles plucking at sweetly tuned metal quills. It played a Dalasorian dance tune.

He looked upwards at the plaster ceiling bright with moulded and painted flowers. How many voices overhead? Men or women? The music box was just loud enough to foil any hope of distinguishing them. If he stopped it playing, he'd have to explain himself, wouldn't he? A neat trick.

There was an upholstered loveseat by the muslin-draped window and a small table flanked by two delicate chairs. The walls were hung with silk embroidered with the same flowers that decorated the hall: rain-roses, sweetflax and copper-sickle. Did Lady Alaric conduct business in here or assignations?

He frowned. He hadn't seen her attended by any maid in Toremal. Why did that servant look familiar?

Doors opened above. Feet sounded on the stairs, mingled with laughter and cheerful farewells. Outside he could hear carriages drawing up with a clatter of hooves. He looked at the window. Here on the lower floor, the shutters were securely closed. Even if he could open one quietly, the candlelight would betray his curiosity.

"Good evening." Lady Alaric entered, one silver-ringed hand smoothing woven plaits confining a cascade of chestnut ringlets.

"Good evening." Karn made his bow.

"Thank you. Your arrival reminded everyone of the late hour." A dimple beside her petal-soft lips made her confiding smile all the more attractive. "It wasn't the most exciting gathering but one must return the hospitality of one's neighbours."

Despite the lateness, the noblewoman was bright-eyed and all the oppressive heat did was tint her perfect cheekbones with a blush of rose. Lavender topaz set in silver filigree ornamented her slender neck, though the clarity of the stones couldn't hope to match her remarkable eyes.

Karn admired the calculated perfection of her appearance. The soft swell of her bosom above her white silk gown's low neckline was demurely covered by a frill of silver lace. More lace trimmed her sleeves in matronly fashion. On the other hand, the tightly fitted bodice drew the eye to her slender waist and the seductive swell of her hips.

Decorous enough not to threaten women, who, Halcarion help them, would inevitably look plain beside this beauty, while any man from the callowest youth onward would find her mature serenity deeply alluring.

That suited Karn. Older women could always be flattered by boyish adoration. He cleared his throat.

Lady Alaric raised a silver-braceleted hand and angled her head. "Hamare of Triolle's man," she said after a moment's thought. "You were in Toremal the summer before last. Can I offer you something to drink?"

Karn closed the music box to stifle the tinkling tune. "Thank you, some water would be welcome."

"It is a warm night." She nodded to her maid and the woman withdrew. "How is your master? How does Triolle fare?" she asked briskly.

"My master is well," Karn said courteously, "though puzzled."

"What's gnawing at him?" Lady Alaric raised her perfectly shaped brows. "What will easing his mind be worth?"

"It will be worth your while, my lady," Karn assured her. "I can tell you anything you wish to know about Duke Iruvain's current plans."

She sat on one of the chairs, sweeping her skirts gracefully aside. "I already know all I wish to." She lifted one foot to tug at the ribbons of her high-heeled satin shoe.

"My master will be most grateful for anything you care to share." Karn spread his hands, submissive. "And, naturally, in your debt."

"Goodwill seldom counts for as much as gold." Lady Alaric smiled sardonically. "My dressmaker won't take debts of honour to settle her bills."

Karn allowed himself to relax a little. Hamare had told him Lady Alaric was interested in solid coin, gold and silver, first and last. A generous purse always made for straightforward dealings, easier than twisting someone's arrogance to his own ends, or their lust, their desire for revenge, whatever proved to be his key to them.

"You must put a value on the answers you decide to share with us, and on what I have to tell you of Triolle and other matters. We'll see where that leaves the reckoning." Karn saw that the ribbons of her shoe were knotted. "May I help you with that?"

"Thank you." Mild amusement twitched at the corner of her mouth as he knelt at her feet.

Karn had played the page often enough. It was the work of a moment to loosen the lavender ribbons decorated with tiny heartsease. Supporting her calf with one hand, he drew off the white shoe.

"That's better." Lady Alaric wriggled her silk-stockinged toes.

Karn stroked gentle fingertips down her instep. "Would you like me to rub your feet?"

"Maybe later." Her gossamer petticoats rustled with spicy perfume as she presented her other shoe.

The door opened and the maid entered with a glass ewer of water and two crystal goblets. She showed no surprise at seeing their late-night visitor on his knees in front of her mistress.

"We'll serve ourselves." Lady Alaric waved a hand at the table beside her.

The maid set the tray down and withdrew with an alacrity that suggested she guessed more intimacy might ensue.

"You've been in Vanam a day or so."

"You're very well informed." As he glanced up, Karn saw a glint in her eye. Might they exchange more than just information?

"You left Triolle just after Solstice." She poured the water, thoughtful. "Something Master Hamare learned from the festival's exchanges of letters and gifts piqued his curiosity? Enough to send you all the way to Vanam with the coin to hire fresh horses for every stretch of road."

"It wasn't so arduous." Karn took the goblet and sipped. The water was lightly flavoured with fresh mint. "The roads are dry and clear and summer days are long."

Lady Alaric leaned back and crossed her graceful ankles. "What does Hamare want to know?"

Where to begin? Karn sat cross-legged, a humble suppliant. The golden carpet of thick northern wool was comfortable enough. "Duchess Litasse wishes to know what Sharlac's vassal lords make of Duke Moncan's seclusion."

Lady Alaric shrugged. "They respect his mourning for his lost heir."

"Not all of them." Karn hesitated, as if he were picking an example at random. "Lord Rousharn, for instance. You must have heard that he didn't hesitate to offend Duke Moncan. I believe his wife's here in Vanam?"

"She's gone home. No one was interested in her whining." Lady Alaric looked severely at him. "Don't fence with me, Karn. Master Hamare cannot really be interested in petty noblewomen lamenting their husbands' wounded dignity."

"Indeed." He let his sheepish grin suggest he had been trifling with her. "He does want to know if Duke Garnot of Carluse's whore is in Vanam."

Lady Alaric stared down at him, perfect lips parted. "That's the rumour on the road now?"

"You know different?" Karn took another drink, effortlessly concealing his dislike of mint.

Lady Alaric was amused. "Why's Hamare interested in a runaway doxy?"

"The girl may be willing to trade whatever she knows of Duke Garnot's plans for the coin to put another three hundred leagues between the two of them." Karn shrugged. "Duchess Litasse is concerned that Duke Garnot is still intent on attacking Sharlac."

"Those reports of new silver lodes in Triolle's mines must be true if Hamare's ready to throw good coin after a bad girl." Lady Alaric considered the play of the candlelight on her faceted goblet. "I'm sorry to say you're in the wrong city. Duke Garnot's whore is in Relshaz." Her beautiful face hardened. "She narrowly escaped the choice between accepting Duke Ferdain of Marlier's protection or being confined to entertain his household guard until they tired of her."

Karn had heard as much in several taverns along his journey. "As to Marlier, there's rumour that Vanam merchants are recruiting in the mercenary camps along the banks of the Rel. Do you know anything about that?"

"Only that it's arrant nonsense." Lady Alaric laughed with genuine hilarity. "That tale's so old it has rust on it!"

"I have it from more than one source." Karn felt his pulse quicken. Was she trying to deceive him?

"Do your sources explain what these woolly-minded merchants are supposedly looking for among the wolf's-heads?" she asked promptly.

"They want leaders for a brigade of young exiles." Karn made a show of admitting more than he should. "A handful of men have told me that Markasir and the Gale Crag Men have taken this Vanam coin."

"I have my doubts about your sources." Lady Alaric wrinkled her nose attractively. "Markasir is in Tormalin, teaching elegant young nobles how to hold a sword without cutting themselves before they brave these new lands on the far side of the Ocean." She relaxed in her chair. "We're already twenty-some days into Aft-Summer and a witless cabal of exiles wants to send a rabble of youthful enthusiasts into battle? When the fighting season's all but over? Who are they supposed to be fighting and how are they to be armed or fed? Have you any reports of wheat or weapons being stockpiled anywhere?"

"Not as yet, but if the weather holds, battles have been fought as late as Aft-Autumn," Karn pointed out.

"True," Lady Alaric acknowledged. "Which is when Duke Garnot of Carluse intends to attack Marlier, according to my sources. Which is why Duke Ferdain of Marlier went to such lengths to get his hands on that whore. You'll find Duke Garnot is the one recruiting mercenaries. He's covering his tracks by shining up this old rumour about exiles coming back from Ensaimin to fight. You can tell Duchess Litasse she has nothing to fear on Sharlac's account."

"You've heard nothing among the Lescari here?" Karn felt the first suspicion of doubt. Could Hamare be seeing Eldritch Kin in a curtain's shadows?

"Nothing." Lady Alaric set her glass of water down and looked sharply at Karn. "So, I'll have something from you, if you please. Why haven't we seen warfare in eastern Lescar this summer?"

Karn was content to tell the truth. "Emperor Tadriol has made it very clear to both Duke Secaris of Draximal and Duke Orlin of Parnilesse that he will take it sorely amiss if fighting spills over the River Asilor to threaten Tormalin homes and harvests."

"Tadriol isn't just called 'the Prudent' by the princes of Tormalin's noble convocation. He's more popular with the merchantry than anyone on that throne for three generations." Lady Alaric considered this, her violet eyes shrewd. "Imperial troops will soon be dispatched if mercenaries start plundering the wagons bringing furs and metals and strings of horses south from Inglis and Dalasor."

"I'm surprised you haven't heard this yourself," Karn remarked. "Haven't the rabble-rousers behind all those broadsheets and night letters castigating Duke Orlin of Parnilesse found refuge in Vanam?"

"No one's interested in such things here." Lady Alaric brushed that aside. "But Draximal and Parnilesse could still fight within their own borders."

"Not without mercenaries, and it appears that fighting men see no profit in the notion," Karn said frankly. "Neither duke has enough good coin to pay a warband more than a tenth of the usual hire at the outset. The mercenaries know that the battles will trample the harvests of both dukedoms into the mud. There won't be anything left to sell for the coin to pay them or for them to plunder on their own account."

"Nor anything left for the peasants, whenever they come out from the hedgerows where they're hiding. I don't imagine their cold, hungry winter weighs much in the balance."

Karn looked up at Lady Alaric, surprised by her bitterness. She smiled thinly at him.

"You're Marlier-born, like me. I can still hear it in your voice. We've both lain awake in a ruined hovel knowing that breakfast will be a cup of rain and a taste of fresh air."

He scowled despite himself. "We've both left that life behind us."

"We have." She pointed her toes. "Rub my feet for me?"

"Of course." He set down his goblet and shifted so he could rest her ankle on his thigh.

She stiffened as he pressed strong fingers into her sole. "Tell me your tale."

Karn hadn't expected reminiscence to be part of his payment. He reviewed what passed for his history, as far as anyone still living knew. He wasn't about to share the true tale of his childhood with Lady Alaric or anyone else.

"We were burned out. I lost my family in the confusion. I've made my own way ever since."

"Selling what other folk had abandoned. What you could steal when needs must," she mused. "Selling yourself?"

He looked up to challenge her. "Didn't you?"

"My family and I stayed together." Her glorious eyes were bright with unshed tears. "I had elder sisters willing to sell themselves into marriage for all our sakes."

"Your beauty must have brought you offers." Karn took her other foot in his hands.

"It was the bread that convinced me not to wed," she said reflectively.

"I'm sorry?" Bemused, his fingers slowed.

"Stale bread." She wriggled her toes to prompt him to continue. "When my sisters were about to wed, they each made up their first household book. My mother let them copy recipes from her own. So many puddings and pottages rely on stale bread." Her generous lip curled. "The leavings from some noble's table, so generously thrown to the poor, as long as it's not needed for fattening the pigs. I decided marriage wasn't for me. I was going to eat fresh white bread every day."

"I can sympathise with that ambition." Karn caressed the swell of her calf. "But life can be lonely without family."

He made sure his words were hollow with loss. She was beautiful, and he'd wager all Hamare's gold that she was no shrinking virgin. Taking her to bed would be no hardship, and what might she tell him in the unguarded intimacy following lovemaking? Because he was certain she wasn't telling him as much as she could.

What more might he learn if he wept on her breast, cradled in her arms somewhere between child and lover? Just as long as he could hold himself back until ecstasy washed over her to drown her alertness? As long as he didn't fall asleep straight away. It had been a very long day.

She surprised him by tucking her feet beneath the chair, straightening her skirts as she leaned forward. "I don't think we had better mix business with pleasure." Lifting his chin with one manicured finger, she kissed him gently on the forehead.

Was he imagining the regret in her voice? He looked up at her, guileless. "I won't tell if you won't."

She stroked his cheek, softly chiding. "Don't tempt me."

He twisted his head to kiss her hand. "Another time? When we don't have any business to conclude?"

"We haven't concluded our business here." She sat back. "There's something that you may tell Master Hamare, with my good wishes."

Her sudden seriousness caught Karn's interest. "What might that be?"

"It concerns the propriety of mixing business and pleasure." She looked at him, unblinking. "Master Hamare has been instructing Duchess Litasse in her wifely duty to gather news and rumour from duchesses, vassals' wives, maids and seamstresses. That's only to be expected. However, it would do Master Hamare no good at all if word reached Duke Iruvain that his spymaster has been teaching his bride a whole gamut of wifely skills, in bed and out of it." She shook her head, chestnut ringlets catching the candlelight. "Don't worry. There's been the barest whisper and I've made it my business to crush it. I value Master Hamare too highly to see him brought low by scandal. But he needs to be more careful. They both do."

How did Lady Alaric know? Karn set that question aside with some difficulty. "He'll be in your debt."

"Think nothing of it." She waved a dismissive hand. "Does he love her?"

That was an unexpected question. How could Karn say if Hamare loved Litasse when he had no idea what love might be? All he ever had was duty, and the most that warmed him was satisfaction for a job well done. "I don't know."

"No, I don't suppose you do." Lady Alaric laughed and rose from her chair with a silken rustle. "Now, you must forgive me, but it's late."

He got quickly to his own feet. "May I call on you tomorrow?"

"Naturally." She smiled. "Bring Master Hamare's gold and we'll settle the reckoning for what I've told you tonight."

"Of course." He bowed low. "Less the value of what I've told you."

"Naturally. So, till tomorrow, Master Karn, goodnight." She dipped the briefest of curtseys before heading for the door, only pausing to pull on the bell rope. "My maid will show you out."

As Karn followed, the maidservant was already waiting in the panelled hall. Unsmiling, though not unfriendly, she ushered him through the front door.

She did look familiar. He stood outside, exasperated. If he couldn't recall where he'd seen her, he'd have a hard time sleeping tonight, no matter how weary he was.

He began walking, keeping half an eye open for Watchmen as he tried to think where he could possibly have seen Lady Alaric's maid.

It came to him just as he reached the forbidding gatehouse jealously guarding access to Vanam's upper town. He'd seen her by the gatehouse of that captured bridge in Draximal. Emirle Bridge.

Had it been Lady Alaric in that luxurious coach? Who else could it have been? What dealings did she have with mercenaries that enabled her to pass, only paying a toll of kisses from her maid? A maid who had been affronted but by no means outraged. She hadn't feared rape, not from what Karn had seen.

If Lady Alaric had been travelling in Draximal and Parnilesse that spring, why was she pretending to know so little about the state of affairs in eastern Lescar?

"Where are you headed?" The Watchman guarding the small door cut in the great gate stepped forward to shine his lantern on Karn.

"Just to the western slope of the Teravin," Karn assured him.

The Watchman grunted. "You watch your step and hurry along, lad."

"Thank you." Karn ducked his head through the low lintel, careful not to trip over the high threshold.

Youthful, slightly built and not wearing a sword, he knew he looked like prey for the ruffians who hid in the wooded gullies along with the feral pigs. The Watchman wasn't to know he could pluck a hidden knife from his boot, quick as lightning, to gut an attacker. Karn wouldn't lose any sleep over another death swiftly and silently delivered.

Chapter Twenty-Three

Aremil

**Beacon Lane, in Vanam's Upper Town,
21st of Aft-Summer**

"Where have you been?" Flustered, Lyrlen jerked the door open.

"I'm sorry?" Aremil was taken aback.

"You have guests." Lyrlen smoothed her apron with agitated hands.

"Who?" Branca asked.

Aremil heard Master Gruit's booming voice through the closed door of the sitting room.

"Who's here?" Branca repeated her question.

"Master Gruit and Mistress Charoleia." Lyrlen addressed her reply to Aremil. "But you need your breakfast, my lord."

"We have eaten," Aremil snapped. It was time Lyrlen stopped this nonsense of ignoring Branca.

"How?" The old woman stared at him, astonished.

351

Aremil took a breath. He hadn't meant to mention this. "Branca helped me."

Not for the first time. That had been some days ago, when they had been working in one of the university's libraries. Branca had told him bluntly that there was no point continuing with his studies into Artifice when he was so distracted by hunger. Moreover, she wasn't prepared to waste her time waiting for him to go home to eat in private just because he was too proud to eat in a nearby tavern. If he wanted to continue, he'd accept whatever trivial assistance he needed from her. So he had.

As Lyrlen struggled for words, Branca opened the door to the sitting room.

"Finally!" Gruit's relief vied with exasperation. "Where have you been?"

Branca set the books she was carrying down on the table. "Are we supposed to inform you of our comings and goings?"

"You're not answering to anyone, Master Merchant." Charoleia's waspish tone startled Aremil.

"Saedrin's stones, woman!" Gruit rounded on her before getting his anger in check. "Forgive me," he apologised to Aremil and Branca. "She sent word at first light summoning me like some errant apprentice. We've been waiting all this time and she won't explain why!"

"The delay's on my account, so for my part, I'm sorry." Aremil was concentrating on reaching his chair without incident. He lowered himself down with relief.

"You're looking tired, Aremil." Charoleia was concerned.

"I find it hard to sleep in this heat." Though he had found the cooler air of the early morning refreshing.

"My lord." Lyrlen hesitated in the doorway. "Shall I bring some refreshment?"

Which would doubtless include a cup that she'd insist on holding while he drank. To demonstrate how devoted she was to his interests.

"No, thank you." Aremil gestured towards the tray of sweetcakes and almond and elderflower cordial. "I see you've already provided for our guests."

"I'll make myself a tisane." Branca smiled cheerfully at Lyrlen. "Is there water boiling?"

It would help if Branca made some effort to win Lyrlen over, Aremil reflected. And if each woman's interpretation of his best interests didn't differ so sharply.

"Cakes and tisanes can wait!" Over by the window, Gruit threw up his hands. He glared at Charoleia. "Will you kindly explain yourself now?"

She smiled tautly before turning to Lyrlen. "A tisane would be welcome. Do you have linden leaves and camomile?"

"Please," Aremil interrupted before Gruit had apoplexy. The merchant's face was as red as the poppies embroidered on his linen doublet. "What is so urgent?"

Charoleia sat, twitching the hem of her pale-blue muslin away from Gruit's impatient boots. "I had a visitor last night. A young man called Karn. He's an enquiry agent for Master Hamare, the Duke of Triolle's intelligencer."

"What did he want with you?" Branca sat down beside Charoleia. Dumpy in her dun gown, she looked like the slender beauty's maidservant.

One might have expected Branca to resent Charoleia's poise and beauty, Aremil reflected, while

Charoleia could have dismissed Branca as plain, frumpy and bookish. Yet the two women had been at ease with each other from their first meeting.

"He was calling on Lady Alaric, who's long had dealings with Master Hamare," Charoleia explained.

Aremil wondered idly what this fabled noblewoman looked like. Presumably most unlike Charoleia today, in her high-necked gown devoid of jewellery, her glorious hair modestly braided.

"I hear Hamare's a shrewd man." Leaning against the windowsill, Gruit's temper faded now that they were finally getting down to business.

"Master Hamare is the reason why the dukes of Triolle are still fishing their lakes and hunting their deer," Charoleia said crisply, "rather than bowing their heads as vassals of Marlier or Parnilesse. Iruvain doesn't value Hamare a tenth as much as he should, as the old duke did. He's shrewd and tenacious and his web of informants reaches all the way from Selerima to Bremilayne. He hears nearly as much as I do and he's sharp enough to know that what he isn't hearing can be just as significant. When he finds a gap in his knowledge, he'll often send a man to Lady Alaric, to trade some piece of information he's uncovered in return for her answers to plug the hole that interests him."

"What does he want to know at present?" Branca helped herself to a pale saffron cake.

Charoleia took one. "Where Duke Garnot of Carluse's whore has run to."

"Failla?" Aremil was puzzled as well as concerned. "Why?"

"To see what she knows of Duke Garnot's plans for war this summer. Hamare knows she's been in

Vanam." Charoleia bit and caught cake crumbs in her cupped hand. "I told you he was good. No one else has the slightest notion she came here."

"What did you tell him?" Gruit looked worried.

"That she's in Relshaz." Charoleia finished her cake. "I set that rumour loose in Peorle before Solstice, so he'll hear it from other sources."

"*You* set that rumour loose?" Aremil felt some fraction of Gruit's exasperation.

Leaning on the windowsill, the merchant frowned. "We should have been told."

"Is that so?" Charoleia raised her neat brows.

Lyrlen's knock interrupted Gruit's retort. The servant woman entered with a tray bearing two silver-mounted glasses of steaming water. She made a careful curtsey to Charoleia. "My lady."

At least she had brought Branca her tisane as well, Aremil reflected.

Charoleia took the glass of straw-coloured liquid. "Thank you."

"So is this Karn going to look for Failla in Relshaz?" Branca took her glass. Dark-red threads floated out of the pierced silver ball at the bottom to tint the water. Aremil could smell blackcurrants blended with Aldabreshin speckle-spice.

"He'll go sniffing through the mercenary camps along the banks of the Rel first." Charoleia cradled her glass in her white hands. "Thanks to Gruit's folly."

"What?" Gruit demanded, indignant.

"Do you know why he's interested in those rats' nests?" Charoleia glared at the wine merchant. "Because, as Karn told me in return for news of Failla, Master Hamare believes someone from Vanam is recruiting hired swords. There's talk of a troop of

Lescari exiles riding into battle. Karn's here to find out what lies behind that."

Aremil was dismayed to see Gruit's colour rise not from anger but embarrassment. "What have you done?"

"You said Tathrin told you your mercenary friends will soon reach the mountains east of Wrede." Gruit folded his arms. "Then they'll move south into the hills above Sharlac. This captain-general, Evord, he'll send scouts into Marlier to recruit experienced men. I've just been hinting at the chance of a rich contract from Vanam to make sure the best mercenary bands aren't already embroiled in some other quarrel. It's not as if there's any truth in it, so where's the harm?"

"Sorgrad has been writing to those mercenary captains he particularly wants to retain since before Summer Solstice," Charoleia said acidly. "Now there's the danger that Karn will pick up some trace of Sorgrad's letters while he's following this false scent you've so clumsily laid."

"We began talking about curing Lescar's ills at Spring Festival." Gruit pushed himself away from the window and began pacing. "Summer Solstice has come and gone and still we sit and talk in endless circles. If we're to see anything change, someone has to take action."

"Making ready for successful action takes time," Charoleia said with icy contempt. "All too often, undue haste makes for wasted effort. Captain-General Evord has to bring an army through the mountains and across the White River unnoticed. You have just made that a good deal harder."

"Excuse me." Branca broke into the argument with a raised hand. "If you don't want Hamare hearing some rumour that Sorgrad is recruiting men, why did you send this man Karn to Relshaz in search of Failla?"

"His journey will take him through all the mercenary camps in Marlier," Gruit seized on this argument. "Why not send him off to Selerima if you're so concerned?"

"He'd be going to Relshaz by way of Marlier regardless and it will be a great deal easier to have him killed while he's in the mercenary camps." Charoleia sipped her tisane. "In such a way that convinces Hamare his man was merely unlucky. I may even be able to arrange for ciphered letters to be found on his body, to persuade Hamare that Failla truly is in Relshaz."

"He has to die?" Aremil swallowed hard.

"This will merely be the first death of this enterprise," Charoleia said calmly. "There'll be more dead than you can count once we see the progress Master Gruit's so eager for."

"Someone will count them and grieve for each and every one."

Aremil saw his own revulsion mirrored in Branca's brown eyes.

"Can he not be bought off, this man Karn?"

"No." Charoleia looked steadily at him. "He's utterly loyal to Hamare and besides, he's as hard as hobnails for all he plays the wide-eyed youth so convincingly."

"So we really must do this?" Aremil felt hollow inside.

"We must." Regret coloured Charoleia's words. "I would rather not, believe me. Who knows who Master Hamare will replace him with? Someone better? I doubt it. But someone it will take me some while to identify, that much is certain. I know a good many of Hamare's people and where the threads of his webs run, but getting the measure of whoever steps into Karn's shoes will take time I have better uses for. And I will have to pay handsomely to be sure Karn's corpse can't be laid at my door. Master Hamare is an excellent source of information and I'd just as soon not lose his goodwill."

"Then we'll all answer to Saedrin for our part in the man's death." Gruit looked troubled. "If this is all we have to discuss, I'll get back to my casks of wine."

"We have more business to attend to." Charoleia drank her cooling tisane. "Please, Master Gruit, have some cordial. You are correct, you know, when you say we must make swifter progress or abandon this whole enterprise."

The wine merchant cleared his throat. "I suppose it's been a while since breakfast." He came over to take a glass and a cake from the tray.

Did this strained politeness mean the two of them saw the folly of holding a grudge? Aremil hoped so.

"When Captain-General Evord's army comes down from the mountains, they're going to need feeding. We must get unthreshed wheat and beef and mutton still on the hoof to Verlayne. We need men ready to take it on into the hills and asking no questions." Charoleia looked expectantly at Gruit.

"You can leave that to me," he said. "My men are well used to keeping trade matters confidential and much else besides."

It took Aremil a moment to recall exactly where Verlayne was. Ah yes, it was one of the towns on the White River, the first sizeable settlement after

Hanchet, if one were travelling from Vanam. Travellers not wishing to follow the river all the way to Peorle could take the road southbound out of Verlayne and skirt the western flank of the Lescari uplands. By heading straight for Duryea and the Great West Road, they could cut a lengthy dogleg out of their journey towards Tormalin.

"They will need weapons and amour," Charoleia continued. "Arrows, spearheads and swords. Chain mail and loose links besides, together with plenty of leather thong. I've never met a captain of mercenaries yet who didn't complain he was always running short of it."

"All to be bought discreetly and carried to Lescar without anyone getting wind of it." Gruit's faded eyes grew distant as he contemplated this challenge. "I know people who can get any amount of barrels and casks to Abray for me without raising questions. But we don't want the merchants who trade down the Rel getting curious about goods arriving in their town and going no further. It would be better to carry such supplies to Duryea and leave the high road there."

"What about Duke Ferdain of Marlier?" Aremil frowned. "He must keep a weather eye on mercenary affairs with so many camps within his borders."

"He does," Charoleia confirmed. "So we will keep Duke Ferdain more interested in the gold piling up in his counting-house." She set her empty tisane glass down. "Master Gruit, please convince as many of your fellow merchants as possible that it would be arrant folly to send their goods to Tormalin by way of the Great West Road this season. We want every barge sailing down the Rel so full that they're all but sinking."

Gruit smiled for the first time. "I should be able to persuade some influential guildsmen to ship their goods out of Relshaz on galleys cutting straight across the Gulf to Solland and Toremal. A good few will follow where such bellwethers lead."

"Duke Ferdain of Marlier can amuse himself counting the coin he levies from every cargo on the river." Branca looked thoughtful. "But less trade on the high road means fewer tariff payments filling Duke Garnot of Carluse's coffers."

"Making it all the easier for us to convince Duke Garnot that Duke Ferdain of Marlier is stirring up these fears besetting the merchantry to improve his own revenues at Carluse's expense." Charoleia searched inside her ribbon-tied reticule until she found a small silver square. It looked like a cased mirror to Aremil. "That should stop him looking northwards to the hills beyond Sharlac." The little silver case opened up like a book.

"A memorandum?" Branca leaned over to see Charoleia writing with a fine metal rod. "Without paper?"

"I've always favoured wax for note-making." She made a show of throwing it into the hearth where a vase of scarlet flowers blazed. "As soon as it's melted, whatever I've written is gone for good. You'd be surprised how long paper or parchment can take to catch properly alight."

Gruit munched another cake, brow furrowed. "I can talk up the hazards along the Great West Road, but plenty of merchants still prefer to keep their goods on dry ground. It's not as if there is any actual fighting at the moment."

"We will start some fighting to persuade them," Charoleia said serenely, "and to keep Master Hamare of Triolle looking in quite the wrong direction as well." She gestured towards Aremil's white raven board. "If Hamare gets wind of this enterprise of ours, we may as well forfeit the game."

"Where will this fighting start?" Aremil asked with misgiving.

"Between Draximal and Parnilesse." Charoleia's face was implacable. "As soon as may be arranged."

Gruit narrowed his eyes. "You said neither duke was prepared to attack the other for fear of the Tormalin Emperor's displeasure."

"We can leave the details to Sorgrad and Gren. They'll have Draximal and Parnilesse at each other's throats before the end of Aft-Summer." Charoleia turned to Branca. "We need to speak to Tathrin as soon as possible."

"We need to be able to contact everyone with Artifice," Gruit growled, frustrated. "If there's going to be war in the eastern provinces, we need to warn Failla and Lady Derenna, Reniack most of all. We need them to be able to contact us without having to find a wagoner heading west who's willing to carry a letter!"

"We have two adepts willing to help us," Aremil assured him. "We only need find one more."

Though that was easier said than done. They'd had no luck on their quest that morning. He had only needed to exchange a look with Branca to see she agreed that particular scholar was better left safely studying ancient histories and newly recovered lore, for all her Lescari blood. Not for the first time, they hadn't even broached the subject of Lescar's ills,

merely buying some books as their excuse for the visit
and coming away again.

Aremil was glad he and Branca were being so wary.
He shuddered to think what scathing rebuke
Charoleia might have had for them if she'd heard
whispers of something they had incautiously let slip.
Such whispers could have betrayed them all to this
man Karn. A shiver ran down his spine.

"I can get a warning to Reniack." Charoleia made
another note on her wax memorandum tablet. "That
woman of his who picks rags for the papermakers
keeps courier pigeons, though I don't know where
they fly to."

Aremil assumed she was trying to find out.

"What about the others?" Gruit was still dissatisfied. "Aremil, you promised we would have these
enchantments to help us. Aft-Summer's already half
over."

"You do need to find this third adept as soon as possible." Charoleia looked at Branca. "Time is going to
become increasingly pressing, especially once fighting
breaks out between Draximal and Parnilesse."

Branca looked at her, eyes bright. "If we cannot find
a third adept in the next five days, I will go to Lescar
myself."

"How does that help us?" Gruit protested. "Aetheric magic or elemental, it takes two to speak over any
distance. We still need an aetheric adept here in
Vanam."

"I don't know that any mentor would call him an
adept, but Aremil's learning." Branca's confident smile
challenged him.

"I have a great deal still to learn," Aremil said hastily.

If both halves of summer had dragged for Master Gruit, even these longest days of the year were too short for Aremil. He seemed to spend every waking moment when he wasn't looking for Lescari exiles studying and attempting enchantments and discussing the possible reasons for his modest successes and all too frequent failures with Branca.

"Can you use whatever you've learned thus far to reach Tathrin?" Charoleia asked. "So he can tell Sorgrad to set about causing trouble between Draximal and Parnilesse?"

"He can," Branca said confidently.

"Then please do so, Master Aremil, as soon as possible." Charoleia stood up. "I'll have a warning sent to Reniack before nightfall. He should get it inside six or seven days. In the meantime, Master Gruit, kindly set about making those arrangements for supplying our troops as soon as they reach the lowlands."

"Don't you want to hear what young Tathrin has to say?" Gruit looked uncertainly at Aremil.

"Not particularly. I don't need to know what Sorgrad has in mind either." Charoleia smiled. "Shall we go, Master Gruit? There's nothing to see when Artifice is worked. It has none of wizardry's thrills and magelight."

She had seen it in his face, Aremil realised: his horror of trying to work Artifice with an audience.

"Very well, then." Gruit looked disappointed all the same. "I'll bid you good day and be on my way." He favoured Charoleia and Branca with a half-bow and, nodding to Aremil, he left the sitting room.

"I should have remembered how readily Poldrion's demons fill idle hands with mischief. Still, seeing to Evord's supplies will keep him busy enough for the moment." Charoleia looped the ribbon of her reticule around her wrist. "Let me know how you get on contacting Tathrin." Her glance went from Aremil to Branca.

"We will." Branca escorted her to the door.

"Goodbye." Aremil drew a deep breath.

Branca closed the door and leaned against it. "Do you want some time to prepare yourself?"

He was tempted to say yes, to ask for all the books he had been reading, for the erratic notes he had so painstakingly scrawled. Branca hadn't cared about his penmanship, merely insisting that the best way of committing such things to memory was writing them down.

"No." He shifted in his chair as cramp threatened his weary limbs. "If this is to work, I need to be able to summon up the concentration at a moment's notice, don't I?" He folded his limp hands in his lap and closed his eyes.

"That's true enough." The rustle of linen told him Branca was sitting down.

If he failed, she could always reach out to Tathrin. Sorgrad would still get his orders from Charoleia.

If he failed, Branca would have to stay here in Vanam. Safe. He'd be sacrificing his own pride, of course. As far as everyone else was concerned, he'd remain the cripple confined to his sitting room. They'd still admire his intellect and accept that his connections were of some use, but they'd be free to despise him for never taking the risks they chose to face. Was that so great a loss? No one had ever thought him anything more than a cripple.

"You can do it, you know," Branca said conversationally. "You've reached through the aether to me a handful of times now."

"The mountains east of Wrede are rather further away than the lower town's back streets."

She would know if he was deliberately failing. Whether through Artifice, or just some unlooked-for felicity, she seemed to know him as well after half a season as Lyrlen did, who'd looked after him his whole life. Aremil smiled. He couldn't help it.

Drawing a steadying breath, he saw Tathrin in his mind's eye. Tall, straight-limbed, dark-haired, strong-featured. He could feel the chair beneath him, hear the soft clink of glass as Branca poured herself some cordial. Years of separating his mind from the pains of his twisted body helped him focus his attention on Tathrin.

Al daera sa Tathrin ne fol. Sast elarmin ash feorin el sur.

This was the hardest part. This was where he had initially despaired. Where his strenuous efforts had come to nothing for so many infuriating days, the words hopelessly mangled by his awkward jaw, his recalcitrant throat.

He might just as well try picking up a lyre, he had spat at Branca when she'd dragged him out to dine in the lower town after a fruitless afternoon's struggles. How could he ever hope his weak and clumsy hands might play something like the lilting ballad that a Forest minstrel had been favouring them with?

Tathrin. Tall, straight-limbed, strong-minded despite his diffident manner. Capable of surprising boldness and generosity. It wasn't enough merely to picture him. He had to summon up all that Tathrin was, his character and his spirit. If you think of the person you wish to reach as an instrument, Branca had said, you have to hear the music inside your head as well.

Al daera sa Tathrin ne fol. Sast elarmin ash feorin el sur.

Now the words flowed smoothly. He shaped them slowly, far more slowly than Branca did. The rhythm and the flow, both were crucial. Straining to control his breathing, he could do it. It hurt. His ribs ached, his throat, even, bizarrely, his stomach. That didn't matter; pain was something he had always lived with.

Al daera sa Tathrin ne fol. Sast elarmin ash feorin el sur.

Now he could feel the sensation of speed, even though he knew perfectly well that he was still sitting motionless in his chair. He and Branca had been speculating about that, about how an ability to divide one's mind, to separate one's perceptions, might determine who could work Artifice and who couldn't.

Was this why scholars of history fared so well, so used to seeing a question from as many points of view as possible, while wizards and alchemists and mathematicians dealt with absolute success or failure, whether of their spells, their compounds or calculations?

He had to keep the rhythm. He had to keep his mind's eye focused on Tathrin.

Al daera sa Tathrin ne fol. Sast elarmin ash feorin el sur.

His eyes were still closed but now he could see. Whatever part of his mind was doing this soared above a parched grassy hillside. In a sparsely wooded gully, he saw shelters woven from hacked branches. Armoured men moved between stone-ringed hearths dug into the dusty ground. More sought shade beneath the withering leaves.

Two tents stood beside a stream tumbling down a rocky scar. Tathrin was standing in front of one, his hands eloquent as he argued with Sorgrad.

"Tathrin." Aremil's aetheric perceptions told him he was standing in front of his friend. At the same time, he knew full well he was doing no such thing. He just had to believe both things were true.

"Yes?" Tathrin looked around, startled.

"Good," said Sorgrad, satisfied.

"I wasn't talking to you," Tathrin snapped. "Aremil?"

"I'm here." With a thrill of disbelief, he felt the heat of the upland sun and smelled the sun-scorched turf. With a shock, he saw how Tathrin's journeying had changed his friend. His hair was cropped as short as any felon's, while his face and forearms had been deeply tanned by this outdoor life. Grazes criss-crossed his knuckles.

Aremil struggled to reconcile the outdated image of Tathrin he carried in his mind with the new reality that Artifice was showing him. He felt the enchantment begin to weaken, fragile as a fading song as some minstrel wandered away.

"I have a message for Sorgrad from Charoleia," he said quickly. "Listen, and concentrate."

Chapter Twenty-Four

Karn

Sanlief Manor Demesne, in the Lescari Dukedom of Marlier, 36th of Aft-Summer

He timed his arrival carefully. Late in the day meant men and women were relaxing, anticipating their evening meal. Plenty would already be drinking, restraints loosening. Walking the last few leagues gave his horse some chance to recover. Few things prompted more curiosity in a mercenary camp than someone arriving on a mount ridden half into the ground.

Ahead, the woods were parched and dispirited despite the morning's perfunctory rain. As the trees drew closer to the track, Karn saw movement in the undergrowth. Stealthy, but not men moving with the effortless ease of practiced mercenaries sliding through woodland.

A tentful, he judged, four or six. Out to rob him? Or believing those ballads where an untried youth bests a true mercenary, who's so impressed that he recommends his captain let the lad sign his name on the muster roll?

Karn rode onwards. The most such hopefuls could expect was being rounded up and driven like cattle ahead of experienced men, to blunt an enemy's swords or to flush out lurking foes by stumbling upon them.

He might just as well be done with them. Pulling up his horse with an oath, Karn dismounted and lifted up one fore hoof, as if he'd felt the beast pick up a stone.

"Stand and declare yourself!"

Karn straightened up to see he'd drawn four youths out of cover. Wet, dirty and, judging by their gaunt faces, hungry. He didn't recognise any of them. Too stupid to be a threat. There was no more movement in the undergrowth to show they'd left any of their number in reserve.

"You stink," he said with contempt. "Are you shitting in the ditch where you're sleeping?"

That was good enough to draw one of them a few paces forward, a stained hunting knife in his hand, more suited to gutting a deer than killing a man.

"There's a toll to pass this way," the youth said boldly.

Karn laughed. "Does herself know you're snapping at travellers' heels?"

"Who?" One skulking at the rear betrayed how recently he'd arrived.

"He means Ridianne. She knows to leave the woods to us," the one with the knife sneered.

Karn shook his head regretfully. "No, she just knows anyone who can't kick shit like you off his boots isn't worth talking to."

"Shut your mouth and give us your coin." The angry youth with the knife took another step forward.

"And food." He was half a head taller than Karn and close enough to wound him now.

Karn dropped his horse's reins. "Take it," he invited.

The nameless youth thrust his knife towards Karn's belly. Satisfied, Karn stepped sideways so the blade missed him by a hand's breadth. As he moved, he punched hard up under the bold youth's jaw. As the youth staggered, Karn seized his knife-wrist and forced it down. He didn't punch him a second time, but rather reached out and wrapped his arm around the boy's neck, trapping his head. Bent over backwards, the youth struggled, his filthy and broken fingernails scrabbling at Karn's sleeve. Still holding the knife well clear, Karn only needed one wrench to snap the youth's neck with a grating crunch of bone.

These scum really did stink. Karn stepped back and let the dying lad fall to the ground, limbs twitching in helpless spasm. The sinking sunlight shone dull gold on urine puddling around the corpse.

The three remaining youths stood aghast.

"Take yourselves off to the shithole you've been cowering in." Karn knocked the deer knife out of the dead boy's fingers with the toe of his boot. "Or I'll cut out your tripes with your friend's knife." He flipped the knife up and caught it.

The three boys backed away and broke, racing for the dubious safety of the tangled bracken.

That suited Karn. Arriving with fresh blood on his clothes would attract as much attention as riding a sweating horse. He didn't have time to waste killing fools, either. Ridianne didn't like interruption while she dined, so her hall doors would soon be closed to all but her most trusted associates. Karn didn't flatter himself that he was among that company.

His mount hadn't run far. Karn sprang back into the saddle and urged it into a trot.

As he had expected, the broad expanse of turf between the woods and the River Rel was dotted with campfires. Each encampment had twenty or so tents, the captain's pennant hanging limp above the heart of each gathering. There was no wind to draw out the standards and show Karn their badges. He rode thoughtfully along the tracks judiciously separating the warbands. There were fewer than he had expected.

He approached the bridge of solid ground cutting across the stone-walled ditch that ringed Ridianne's fortified manor house. When the rest of the trees surrounding it had been cleared, the oaks had been left out of respect for Talagrin. Ridianne wouldn't risk displeasing the god of the hunt.

A woman, shirtless beneath a leather jerkin, sat in a spreading tree's shade, picking her teeth. "I'll have your name and your business." She didn't get up from her stool.

"My name is Lec and I ask for audience with her ladyship." Karn made sure his tone was neither aggressive nor supplicant. Twenty men would come running at the first sign of trouble. Twice that number would come for the entertainment of seeing a trouble-maker kicked to death.

"Who do you ride for?" The woman warrior spat out her wooden splinter.

"Hamare of Triolle." Karn twisted in his saddle to show that his swords were already securely tied up in the centre of his roll of blankets. "I have two hand-and-a-half blades and one boot knife."

"What's on your belt?" The warrior raised a languid hand.

"Just an eating knife." Karn raised his arm so the woman mercenary could see it was no longer than a man's forefinger. He saw another man closer to the manor house's erratic stone wall shove a lad in their direction.

The boy came running, brushing a hand to his sandy forelock in a brief salute as he arrived.

The woman on the stool nodded. "Take him to the gate."

Karn dismounted without being asked and followed the boy along the scar worn in the turf by countless boots and hooves. The ditch divided those mercenary troops Ridianne trusted from those on whom she was reserving judgement. Within this inner circle, he could see tents crowded close together, right underneath the shadow of the manor's outer wall.

He could see sufficient blazons to identify these collared dogs. Marlier's silver-grey swords made a triangle around the coiled menace of a loathly worm. Beyond, a toad squatted on a blue shield with the same three swords ranked above it. So Ridianne was whistling up the mercenary troops who had taken Marlier coin for so long they'd earned the right to blend the dukedom's insignia with their own. She wouldn't be doing that without Duke Ferdain's orders.

Though there were mercenaries with other allegiances here, Karn noted. A pale round drum painted on the canvas tents beyond identified the next troop, smoke curling around the fire-basket in its centre. So that war band was more usually at Draximal's beck and call.

They approached the timber-framed gatehouse. With river mud mixed into the plaster, the walls looked russet in the fading sunlight.

"Not so many unchained curs here," Karn remarked. "More men on the leash, though."

The lad shrugged. "I wouldn't know."

Karn didn't take that amiss. The lad had the wary poise of one who'd grown up knowing nothing outside this world. Even those few words showed he'd heard nothing but mongrel accents since he'd been born to some mercenary or some mercenary's whore. He might even be one of Ridianne's whelps. Karn wouldn't put it past her to see to it that any arrogance was knocked out of her sons by making them run such errands.

"Has there been fever here again?" Karn sharpened his words with apprehension. Perhaps fear would open the lad's mouth.

"No, it's been a dry season, Ostrin be thanked." The boy's eyes dulled briefly with dreadful recollection.

"Dastennin be thanked for that." Not that Karn feared the camp fever that wise women said was stirred up when rain gathered in stinking sumps under the hedgerows. He didn't fear mulberry fever or even snowy rot. If he hadn't succumbed to such contagions as a starving child, he wouldn't now.

He waited to see if the boy would say more, but the lad stayed silent until they reached the studded double gates where a swordsman stood guard.

"Name of Lec. Asks for an audience."

The swordsman shrugged his own lack of interest. "Wait there." He slipped through the narrow gap between the gates.

Karn admired the fox's skull nailed above the archway, a few rags of desiccated fur still clinging to it. "Did herself hunt that down?"

The boy didn't respond.

Karn contented himself with untying his modest bundle from his saddle as he continued surveying the insignia on the tents further round the manor house wall. None were showing the black boar's head of Carluse. That was hardly unexpected. Ridianne's ties with Duke Ferdain were far too close for any warband wearing Duke Garnot's collar to come here.

The green grebe of Triolle was nowhere to be seen either. Since his accession, Duke Iruvain kept his most trusted troops of hired swords inside Triolle's borders. Master Hamare had made certain those who refused to stay had stripped the ducal bird from their badges. Karn had carried the gold that paid such loyal mercenaries to force their erstwhile allies to comply at sword-point.

Karn frowned. Over beyond a sprawl of tents where the antlers of Sharlac's russet stag bracketed a white rose, he saw Draximal's fire-basket flanked by leafy branches.

Duke Ferdain of Marlier had long been on good terms with Duke Secaris of Draximal, mostly on account of their mutual suspicion of Duke Garnot of Carluse. If Marlier didn't detest Parnilesse with the same vigour as Draximal did, there was always rivalry between Duke Ferdain and Duke Orlin for coastal trade. Draximal's dogs were always assured of a warm welcome in the mercenary camps along the Rel.

But why wasn't Duke Secaris of Draximal whistling up all his faithful hounds, if warfare with Parnilesse was imminent?

As Karn frowned inwardly over this puzzle, the guard re-appeared.

"She'll see him."

"I'll take your horse." The lad reached for the reins.

"Thank you." If Karn needed to leave here in a hurry it wouldn't be on that sluggard. He knew that the only horses trained to jump the broad, open ditch without baulking were stabled inside Ridianne's manor.

He went in through the tall gates, his gear under his arm, his demeanour meek. He had no hope of drawing a sword from his bundle fast enough to foil an attack. Inside her walls, Ridianne's personal company of swordsmen all carried at least one long blade as well as a plethora of daggers. For the present, none of them paid him any heed. They were more concerned with watching the men wearing different liveries who were trooping up and down the stone stairs to the great hall's undercroft. This slate-roofed hall was the tallest building within the protective circle of the stone walls. The rest were all later additions crudely built and thatched with reeds.

Karn knew better than to try going up the flight of steps rising to the great hall's door unescorted. He caught one of the guards by the elbow, another sandy-haired man with Ridianne's blazon painted on the back of his deerhide jerkin: long sword, small sword and dagger all impaling a limply dangling dog-fox on the scarlet ground of Marlier's ducal flag.

"I'm to speak to herself."

"She's about to sit down to her meat," the swordsman warned.

Savoury scents coming from the kitchen on the opposite side of the yard were making Karn's mouth water. "I won't take up much time," he promised.

The swordsman grunted. "Follow me."

"My lady." Karn bowed as soon as he stepped into the cool gloom.

"Lec. I hope you're well." Even after so many years her accent was unmistakably Caladhrian.

He could hear Ridianne more easily than he could see her. The low sun shone in through tall west-facing windows and struck sparks in the smoke rising from a long hearth in the centre of the floor.

She chuckled. "You have until that arse of a cook finishes shouting at his scullions. What do you want?"

Ridianne was sitting in a high-backed chair of carved black oak behind the long table at the head of the hall. A double handful and more of her sons and favourites sat on benches all around, watching Karn with idle interest.

He bowed again. "My master wishes to know which dukes are calling their favourite hounds to heel. He hopes you're having a pleasant summer."

There was no profit in lying. Ridianne would inevitably hear what questions he was asking around the camp. Trying to gather news without her approval would see him beaten bloody and thrown into the manor house ditch to scramble out or die in the depths, no concern of hers.

"Wine?" Ridianne jerked her head and two men stood to leave the bench on the opposite side of the table empty for him.

"Thank you." Karn took a seat and kicked his bundle beneath it.

"I'm spending these long summer evenings counting all the silver we're being paid to chase footpads and bandits back into Carluse and Triolle." Ridianne poured wine from her own flagon into an empty pottery goblet, her hazel eyes bright. "Besides counting the gold we've earned hiring out as guards for the merchants shipping their goods down the Rel."

Duke Ferdain of Marlier's brindled vixen was still a good-looking woman even if she was grey-headed now. Her once-auburn hair was short and ragged, hacked off with a knife. She'd first cut it herself, newly widowed and beggared by Caladhria's laws denying a wife any part in her husband's estate. Whether her lord had married her for love or lust, she'd brought no dowry to the marriage to reclaim on his death. That cropped head had become her mark when she'd taken up arms to fight the son of her husband's first marriage who refused her more than a single mourning gown. She'd thrown it in his face, taking instead to the black breeches and doublet that she still wore.

"Duke Secaris of Draximal can spare so many of his best hounds to hunt with you?" Karn took the goblet. "When everyone expects Duke Orlin of Parnilesse to attack before the turn of For-Autumn?"

Ridianne shook her head. "They won't fight. Both their valiant Graces are too scared of Emperor Tadriol."

"That's not what I'm hearing in Vanam." Karn was careful to make it clear he doubted himself, not her.

"What do they know in Vanam?" Ridianne grinned.

"What indeed?" Karn pretended to take a sip of his own wine. "They say, in Vanam, that someone's looking for mercenaries to lead their bold youths in a campaign to force peace on Lescar."

"The news drew off half the scaff and raff hiding in the woods." Ridianne chuckled with amusement. "I wish whatever fool's planning such folly the best of luck with those scum."

All the other men in the hall laughed. Not for the first time, Karn wondered which of Ridianne's numerous sons were Duke Ferdain's bastards. If she hadn't been able to reclaim her lost home, she'd certainly proved that her Caladhrian lord hadn't been ploughing a barren field when he left her childless.

Had her stepson, born to her dead husband's first wife, ever wondered about his own mother's fidelity? Or did he just appreciate his mother's resourcefulness in presenting her lord with his sole heir, irrespective of who might have begotten him?

Karn swirled the dark wine around in his yellow-glazed goblet as he waited for the merriment to fade. "So who's recruiting the dusty dogs and mucky pups? I see fewer troops than usual camped between here and the river."

"They're in Caladhria, eating themselves fat and lazy. Coastal lords are shitting their breeches in case corsairs from the Southern Seas come raiding again this year." Ridianne waved a dismissive hand. "Or they're in Tormalin, begging for a berth on a ship heading to this new land across the Eastern Ocean." She narrowed her eyes. "No one ships out without Arkady the Red's say-so. He and Markasir and Lerris the Mason have all the gold there sewn up tight in their own pockets." Her grievance rang true to Karn's ears.

He frowned. "You don't think some of the loose dogs are sniffing around Carluse? I hear Duke Garnot begrudges Marlier's revenues from the river trade. That he's planning on taking a share."

"Duke Garnot of Carluse is only hiring proven war bands." Ridianne looked past him as the main door opened. "We'll whip them and send them crawling back with their tails between their legs, never fear."

Karn could believe that. However much gold Ridianne had seized from her erstwhile stepson and paid to Duke Ferdain of Marlier for the right to reclaim and rebuild this long-derelict holding, she had earned it back twenty- or fortyfold in his service since.

He turned to see a covey of youths carrying platters of meat and bread, bowls of pease and spiced vegetable pottage.

"You're in our place." The two men who'd yielded to him stepped forward.

"I beg your pardon." Karn stood up. "May I beg your protection overnight, my lady?"

"Stay in the outer camp." Ridianne took out her jewelled eating knife and polished it with a linen kerchief.

He remembered one last thing as he bent to recover his bundle. "My lady, have you any news of Duke Garnot's whore? There was talk of her hiding out in Relshaz."

"Not that I've heard, and I would hear." Ridianne reached for a partridge dripping with fat and began dismembering it. "If she has the sense Saedrin gave a ewe-lamb she's on the far side of Ensaimin and still running."

"Of course. Thank you." Karn bowed again and left, thoughtful.

Of all the mercenaries Duke Ferdain could use to guard a prisoner like Duke Garnot's doxy, Ridianne would be his first choice. She had more women in her pay than most captains-general, and no man under her command would lay a finger on the girl and risk her displeasure. Was the brindled bitch lying? Why would she?

So should he believe Ridianne or Lady Alaric? The old vixen knew every dog sniffing under another's tail or pissing on a tree in her territory but not much of what went on beyond it. The cold beauty had informants everywhere, according to Master Hamare, second only to his own. But the more Karn travelled, the more he was hearing that weighed against Lady Alaric's words.

Had she been fooled or had she deliberately lied to him? Irritated, Karn couldn't decide. Regardless, he was hungry. Coming down the steps from the great hall, he looked around the courtyard for someone who could offer him food as well as useful conversation. Someone who'd be camped beyond the ditch. Ridianne would see him flogged if he disobeyed her and found a bed within the boundary circle.

"Ulick!" He raised a hand as he saw a familiar face and, better yet, a dusty dog blazon.

A rotund mercenary broke off his conversation with a woman whose badge showed Marlier's three swords braided together with cords. He came to the bottom of the stone stair. "What can I do for you, friend?"

"I'll take a bowlful of whatever's in your pot this evening," Karn replied hopefully.

Ulick nodded. "How's Master Hamare?"

"He's well." Karn knew Ulick's main concern wasn't Hamare's health. "As generous as ever to his friends."

"Good," Ulick said with feeling.

"You're quartermastering for Beresin Steelhand?" Karn nodded at the brooch pinned on Ulick's worn grey jerkin.

"Fetching and carrying for his supply sergeants." Ulick looked gloomily at the miniature gauntlet curled into an aggressive fist. "You heard Shoddy Nair died?"

"I did, and I'm sorry for it," Karn said with every appearance of sincerity.

No wonder Ulick was unhappy. He'd fought long enough to earn the right to the safer life of a quartermaster. Karn knew the older man had been saving up his coin for the day when he couldn't keep up with the marching pace. With Shoddy Nair dead, he'd fallen a good few rungs down the ladder and the chances for skimming off private profits were less on every step.

"I expected you to be in Tormalin with Markasir," Karn remarked as they walked out through the gate.

Ulick looked at him, surprised. "Markasir isn't in Tormalin."

Karn jerked his head back towards the manor. "Herself seems to think so. Him and Lerris the Mason."

"Lerris is there but not Markasir." Ulick was quite certain.

So Lady Alaric might know more than Ridianne.

"He's in Carluse, then?" Karn queried.

"No." Ulick was just as certain of this.

"Where is he, then?" Karn reached for the purse on his belt.

"I wish I knew." Aggrieved, Ulick ran a hand over his stubbled jowls. "Find out and I'll do more than fill your belly from our stew pot. Markasir might just as well have run off through a rainbow to live with the Eldritch Kin. I can't get word of him anywhere."

"You don't think he's part of this plan to raise a force from the Lescari living in Vanam?" Karn ventured.

Ulick scorned the idea. "If he is, that knock on the head he took fighting for Draximal cracked his skull and let his wits leak out."

"You don't reckon there's anything to that?" So was Lady Alaric right? Karn was growing irritated.

As they walked over the earthen bridge to pass beyond the ditch to the outer camp, Ulick surprised him again. "There's something to it, no question. Some fool's wasting his coin and more fools will be losing blood. But Markasir's no more part of it than Glaive Tibbat. I could get a decent place on his muster," he said with feeling, "if I could only find the lanky bastard."

No one knew where Glaive Tibbat was either? Or rather, Ulick didn't know. The captain of the Steelhands might.

"Is Beresin dining with herself?" Karn didn't recall seeing the scarred mercenary in Ridianne's gloomy hall.

"Not tonight." They reached the Steelhand encampment and Ulick gestured towards a low tent whose sides were secured with iron hoops hammered into the hard ground. Two muscular men stood guard.

"Anyone I know?" asked Karn, mildly curious.

"No." Ulick waved a hand to the hard-faced woman tending a blackened cauldron on the fire. "This is Karn, a friend of mine."

Shrugging, the redhead plucked a wooden bowl from a basket and slopped cabbage and broth into it. "Bread's over there."

"Thank you." Karn took a torn hunk from the next basket.

Ulick accepted his own meal and led the way to an empty patch of grass, fishing a horn spoon out of a pocket.

Before Karn could frame his next question, Beresin, captain of the Steelhands, came striding through the tents.

"Bring out the prisoner!"

Always a good time to administer discipline, when every swordsman would be coming back for his food. Karn chewed on the bread, dense with the oats used to bulk out the wheat flour at this season.

The muscular guards unlaced the black tent's flaps and one thrust an arm inside.

"I'm coming." A shock-headed youth scrambled out of the low doorway, breeches grass-stained, shirt filthy.

Standing by the fire, Beresin's long black hair was drawn into a tail, emphasising his beak of a nose. A blow that had nearly cost him an eye left a dark scar down his forehead, cutting through his eyebrow and carving a deep notch into his cheekbone. Despite the heat of the season, he wore plate mail over black trews and padded jerkin. The last of the sunlight gilded the metal.

"Do you admit your offence?" he barked.

The youth was still flushed and sweating from his airless confinement. "I didn't know!"

He flinched as one of his captors ripped his shirt clean off.

"Dearie me." Karn took another spoonful. There was a good measure of bacon shredded among the cabbage.

Ulick leaned close, his voice low. "Save some of your bread. I've got cheese in my tent."

"You're showing a Steelhand tattoo." Beresin drove a plated finger into the lad's upper arm. "Has he earned it?" he roared.

"No!" The mercenaries' condemnation was unequivocal.

Beresin held out a blacksmith's rasp and plucked a knife from his own belt. "You can scour it off or cut it out."

At least the lad had the sense not to refuse to do either. Karn's spoon hovered over his bowl as he waited to see which torment the boy chose.

"It's a shame," Ulick remarked as the boy took the blacksmith's rasp in a shaking hand. "He's just overeager."

"You're sure Markasir isn't in Caladhria?" Karn ate another mouthful of bread. "Or the Glaive and his men?"

"Not that I've heard." Ulick raised his voice over a yelp of pain. The boy had tried a tentative swipe with the rasp.

"Let me know if you do hear anything." Karn saw the youth decide resolute action was the only way to be rid of his unsanctioned tattoo.

"As long as it's worth coin in my purse." Ulick winced.

The boy was scraping at his arm hard and fast. He kept his clenched fist raised, blood soon dripping off his elbow. More blood trickled down his beardless chin as he bit his lip to stop himself crying out.

Karn counted thirty strokes of the rasp before Beresin stepped forward with a clashing clap of his armoured hands. "Enough!"

If he said anything more, it was drowned out by cheers and whistles from the rest of the troop.

"Will that have taken the tattoo off?" Karn wondered.

"It will by the time I've tended it," Ulick promised. He stuck his spoon in his pocket and slurped the last of his broth. "Take this back to Shash or I'll never hear the last of it."

"Gladly." Karn set Ulick's bowl on the grass as he scraped up his own last mouthful.

As the fat man hurried towards the bleeding youth, Beresin intercepted him to exchange a few words. Karn guessed the ashen-faced lad would be boasting the gauntlet tattoo on his other arm one day, with Beresin's full approval. As long as Ulick kept the wound from festering and killing him.

What could he usefully do while Ulick was tending the fool boy? After taking both bowls back to the cook, Karn left the tents and walked towards the gliding waters of the Rel. With the sun now sunk below the horizon, only the afterglow reflected from the river. The water was well below the banks where the flourishing vegetation was showing no sign of the long dry spell. He could smell meadowsweet.

The assault from behind was so unexpected that Karn was knocked sprawling. He raised his arms to protect his face as he fell forward, ready to roll away from whatever second blow his assailant had ready. But he couldn't bend or roll. Even the attempt sent a shock of searing pain through him. He could barely catch his breath for the agony.

Lying face down, unable to move, Karn realised he'd been stabbed. Wet trickled into the hollow of his spine, warm and then, oddly, quickly cold. He was bleeding. Was the knife still in him? He reached clumsily round, trying to find a hilt.

Someone grabbed his flailing hand. Another someone seized his other arm. They were dragging him, hanging limp, face down and helpless. They were running, his feet trailing uselessly on the ground.

Who were they? The boys from the track through the woods? Karn choked on a stink of horse dung. Coughing was impossible, his lungs paralysed by the torment wracking him.

His captors dropped him. He couldn't do anything. They grabbed him again, one taking his hands, the other his ankles. They lifted him up and swung him sideways, doubling and redoubling his agonies. Karn tried to scream as he was flung out to land in the river with a noisy splash.

The cold shock momentarily revived him and he rolled to get his face out of the water. He tried to spread his arms and legs to stop himself sinking. Hadn't anyone heard the splash? He couldn't hear any shouts on the riverbank.

Was this how he was going to die? As his senses floated away, the dark waters closing over his face, he felt curiously relieved.

CHAPTER TWENTY-FIVE

Tathrin

Upstream from Emirle Bridge, in the Dukedom of Draximal, 37th of Aft-Summer

"ANOTHER HAND OF runes?" Gren tossed the three-sided bones from one hand to the other.

"Can't we run through some sword-work?" Tathrin would far rather be seeing if he could finally prod Gren with his sword-point. After daily practice bouts through nearly both halves of summer, he was starting to think he might manage it sooner rather than later.

Gren shook his head. "Someone wandering where they shouldn't might hear us."

"This is a ducal hunting forest." Tathrin looked around the clearing where they'd camped overnight. "I've seen no sign that anyone ever comes here."

"Only because you don't know what to look for." Gren threw a pair of rune bones, one hand against the other. Water landed upright, stronger than the Fire opposite. "I've seen snares. Fear of Duke Secaris or his rangers won't stop a man needing meat to feed his family. If some poor bastard does stumble across us, we'll just have to kill him. Then we'll have ten more beating the underbrush when he doesn't come home. Sorgrad won't be pleased to find us knee-deep in peasants."

Another thing Tathrin had learned through the summer was that Sorgrad's displeasure settled any argument as far as Gren was concerned.

The Mountain Man picked one of the nine bones out of his palm and studied the symbols on its three faces: the Salmon, the Reed and the Sea. "You don't like playing runes, do you?"

Tathrin had also learned that while Gren was as straightforward as a knife to the heart, he wasn't stupid. "I prefer the challenge of white raven."

"I like more excitement. You never know which way the runes are going to fall." Gren shook his head. "Playing raven's never going to change your life. If the runes are running your way, an evening's play could see you taking everyone else's coin home."

"Which could see someone cracking your skull on the way there so they can steal it back," Tathrin retorted. He hitched at his shirt. Thanks to the swordplay, it was uncomfortably tight across the shoulders now, whereas his breeches were markedly looser and he'd had to make a new hole in his belt with his knife.

"True enough," Gren acknowledged, idly examining the rune bearing the Eagle, the Broom and the Plains. "That's why our friend Livak used to travel with Halice. Now, she—"

"Won all the long lad's coin?" Sorgrad appeared, filthy and picking dead leaves out of his yellow hair.

Tathrin had initially wondered if he was using his unsanctioned magic to vanish as he scouted ahead on their journey. He'd finally concluded Sorgrad was merely very stealthy and perfectly willing to sacrifice his usual spruceness for the sake of going unseen.

"Not yet." Gren grinned.

"Well, put your runes away. It's time you learned how not to get killed in a knife fight," Sorgrad told Tathrin.

Gren's blue eyes brightened to rival the cloudless sky. "It's tonight?"

"I said we'd start this war before the end of Aft-Summer," Sorgrad confirmed.

"Are we here to begin recruiting a proper army?" Tathrin asked, apprehensive. "With Arest and his mercenaries?"

Twenty men sharing seven tents. A fifth of a company. That's how many men were up in the hills with Captain-General Evord: the handful of Solurans who'd come with him, and a scattering of Mountain Men who'd joined them on their long journey through the uplands. Granted, a good few weather-beaten men and a few daunting women had come and gone, promising to bring their warbands to join Evord's muster, but Tathrin would believe that when he saw it. How were they ever going to achieve anything worthwhile before the end of For-Autumn and the Equinox Festival drew the fighting season to a close?

"Arest and the lads are still holding the bridge?" Gren asked. "You got close enough to be sure?"

Sorgrad nodded. "Breaking them out of there will make for a nice distraction to set all the dukes fretting, just like Charoleia wants."

"As long as you keep your mouth shut," Gren warned Tathrin.

"Accidents happen in the best-regulated companies." Sorgrad's smile was cold enough to chill him despite the afternoon sun. "Besides, we'll be meeting more mercenaries soon enough and a long lad like you with no blazon to protect him could catch the eye of someone wanting to make their name with an easy kill."

"Especially short-arses. They're always troublemakers." Gren shook his head, oblivious to any irony.

"No one needs to know I can work wizardry," Sorgrad continued, "so keep your mouth shut about that as well."

"What—?" Tathrin blinked and tried not to swallow.

Gren was standing in front of him, one hand on his shoulder, the other holding a dagger across his throat. The slightest movement would shave off the bristles under his chin, Tathrin thought inconsequentially. Mountain Men kept their blades astonishingly sharp.

"You have to move quicker than that," the blond man reproved.

"You're not going to learn how to fight with a knife and win. All you need to know is how to keep yourself alive. Same as you're only practising with that in case you get caught up in a battle by mistake." Sorgrad nodded at Tathrin's sword.

He was a little comforted to realise he'd instinctively reached for his weapon. Not that he'd have been able to draw it before Gren had cut his throat.

"Manage not to get gutted and one of us will settle whatever quarrel's going on. Now, watch," Sorgrad instructed.

With another lightning-fast move, Gren had the blade at his brother's throat, the same grip on his shoulder.

"End up pinned like this and you deserve all you get." Sorgrad stepped back and nodded at Gren. "So don't get pinned."

This time, as Gren reached for his shirt, as the dagger came sweeping up, Sorgrad stepped sideways just as fast. He shoved the back of Gren's elbow so hard that the knife swept past him, cleaving nothing but empty air. The calculated force of the blow twisted Gren half-around, leaving his back open to Sorgrad's own blade. Tathrin hadn't even seen the older Mountain Man draw the weapon.

"Watch again," Sorgrad commanded.

Tathrin concentrated intently. He already knew Gren could kill him without breaking a sweat if he chose to. He also knew the Mountain Man wouldn't lose a wink of sleep over it. But he would never wound him deliberately in one of their practice bouts, and he was far too skilled with his sword to injure a novice by accident. Which didn't mean Tathrin wouldn't get a nasty scrape if he made an egregious error, to remind him to pay closer attention. He'd been picking scabs off his knuckles all summer.

"*Tathrin?*"

He shivered, startled. He couldn't help it.

"*Tathrin?*"

"Yes?" He tried not to sound too reluctant.

"*It's Aremil.*"

"Yes."

His friend's voice was no longer the almost imperceptible whisper it had been at first. It was like having Aremil standing behind him. Tathrin felt the skin between his shoulder blades crawling, as if he was being watched by someone he could never catch sight of.

"*Where are you?*"

"Some way upstream from Emirle Bridge." As he spoke, Tathrin felt recollections of these latest stages of his interminable summer's travels running through his mind.

As soon as Charoleia had ordered Sorgrad to distract the dukes, he and Evord had consulted briefly and Tathrin was told to ride south with the two brothers. As soon as they were half a day away, Sorgrad's magic had carried them to a remote corner of Carluse. Even fleeting recollection of that uncanny journey made Tathrin's head swim. They'd skulked around the byways until Sorgrad found the travelling maltster whom Charoleia trusted to get a message to Failla. Then Sorgrad had announced they were going to Draximal, back to the bridge where Tathrin had first found them. And still no one would explain exactly what was going on.

"*I see.*"

Aremil was envious, Tathrin realised with incredulity, of all the new places he had seen, of the people he had met, of his newfound skills as a swordsman. Did he think Tathrin was enjoying some adventure fit for a minstrel's ballad? Those tales all left out the wearisome reality of endless walking and riding, snatching indifferent meals and broken sleep in hedgerows.

"*Forgive me.*"

Tathrin was shocked to feel the depth of Aremil's chagrin. In the next breath, he sensed his friend's unease.

How did he know what I was thinking? Could Aremil pick whatever he liked from Tathrin's thoughts?

"*I would never do that!*"

But Aremil saying he wouldn't do something wasn't nearly the same thing as saying he couldn't. Tathrin tried to bury his instinctive response in some dark recess of his mind. His head was abruptly filled with a silence so loud that it drowned out the snatches of birdsong amid the papery rustling leaves.

"It's the cripple?" Gren was watching with interest, his dagger sheathed.

"*Charoleia wants to know if this friend of Failla's has arrived yet.*"

"Not yet," Tathrin replied.

"Reher should arrive before sunset," Sorgrad said. "Then we'll move to the bridge—"

"Please." Tathrin shut his eyes, shaking his head. "I can't do this if everyone's talking at once!"

"*I'm sorry.*"

Tathrin swallowed. "Sorgrad says this man Reher should—"

"*I heard.*"

That was new, and unwelcome.

"*I wouldn't hear anything you didn't want me to.*"

Aremil's earnest assurance couldn't quite cover the hurt Tathrin knew his friend was feeling. But how did he know Aremil was feeling hurt?

"Well?" Sorgrad's eyes were as opaque as blue slate.

Tathrin looked at him, exasperated. "Instead of being so secretive and asking me and Aremil to pass mysterious messages to Charoleia, why don't you just explain your plan? Aremil can hear you perfectly clearly."

Sorgrad pursed his lips for a moment. "I scouted downriver last night and this morning, and Arest and his company are still holding the bridge at Emirle. The Duke of Draximal has filled the town with a couple of companies of his militia and there are more dug in on the far side. Duke Orlin of Parnilesse's militia are huddling in the woods half a day's march to the south. No one's shuffled their feet since Solstice."

"What now?" As Tathrin spoke, he heard Aremil's voice echoing the selfsame words in his head.

"Now we persuade Arest to break his men out of their cosy billet. Half of them can convince the Draximal militia that the Parnilesse forces have finally stopped sitting around polishing their weapons and attacked. The rest can send Parnilesse's militiamen running all the way to their duke swearing blind they've been attacked by Draximal."

"That should be good for a few days' skirmishing," Gren said cheerfully.

"We need more than that," Tathrin objected. "Captain-General Evord needs time to raise his army."

"As soon as Reher joins us, we can set this whole border ablaze," Sorgrad promised. "Evord will have all the time he needs."

"How?" Tathrin's irritation grew.

"Hush." Gren disappeared into the undergrowth.

Sorgrad silently raised a finger to his lips as he retreated behind a tree.

Tathrin gritted his teeth and edged backwards into the cover of a leafy birch.

"*What is it?*"

"I don't know." Tathrin could barely hear his own whisper, but he still had to speak if Aremil was to hear him. Just thinking the words was never enough. But now every time he opened his mouth, Tathrin thought uneasily, it seemed his thoughts were laid ever more open to Aremil.

He stood motionless, his sweaty shirt clinging to his body in rank folds. If he moved, he'd get a tongue-lashing from Sorgrad, same as he had done on their hunts up in the hills.

"*I cannot stay with you much longer.*"

Aremil's voice sounded further away.

"Till tomorrow," Tathrin breathed.

"*Very well.*"

The unseen presence faded reluctantly. Tathrin was ashamed at how relieved he felt. Aremil was his friend.

"Here we are." Gren's cheery return provoked a glossy thrush into a chatter of alarm.

Tathrin knew he'd never met this friend of Failla's. He'd have remembered him, no question. There were precious few men who could look Tathrin in the eye and fewer still he had to look up to. He'd be looking up to Reher, unless he was standing on a step. He'd be minding his manners, too, given the black-bearded man's massive shoulders and his forbidding scowl.

"I'm Tathrin." He hesitated between offering the arm-clasp that he'd seen the mercenaries using and a more usual handshake.

Reher shook his hand, oblivious to Tathrin's dithering. "Good to meet you."

It was good to hear another Carluse accent. With the sleeves of his loose linen shirt rolled up, Tathrin noticed tiny black scars pitting the man's hands and arms. His sister's husband bore the same marks. "You're a smith? Or a farrier?"

"A smith." Reher's scowl deepened. "When I get the chance to work an honest trade."

"I'm Sorgrad." The Mountain Man was all business. "What did Failla tell you?"

"That you have need of my particular talents." Reher's dark eyes glowered beneath the tumble of black curls sticking to his sweaty forehead. "In some scheme to finally bring peace to Lescar."

"There'll be fighting and dying along the way." Sorgrad looked steadily at him.

Reher shrugged one muscular shoulder. "No different from half my lifetime."

"Come on, then." Gren was gathering up their gear, impatient as a hunting dog seeing his master pull his boots on.

"Suits me." Reher shifted a grubby canvas sack from one shoulder to the other.

Tathrin hurried to gather up his own bag and tightly rolled blanket. Sorgrad and Gren were already moving away and this blacksmith Reher followed close behind. For a big man in heavy boots, he moved remarkably quietly through the dense summer undergrowth.

Had he seen Failla? Tathrin knew she had gone back to Carluse. Was she still safe? Aremil had told him she was, as far as he knew, but Charoleia seemed to share as little with Aremil as Sorgrad did with him. How soon would this woman Branca find someone to travel to Carluse and use aetheric enchantments to make sure Failla stayed safe? So many questions burned under his tongue. Perhaps he'd get a chance to talk to Reher when they next halted.

But they didn't stop. They left the dense woods unscarred by woodsmen's axes to walk cautiously through coppiced stands of hazel and beech. Soon after that, the sky opened up above them and they followed hedgerows bracketing sunken lanes that divided fields of standing grain from land given over to hay. In the distance Tathrin saw farmhouses, all surrounded by solid stone walls, readily defended in this imperilled region. Not so very different from the farmsteads on the far side of Losand, he realised, where Carluse territory ran up against Sharlac lands, only separated by the narrow width of the Great West Road.

They had to move slowly and quietly, with Tathrin and Reher walking bent almost double. Every hay meadow was busy with men wielding scythes, women following after to turn and spread the tangled grass. Children and dogs alike chased the mice fleeing for the refuge of the hedges. Here and there some of the wheat was already being cut, ripened to golden perfection by the hot summer sun.

If Duke Secaris of Draximal sent his personal guard to root out some explanation for whatever mayhem Sorgrad had planned, Tathrin knew these harvesting peasants would find a pair of Mountain Men and a couple of uncommonly tall Lescari unhelpfully memorable. But Sorgrad had reconnoitred a path that took them towards the river unseen.

They left the wheat fields and the land turned to damper, greener pasture. Curious cows watched them, beef cattle fat and placid, milking herds chewing, udders hanging heavy. The hedges around the grazing were quite unlike those Tathrin was used to. He hadn't noticed as he walked along the high road on his earlier journey, but now down among them, he saw that steep-sided banks half as high as a man enclosed each field, dense tangles of hedges growing on top.

Sorgrad signalled a stop just before the next gate. Tathrin took a drink from his travelling flask. His back was aching viciously. He offered Reher some of the water as a haywain rattled along the unseen lane.

Gren caught Tathrin's eye as the noise faded. "These cursed fields are why Parnilesse never gets the upper hand over Draximal," he whispered. "It's a drunkard's nightmare fighting through here, all ambushes and counter-strikes and ten men dead for every plough-length."

Sorgrad signalled with a silent hand and they crossed the next pasture to the shelter of a tangled blackthorn hedge. Sorgrad pointed to a curve of pollarded osiers sprouting grey-green withies. Tathrin nodded ready understanding. The river lay beyond the line of trees.

Reher picked a stray thorn out of the loose weave of his homespun breeches. "Can you swim?"

"Sorry?" Tathrin was remembering how itchy homespun could be. But at least Reher's clothes were neat and new. His own breeches and doublet of fine Vanam broadcloth were sadly worn and faded and his shirt was so stained no laundress could save it. "Yes, I can swim."

"Strongly enough to save a drowning man?" Reher grimaced. "Because I can't."

"I hope so." Tathrin did his best to sound confident.

Thankfully, when Sorgrad waved them forward through the osiers, he saw that the river fell far short of the boisterous torrent they'd ridden in Aft-Spring. It had sunk so far in the centre of its wide bed that shallow islets had broken through the sluggish flow, some sprouting clumps of weeds.

"There's no one on the banks." Tathrin looked up-and downstream.

"No one goes fishing till the harvest's home," grunted Reher.

"Do we have a boat?" Gren looked around.

"Of course," Sorgrad said scornfully. He slid down the crumbling clay bank and hauled a marsh hunter's punt out of a tangle of washed-up branches.

"Aren't we waiting till dark?" Tathrin looked up at the afternoon sky.

"It'll be dusk by the time we reach the bridge." Sorgrad dragged the shallow-sided boat towards the water.

"Do we have oars?" Tathrin tried to sound offhand.

"A paddle." Gren wasn't about to relinquish it.

"Get in, lie low, and we'll let the river do the work." Sorgrad waded into the water.

Gren sprang into the prow and knelt there, alert.

Tathrin shared an eloquent glance with Reher as they climbed cautiously aboard.

"Lie flat," Sorgrad ordered.

The two tall men stretched out as best they could. It was cramped and uncomfortable, and water soon seeped through the planking. Tathrin tensed as Reher shifted his bulk and the punt rocked alarmingly.

"Best to lie still." Sorgrad was crouching in the stern, watching where the current might take them.

The waters whispered on the other side of the planks. The chill of the river soaked the back of Tathrin's shirt and breeches and the marshy odour grew steadily stronger. Add the reek of his own sweat and Reher's and he wondered wryly if the mercenaries holding the bridge or the militias penning them in would need to see the little boat approaching. Surely they would just smell them coming?

He lay still and looked up at the cloudless sky, the blue growing steadily richer as the sun slid towards the horizon. This was at least preferable to the first trip he'd taken on this river.

What did Sorgrad or Gren have planned? Why had they gone to such lengths to bring Reher here? Doubtless Arest and his band of mercenaries could use a blacksmith's skills but why bring Reher to Emirle Bridge to fight in this battle? One man, however strong, surely couldn't make that much difference?

"You've known Arest for years, right, Sorgrad?" he said suddenly. "Why do you need me and Reher along to talk him into your plan?"

"I need you because you're the one Aremil talks to." Sorgrad shifted slightly.

"Can't he talk to you?" He remembered Sorgrad's magebirth. "Or to Gren?"

"That's not a good idea." Sorgrad's tone sent a colder shiver down Tathrin's spine than the river water he was lying in. "If he's caught unawares, Gren tends to lash out."

Tathrin heard a hiss as the paddle bit into the flow and Gren chuckled. "Some *sheltya* bastard tried getting inside my head once. He soon regretted it."

"What are you talking about?" Reher demanded.

"Never mind," Sorgrad said repressively.

Sheltya. These mysterious adepts who wielded their Artifice in remote mountain valleys. Tathrin had seen no sign of Sorgrad fearing anything but he certainly treated these unknown enchanters with wary respect as well as mistrust. They could pluck thoughts out of a man's head if they wanted to, without him even knowing—that's what Sorgrad had said. Reniack had talked about enchantments that could find out all a man's secrets.

Was that why Sorgrad told him so little of his and Evord's plans? Tathrin suddenly wondered. Because he didn't trust Aremil not to pick things out of his mind? Not so long ago, that notion would have angered him. Now he wasn't inclined to be so affronted. Not when every time Aremil used Artifice to contact him, he seemed to see deeper into his friend's thoughts and feelings, just as Aremil saw further into his. Would bringing more adepts into their conspiracy mean he'd have strangers uncovering his innermost thoughts?

Uncomfortable, Tathrin turned his thoughts instead to the concerns that he knew he and Aremil shared. Where was Captain-General Evord going to get his army from? Just what could they hope to achieve before Aft-Autumn and then For-Winter put an end to all campaigning? The Mountain Men and the Solurans were supposed to be experts in waging war. Weren't they gambling everything on decent weather lasting past the Equinox?

He turned the endless questions over and over in his mind. Was there any way he could phrase a query that might prompt Sorgrad into an unguarded answer? He was tired of the Mountain Man's sarcastic answers that didn't actually tell him anything.

Chapter Twenty-Six

Tathrin

Emirle Bridge, in the Lescari Dukedom of Draximal, 37th of Aft-Summer

"THERE'S LIT WINDOWS in that village." Gren was kneeling in the prow, crouching so low that his chin rested on the rail.

Propping himself cautiously up on his elbows, Tathrin looked over the shallow boat's side. The day was definitely turning to twilight. "Where are we?"

"Nearly there," Sorgrad said.

Reher was snoring. Gren reached back to shake his massive shoulder. "We're coming up on the bridge."

Tathrin saw torches lit on the watchtowers at either end. The illumination threw the water and everything between the defences into deep shadow.

"Don't stare at the lights," Sorgrad chided him. "They're just to keep the militia looking and ruining their night sight."

"Don't move till I say." Gren reached for a coil of rope.

After the drama of his first arrival, Tathrin's second landing on the bridge was blessedly uneventful. A mercenary waiting beneath the arch caught the rope Gren tossed and drew the punt gently against the central pillar's footing.

"All quiet?" Sorgrad stepped lightly onto the stone stairway.

"Cursed boring," the swordsman growled.

"We'll see what we can do about that," Gren promised.

"Shall I take your gear?" With dry stone safely beneath his boots, Tathrin turned to Reher.

"Thank you." The big man answered Tathrin with a wry smile. "I don't like water and it doesn't like me." He handed his canvas sack to Tathrin and clambered awkwardly out of the shallow boat.

"Where's Arest?" Sorgrad asked.

The mercenary jerked his head. "On the east gate."

As they climbed the narrow spiral staircase, Tathrin wondered if the burly captain would insist that Reher strip to his underlinen to prove he had no mercenary tattoos.

"Going to see Arest." Sorgrad passed through the side room of the bridge's central tower with a brief wave. The swordsmen sitting round a game of runes barely looked up.

Outside Tathrin heard the clip of an iron shoe as one of the horses stabled in the archway shifted. The roadway was dark, all the lit torches confined to the outer faces of the gates at each end. Tathrin still listened for the spiteful chirp of arrows coming out of the darkness. How many militiamen were camped on the banks? Could Arest's men break out, as Sorgrad planned?

A solitary watchman stood by the oak door of the eastern gatehouse.

"Zeil? Where's the boss?"

Tathrin wondered how Sorgrad could recognise anyone in the gloom. But it was Zeil.

"Up top."

A narrow stone stair built into the width of the wall ran up to the room above the gate. Arest was leaning against the portcullis mechanism, looking out of a crossbowman's firing slit. Tathrin peered through another one. Campfires beyond the causeway were bright dots in the distant darkness.

Arest reached for a candle lantern hung on a nail and slid its metal shutter up to let out more light. "Don't fret, lad. At least a third of those fires are false lures, just lit to make us think they have more men than they do." He looked at Reher. "Who's this? A new recruit?"

Arest was half a head shorter than Reher but broader in the shoulder and sturdier in the leg. Tathrin wouldn't know who to wager on, if the two men were to wrestle.

"He's a smith with a talent for starting fires." Sorgrad grinned. "Now, Lady Alaric reckons you'll be bored with this game by now."

"I'll say." Arest spat on the floor. "Orlin, pissing Duke of Parnilesse, hasn't sent us a copper penny, for all his promises of gold for every day we hold the bridge. Duke Secaris of Draximal, the horse-kisser, he's not offering anything to get his river crossing back."

"How's the pickings hereabouts?" Gren was still counting campfires.

"We can keep ourselves fed. Send out boats at dawn and dusk and foraging parties give the militiamen the slip easy enough." Arest scowled. "Beyond that, anywhere within reach is picked clean of dainties and there wasn't much to send home to mother to start with. As for entertainment, Halcarion's tits, it's impossible to find a willing whore. Try for a taste of honey and you risk a pitchfork up the arse while your breeches are round your ankles."

"So you and the boys would take a hire from Lady Alaric?" Sorgrad asked.

Arest's narrow eyes brightened. "Her word's always gold in the hand."

"She wants you and the lads to break out on both banks to start a panic." Sorgrad gestured back towards the town. "Convince the Draximal militia that Duke Orlin of Parnilesse is trying push his border north to the bridge." He nodded in the direction of the causeway. "Go through those peasants like a dose through a sick horse and kick the Parnilesse militia so hard they run back to Duke Orlin screaming that Duke Secaris of Draximal is seizing all the forest up to the southern margin."

Arest looked doubtful. "Why would anyone believe either duke's found stones that big in his codpiece?"

Sorgrad smiled. "Because every militiaman will be running with his breeches on fire, swearing by every god from Saedrin down that the enemy's got a wizard."

Arest was astonished. "Lady Alaric wants to spit in the Archmage's eye?"

"Lady Alaric has found this smith who knows all the secrets of Aldabreshin sticky fire." Sorgrad nodded at Reher. "There isn't a peasant between here and the sea who can tell the difference between that and real magecraft."

Arest looked thoughtful. "But the dukes will have seen real wizardry. They'll know when they're looking at a sham."

"They're not here to see it," Sorgrad pointed out. "All they'll know will be twice- and thrice-told tales."

"Which will have them pissing themselves regardless, for fear their enemy's found some secret ally, renegade mage or Aldabreshin alchemist." Arest rubbed a broad hand over his chin, bristles rasping in the silence. "What's Lady Alaric got coming to the boil that needs this much lamp oil thrown on the embers here?"

"She'll bar her door to me if I tell you." Sorgrad shook his head, regretful. "Tighter than Saedrin locks the door to the Otherworld. But when you break out of here, head west across the Triolle hills and then cut north to the uplands above Losand. You'll find Captain-General Evord there, and you can tell him I sent you."

"Evord's back in the game?" Arest looked keenly interested.

Warfare was just a game to these people? Tathrin hid his contempt behind an impassive face. Innocent men and women were no pieces to be played and discarded, lives worth no more than copper cut-pieces won and lost in a game of runes.

"Only take men you know he'll accept on his muster," Gren warned.

"Do you think I'm a fool?" Arest's scorn was half-hearted. Clearly, he was already thinking ahead.

Letting the others go down the stair ahead of him, Tathrin caught Sorgrad's elbow. "How much mayhem will Arest and his men wreak as they pass through Triolle and Carluse?" he asked in an angry undertone.

"Very little." Sorgrad shook his hand off. "Harvest's been good, so the farmers can buy them off with bread and beer and maybe a pig-killing."

Gren's sharp ears heard their exchange. He looked back. "They won't be idling in hopes of casual plunder, long lad. Not if there's a chance of signing onto Evord's muster roll."

"Don't begrudge them food and drink along the way, not if you want them to fight for Lescar's peace." Sorgrad looked up at Tathrin, his eyes hard. "Not when some of them are going to bleed and die for it."

Reher turned, his face shadowed by some grim memory. "There'll be blood on all our hands before morning. Get used to it, friend."

Tathrin swallowed and couldn't find anything to say.

He followed the others back to the central tower and up to the wide room spanning the whole bridge. It was as loud and rowdy as he remembered. Mercenaries huddled over rune games in different corners and others were laughing raucously as they swapped tattered broadsheets. Lewdly illustrated tales and graphic accounts of hanged felons' crimes, Tathrin guessed. Over by the windows, men and women dipped horn cups into open barrels, talking loudly with expansive gestures, ale slopping to dampen the flagstones. Sorgrad and Gren were already by the fireside, greeting old friends and being offered their choice from the seething pots in the hearth.

"I don't suppose their food will choke us." Reher glanced at him.

So whatever else he might be, the blacksmith didn't count himself a mercenary. That was some comfort to Tathrin. He nodded, accepted the offer of a bowl of fishy stew with a brief word of thanks and found a space to sit. As he ate, he watched Arest moving from group to group, talking in low tones. Around the room, all eyes were intent on the captain. As Arest moved on, dark heads, red hair and tangled black curls drew close together in quiet debate. Every so often someone wandered over to the hearth to exchange a few words with Sorgrad or Gren.

"No one owns the river fish, so no one's been robbed to feed us." Reher came to sit beside him with a second steaming bowlful.

Before Tathrin could answer, a mercenary hunkered down in front of them. It was Jik, the tall, thin man who'd taken his dagger till Sorgrad made him give it back.

"They say you know about sticky fire?" He looked sceptically at Reher.

"Do they?" The smith's bearded face gave nothing away.

"Where's the makings of it?" Jik looked at Reher's canvas sack.

"Only a fool would bring such things anywhere near a live flame." Reher used his spoon to point towards the hearth.

Jik grinned. "Right, then."

Tathrin watched him walk casually back to the men who'd first captured him when he was trying to find Sorgrad and Gren.

"You've seen how dry the woods and fields are. Sticky fire could set half the dukedom alight, couldn't it?" If only half the tales that minstrels told were true, the Aldabreshin concoction was all but unquenchable.

"You think we'd really use such gods-cursed stuff?" Reher said in a terse undertone.

"Then what's the plan?" Tathrin was confused.

"Sorgrad sets the fires on one bank and I set them on the other. We have the same talent for it." Reher glowered at him. "Don't breathe a word about that."

The blacksmith was a wizard? Tathrin nodded mutely and ate his fish stew.

Reher went over to the fireplace and exchanged a few words with Sorgrad. The Mountain Man glanced at Tathrin. Arest joined the two men for a brief conversation.

The atmosphere in the room was changing. Tathrin saw the rune bones swept up and the ragged engravings folded away. Men were running whetstones along swords and daggers. He watched one pox-scarred man test the edge of his blade by shaving the dark hair off his forearm. Gren was wont to do the same. One of the men who'd been drinking deepest from the ale barrels thrust his fingers down his throat. Tathrin felt his own gorge rise as the man stuck his head out of the narrow window and vomited noisily.

Sorgrad and the blacksmith came over. "Tathrin, you stick with me like a calf to its cow and you'll be safe enough. Reher, you're going over to the eastern bank with Gren. Once the peasants are pissing themselves for fear of magefire, Gren will see you safe back across the river. He knows where we're meeting up."

"Don't fret." Gren appeared at the big man's elbow. "I can't lose someone your size."

Tathrin cleared his throat. "Should I sharpen my sword?"

Gren chuckled. "Only if you want to give the lads a laugh. You use a whetstone like you're cleaning a ploughshare."

"Ploughman's an honest trade." Reher's stare challenged Gren.

"True enough," the Mountain Man said equably.

"Just sit still and don't get underfoot," Sorgrad advised Tathrin.

The Mountain Man talked to him like his mother. Galling as Tathrin found it, he decided this wasn't the time to rebuke him.

Sorgrad turned away with Gren to talk to some other mercenaries. Reher sat down beside Tathrin again.

"So whereabouts are you from?"

Sorgrad had told Tathrin to share nothing of his background with the mercenaries. But Reher wasn't a mercenary. He was from Carluse, and if he was a wizard, perhaps Tathrin could trust him to take word to his family. Because, as Tathrin was realising with a sinking feeling, he was going to be in a battle tonight. Would Sorgrad keep him alive?

"My people keep an inn on the Abray Road."

"I have family in Losand," Reher remarked.

Tathrin dragged his attention away from the mercenaries' ominous preparations. "What are their trades?"

"Pewtering." Reher stretched out a broad hand and clenched it so the muscles in his forearm corded. "My uncles reckoned I had the build for heavier work, so I was apprenticed to Master Findrin, the smith in Carluse."

What had befallen Reher's father, Tathrin wondered, that his uncles were making such decisions? "My father buys pots and pans in Losand. What's your family's mark?"

"The dog-rose." Reher looked at him.

Tathrin grinned. "I've cleared a fair few of those plates and tankards from the taproom."

Reher's smile was white against his dark beard. "Pleased to hear it."

Tathrin looked to be sure no mercenary could overhear them and chose his words carefully. "You didn't want to pursue other opportunities? Given your natural aptitudes?"

The big man's face darkened. "Not when I'd be forbidden to use whatever skills I learned to help my kith and kin."

"Were you in Losand when Sharlac last attacked?" Tathrin wondered.

Reher's fast-fading good humour vanished. "Not in the town. Nearby."

Seeing the bleakness in the smith's eyes, Tathrin shrank from asking anything more.

Reher got to his feet and beckoned to Sorgrad. The two of them retreated into a corner, the smith looming over the Mountain Man.

Tathrin couldn't help wondering. They'd said Lord Veblen, Duke Garnot's bastard son, had been shrouded from head to toe when he was put on his funeral pyre. They'd said he'd been horribly burned when some Sharlac scum had thrown flaming oil all over him. The treacherous cowards had been out to avenge the death of Lord Jaras, Sharlac's heir, at Veblen's courageous hand. Was that really what had happened? Might Reher have used his wizardry to kill

Veblen, captain of Carluse's militia? If so, to what end?

He recalled the talk in the taproom once the dead had been recovered from the fields around Losand and the smoke from the funeral pyres had blown away. If Lord Jaras hadn't died, Sharlac mercenaries and militia would have ridden roughshod right into Carluse. But Jaras had died and Sharlac's attack was blunted. If Veblen had lived, Carluse militia and Wynald's Warband, Duke Garnot's favoured mercenaries, could have followed up their advantage and carried the attack on into Sharlac. But Veblen had died and that meant the Carluse forces had to settle for chasing the invaders back to the border.

Tathrin sat and studied his boots. Reher knew Failla, and Failla was close to the priests and guildsmen who secretly connived to keep the ordinary folk of Carluse safe from fighting. How closely was Reher involved in their schemes? Could they be so ruthless as to kill their own duke's son? His father knew some of these men. Had he wondered the same as Tathrin? Could his father approve of such callousness? Would that make it easier for Tathrin to explain himself, and everything he was doing this summer, when the time came?

Not wishing to pursue that line of thought, he turned his attention outwards and scanned the room, only to notice women armouring themselves alongside the men. A sturdy matron who looked as if she should be sweeping out her kitchen stripped off her tattered gown and donned buckskin breeches. As she stood, half-naked, turning her padded arming jacket the right way out, no one spared her heavy breasts a second glance. A younger woman, lightly built but harsh-faced, held out her arm as a swordsman buckled on her vambraces. As soon as he was done, she did the same service for him. With a shock, Tathrin realised a warrior almost as tall as him was another girl when she laughed at another mercenary's jest, kneeling to secure her metal-plated boots.

Men and women alike were winding bandages and checking pots of salve. Some spread sticky concoctions on linen rags that they carefully stowed in pouches on their sword-belts. Donning helms that made it difficult to tell men from women, Tathrin saw that all of their faces were grimly determined.

What kind of woman chose life with a mercenary band? Had they no family, no friends to shelter them from whatever calamity had deprived them of hearth and home? Tathrin knew there were such unfortunates. He'd seen maidens, desperate mothers and grey-haired matrons among the beggars trailing along the verges of the Great West Road. Had these bolder women chosen this dangerous life in preference to the insults and perils of whoring to keep from starving?

What had driven Failla to play the strumpet in Duke Garnot's bed? Tathrin wondered. Did it matter? Wasn't her help in their quest to bring peace to Lescar enough to persuade Drianon to forgive whatever sins against chastity and motherhood the goddess might hold her to account for? Where was Failla? Was she safe? Whatever Tathrin's misgivings about Aremil sending some unknown adept to travel with her, it would be a relief to know what had become of her.

"Here." Gren walked up and dumped a roll of chain mail at his feet. "You may as well look the part." He dropped a round helmet on top of it and walked off.

Standing up, Tathrin tried to don the hauberk like a tunic, but the slithering links didn't stretch like cloth. With it halfway over his head, he realised his arms and shoulders were firmly stuck. For one horrible moment he thought he was going to have to ask for help. His shoulders sagged, something slipped and he was able to wriggle free.

Red-faced, he paused and watched how the other men threaded their arms through their hauberks' sleeves before throwing the weight upwards. Ducking their heads inside, they shook themselves like dogs as the steel rings flowed down their bodies. Taking a deep breath, Tathrin did the same, grimacing as the pinching links ripped stray hairs from his head.

"Zeil, you're leading the horsemen along the causeway. I want you kicking Parnilesse arses before dawn." Arest strode into the centre of the room, massive in his gleaming hauberk, swinging a round shield broader than Tathrin's arm was long. His black helmet shadowed his face, his voice harsh and commanding. "The rest of you, Jik's got weapons we've taken off the locals out on the bridge. Take some to throw down and make this look like a real rout."

With that, he walked off.

Tathrin had been expecting some words of encouragement. Fear congealed the fish stew in his belly. How could he need to piss so urgently when he'd only drunk water and precious little of that?

"Stick close to me." Sorgrad shoved his shoulder.

Mute, Tathrin followed him down to the bridge. Zeil and the horsemen were already galloping out of the far gate. Sorgrad stooped to pick up a stained and notched sword from a heap on the roadway. Tathrin grabbed a pike with a broken haft. As they reached the gatehouse facing the sleeping town of Emirle, mercenaries were throwing the torches into the river, their shouts drowning out the hiss of quenched fire. There was enough moonlight to see by without them, with the Greater Moon full and the Lesser still at its half.

"Ware! Ware! Ware!" Sorgrad banged the notched sword on the small metal shield strapped to his other forearm.

The mercenaries took up the cry, roaring obscenities as they clashed purloined weapons in mock combat. The same commotion rose at the other end of the bridge, echoing down the river. Whatever their birth, Tathrin realised, Arest's men were all yelling with Draximal and Parnilesse accents. It sounded like battle to him.

Mercenaries were at the bridge's gatehouse, sliding the timbers barring it out of the sockets in the stonework. As the gates swung open, the swordsmen ran out, every warrior staying within reach of his neighbour's protective blade. Half were crying out desperately for assistance, the rest shrieking vile threats or cheering loudly for Parnilesse as they ran up the slope towards the walls of Emirle Town. Tathrin saw the first startled lights being kindled along the ramparts.

"Come on." Sorgrad ran to the end of the bridge and threw the notched sword down among the scorned weapons littering the road. Tathrin tossed the broken pike after it.

Sorgrad turned and flung his hand out as if he were strewing sawdust onto a treacherous floor.

Scarlet flame sprang out of the darkness and rolled along the pounded earth. Where the red fire touched a weapon, the blade glowed white hot, as if it had just been taken from the heart of a forge. Leather bindings and wooden hafts flared to ash in an instant of ruby flame. Blades melted into puddles reflecting the eerie magelight.

Tathrin took a hasty step backwards, seeing the liquid metal running together like quicksilver. How could anything burn with such an improbable colour? How could anyone mistake this unearthly fire for anything but wizardry? He could feel the searing heat on his face.

Molten metal pooled beneath the gates of the bridge. Sorcerous fingers crawled up the ancient weathered wood, glinting savage red. Silver threads spun off to ease themselves into knots and crevices. Inside a few breaths, the timbers split. A handful of men with axes couldn't have done as much damage if they'd hacked at the wood for a long summer's day. The iron bindings screeched with protest, stretching like softening wax.

"That'll do." Sorgrad turned towards the town.

Tathrin saw a shadowy void in the wall, piercing pale stone reflecting the red of the magefire. Who had been fool enough to open the town's gates? He followed Sorgrad up the slope. What else could he do?

As they ran through the arch of the gate, unchallenged, he saw lights in windows. Shutters slammed open on shouts of alarm. Arest's mercenaries were running up the main street now, kicking in doors and smashing lanterns hung out by conscientious householders.

Gouts of red fire dripped from Sorgrad's fingers as he set the town's gates burning. Tathrin watched, dumbfounded. How could the Mountain Man do such a thing? How could anyone be born with the ability to command the fleeting mystery of fire? How could Sorgrad use his talent to wreak such havoc? What else could he do, if he chose to? What could he do to a living thing?

"Shit!" Tathrin flinched as a rivet sprang from the tortured gate and struck a chip from the stonework beside him.

"Come on."

Dragging his gaze from the burning gates, Tathrin followed Sorgrad along the road into the little town. He was sweating, yet at the same time chilled to the bone. Shouts and screams came from all directions. Weapons clashed, glass shattered and wood splintered. All around, men and women were screaming. Sorgrad loped on ahead, looking this way and that, his sword ready.

Drawing his own blade with a trembling hand, Tathrin smelled smoke. A whitewashed wall reflected the orange glow of ordinary fire running out of control. A girl ran shrieking from an alley, her white nightgown splashed with dark vileness.

Sorgrad let her pass before heading into the shadows she had fled. Hurrying after him, Tathrin nearly fell as he skidded on slick cobblestones.

"You bastards!" A townsman raged at Sorgrad, a murderous billhook raised.

The Mountain Man's sword met the stroke before it could descend. He smashed the small shield on his forearm into the man's face. The townsman fell backwards, his head hitting a windowsill with a sickening crack. Sorgrad bent over him, forcing his head back to bare his throat. A stray gleam of moonlight caught the blade in his other hand.

"No!" Tathrin couldn't see an innocent man's throat cut. "You can't kill him." He tightened his grip on his own sword. Was this how he was going to die?

Defending someone he didn't even know from Sorgrad?

"That windowsill's smashed his skull. He's better off dead than lingering." Sorgrad thrust the narrow dagger into the man's eye and straightened up. He frowned at the wet cobbles. "Where's all this blood come from?" He stepped into a black shadow cast by a nearby gable. "Ah, sheepshit."

"What?" Tathrin took a reluctant pace after him.

"It's Jik." Sorgrad snapped his fingers and a scarlet flame danced on his palm.

Tathrin saw Jik sprawled gracelessly in the dirt. A massive gash split his head just in front of his ear, running down his neck. Bone and gristle shone in the murderous wound, the exposed skull rosy in the light of Sorgrad's magefire.

"Go and fight Poldrion's demons, old pal." Sorgrad tilted his hand and dripped ruby magic onto Jik's bloody chest. "Till they're the ones hammering on the door to the Otherworld just to get away from you."

"But he's not dead!" Aghast, Tathrin saw the magelight shimmer. Jik's chest struggled to rise.

"You think he can be saved?" Sorgrad asked savagely. "You think he'd want to be thrown into some charnel pit to rot like vermin?"

"But—" Tathrin gagged on the stink of burning flesh.

The flames of the magefire sprang up as if fanned by the Mountain Man's anger. A spasm racked Jik from helmet to boots. His corpse writhed, hands drawn up as if to ward off some hideous foe. The hobnails on his boots scraped the cobbles. A moment later, a charred and splintered skeleton lay wrapped in the smouldering remains of Jik's clothes. His helm was twisted and blackened, patches of his chain mail melted.

Tathrin whirled around to vomit up his supper.

"This way no one can identify him as Arest's man," Sorgrad added with vicious satisfaction. "He's just another victim of Parnilesse's treacherous mage." He snapped his fingers and the sorcerous fire vanished. "Come on. We don't want to get left behind."

That prospect was too hideous to contemplate. Wiping his mouth, his throat seared with sickness and loathing, Tathrin followed Sorgrad along the alley.

The Mountain Man looked around warily as they emerged into a deserted street. "We should make sure no other friendly bodies need an impromptu pyre. Then we find Arest and whoever else comes safely through the night. We wait for Gren and Reher and then we head back to Evord."

"How could you do that?" Tathrin spat bile into the gutter. "Have you no conscience at all?"

Sorgrad looked at him, his angular features cold in the moonlight. He looked older than Tathrin usually thought him, more dangerous than ever. "Why do you think I'm helping you people?"

"What?" Unnerved, Tathrin retreated a step.

"I'm not just in this for the coin, long lad, or for the fun and games like Gren. How many friends do you think I've seen die? How many more do you think I've had to give a quick death like Jik? Or killed like that poor bastard who was only trying to defend his home? I've lived like this since I was younger than you. I've seen more bloodshed than you'll ever know and I've had a bellyful of it. Now come on, before I have to cut anyone else down just to save your lanky skin!"

The Mountain Man broke into a measured run. Dizzy and nauseous, Tathrin followed. What else could he do?

CHAPTER TWENTY-SEVEN

Litasse

**Triolle Castle, in the Kingdom of Lescar,
2nd of For-Autumn**

"WHAT HAVE YOU heard?" Litasse didn't wait to
knock, shoving open the door to Hamare's study.

He looked up from his letter, his eyes blank with
shock. "How did you know?"

"What?" She halted, perplexed. "The whole castle's
in an uproar!"

She'd finally had to slap some sense into her maid,
just so the silly girl would finish dressing her hair so
she could leave her chamber.

"You're talking about this bridge in Draximal?" He
looked down at his letter again.

"What else would I be talking about?" Litasse saw
that Hamare's haggardness was far beyond his usual pallor. She closed the door. "What are *you* talking about?"

He set the letter carefully down and smoothed it out.
"Karn is dead."

"You said he was travelling through the mercenary camps." Litasse sank onto a chair. "Those are dangerous places."

"Not for Karn." Hamare looked up. "Besides, he was among friends. One of them sent me word."

"What happened?" Litasse didn't want to think of Karn being dead. Hearing that nameless, faceless militiamen had died in Draximal was one thing. Knowing that hapless peasants had been burned out of their homes was distressing but a regrettable part of life. Karn was someone she had known, someone she had talked to.

"There's a woman called Ridianne who keeps a leash on some mercenary companies for Duke Ferdain of Marlier," Hamare began.

Litasse nodded. "I know all about that scandal."

Hamare waved the irrelevance aside. "Karn was asking questions there. He disappeared in the night."

"Couldn't he simply have left?" Litasse wondered.

"Not without taking leave of Ridianne." Hamare sighed. "And if he did slip away, he'd make sure no one called attention to his absence by asking awkward questions. Besides, this friend of Karn's found fresh blood on the grass the next morning, in a hollow by the river."

"I'm so sorry." Litasse knotted her fingers. The hollowness in Hamare's eyes was a painful reminder of the horror of learning her brother Jaras was dead.

"Ridianne turned the camp upside down. They couldn't find anyone with fresh wounds to explain the blood. All had—" Hamare glanced down at the letter again, eyes hooded. "She did discover that Karn had beaten off an attack by some ruffians earlier in the day. We can only suppose they caught up with him in the darkness." He screwed the letter up in sudden fury. "What a stupid, pointless waste of his life!"

"I'll have to tell Valesti," Litasse realised suddenly. "But he had no family, surely?" Did that make it better or worse?

Hamare gazed towards the window, eyes unseeing. "All his family were killed when he was a child. He told me about it once. A great swathe of Marlier and Carluse was laid waste over one summer. All the crops had been burned, all the cattle stolen or killed. There was famine in the autumn and some desperate men decided their wives and children would fare better enslaved or in the Otherworld instead of starving through the winter. Karn said they drove the women and children into a camp full of drunken mercenaries and then started attacking the swordsmen with their cudgels and axes. Karn said he saw his father force his mother onto a mercenary's blade, to be certain she died before him. He doesn't recall anything after that, until he woke in the night in a ditch full of corpses."

"That cannot be true." Litasse recoiled from such a tale.

"Karn wouldn't disappear without telling me what he'd learned. And if someone's had him killed, there's definitely something to be learned." Hamare was scowling, though not at Litasse. "In Vanam, as likely as not."

"You still believe there's something in this tale of an exiles' brigade gathering?" Litasse looked doubtfully at him.

"If not in Vanam, somewhere," Hamare said savagely.

"What could a few bands of hired swords do?" Litasse protested.

"How much better do you think these exiles would fare," Hamare challenged her, "if their bold youths were led by real swordsmen?" His expression darkened further. "I want to know what part Lady Alaric has played in all this. Karn wasn't sure he trusted her. And Pelletria tells me there's fresh rumour that Duke Garnot's doxy has been seen in Carluse."

"What in the name of Poldrion's stinking demons is going on?" Duke Iruvain threw the door open so hard it crashed against the wall. "Hamare?" Irate, he strode up to the table and swept a sheaf of papers to the floor with an angry hand. "You spend all my silver gathering this stable litter? You don't know that there are wizards in Draximal?"

Litasse froze in her chair as the spymaster shouted back, frustrated.

"There's only so much I can discover. Some secrets are kept from everyone." Hamare rose to his feet. "And who's to say this is even true!"

"The men who whipped their horses half to death to bring me the news that Emirle Bridge has burned to its foundations," Iruvain bellowed back. "That the woods along Draximal's border with Parnilesse are ablaze. Every vassal lord along our eastern border tells me he's overrun with clamouring peasants who've risked drowning in the Anock and taking a beating from our militias rather than face magefire burning the roofs over their heads!"

"All of which is as much an unwelcome surprise to Duke Secaris of Draximal and Duke Orlin of Parnilesse," Hamare retorted. "Their private letters are as full of confusion and outrage as any you've had from your vassal lords." He brandished a handful. "They're promising vast rewards for anyone who can bring them the truth of what went on."

"You expect them to admit their own guilt?" Iruvain threw up his hands. "Defying all honour, custom and the Archmage besides?"

Litasse spoke up. "I've had letters from the duchesses of both Draximal and Parnilesse, my lord. They're pleading their innocence, begging me to believe them."

"Which only proves Duke Secaris has enough sense to keep his mouth shut inside his bed curtains." Iruvain waved her away impatiently. "Along with Duke Orlin. Hamare, who's responsible for this outrage?"

"Neither duke." He had no doubt. "Neither would have acted without a plan to follow up such a bold move. Neither would risk every other dukedom uniting against him, with the blessing of Tormalin's Emperor and Caladhria's barons." Hamare threw the letters down. "What do we see? No moves by Draximal or Parnilesse. No mercenaries erupting from ambush, no militias thrown into the fray. Neither side has done anything but panic as chaos burns along their border."

"They've done nothing that *you* know of," spat Iruvain.

"If there was anything to know, I would have learned it." Hamare was adamant.

"You didn't know one of them was suborning a wizard," Iruvain shouted.

Hamare shook his head. "We don't even know that wizardry was worked."

Iruvain stared at him. "Woods and fields and houses burned for a night and a day, with scarlet fire that couldn't be quenched."

Hamare shrugged. "The Aldabreshi have sticky fire and Misaen only knows what other foul alchemies. One of their warlords visited Emperor Tadriol not so long ago, not for the first time. Who knows what knowledge came north with him?"

Iruvain looked contemptuously at the spymaster. "Do you have the least shred of evidence to suggest an Aldabreshin alchemist has set foot in Draximal or Parnilesse?"

"No, Your Grace, I do not," Hamare said steadily. "Just as I have no shred of evidence that either Duke Secaris or Duke Orlin has attempted to suborn a wizard. Believe me, Your Grace, I would know about that. I make it my business to keep a very close eye on any mage who might be bought or coerced."

Iruvain narrowed his eyes. "Why would you do that?"

"Because there are persistent rumours that barons along the Caladhrian coast are seeking magic to defend them against the corsairs raiding up from the northernmost domains of the Aldabreshin Archipelago." Hamare's voice was determinedly reasonable. "They have made repeated representations to the Archmage and to the Council of Hadrumal. Since the Aldabreshi murder any wizard they capture, they argue these corsairs are just as much Hadrumal's foes. Rumour has it some mages in Hadrumal and a few of those living on the mainland agree. One might be persuaded to act, for the right price."

As far as Litasse could discern, Hamare was telling the truth. He wasn't telling the whole truth, though. Couldn't Iruvain see that?

"Rumour." Iruvain's lip curled. "You spend your days mired so deep in suspicion and supposition that you cannot see what's in plain sight. Draximal and Parnilesse have gone to war!"

"A war that neither side has prepared for! At the very turn of Aft-Summer into For-Autumn? When we could be only half a season from weather that will put an end to all campaigning? At very best, they'll be bogged down by the end of Aft-Autumn." Hamare shook his head, obdurate. "When fighting will outrage the Tormalin Emperor, after both these noble dukes have been so desperate to placate him?"

"Then what is going on?" demanded Iruvain, infuriated.

"Have you never seen a festival trickster pretend a rune bone has vanished from his closed fist only to reappear behind someone's ear?" Hamare bent to retrieve the papers the duke had swept from the table. "Someone wants us looking the other way."

"Who?" Iruvain stared down at him.

"Caladhrians have been selling their harvests for fat profits to Vanam merchants, but there's no sign of that grain reaching their markets." Hamare searched among the papers on the table and found another letter. "Someone has been buying up quantities of cloth and canvas and leather but no one knows where the goods have been shipped. Someone's been quietly making ready for war."

"Draximal or Parnilesse," Iruvain retorted.

"No, Your Grace," Hamare said swiftly. "Vanam."

"Vanam?" Iruvain's incredulity warred with anger. "This again?"

"Let him speak, my lord," Litasse said, irritated.

Hamare slid her a warning glance before continuing. "Every thread I pull on leads back there. Even muckraking rabble-rousers have been printing their lies in

Vanam. Accusing Duke Secaris of suborning wizardry. Condemning Duke Orlin for bringing magecraft into Lescar." Hamare held out a crudely printed leaf, then another and another. "I have others fanning the flames of panic with identical tales of supposed atrocities on both sides of the border. I know the style of old. They're all written by a man called Reniack, who's made it his life's work to attack Duke Orlin in pamphlets carried along the high roads and round the taverns by ballad singers and beggars. He was last heard of in Vanam."

Iruvain thumped the table with a clenched fist. "What's your point?"

Hamare threw the papers down. "Now Reniack's condemning all the dukes of Lescar. Declaring that the common folk have suffered so much for so long, for the sake of noble quarrels they have no part in, that their noble lords have forfeited all right to their fealty. Saying bringing magic into battle is the final treachery that cannot be forgiven. He knows what's going on. He knew what was going to happen. All these slanders were printed and ready, Your Grace. They were being shared around the alehouses and the market squares of both Draximal and Parnilesse inside a day of this so-called wizardry."

Hamare reached for a dog-eared missive, a narrow slip of paper curled around the fragment of its seal. "The same treachery is surfacing in Carluse. Guildmasters are no longer content merely to help the common folk send their sons and daughters away in secret. Now they're saying no duke can be trusted. That Duke Garnot would have been the first to use magic if he thought he could get away with it. They're saying so in the very same words that this man

Reniack is using in Parnilesse. The selfsame contagion is spreading in Marlier and Sharlac."

"What did you say?" Iruvain stared at him. "About the guildmasters of Carluse?"

Hamare set his jaw. "There have been rumours, for some years now, of disaffection within Carluse. You've heard the tales of these mysterious Woodsmen."

"I've heard Duke Garnot laugh at them," Iruvain asserted.

"I suspect these tales are deliberately spread to cover the truth." Litasse saw that Hamare's calm tone was costing him visible effort. "The truth being a conspiracy among Carluse's priests and guildsmen to send youths and maidens away to family and friends beyond Lescar's borders. They tell the duke's reeves they have died or married away. I also suspect some priests hide coin in their shrines when Duke Garnot sends his mercenaries collecting levies."

"You knew such treachery was undermining one of Triolle's allies and you said nothing?" Iruvain said slowly.

"I cannot burden you with every rumour, Your Grace, not until I have satisfied myself as to the truth of them." Hamare's attempt at humility was unconvincing.

"Satisfied yourself?" Iruvain's voice was cold. "You take too much on yourself, Master Hamare."

Litasse shifted in her chair. "Carluse is no friend to Triolle."

"I say who our friends are!" Iruvain rounded on her. "And you are Triolle's duchess. I'll thank you to remember that!"

"Duke Garnot's missing whore is niece to a priest deeply implicated in these plots, Your Grace," Hamare said loudly. "She fled to Vanam where she had dealings with this agitator Reniack. Where rumours persist that a band of exiles is preparing to raise arms against Lescar."

"Rumour?" Furious, Iruvain threw an inkwell at Hamare. "Is rumour burning the far banks of the Anock? If you continue to waste my time with this nonsense of Vanam, I'll have you whipped to your senses!"

"My lord!" Litasse sprang to her feet.

He glared at her. "What are you doing here, my lady wife?"

She stiffened as she saw his anger cool to be replaced with sharp curiosity.

"I'm looking for some truth amid all this frenzy, just like you," Litasse said with asperity. She kept her eyes fixed on Iruvain, not daring to look at Hamare. "I have had as many hysterical letters from our vassals' ladies as you've had from their lords, my husband."

Out of the corner of her eye, she could see Hamare, black ink splashed across his face and the white collar of his shirt.

"It's a shame our vaunted intelligencer has lost his way so completely amid this blizzard of paper." Iruvain's scowl dared Hamare to speak. "But his failings are my concern, not yours." He gestured towards the door, his face hard. "Calm your servants, my lady, and forbid all foolish gossip until we really know what's going on in Draximal!"

What did he expect her to do? Stand over every scullion up to his elbows in greasy water? Follow every chambermaid around the castle to make sure they didn't speculate over their dusting? But Litasse had never seen Iruvain so furious. She nodded a prudent farewell. "Of course, my lord husband. Master Hamare, good day to you."

A bruise was darkening his cheek where the inkwell had struck him. He didn't smile but his eyes warmed to her. "My lady."

Iruvain didn't even do her the courtesy of opening the door before he turned on Hamare again. "Show me everything you have had from Draximal and Parnilesse in the past three days."

Litasse opened the door for herself and went out. She would have stopped on the far side, stooping to listen at the keyhole if need be—could Iruvain have been serious when he'd threatened Hamare with flogging? But two men from Iruvain's personal guard stood outside, imperfectly concealing their curiosity. What had they overheard?

"Your Grace." One of them bowed.

Was she imagining the insolence in his face? "Good morning."

"My lady." Valesti was waiting by the stairs, keeping her distance from Iruvain's attendants. Litasse could see she was as keen as the swordsmen to know what Hamare had said.

"We have letters to write." Litasse hurried down the stairs. "Send word to the stables to have couriers ready."

If Iruvain wouldn't listen to Hamare, she would at least do the spymaster the courtesy of taking his arguments seriously. Whatever was afoot, he had convinced her that this strife in Draximal was only part of some wider threat. Was there something going on in Vanam? She was inclined to think so now. If Iruvain wanted proof, she would do all she could to obtain it. She knew vassals whose ladies had cross-border ties that strained their loyalties. She knew which ones quietly traded with the furthest-reaching merchants. If they couldn't tell her what she needed to know, they might well know who else to ask.

It was only a pity that Duke Garnot of Carluse seemed to be as much a victim in all this as Duke Secaris of Draximal or Duke Orlin of Parnilesse. But that still didn't mean Duke Garnot wasn't the villain she knew him to be.

"What did Master Hamare say, Your Grace?" Valesti followed so close that she trod on Litasse's silken hem.

"Nothing of consequence." Litasse didn't dare look at her, in case the maidservant read the lie in her eyes.

She would tell her later. Whatever there had been between Karn and Valesti was done, wasn't it? She couldn't afford the delay the foolish woman's tears might cost her. It would be best to get her letters on the road before Iruvain finished berating the spymaster. What His Grace her husband didn't know about need not concern him.

Chapter Twenty-Eight

Aremil

**Beacon Lane, in Vanam's Upper Town,
4th of For-Autumn**

How soon would early risers find the mornings starting to darken? For-Autumn would quickly see night's bells encroaching on servants' duties. Though at least it was a long half-season this year—forty-eight days.

Aremil carefully unlatched the shutters. The waning Greater Moon and the last shaving of the Lesser Moon were still visible in the pearlescent sky. He smiled as he recalled Tathrin's frustration with the vagaries of the calendar. Given that the Solstices and the Equinoxes marked fixed points in the year, why couldn't the intervals between them be divided equally as well? Why did the turn from winter to spring or summer to autumn have to be decided by the erratic phases of the two inconveniently synchronised moons?

Aremil's face turned solemn again. What could they possibly achieve in forty-eight days? Did Captain-General Evord plan on fighting right through the Equinox and the Autumn Festival? How long would the weather stay fine into Aft-Autumn? Fine enough for warfare? It was almost enough to persuade him to nail a prayer to the door of Dastennin's shrine. Or should he beseech Talagrin's favour? Why bother, when he had scant faith in any god or goddess?

He folded the wooden panels into the sides of the window embrasure and looked at the silent street. Those who could sleep would still be in their beds as the echoes of the darkness's final hour floated over the rooftops. Those who weren't setting out on a journey so urgent that every daylight hour must be spent on the road today.

He heard cautious footsteps on the stairs.

"I'm in here," he said quietly. It wouldn't do to wake Lyrlen.

"You're awake?" Branca entered the sitting room. She wore a plain green gown and a grey travelling cloak hung over one arm.

Aremil smiled crookedly. "I wanted to say good-bye."

"You couldn't sleep?" Branca looked at him.

He hesitated. "That too."

Every time he'd closed his eyes, he'd pictured the bodies Tathrin had tripped over on his nightmarish flight through the panicked town. He'd felt Tathrin's disgust at the jovial unconcern of Sorgrad and Gren when they'd caught up with Arest. Regrouping, making only a perfunctory count of the men who had died, the mercenaries had laughed as they'd drunk themselves foolish on purloined spirits, all the while mocking the peasants they'd so easily terrified. Only Tathrin and the newcomer, Reher, had stood silently apart, seeing no cause for celebration.

More disquieting still, Aremil knew he had only seen that chaotic night through Tathrin's subdued recollections. How much worse had it really been? How far had mage-kindled fires spread through the parched trees and fields? As Tathrin and Sorgrad had waited for Gren and Reher to rejoin them, the skies on the far side of the river had been black with smoke.

Branca pursed her lips. "I'll make us both a tisane."

"That would be welcome," Aremil admitted. Getting himself out of his bed in the back room was one thing. Dressing himself was quite another. With the hottest summer nights now past, the dawn was none too warm.

As he tucked his chilled feet under the hem of his chamber robe, he heard Branca stealthily filling the kettle. The scrape of the grate told him she was rousing the slumbering fire with a scatter of fresh coal. Aremil tensed. Thankfully, there was no sound of Lyrlen rousing.

Branca came back, pushing the door closed. "Being able to share Tathrin's thoughts over so many hundreds of leagues is all very well until he encounters something we'd rather not know about."

"I may not wish to know about such slaughter but I need to," Aremil said sombrely. "If I'm to answer for what we're starting."

"Answer to whom?" Branca cocked her head. "Saedrin?"

Aremil had learned that she had less faith in gods or goddesses than he did. "To the folk of Lescar. There'll be an accounting, some day."

"True enough." She sighed. "These deaths in Draximal, are they the first stones heralding the landslide?"

"That all depends on this Soluran captain-general." Aremil didn't hide his frustration. "And how soon he can raise this army that Sorgrad keeps promising us."

"Charoleia is still confident," Branca said thoughtfully. "Failla and Lady Derenna have prepared the ground to good effect if their letters are to be believed. Duke Garnot of Carluse and Duke Moncan of Sharlac will find it hard to rouse their militias to oppose Evord and his men."

"Difficult, but not impossible." Aremil felt his throat tighten. "You must be careful, you and Lady Derenna. Failla says Duke Garnot has his mercenaries beating the bushes to flush out these mysterious Woodsmen."

"Sharlac will be a safer place than Carluse or Parnilesse," Branca said firmly. "Duke Moncan is still closeted inside his castle walls while Duke Orlin is chasing rumours of Draximal invasions here, there and everywhere."

"I wish we knew what Reniack was up to," Aremil said with feeling.

"You'll find out as soon as Jettin catches up with him—" Branca broke off as if to listen for something again. She shook her head. "Besides, his broadsheets turn up here soon enough. You've read them. Why do you suspect he's doing anything more than convincing folk it was Duke Orlin of Parnilesse who sent some renegade mage against Draximal and vice versa?" She sprang to her feet. "The kettle!"

As she hurried to the kitchen to stifle the rising note, Aremil looked at the brightening sky. He had no reason to mistrust Reniack, nothing that he could put his finger on, anyway. Perhaps it was just because the man was someone he didn't know, so far away, his letters so infrequent. Still, Branca was right. They'd know what the rabble-rouser was up to once Jettin joined him.

There was no denying that Reniack's lies were convincing. Judging by the gossip among the wagoners that Gruit reported and the rumours Charoleia was hearing, all the eastern Lescari, from dukes to dungshovellers, feared that their foes had wizardry to call on.

So it shouldn't occur to anyone that aetheric magic was at work in their lands. Branca should stay all the safer, her and the other Artificers, and all the other conspirators. As long as Branca stayed well away from any fighting. He looked down at his hands, so weak and useless.

"You'll find you fare better with aetheric enchantments if you can set certain things aside."

Aremil looked up as Branca re-entered the room carrying two tisane glasses. "What do you mean?"

"Your father," she said with uncharacteristic hesitation as she set the glasses down on the table. "He's Duke Secaris of Draximal."

Aremil swallowed hard. "Lyrlen told you?"

"Hardly." Sitting on the brocaded settle, Branca's scorn was momentary. "I saw him in your memories," she explained apologetically.

"I see." Aremil immediately regretted the coldness in his tone.

"I didn't go looking," Branca retorted with more of her customary spirit. "I can't help feeling what's colouring your thoughts. Especially when it's stifling your Artifice."

Aremil reminded himself fiercely that Tathrin had been feeling echoes of his emotions, and his friend hadn't had the least training in Artifice.

"Forgive me," he said stiffly. "I know you'd never deliberately intrude."

But what exactly had Branca learned from his unguarded thoughts? When he didn't know himself where his feelings for her were leading, beyond the admiration and affection he could no longer deny.

More to the point, was she right about what was limiting his Artifice? When he was going to be the only link between Vanam and those braving the dangers in Lescar? He couldn't bear the prospect of proving unequal to playing his part.

"What exactly must I set aside?" he asked curtly.

"You're worried that your birth will somehow be betrayed. You're afraid that people will think you're raising a revolt just to get revenge on your father." Branca's face was sympathetic. "You're worried that they might be right, because you do resent him and all the decisions he has made that have governed your life for so long. On the other hand, you know full well you should be grateful for comfort that so few people with your afflictions will ever know. Few of those sound in mind and limb are granted a life of such privilege, come to that. And you should be grateful," she said frankly.

He waited a moment until he could be certain he had control of his voice. "I am."

Branca shrugged. "So acknowledge there's no reconciling your gratitude and your resentment and stop struggling with such an impossible task. I've told you that the best practitioners of aetheric magic are the most dispassionate. You've already shown your talent for rising above petty distractions, so I know you can do it."

"I'll do my best." Aremil cleared his throat. "I keep sensing what Tathrin feels when I reach through the aether to him and I know he hears some echo of my thoughts. But I never know what you're thinking. Why is that?"

"Practice." She sipped her tisane and winced at the heat. "The ability to guard your thoughts will come the more you hone your skills. You should be grateful that you feel things so passionately," she continued reflectively.

Aremil was puzzled. "Even though you say the best Artificers can deny their emotions?"

"At one and the same time, the best Artificers are those for whom commitment to their craft becomes an all-consuming desire." She smiled ruefully. "Another conflict that pulls us this way and that until we can find the balance point and thus improve our skills."

Aremil shook his head. "I can't be grateful for emotions that are holding me back at the worst possible time."

"Well, I wouldn't be going to Lescar at all if you didn't believe in your cause so fervently." Branca blew on her tisane to cool the cloudy red liquid. "I've no doubt some people will misunderstand your motives when everything's out in the open. Some will accuse you out of spite or just to secure their own advantage. But you know the truth and so do I."

Aremil swallowed. "Since when?"

"Since that day in the physic garden." The faint spark of mischief in her eyes warmed him.

"I've been wondering about that," he said with a crooked smile. "Since you told me that tale of ancient kings locking Artificers away, to lie in cold dungeons surrounded by their own filth so that discomfort crippled their ability to work enchantments. Presumably taking a cripple out into the hot sun and making him struggle along on his crutches made it all the easier for you to see my motives?"

"I did tell you I wanted to know your intentions." She was unabashed. "I didn't go looking for secrets, though. I just read what was there to be seen most clearly. Be thankful that I did."

"I'm thankful for more than that," Aremil said unguardedly.

"As am I." Branca finished her tisane with a swift gulp and took up the other glass. "This is cool enough for you now."

"Thank you." Aremil was past worrying that Branca would spill food or drink on him. As she held the glass to his lips, he sipped the steaming water. The welcome warmth of steeping ginger and honey-soaked spice-berries eased some of the tension wracking him.

"When do you think Master Gruit's coach will be here?" he wondered aloud.

Whenever it came would be too soon for him. He didn't want to see Branca leave.

"Jettin's no early bird," Branca commented, "but Kerith was staying at his lodgings last night and he's always a prompt riser."

"Indeed?" Aremil couldn't help wondering how Branca came to know so much about either man's demeanour first thing in the morning.

He'd better put that aside, lest it hamper his Artifice or betray his small-mindedness to Branca. Petty jealousy of men who'd known her before he had, who'd shared in the rediscovery of aetheric magic, was pointless. It was ungrateful, too, when Jettin and Kerith were about to risk Talagrin only knew what dangers for the sake of their common Lescari blood.

"Enough?" As Aremil nodded, Branca took the glass away. "Can you sell some books for me while I'm away?"

"Sell them?" Aremil was bemused.

"We can't all afford to keep bookbinders' and joiners' wives in velvet." She nodded at his crowded bookcases with a teasing smile. "I brought a list of the ones I can do without. I'll leave you my keys and you can send one of Master Gruit's apprentices to fetch them. That'll clear a shelf in my lodging for the titles I need next, so that we can continue our studies when I get back." She put the glass down and searched her cloak for an inner pocket.

"I'll have them ready," Aremil assured her.

Branca paused, her hand hidden in the folds of material. "Bought with the coin earned by selling the others."

"Naturally." Aremil didn't need Artifice to know that Branca loathed being indebted or obligated to anyone. He wondered if that had hindered her studies in aetheric magic. Had some mentor at the university told her to set such things aside?

He turned to the side table beside him. "I have something for you." He held out a small linen-wrapped package, fighting to stop his hands shaking.

"What is it?" Branca took it and teased the knotted cord undone. The undyed cloth slid away to reveal a gleaming silver oblong.

"You'll need a memorandum case as you travel," Aremil ventured. "I asked Charoleia where I might find one like hers."

"It's lovely." Branca turned it this way and that. She looked at him, more bright-eyed than he'd expected. "Did you choose it yourself?"

"I did." Aremil had thought the engraving of the goddess Arrimelin weaving dreams in her bower was charming.

"That'll make it all the easier for you to picture it." Branca busied herself folding up the linen square. "When you're sending your thoughts to find me."

"Indeed." Aremil knew he'd be able to fix his thoughts on Branca regardless.

As she tucked the silver case into the pocket in the seam of her skirt, they both heard wheels growling on the street outside.

"Here's Master Gruit's coach." Aremil tried to sound brisk.

Branca donned her cloak. She found the list she'd been looking for and set it down on the table, weighting it with a key knotted on a medallion's chain. "Keep these for me. I've told my landlord I'm away attending family matters. Tell whoever you send to collect the books to show him my father's guild insignia." She managed a faint smile. "Then he won't send for the Watch and have the lad arrested for housebreaking."

"Of course." Aremil nodded. "Now, quickly, hurry."

Her books could stay where they were. He'd sent Lyrlen to the booksellers' by Misaen's shrine to ask what they would charge for the tomes Branca wanted to sell. Then he'd buy them himself at whatever outrageous price those scoundrels thought they could demand from an unworldly old woman. Master Gruit could take that purse and bargain his hardest for the titles Branca wanted to buy. Aremil would assure him that such knowledge was essential for the success of their whole enterprise.

The doorbell rang.

"Where are your crutches?" Branca looked around.

"I'll say my farewells to you here." Aremil shrank from appearing before the other Artificers in his night-clothes.

"I'm coming, I'm coming."

They both looked up as Lyrlen's bedchamber door opened. An impatient hand rattled the door knocker.

"I'm coming!" the old woman called irritably down the stairs.

Branca drew a deep breath. "I had better go."

"Be careful." Aremil felt anxiety twisting his face.

"I will." She stooped and kissed his sunken cheek.

Their eyes met and Aremil saw that her uncertainty equalled his own, and not just about this journey.

Straightening up, she busied herself with her cloak ties. "Take good care of yourself."

"Lyrlen sees to that." Aremil tried to make a joke of it.

Branca bit her lip. "We'll talk about that, when I get back."

Before Aremil could ask what she meant, she hurried from the room. He heard Lyrlen in the hall, the two women talking over each other as the door was unbolted. A man's voice out in the road was incomprehensible, overlaid with the stamp of horses' hooves.

Aremil grabbed his crutches and heaved himself out of his chair. He reached the window just in time to see Branca climbing inside the coach. Master Gruit's lackey was strapping her travelling chest to the already laden roof.

A draught shivered through a sheaf of papers on the sill as the front door slammed.

"That's that," Lyrlen said with satisfaction. She entered the sitting room and her mouth fell open in astonishment. "My lord?"

Aremil expected her to chastise him for presuming to get out of bed without her help, not to see such hurt in her expression.

"I couldn't sleep," he said apologetically.

"Do you need me to send for the doctor?" she asked anxiously. She took his hands between her own. "Oh, you're so cold!"

"There's nothing amiss," Aremil assured her. "I just wanted to see Branca safely on the road."

"Best I mix some poppy tincture in a little wine," Lyrlen said tartly. "You can go back to bed for a few hours."

"I may as well start the day early." Aremil tried not to rebuke her. "Then I'll sleep all the better tonight."

He wasn't going to take any apothecaries' concoctions to blunt his Artifice when he needed to be able to reach through the aether to Branca.

"Very well." Lyrlen rallied. "Do you want to wash and dress, or breakfast first?"

Aremil saw her look around the room. As the tisane glasses caught her eye, her lips thinned.

"I was cold," he said firmly. "Branca was merely doing me a service."

"And herself." Lyrlen sniffed.

"Surely we don't begrudge our guests a glass of warm water," Aremil said more curtly than he intended.

Lyrlen looked at him, and this time Aremil saw something like fear in her faded eyes.

"There's bread in the crock and preserves laid ready. I told her last night but the girl's always so brusque. If you'd wanted me to get up and see her fed, my lord—"

"No, don't worry." Of course Branca would have had something to eat in the kitchen if she'd wanted it. "Yes, please, I'll take my breakfast before I dress. Then I have some errands for you to run."

"As you wish, my lord." Looking happier, Lyrlen slid her arm under his own to help him back to his chair. Once he was seated, she tucked his robe warmly around his knees before catching up the offending glasses. "I'll make you some porridge, with a little honey, my lord. That'll set you up nicely for the day."

Aremil had been about to ask for bread and jam. He could eat that without assistance, albeit messily. If Lyrlen made porridge, she would insist on feeding him. He hid his irritation.

"Thank you. That will be lovely."

He hadn't liked to see the fear in her old, loyal face, though. If cosseting him would reassure her, he could put up with it. For the present.

Chapter Twenty-Nine

Failla

**The Leather Bottle Inn, on the Dromin Road,
in the Lescari Dukedom of Carluse,
24th of For-Autumn**

She leaned back and closed her eyes. Stretching out her legs, her mud-spattered skirts hung heavy around her booted ankles. The settle in the parlour was unpadded, high-backed and narrow-seated. She didn't care. Her head ached with tension aggravated by every thud and shout from the bustling courtyard outside.

"I've paid for this parlour and the two bedrooms up above." Nath kicked the door closed and dropped their bags. "I don't think that woman believes we're map-makers," he observed, lighting the half-burned candles on the mantel with a taper he'd been given. "Or brother and sister, come to that."

Failla opened her eyes and glared at him. "So leave the door ajar so no one can imagine scandal."

"If we don't want to be fodder for local tittle-tattle, why stop at an inn at all?" Nath demanded, as if they hadn't already had this dispute on horseback. "Or spend good coin on rooms we'll be abandoning at midnight? We can't leave it any later and still hope to meet this Artificer at first light. Won't riding out with the rising moons give the gossips hereabouts something juicy to chew on?"

"Duke Garnot has his dogs hunting for Woodsmen on the byways, not the high roads. An inn this busy sees people coming and going at all hours. No one will notice us." Failla was counting on it. She closed her eyes again so she wouldn't have to look at Nath as she lied to him. "There's no need for us both to go to this shrine. You meet this man Kerith and bring him back here. I have those letters to read and answer and Drianon's mercy, I'm tired and I'm filthy. I want a bath and some sleep in a real bed," she said petulantly.

"You don't think I'd like the chance to brush the muck off my clothes?" Nath snapped. "Or to wash? I smell worse than my horse!"

It was unlike Nath to lose his temper. Failla hid her alarm. "Forgive me, I know you're tired, too. You and this traveller should both come here to rest, before we go onwards."

Nath was untouched by her apparent concern. He carried a candle over to the parlour's indifferently polished table and dropped heavily into one of the wooden chairs. "Are any of those letters that saddler gave you for me?"

"I think so." Business was as good a way to distract him as any other. Failla sat up to find she had stiffened even in those few minutes sitting down. She grimaced as she bent to unbuckle her travelling bag. "Could we have some wine?"

"We can ask." Nath wearily rattled the brass bell standing on the table.

Failla sorted through the letters passed to them by the guildmasters' most recent courier. Uncle Ernout's friends hadn't let them down yet. "This is Sorgrad's writing."

Nath flexed his grimy hands, rubbing them on his breeches. "Where are they?" he wondered with savage exasperation. "Halfway through For-Autumn and there's no sign of them coming down from the hills."

"Hush." Failla tossed the letter to him and went to the door, just in case there was anyone in the passage to overhear. There wasn't. "Maybe that letter tells us."

"This is cracked." Nath was studying the wax seal closely.

Alarmed, Failla went to see. "Has it been opened?"

"No, just roughly handled." Nath ripped it open, infuriated. "How many days have we lost, waiting for news to pass from hand to hand like this? There's no chance this side of the Otherworld that I'll be home for Equinox."

Nath spoke of his family often enough and Failla was glad of it. Devotion to his absent wife meant he'd never once looked at her with speculative eyes. She only hoped homesickness was the reason for his uncharacteristic ill-temper.

"Everything will move more quickly once this Kerith joins us. We'll be able to get word to and from Vanam much faster." She examined her own letters. "There's no sign that any of these have been interfered with." Snapping the wax seal, she unfolded the first one.

"Is there anything I should know?" Nath asked sourly. "Or anything you're allowed to tell me?"

"I don't like keeping secrets, but my uncle won't have it any other way." She looked at him with carefully judged anxiety. With luck he would think all her secrets were concerned with safeguarding the guildmasters and their fellow conspirators. "You've seen how keen Duke Garnot is to run the Woodsmen to earth."

Nath stared at his letter. "I hope this Kerith can tell us why. Do you suppose Charoleia knows what's stuck a burr under Duke Garnot's saddle?"

"I hope so." Failla said honestly. Travelling through Marlier to distribute Reniack's broadsheets had been nerve-wracking enough, where no one knew her beyond a few of Duke Ferdain's servants. Back in Carluse, with Wynald's Warband riding the roads in search of unknown rebels, she was as tense as an overwound harp string. But she and Nath had found so many willing ears for their message. She could almost believe this crack-brained plot stood half a chance of success.

She hid her other concerns. If this Artificer's enchantments could see into someone's thoughts, would he use them on her? Better not arouse his suspicions and give him cause to try. Which only left her with tonight. As long as Nath agreed to ride on alone, curse him. How would she persuade him in his current mood?

An elderly woman in a worn black dress looked round the open door. "I heard the bell. Can I help you, Master? My lady?"

"A jug of wine and two goblets, if you please." Nath's voice was still harsh with strain.

"Of course." The woman bobbed a half-curtsey, an amiable smile on her hook-nosed face.

Failla saw her keen eyes taking in their baggage, the letters on the table and their travel-stained clothes. Inn servants were always nosy. Hopefully hearing her and Nath squabbling should convince the old crone that they were indeed brother and sister.

She returned to her letters. Unravelling the Ashgil glover's circumlocutions wasn't easy. Finally she was satisfied that he'd done his best to persuade his fellow craftsmen that standing aloof would be their safest course if, by some unimagined chance, warfare returned to Carluse.

"You wanted wine?" A different maid, neatly aproned, soon appeared with a tray.

"Yes, thank you." Nath raked his fingers through his tangled hair. "Draw the curtains and close the door, if you please."

Failla didn't look up, opening her next letter with her belt knife. All the better to convince the servant there was nothing lover-like between them.

The maid poured some wine and pocketed the coin Nath gave her, the latch clicking behind her.

He sprang to his feet. "They want maps of Sharlac as soon as possible." Kneeling by their baggage, he unstrapped his writing case. "As many as we can draw up. And everything we can tell them about the state of the roads in Carluse, and Marlier after that."

"Why?" Failla's fingers tightened, creasing the letter.

"Why do you think? It's finally starting." Nash leafed through some parchments. "Let's see what we can do to bring it to a swift conclusion. I surveyed a good deal of Sharlac last year." He quickly set pens, inkwells and paper on the table. "Let's hope nothing much has changed."

Failla moved the wine jug. "Where are they, Sorgrad and Gren? And Tathrin?"

She would so much rather be travelling with him, even at the price of the Mountain Men's escort. She stifled fleeting recollections of their walks in Vanam, their easy conversation about places and people they both knew.

"We meet them the day after next." Nath emptied his goblet with a single swallow. "Six leagues out of Abray on the Great West Road at a tavern called the Pipe and Chime."

"I don't know it." Failla could only hope that meant no one would know her.

"We can spend this evening making fair copies until we have to leave to meet Kerith." Nath unscrewed his metal flask of ink and carefully filled the wells. "Then we can cut along the forest road from the shrine to reach the highway."

Failla had long since learned to tell when a man wasn't about to be gainsaid. "Very well."

"You take the main highway maps." He began trimming a quill. "The byways are more complicated, so I'll do those."

Failla reluctantly took a sheet of paper and chose a pen. How could she get away from Nath now? As she drew careful lines, she thought furiously.

They worked in silence until the third chimes struck. Nath scowled as he saw how few sheets she'd copied. "Can you work any faster?"

"Not if you don't want them blotted." Failla continued working, her hand steady. She still saw no solution to her own problem, though.

Nath bent over his own work. "I could do with some supper."

"I'll see what the kitchen can offer." Failla set down her pen with a snap.

She found the kitchens at the rear of the long building. The older woman who'd answered their bell was nowhere to be seen but the aproned maid was talking to a cook kneading dough.

"My lady?"

Failla smiled ruefully. "My brother has just had word of an urgent order for our maps. Could you serve us some food in our parlour while we work?"

The cook paused in her kneading. "There's breast of veal with a green sauce and batter puddings. With apricot pies and crayfishes?"

"That will be lovely, thank you."

Failla walked slowly back to the parlour. Nath didn't look up, intent on tracing a fine line. Failla took up her pen again and, still working as slowly as she dared, waited to hear footsteps outside the door. Making sure Nath couldn't see her face, she reluctantly unlocked her most painful memory. Tears slowly filled her eyes.

As she heard the maid approaching, she swept up the sheets of paper. "Here's our supper." Tipping an inkwell so that the black tide only flooded her own work wasn't easy but she managed.

"Drianon's tits!" Nath sprang up, clutching his painstaking copies.

"I'm so sorry." Deftly catching the sliding ink on the topmost sheet, Failla let the brimming tears spill down her cheeks.

"Master?" The aproned maid opened the door, another carrying a laden tray behind her. "Your supper?"

"What? Yes, thank you. Just put it down over there." Nath managed curt politeness but his face was burning with anger.

Failla took her chance to drop the ink-stained pages into the sooty hearth and huddled on the settle, her face in her hands. The maids left the food and made a hasty exit.

When Nath stopped swearing, Failla looked cautiously through her fingers. He was sorting through his own copies, checking to see if any of them were ruined.

"It's not as bad as it might have been," he said with a visible effort.

"I'll start again. I can work all night." Failla wiped tears from her cheeks with trembling hands. "If you meet this man Kerith and bring him back here."

"I suppose so." Nath sat down, leaning heavily on his elbows, his head hanging.

"If you're going to be riding all night, why don't you get some sleep first?" Failla hoped she sounded as if she'd just had the idea. "I can finish my copying and yours, too. Then I can sleep while you're on your way back. We'll both feel better."

Nath looked too weary to suspect anything. "I suppose so."

"Have something to eat," Failla urged.

Without waiting for his answer, she served them both. Despite her hunger she took only a small portion to maintain her pretence of distress. As they ate, she kept Nath's goblet topped up with the vinegary wine. Their long day's travel and the food and the drink soon had him yawning.

"I had better get some rest," he allowed, "or I'll fall off that cursed horse and end up snoring in a ditch."

"I'll come and wake you," Failla promised as she stacked their dirty plates on the tavern's tray.

As soon as he left the room, his travelling bag under one arm, she hurried to retrieve the papers she'd dumped on the cold ashes. The bottom few were too dirty to be salvaged and the ink had soaked the topmost. She tucked the rest inside Nath's writing case for safe keeping and redrew the ruined ones, working more swiftly than she had done all evening. By the time the fifth chime of the night sounded, she had copied a further handful and three of Nath's more intricate map. That should convince him that she had worked until the candles guttered.

The flames fluttered as the door opened. She froze, startled. Seeing it was Nath, she managed a smile. "I was just about to wake you."

Halcarion help her. Failla could only pray he wasn't about to ask how much she'd achieved.

"I saw that old woman on the stairs and asked her to call me at midnight." Nath rubbed a hand over his stubble, far more his usual genial self. He caught his cloak up from the chair. "I'll be back as soon as I can. Make sure you get some sleep."

"I will." Failla breathed more easily as the door closed behind him. Moving to the window, she eased the curtain aside. Smoky torches lit the courtyard and she saw an ostler bringing Nath's horse from the stables that occupied three sides of the inn's ground floor. As soon as he rode out through the arch onto the high road, she let the curtain fall.

She quickly packed away all the papers, ink and pens and buckled Nath's writing case securely. Gathering up her own bag and cloak along with it, she hurried upstairs. Nath had said their rooms were right above the parlour, hadn't he?

As she reached the top step, the old woman came out of a door opposite. She dropped a hasty curtsey. "I was just straightening the young master's bed and snuffing his candle."

"Of course." Failla nodded at the next door. "Is that my room?"

"It is, my lady." The old woman opened it up for her. "Let me fetch you a light."

Failla quickly stowed the writing case under the bed and left her travelling bag on top. If some ill-chance brought thieves in the night, they were welcome to her dirty linen. Hopefully they'd pay no attention to a case full of paper and pens. As for spies, mere maps could say nothing definite. She had all the incriminating letters in her pocket. Better not forget to read and answer them before Nath and this newcomer returned in the morning, she reminded herself. She slung her cloak around her shoulders.

"My lady?" Returning with a fresh candle, the old woman halted, surprised.

"My brother's riding to our patron's house without one of his commissions." Failla flourished the spoiled sheets of paper, folded into a convincing pretence. "If I hurry, I should catch him."

"You're riding out alone, at this hour?" The old woman was horrified.

"He's only just left, and there won't be anyone on the road." Failla was counting on that. Her luck had held thus far, thank Halcarion.

"My lady, at least take a groom with you."

"I'll be back soon." Failla brushed past the servant and headed for the stairs.

Down in the courtyard, a heavy-eyed ostler fetched her horse without comment. The timely arrival of a coach with a lame horse prompted a flurry of activity and she made her escape. The road was deserted. Even the hardiest beggars had found some hedgerow to sleep under by now. Riding out into the night, she paused only once.

Looking up, she was relieved to see that the day's clouds had yielded to a clear sky. With both moons waxing past their halves, there was plenty of light.

Looking back at the village spread out beyond the inn, she saw candles in a few unshuttered windows. The fire-baskets on either side of the inn's gateway burned brightly, showing no one following her. No one to see she was riding in quite the opposite direction from Nath.

CHAPTER THIRTY

Failla

The Dromin Road, in the Lescari Dukedom of Carluse, 24th of For-Autumn

"COME ON, HORSE." She stroked the reluctant animal's neck before urging it on with ruthless boot heels.

It had been easy enough to find the waymark stones on the high road. Now she was on the lesser byways, she had to search the leafy shadows for their pale gleam. Each one marked a league closer to Carluse, but she couldn't worry about that. She couldn't fret about beggars or footpads or worry that some scum from Wynald's Warband might stumble across her. This was her only chance. She had to take it.

Sooner than she expected, she saw the stone marking twenty-eight leagues from Carluse Town on this road. Weak with relief, she urged the horse down a track branching north. Finally, she turned down a narrow rutted lane. The horse snorted and baulked. Despite her frustration, Failla let the weary beast pick its own path in the half-light. She'd be hard put to explain to Nath how the animal had lamed itself overnight in a stable. The last thing she needed was him challenging the ostler and learning she'd ridden out alone.

As the lane cut across a shallow crest, she could see the little farm nestling in the side of the valley. There was no sign of light, nor any smoke rising from the chimney at one end of the long, low roof.

Her frustration gave way to apprehension. What welcome could she expect? Dismounting at the gate, she led the horse past the byre and the pigsties where the fattening weanlings were safely penned up for the night. The scent of cows and swine hung heavy in the air and her mount snorted loudly. The farm's own plough horse responded with a curious whicker. A single goose cackled briefly in the darkness.

"Hush." Failla stroked her mount's nose before it could whinny. She unbolted the top half of the stable door and tied her reins to it. She knew the plough horse of old. It would raise more racket than Poldrion's demons if its curiosity went unsatisfied.

A window under the edge of the thatch rattled. "Who's there?"

"Failla." She felt her palms sweating inside her gloves.

There was a moment's startled silence. "Failla?"

A second voice murmured in the bedroom, impossible to make out.

"Wait there." The window snapped shut.

Failla hurried past the well and the dairy to the farmhouse door.

Bolts scraped and a white-gowned figure stood in the darkness. "What do you want?"

"I need to see her," Failla pleaded.

"In the middle of the night?" The figure made no move to let her in. "Where have you been?"

"I can't tell you. But Uncle Ernout knows. Please, let me see her," begged Failla.

"Have you brought any coin for her keep?"

"No, I couldn't." Failla was miserably conscious of her empty purse. "But there's something you need to know. Can I come in?" She held out beseeching hands.

The figure in the doorway stepped back. "I suppose so."

As Failla entered, the nightgowned woman went over to the hearth and stirred the banked fire to a sullen glow. "You're pregnant again? That's why Duke Garnot's sent you away?"

"No." Failla knew she should have expected that. "I'm carrying messages for Uncle Ernout."

"Saedrin send his schemes are prospering," the woman said grudgingly. "But don't tell me what they are," she warned.

Unable to contain her anxiety, Failla paced back and forth on the far side of the well-scrubbed table. "There's going to be fighting, Lathi."

"With Marlier or Sharlac?" As the woman tossed a handful of kindling onto the fire, the light illuminated her frightened face. She was much the same age as Failla, her features in the same mould.

"Neither." Failla bit her lip. "You mustn't say anything, not even to Uncle Ernout. He knows it's coming but I shouldn't be telling you. But I want you to be ready, so you're prepared."

"For what?" The woman gripped the poker like a weapon.

"Fighting will start in the north, any day now." Failla clenched her fists. "Not Sharlac invading but an army coming down from the hills to overthrow Jackal Moncan, and then Duke Garnot and all the rest. To bring us real peace, once and for all."

Lathi was aghast. "When did armies ever bring peace?"

"Uncle Ernout thinks this one will. Please, Lathi," Failla begged desperately, "let me see her. I can't stay long and I don't know when I'll be close by again."

The white-gowned woman bent to light a spill and then an oil lamp. "You mustn't wake her."

"I won't." Failla swallowed salty tears, her heart twisting inside her.

She followed Lathi up the narrow curving stair. At the top, she looked fearfully through the narrow door to the canopied bed. Lathi's husband was a silent heap beneath the blankets. Failla couldn't blame him. Far safer for him not to be involved.

Lathi eased the latch and opened the door to the loft over the stable.

Failla heard a sleepy protest and her heart leaped. It couldn't be helped if the children woke of their own accord.

"Hush, hush," Lathi soothed and the murmur subsided.

Now all Failla could hear was peaceful breathing. She swallowed fresh tears.

"You wanted to see her." Lathi moved aside.

Hesitating on the threshold, Failla looked at the four little girls in the rumpled bed, their brothers curled up like puppies on a pallet beneath the low window.

"Which one is she?" Failla thought her heart would break. All were so alike in their creased chemises, dark hair strewn across the lumpy bolster.

For a long moment, Lathi didn't answer. She cleared her throat. "If you don't recognise your own daughter, I'm not going to tell you."

"Lathi!" Failla choked on a sob.

"No." Lathi forced her out of the room, shutting the door. "You gave her to me to raise as my own. We all agreed that was safest." She pushed Failla towards the stairs.

Failla couldn't speak for silent weeping, stumbling on the edge of her cloak and nearly falling.

Lathi followed her down to the kitchen with the merciless truth. "As far as anyone knows, they're sisters, not cousins. If no one knows different, not even you, no one can betray her to Duke Garnot. You don't think they'd use her against you, against Uncle Ernout? What life would she have if Duke Garnot and his bitch of a wife took her from us? What happens to her if Wynald's bastards catch up with you? Once they've beaten the truth of whatever it is you're doing out of you? They'll come here and burn the roof over our heads. You know they will." For all her hard words, firelight shone on tears trickling down Lathi's face. "I'm sorry, Failla, you have to go. I'm grateful for the warning, but you have to go. Please!"

"I'm going." Failla tried to wipe her tears away. They wouldn't be stemmed.

"How far must you ride?" Lathi asked with belated solicitude.

"If you don't know, you can't betray me," Failla said harshly.

Fleeing into the yard, an aching realisation prompted fresh, uncontrollable tears. She didn't even know her daughter's name.

As the farmhouse door bolted behind her, she hurried to the stable, untied her horse's reins and dragged the bemused beast to the mounting block. Pausing only to scrape more tears from her face with her cloak's harsh wool, she set off, hands and heels more brutal than the innocent animal deserved.

By the time she was approaching the inn, her tears were exhausted. She locked the night's sorrow in that same remote corner of her heart where the memory of giving up her baby girl lived. She hadn't even let the infant suckle. Lathi had said that was best, if she were to carry the fewest marks of motherhood on her body.

The fire-baskets on either side of the archway still burned bright. Failla pulled up her hood to hide her wretched face. The courtyard was quiet, the clock striking eight chimes on its muted bell. A sleepy youth emerged at the sound of her horse's hooves and Failla handed him her reins without a word.

What must she do now? Beyond washing her face and hoping her eyes weren't too red and swollen in the morning. As she drew her cloak around her, she felt the letters in her pocket. She could make sure they were all read and answered before morning. There was no way she could sleep, after all.

She hurried up the stairs as quietly as her boots allowed. Opening her bedroom door, she was startled to see the candle was alight.

"Come in."

Failla looked nonplussed at the old woman sitting on her untouched bed. Nath's writing case was open on the floor before her and she was leafing through the newly copied maps.

"Robbing us?" Failla gasped. "I'll have you turned out on the road for this!"

"Ah, now there's your first mistake." The old woman looked up with a pleasant smile. "I'm no servant here, no more than that lad's your brother."

"What?" Failla stared at her.

"Duke Garnot's doxy had no brothers, nor sisters neither. She'd never have had to trade her virtue for his bed if she had. So, where have you been?" The old woman put down the maps. "Not sneaking away to some lover, that's for certain. You made your bargain and you stuck honestly by it. Whatever Duchess Tadira might say, you're no whore. You're hard to follow, though, I'll give you that."

Failla noticed an unfamiliar cloak on the floor and fresh dirt on the old woman's boots. She clenched her fists and took a pace into the room, shutting the door behind her.

"Raise your hand to me and you'll be sorry, my girl." The old woman drew a thin-bladed knife from a scabbard hidden among her skirts. She shook her head with a chuckle. "Don't worry. I don't work for Duke Garnot of Carluse, or his duchess. I shan't give you up to either of them. Not if you tell me why you fled Garnot's protection. Not pregnant again, I see." She nodded at Failla's slender waist. "Not like the year before last. My compliments, my lady, on managing to keep such a thing secret."

"What do you know about that?" Failla wondered if she could cross the room fast enough to turn the old woman's knife against her without being too badly cut herself. This vile hag might be bold but Failla was certain she was stronger. But what then? How could she explain away a bloody murder? Could she commit such a crime? She quailed inwardly at the thought.

"I don't know as much as I'd like," the old woman admitted, "nor as much as I could have discovered, given time. My master has me searching out more urgent secrets now."

"Your master?"

"Master Hamare." The woman looked at Failla. "Who will want to know what's in those letters you're carrying. So hand them over, there's a good girl. You can have them back when I've read them and your friend need be none the wiser."

It took Failla a moment to recognise the name. "Duke Iruvain's intelligencer? You expect me to betray Carluse to Triolle?"

"Whatever you're doing, it's not for Carluse, or at least not for Duke Garnot." The old woman tucked her knife away. "I'm not your enemy, you silly girl. It's all one to Triolle if Duke Garnot finds his militia's no more a defence than some worm-eaten pikestaff thanks to your guildmasters and their plotting." She looked down at the maps. "So tell me, why are you and that Tormalin-born lad tracing out every highway and byway running through Carluse and Sharlac? What were you doing in Vanam? I know there's more to this than disaffected priests and craftsmen hatching some scheme. Don't try telling me different," she warned.

Failla thought fast. "The guildmasters are recalling all the apprentices they've sent away these past years."

"Why?" The old woman frowned.

Failla feigned reluctance before answering. "To defend Carluse against Sharlac."

"Sharlac?" Now the old woman was genuinely puzzled. "Duke Moncan's barely set foot outside his castle since his son was killed."

"That doesn't mean he's not plotting," Failla spat with all the loathing she felt for Sharlac and his dead heir. "What better cover for the Jackal's schemes than having everyone think he's crippled by grief? You don't think I'm doing this for Carluse? I'm doing it for Lord Veblen!"

Failla saw mention of Duke Garnot's baseborn son instantly catch the old woman's attention.

"The doxy and the bastard? That's long been one of Duchess Tadira's tales."

"He was my friend," Failla said tightly. Why was the truth harder to tell than lies?

"Nothing more?" The old woman raised her thin brows.

"Nothing more." Failla kept her face impassive as she searched her recollections for whatever half-truths and misdirection she might use to make these lies more convincing.

"The letters," the old woman demanded. "Let's see what they say."

Turning to reach inside her cloak, happy to hide her face lest she betray some relief, Failla threw the letters, sealed and unsealed, at her tormenter.

The old woman let them fall to the floor and across the bed without comment. Picking up the nearest, she slit it open with her knife and leaned close to the candle to read it.

Failla could only thank Saedrin that Uncle Ernout had been so adamant that the guildmasters' plotting and the Vanam conspiracy remain separate. Only the fact that war was to come from the north had been shared among his people. None of these letters could betray the full truth of the assault. All the same, she stood, tense and fearful, until the vile old woman had finished reading every letter.

"This glover wastes a good deal of ink saying nothing much to the point." She looked up, dissatisfied. "So where is this map-maker you're travelling with? What took him off in the middle of the night? Don't tell me he has some lover or bastard child tucked away. He's not laid a finger on another woman since he wed, that one."

"He went to meet someone bringing news from Vanam." Failla let her shoulders sag, defeated.

"What news?" the old woman demanded.

"How should I know?" Failla protested.

"You'll see me again soon." The old woman stood up. "You can tell me then."

"No," Failla objected. "It'll do you no good to dog my footsteps. If I'm seen associating with strangers, I'll be cut out of everything."

If she was being followed, she had no hope of retrieving her gold from Uncle Ernout or stealing her daughter away from her cousin Lathi.

"Then don't be seen." The old woman was implacable. "You've had plenty of practice at that. When we next meet, I want to know everything you and your people think you know about Sharlac's plans."

"No." Failla shook her head, pressing herself back against the door. She couldn't do it. She couldn't betray everyone like this. "I won't help you."

"No?" The old woman queried. "When your daughter's safety depends on it?"

Failla's blood ran cold. "My daughter?"

"I know that much, even if I don't know where you've stowed her." The old woman shrugged. "Not yet anyway. Of course, if I'm busy sending word to Master Hamare about these schemes of your Guilds and Jackal Moncan's deceits, I'll hardly have time to go searching for the precious mite, will I?"

How hard could it be to strangle someone? Nath would help dispose of the body, surely? He'd have to, once she explained how the duke had sent someone to exact his revenge upon her. Failla felt her fists clench once again.

"You won't find her at all if I kill you here and now."

"Do that and my master will just send someone else to dog your footsteps." The old woman was unconcerned. "Someone far less sympathetic to your plight, you can be sure of that. I've left letters to be sent to my master if I turn up dead, or even if I don't turn up at all. They'll tell him everything I've learned so far. As it stands, Master Hamare knows nothing of your child. Kill me and he will. She'll be a new piece thrown right into the middle of this game board. Help me, and no one else need know she was ever born."

"This is your price?" Failla set her jaw. "For your silence?"

"It is." The thin blade shone in the old woman's hand. "So stand aside and I'll bid you goodnight before your so-called brother comes back."

Failla moved away from the door. What else could she do?

"Who are you?" she burst out.

"You can call me Pelletria, dear." Coming close, the old woman patted her hand reassuringly. "You've known me for years, haven't you, back at Duke Garnot's castle? That's what you'll be saying if I come a-visiting when that so-called brother of yours is around. Oh, and don't think of running, dear. You won't lose me a second time, so all you'll do is lead me straight to your little girl. If you run without her, well, I'll just have to take her under my wing when I do find her, to keep her safe. And we'll still find you. Master Hamare has eyes and ears in every town and city between the Ocean and the Great Forest. Now, you make sure you get some sleep, my dear, or there'll be no roses in your pretty cheeks come the morning."

The old woman left, smiling kindly.

Failla stood, silent, motionless, for a long moment. Slowly, she restored all the copies of the maps to Nath's writing case. Finally she began gathering up the opened letters. She had to see them answered before he came back.

Sitting on the bed, clutching the papers, she desperately tried to weave a tissue of lies that might hide these latest secrets come to torment her. What falsehoods could she tell this woman Pelletria, to pass on to Master Hamare? How much truth would she have to use to salt the deceit to make it palatable? How much was she prepared to trade for her daughter's safety, even if the child was already lost to her?

Chapter Thirty-One

Tathrin

The Pipe and Chime Tavern, in the Dukedom of Carluse, 26th of For-Autumn

"There they are." Sorgrad stepped out of the gate recess in the high stone wall that flanked the highway.

"They've taken their own sweet time about it." Gren was sitting aloft, eating apples plucked from the orchard within. "Still, a chance to flirt with a pretty girl's always worth waiting for."

From what Tathrin had seen, Gren flirted with any maid old enough to wed and any matron still young enough to have her own teeth.

The two men rode either side of Failla. Tathrin saw her look at him and speak briefly to her escort. All three urged their horses towards the gateway.

"Sorgrad and Gren?" Like them, the first man wore buff breeches, a plain linen shirt and dun jerkin, the workday clothes that every second man on the road seemed to favour. He was a few years older than

Tathrin and blessed with the square shoulders, strong features and clear eyes that Tathrin's sisters always found so attractive.

Tathrin was glad he'd insisted on buying some new clothes to replace those he'd worn to rags up in the mountains, otherwise Failla could have mistaken him for one of the beggars on the road. Then he recalled his hair, long since grown out of his scholarly crop. He'd trimmed it with his knife as best he could on the long journey through the uplands but it must still look unconscionably ragged.

"You must be Nath." Sorgrad offered his hand. "You have some maps for me?"

"Yes, and here they are." The newcomer smiled, relieved, and handed over a package of oiled cloth sewn tight.

"And who are you, friend?" Gren asked Failla and Nath's companion with lively curiosity.

"Kerith." The other man, darkly bearded and solidly built, shifted in his saddle with evident discomfort.

Gren smiled sunnily. "Don't worry, your arse'll soon toughen up."

"Mind your manners and look after these." Sorgrad handed his brother the package of maps.

So this was the Artificer. Not long off the coach from Vanam and still wearing the long-sleeved black tunic and dark breeches customarily seen around the upper town. He also wore the university's silver seal ring.

"You're very welcome, Master Kerith, but you'll find precious few scholars on these roads," Tathrin said politely. "Riding on in those clothes risks calling attention to yourself. You might wish to change."

"We've thought of that," Nath said quickly. "Failla and I have been travelling as map-makers on our way to take up a commission from a suitably distant lord. Kerith's going to be a tutor freshly hired to give that lord's sons their winter season's lessons."

"Just as long as you all stick to the same story." Sorgrad dismissed the matter. "What's the news from Vanam?"

"I have one letter from my Lady Charoleia and two I was given in Verlayne." Kerith unbuckled a pouch slung across his chest and looked quizzically at the Mountain Man. "If you're Master Maspin? The lad who insisted I take them was quite certain that's who I'd be meeting and Lady Charoleia did say I should look out for the name."

Sorgrad grinned. "That's me. Some of the time, anyway."

"Shall we go and wash the dust out of our throats while you read?" Nath looked hopefully at the tavern as he dismounted.

Tathrin noted how deftly he managed the sword hanging from his belt. Was he as accomplished when it came to fighting with it?

"We've already eaten and we'll be riding on." Sorgrad opened the first letter. "But please, dine at your leisure."

"The food's very good," Tathrin volunteered.

"That's welcome news." Failla favoured him with a sweet smile. "Nath keeps finding inns where swine would turn their snouts up at the fare."

"There's hardly been much choice," he protested.

There was nothing lover-like in that exchange, Tathrin thought with private satisfaction. Though Failla did look dreadfully weary. Dark smudges hollowed her eyes and her smile was strained. Her vulnerability roused his protective instincts. "You should stay here overnight," he advised. "Make sure you're properly rested."

"Master Gruit has all the supplies we've asked for ready and waiting, but Charoleia says too many people are starting to take notice of what's going on." Sorgrad studied the letter again and shrugged. "That's hardly a surprise, now that everything's about to come together."

"Is it?" As Failla looked at Tathrin, her desperation startled him. "Truly?"

"I believe so." To his chagrin, that was all he could tell her. When would Sorgrad start trusting him with the plans for Evord's army?

"Different people noticing different things in different places isn't too much of a concern." Sorgrad tucked the letter inside the breast of his jerkin and opened the next. "As long as no one can see all the pieces moving after each other, they can't guess the play on the board."

"You say Captain-General Evord is about to make his move?" Kerith looked keenly at Sorgrad. "I've been wondering if I should come with you, rather than staying with Nath and Failla. You and Master Evord still have no means of taking the initiative to contact anyone else. Until we're able to recruit another Artificer, you can only wait for Master Aremil to reach out to Master Tathrin." He glanced at Tathrin. "Forgive me, I mean you no disrespect, nor to Master Aremil either."

"I take no offence at the truth. Believe me, I'd be glad to be rid of the burden." Realising too late that might sound disloyal, Tathrin covered his confusion by stooping to gather up one of Gren's discarded apple cores.

"Fighting men run shy of magic, whatever its nature." Sorgrad finished reading the second letter. "Let's leave things as they are."

"Your swordsmen need not know about my Artifice." Kerith dismounted, ungainly proof that he was really no horseman.

"Master Aremil learns what Tathrin knows every second day or so and that suits us well enough." Sorgrad broke the third letter's seal. "You'll be more use helping Nath and Failla. As soon as the storm breaks and Duke Garnot finds his militia won't come when he whistles, his intelligencers will be beating the bushes for whoever's responsible."

"His mercenaries are already sniffing around," Failla said tensely.

"Wynald's Warband are on the prowl?" Gren looked interested. "You could end up in a decent fight before we do."

"Perhaps we should send some swordsmen to travel with Failla and Nath." Tathrin went over to Failla's horse and fed it an apple core.

"Do you want an armed escort to call all the more attention to you?" Sorgrad raised a sardonic eyebrow.

"That won't be necessary." Kerith looked quietly confident. "I believe my Artifice will ensure we travel unnoticed."

"I bet you can keep the duke's spies chasing their own tails." Gren winked at Failla. "Don't fret, sweetheart."

"What about Reniack and Lady Derenna?" She bent to disentangle her dusty blue skirts from her stirrup leather. "Have more Artificers gone to Parnilesse and Sharlac?"

Tathrin stilled her restive horse with a firm hand. "They're scholars, like Kerith."

"No need to tell us," Sorgrad interrupted, looking up from his letter. "What we don't know we can't let slip."

"I'm sorry." Failla ducked her head, the brim of her straw hat hiding her eyes.

"Don't take it to heart," Tathrin said quietly. "They don't trust anyone, those two. Can I help you down?"

"Yes, thank you." Her colour still high after Sorgrad's rebuke, Failla made ready to dismount.

Tathrin took hold of her trim waist and lifted her down to the ground. For a moment she stood so close he could feel her skirts brushing his leg and smell the faint flower scent of her linen. He could imagine he was about to embrace her.

"We do trust some people." Gren's sharp ears had heard his remark. "Charoleia, for one."

"And Halice." Sorgrad shot his brother a grin.

"And Livak." Gren nodded happily.

There was a pause.

"And?" Nath prompted.

Gren pursed his lips. "No, that's everyone."

Sorgrad folded his last letter. "The next time you bespeak your fellow Artificers, Master Kerith, warn them that the dukes of Draximal and Parnilesse have got all their spies searching for the truth about Emirle Bridge."

"More tail-chasing," Gren remarked with satisfaction.

"What did happen?" Nath saw Sorgrad's expression. "I take it we don't need to know?"

Sorgrad just smiled as he buttoned up his jerkin. "Well, we need not keep you any longer."

"It is past time we were going." Tathrin hoped Failla saw he regretted leaving her so soon. "I hope you enjoy your dinner."

"Thank you." She took the reins from him with a half-smile. "But you can at least walk with me to collect your horse, can't you?"

"No horses for us today." Sorgrad inclined his head briefly to Kerith and Nath. "Master Scholar, Master Map-maker, it's an honour to meet you. Stay safe till we next meet, and you too, my lady." He smiled at Failla.

"Where are you going?" She looked at Tathrin, perplexed, as Gren retrieved their gear from the gateway. "On foot?"

"I don't know." He honestly had no idea.

"I believe that's their business, and none of ours." Kerith set his horse walking towards the tavern. "Let's see how good the meat and ale are here."

"I do like a man who can take a hint," Gren approved.

Nath laughed and waved a farewell. "Till we next meet."

Tathrin caught the leather sack Gren tossed to him. He didn't say anything, just stood watching as Failla led her horse away, a fragile figure beside the two tall men. When would he see her again?

"Come on." Gren shoved his shoulder.

Sorgrad was already walking away, around the curve of the orchard wall into a hedge-lined track leading across the fields. As soon as they were out of sight of the road, he searched in the sturdy pouch belted on the opposite hip to his sword. "Let's see what the captain-general's been up to while we've been busy down here."

Tathrin watched as he pulled out a shallow silver bowl that fitted neatly into the palm of his hand.

"Gren, water." As his brother unscrewed the top of his brass flask, Sorgrad found a small vial of ink. "Uncork this, lad."

Tathrin's fingers threatened to cramp as he worked the stubborn stopper free. "What are you doing?"

"Scrying." Gren beamed with simple pride in his brother's magecraft.

Taking the ink, Sorgrad let a drop fall into the water. As the silver clouded, he passed his other hand across the bowl. A faint green light rose to give his face a sickly hue.

Tathrin had heard of scrying. He'd never imagined he would ever see the spell worked.

"Come and look," Sorgrad offered.

Unwilling, yet irresistibly curious, Tathrin peered into the bowl.

He caught a brief glimpse of a sprawl of tents, stone-ringed fire pits scattered between them, with picket lines for horses marking out regular squares beyond. Figures were moving everywhere. Trying to focus on one individual made him suddenly dizzy, his stomach lurching. He stepped back, pressing the back of his hand to his aching eyes.

"There's something about my magic that turns your stomach, isn't there, lad?" Sorgrad tipped the inky water away. "Well, try to hold on to your supper because that's where we're heading."

"But you said a wizard can't go where he's never been." Tathrin's gorge rose at the prospect of being caught up in the uncanny sensations of Sorgrad's magic again.

Before he could gather his thoughts, the rough stone wall of the orchard vanished in a rush of white light. Perhaps it wouldn't be so bad if he kept his eyes open? He did his best, to no avail. As he lost all sensation of weight and substance the light shattered around him, crazed with a violent purple glare. He shut his eyes and swallowed hard as nausea surged up his throat. The sensation of being lost in the magic was endless. Just when he thought he could bear it no longer, his feet hit the ground. The shock struck right through him, like the retching pain when he'd fallen from a tree and broken his arm as a child. Tathrin collapsed to his hands and knees and, despite all his efforts, vomited.

"Try drinking something stronger than ale before we do this again," Gren said with rough sympathy. "Like when you need a bad wound cleaned. If you're going to end up emptying your guts regardless, you may as well get merry first."

Tathrin forced himself to his feet. "Where are we?"

"Within a short walk of Evord's camp." Sorgrad held out a leather-bound bottle.

"Thank you." Tathrin took a swig, expecting water to rinse out his mouth. Instead white brandy stung his sore throat. Taken aback, he swallowed and coughed.

"Better?" Sorgrad grinned at him.

"I'm not sure." Eyes watering, Tathrin pinched the bridge of his nose. He tensed as the aromatic spirit traced a hot path to his belly, but the sickness had passed. The dizziness took a moment longer, though that might have been the liquor.

"Come on." Sorgrad started walking.

Taking a deep breath, Tathrin realised that these hills and woods were fragrant with autumn. Down in Lescar, summer's warmth lingered during the day even if the nights were growing a trifle chilly. Up here the trees showed gold as well as green and the damp scent of an early mist still hung around the dell. At least the freshness lessened the headache thumping behind his eyes.

Was it his imagination or did magic make him even more nauseous now that he'd seen what evil could be wrought with wizardry? But he had felt queasy the very first time Sorgrad had shifted them from place to place in the blink of an eye, when he'd had no real idea what the man was capable of.

He took another breath and hurried after the two brothers. "Where are we, exactly?"

"Dalasor, maybe. Or Caladhria." Gren shrugged. "You know the hills where the headwaters of the Rel rise? East of the White River?"

Tathrin pictured maps of the high ground to the north and west of Lescar. The hills dictated the routes of the two roads running eastward out of Ensaimin. The Dalasor Road crossed the White River at Hanchet and headed over the Dalasorian plains to Inglis. The Great West Road left Ensaimin by way of Peorle and cut across Caladhria, crossing the Rel at Abray before tracing a line to the south of the hills through Carluse, Sharlac and Draximal.

"So this is Carluse land?" A chill replaced the heat of the white brandy in his belly. Then battle really was about to be joined.

"Duke Moncan of Sharlac would argue the roll of those runes." Gren shrugged. "Duke Garnot's writ runs further south where the lead mines are. Up here, no one cares. The land's worth nothing, not to lowlanders anyway."

Tathrin could see why. The hills were too steep and rocky for grazing, with broken screes tumbling across scant turf. While plenty of trees sheltered in the hollows, they were too squat and twisted to be cut for useful timber.

Sorgrad crested a rise. "Which makes this an excellent place to gather an army not made up of lowlanders."

Standing on the ridge, Tathrin saw that the array of tents was far more extensive than the glimpse he'd had through Sorgrad's scrying. Trying to count the mercenary company standards flapping where the wind caught them, his best guess was somewhere between thirty and forty. Tathrin wouldn't have imagined it could be possible to gather so many thousands of men, women and horses in this barren land.

The Dalasorians travelled light without camping gear, so their bicoloured pennants flew over shelters deftly wrought from branches that clustered on steeper slopes beyond the narrow floor of the valley. There weren't quite as many of them as there were mercenaries, but Tathrin didn't think their numbers fell far short. Beyond the formal horse lines, where shirt-sleeved figures groomed stolid mounts, newly split wood fenced off enclosures where younger horses bickered and whinnied.

The regular beat of hammering underpinned the murmur of all the people moving around. Steel flashed in the sunlight as companies of men practised their sword-work on the far side of the shallow river. Barely giving the swordsmen elbow room, horsemen drilled their steeds in rapid turns, urging them into sudden gallops before pulling them up short.

"You can tell Master Aremil about all this now," Sorgrad said with satisfaction.

Tathrin scowled. "If we had an Artificer here, we could let Aremil know at once, and Charoleia."

Gren smiled. "Charoleia won't need telling. She knows she can trust us to get the job done."

"You still don't trust me." Tathrin was still aggrieved.

"Are you ever going to drop that bone?" Sorgrad looked at him, exasperated. "It has precious little to do with trust."

A brassy blast ringing across the valley interrupted him.

"They've seen us," Gren observed.

Sorgrad jerked his head towards the sound. "I don't trust or mistrust you, or Aremil, come to that, any more than I trust or mistrust a signal horn. But once that horn's been sounded, I have no way of knowing how far away it's been heard, who's heard it and what they make of that knowledge. There's no way to recall the noise any more than you can get a loosed arrow back before it lands. If there's any chance my enemies might hear something and make use of what they learn, the safest thing is to leave that cursed horn unblown until I really need it."

Before Tathrin could find an answer to that, a handful of blond men emerged from a thicket he would have sworn was too sparse to hide a newborn fawn.

"Here's something I have to trust you with," Sorgrad said quickly. "Don't tell anyone how we got here or what you know of my magic. And keep your mouth shut about Aremil picking your brains with his Artifice."

"If you say so." Tathrin looked apprehensively at the approaching Mountain Men.

The leader of the newcomers nodded and spoke to Sorgrad, who answered in the same tongue. Then the unknown Mountain Man looked at Tathrin and said something.

"I'm sorry." He tried for an apologetic smile.

The Mountain Man responded with a rueful shake of his head and the rest laughed along with Gren.

Tathrin felt his colour rising. "Do I get to share the jest?"

"No," Sorgrad said briefly. "We need to report to the captain-general."

He walked down the slope, chatting to the leader of the sentries. Gren was sharing another joke with two others, still talking in the mountains' baffling language.

Gritting his teeth, Tathrin followed. He looked around the valley, intent on committing every detail to memory since he was the only one who could give Aremil a vision of this army. First there were the mercenaries, all looking much the same as Arest's men and women. Each company's tents were all grouped around its standard, none of the blazons showing any element of a ducal badge.

Then there were the Mountain Men. Tathrin knew Aremil would want to know how many had joined them on their march through the uplands. Sorgrad had boasted a thousand would answer his summons. Tathrin couldn't vouch for that, but he guessed the total couldn't be far short now that those who'd been making their own way through the hills had joined this final muster. Stocky and blond, hard-faced, they moved silently through the mercenary tents, exchanging barely a word here and there, and for some reason he couldn't fathom, usually stopping to watch Tathrin pass by.

Did they think he was Dalasorian? They were all dark-haired strangers, taller than the tallest Mountain

Men. With hands and faces tanned like his from the summer sun, men and women alike were breeched and booted. The only difference in the women's dress was the bright embroidery decorating their tunics. Tathrin had never seen the like, nor heard any language like theirs, different again from the Mountain tongue.

"You should take a wander tonight." Gren nudged him in the ribs as a girl sat fletching arrows by a fire called out to her friends. "I reckon you've caught her eye. Dalasorian girls take some bridling but it's well worth the effort."

Tathrin looked at the girl busy with her arrows. Dalasorians weren't to be trusted. His grandmother had told him that. They came and went in the night, never staying in one place long enough to raise a decent roof over their heads. That black hair was the mark of the old plains-people's blood running in their veins. The plains-people had been friends and allies of the Eldritch Kin. Until they had vanished in some catastrophe that his grandmother had been curiously vague about, only insisting it was no more than justice visited on them for their godlessness.

While the girl didn't look particularly godless to Tathrin, he still preferred Failla's gentle appeal to the bold challenge in the Dalasorian's dark eyes when she realised he was looking at her.

"Master Tathrin! It's good to see you again."

It took him a moment to realise Captain-General Evord was addressing him. Appearing from behind a tent, he looked as fresh as if he slept every night in a feather bed and rose to bathe and breakfast in Imperial Tormalin luxury.

"What do you think of our army?" the grizzled Soluran asked.

"I don't know what to think, my lord," Tathrin said honestly.

Evord looked more closely at him. "Are you unwell, lad?"

He hesitated. "Something I ate disagreed with me."

"Let's get you a tisane to settle your stomach." Evord snapped his fingers at Gren. "I take it that's for me?"

The Mountain Man grinned as he handed over Nath's carefully bound package of maps, his comment unintelligible.

Evord chuckled and answered in the same tongue before reverting to Tormalin. "Go on, both of you, introduce yourselves around the camp. I want to talk to our young scholar."

"Let me do the talking and don't play the fool," Sorgrad told Gren sternly as they walked away. Gren was laughing.

The captain-general headed down the slope and Tathrin lengthened his stride to keep up. "I didn't expect to see so many Mountain Men."

"Does that bother you?" Evord looked keenly at him.

"I don't know how I'm going to make myself understood, sir," he admitted.

"Most of the Mountain Men speak enough Tormalin for trading or barter." Evord's glance took in every detail of the camp as they passed through it. "Dalasorians are more fluent, for the most part, and those born among the northern clans grow up speaking as much of the Mountain tongue as their own." He gestured towards the collections of tents with pennants fluttering above them. "Most mercenaries can make their way through a fight, a tavern or a brothel in at least three languages. Will that help or hinder us, do you think, once we reach the lowlands?"

Evord was a scholar. Tathrin had learned that when they had first met and the Soluran had interrogated him about every detail of the Vanam conspirators' plans. He was going to be questioned again, he realised, to prove his understanding.

"If most of our army can use the Mountain tongue," he said slowly, "no duke's militiamen will know what's being shouted around them."

"Quite so," Evord said approvingly. "Though of course that'll be less of an advantage against other mercenaries. Still, even a featherweight can tip a balance."

"That's not the only reason you've recruited in the mountains and Dalasor." Tathrin felt on surer ground.

Evord's smile broadened. "What do you know of Mountain customs, lad?"

"Very little." Tathrin couldn't help an exasperated look at Sorgrad's back.

"You and the rest of the lowlanders." Evord was unconcerned. "Well, lad, up in the mountains, women hold the land in perpetuity. Each one in a kinship is granted a share in the forests and mines for her lifetime. They almost always live out their days and die in the valley where they're born. That's failure and dishonour for a man. Once boys are grown strong enough, they're taught to work in the forests and the diggings under the guidance of their fathers and uncles by marriage. Once they're young men, they must set out to find a new home. As they travel, they work to accumulate the gold and silver that proves they're fit to be husbands and fathers. That's the only way they'll find a bride willing to let them work whatever forests and mines come as her marriage portion."

"They'll be fighting in hopes of earning enough gold to go home and wed?" Tathrin could only admire the absurd simplicity of it.

"There are a great many young men up in the hills who are keen to start sowing their seed for the next generation." Evord gazed around the camp. "Give it fifteen years or so and those sheep farmers who've been annexing Mountain lands to the north of Ensaimin won't find it so easy."

Was the price of bringing peace to Lescar going to be warfare plaguing some other innocent folk? That wasn't so amusing. Tathrin cleared his throat. "And the Dalasorians?"

"We'll have an advantage in numbers overall against Sharlac and we will certainly have the edge in battle-hardiness, but I want cavalry to weight the scales in our favour as well." Evord turned down a trampled path between two lines of tents. "No Lescari duke ever trusts his militia with horses, so your countrymen are unused to fighting against mounted men or with their support."

"Why would Dalasorians lend their aid?" Tathrin wondered.

"For coin, plain and simple. Merchants going up and down the roads to Inglis seldom barter for goods." Evord smiled. "We've promised them the pick of the horses we capture, too. Needless to say, Duke Garnot of Carluse's stables are of particular interest."

Tathrin tried to laugh. All he could see was blood-stained Dalasorians galloping through Carluse Town, hacking down men and women no different from his own family. Men and women who could be Failla's kith and kin.

"Captain!"

Sorgrad was walking rapidly towards them, his expression intense. Gren followed, silently ominous.

"Thyren says some mercenaries who went out hunting last night haven't come back yet." Sorgrad gestured towards a Mountain Man.

Evord looked levelly at Sorgrad. "We must accept that a certain number will desert once battle becomes a certainty. So we'll give them till this evening. If they haven't returned by then, we strike them from the muster."

Sorgrad shook his head. "These are Arest's men. They wouldn't desert."

Tathrin wasn't so certain. "Couldn't they be heading to Sharlac or Carluse to earn some safer coin by raising the alarm?"

"Not Arest's men," Gren said stubbornly.

"No one leaves this camp with a horse, so anyone fleeing has a long, hard walk before they can alarm anyone." Evord spared Tathrin a glance. "And do you think anyone would believe such wild tales? Besides, no one knows the plan of campaign but me and my lieutenants. No betrayal would tell Sharlac or Carluse where to prepare a defence."

"Captain, all the roads of Carluse are lousy with enquiry agents. It's not beyond possibility that some of them have found their way up here."

Tathrin had never heard Sorgrad pleading before. He found it disconcerting.

Gren looked more cheerful. "If they have, they need their throats cutting."

"True enough." Evord nodded. "Very well. See if you can track down Arest's strays."

"Come on." Sorgrad snapped his fingers at Tathrin.

"What do you want me for?" he asked, startled.

Sorgrad looked at him, exasperated. "To pass back whatever we find to Aremil so he can tell Charoleia."

"Discreetly," Evord reminded them both with a meaningful look.

Chapter Thirty-Two

Tathrin

**Captain-General Evord's Camp,
in the Uplands East of Verlayne,
26th of For-Autumn**

SORGRAD CUT SWIFTLY between the tents towards Arest's wyvern pennant, Gren hurrying along at his elbow. Tathrin followed unwillingly. As they reached the open space ringed by the Wyvern Hunters' tents, he heard a familiar voice.

"Next time don't force it."

"Reher!" Tathrin had more than half expected that the blacksmith would think better of using his illicit magecraft to further their conspiracy and cut loose from Arest. But Reher was standing by a fire, his anvil and tools to hand. "You found some honest work, then?"

"For the present." Shirtless beneath his leather jerkin despite the chill in the air, Reher looked more muscular than ever. "What's the news from the south?"

"Later," Sorgrad interrupted. "Where's the captain?"

"Arest?" Reher tossed a newly mended cooking pot to a sullen youth. "Out trapping scrawny goats with Zeil and some others."

"Sheepshit," Sorgrad cursed.

"Goatshit, surely?" Gren chipped in, irrepressible.

Sorgrad shot him a lacerating glance. "Reher, who went out last night and didn't come back?"

Reher weighed a hammer in one hand. "Macra and his tent-mates."

"They wouldn't desert." In the blink of an eye, Gren was wholly serious. "Are Arest and Zeil really hunting dinner or trying to track them?"

Reher shrugged. "A little of each."

"Which way did they go?" Sorgrad demanded.

"We've had warnings of spies," Tathrin explained quickly.

There was a moment's pause before Reher spoke. "I'll show you."

Gren threw his bag and blanket roll at the sullen youth. "You, find a tent for our gear."

"Put their gear with mine," Reher advised. "This way."

Tathrin hastily donned his sword and dumped his baggage. Hopefully the discipline in Arest's camp meant he'd come back to find his possessions intact.

Reher lengthened his stride as he led them up a narrow gully. Tathrin felt the uneven ground pulling painfully at his leg muscles. At the top, three yellow-headed sentries appeared out of a fold in the stony ground. Gren said something and they retreated with a brief nod.

Tucking the hammer he still held inside his jerkin, Reher used his hands to negotiate the steepest section.

He led them across a rocky shoulder of barren ground before pointing down a treacherous slope towards another valley. "That's where Arest said they were going to hunt."

Tathrin was surprised how soon the valley sheltering Evord's army dropped out of sight and hearing. Just how far were they from the nearest road or village or even an isolated upland farmstead? Tens of leagues, surely?

Any spies combing these trackless lands would only stumble upon Evord's encampment by accident. Unless they stumbled across some foraging swordsmen and beat the truth out of them. Was that what had happened?

"Have you tried scrying?" Despite his lesser height, Sorgrad had no difficulty keeping up with Reher.

Reher shook his head. "It's water magic and my affinity's with fire."

"I'm born to fire and air and I learned." Sorgrad reached for his silver dish. "When we have a few moments to spare, I'll show you the trick of it."

"You think we'll have any spare moments this side of Solstice?" Reher watched with ill-concealed curiosity as the Mountain Man poured water and dripped ink.

"Who knows?" Sorgrad peered into the luminous bowl. "Now where do you suppose that is?

Tathrin held back, the memory of his nausea still swirling in his gut.

Reher looked, his black brows knitting. "They're there, are they?"

"Hidden and not moving." Sorgrad looked bleak.

Gren peered into the greenish light. "That's no place to be planning an ambush."

"I know those trees," Reher said suddenly. "This way."

He scrambled down the slope and cut across the stream carving a glistening cleft through the dark rocks. His long legs easily negotiated the awkward gaps between the largest stones.

Tathrin was glad he was tall enough to do the same. Watching Gren jump from rock to rock made his blood run cold. One slip and the Mountain Man risked a fall to injury or even death.

Unless his brother was helping him keep his footing? Tathrin watched open-mouthed as Sorgrad walked straight out across a precipitous plunge, a faint beam of sapphire light supporting his feet.

Reher was watching, too. "That's another neat trick."

"Later," Sorgrad promised. "Are those the trees?"

"I'd say so," Reher confirmed grimly.

"Come on, lad." Gren drew his sword.

Tathrin did the same and gripped the hilt as they advanced on the thicket. "You want me to fight?"

But there was no sign of any enemy. Sorgrad and Gren began cutting at the undergrowth choking the stunted thorn trees. Reher simply tore the sprays apart, his hands seemingly impervious to the lacerating prickles. Tathrin circled around to start clearing the far side.

"Here." All too soon, Gren stopped and shook his head.

"All of them?" Sorgrad stepped closer to see.

Five bodies had been dumped in a deep crack where a thorn tree had taken root. All had been stripped to their shirts, so it was easy to see how viciously they'd been hacked by merciless swords. Two pallid faces were looking upwards. One was frozen in surprise, the other struggling with what looked like puzzled recognition. Tathrin was only thankful he didn't know either of them, and for the cold weather, although carrion flies were already gathering.

As Sorgrad knelt and reached down, Tathrin thought he was going to close the corpse's eyes. He flinched with pointless sympathy as the Mountain Man poked his forefinger into one unseeing eye instead.

"Still moist." Sorgrad tried to move a dead hand. "But stiffened."

"So they died some time last night." Gren's blue gaze was murderous. "How long to catch whoever did it?"

"Perhaps we should have asked Aremil to send us an Artificer after all." Sorgrad glanced briefly at Tathrin. "If Vanam's scholars can read the last moments of the dead in the same way as the *sheltya*." His gaze switched to Reher. "I know you've shunned Hadrumal's training, but do you know anything of necromancy?"

"Nothing, and I wouldn't countenance such sacrilege." Reher stared down, grim-faced. "I can help you regardless. I mended Macra's belt buckle and drew the wire to make links that half the camp has patched their chain mail with."

"But you can't scry," Gren pointed out tersely.

"I can find any piece of metal I've ever worked. If it's close enough, I can call it to my hand." Reher shrugged his massive shoulders. "I thought all blacksmiths could, till my father told me different."

"I've always said there's more useful magic outside Hadrumal's libraries than in them." Sorgrad was keenly interested. "You can show me the trick of that, if you like."

Tathrin retreated from the carnage. "If they died last night, the killers could be leagues away by now."

"Not if they're spies." Gren was adamant. "They won't have got anything out of Macra worth taking back to their paymaster."

"True enough." Sorgrad looked speculatively at Tathrin. "They'll be looking for some other pigeon to pluck."

"What?" Tathrin took another pace backwards.

"Up in the mountains, if a wolf's raiding the flocks, a goatherd tethers a dry nanny out overnight." Gren's smile was far from reassuring. "When her noise draws the wolf, the goatherd draws his bow."

"I'm not a goat," Tathrin retorted.

"We won't let them kill you." Sorgrad looked at him unblinking. "You're our only link with Aremil."

"They won't be expecting magecraft," Reher pointed out.

"If you haven't got the stones for it, go back to the camp. I can play the victim." Gren smiled unpleasantly. "Of course, these spies might catch up with you on the way. Then you'll be all alone without any of us to pull your feet from the fire."

"Think what a tale you'll have for Failla," Sorgrad mused. "Such a hero."

Tathrin stiffened. "I'm in this for the sake of all Lescari, not just to impress Failla."

"Good," Sorgrad said briskly. "Reher, which way?"

Tathrin opened his mouth to protest that he hadn't agreed. He closed it again. The others were already walking away. He followed reluctantly.

Leaving the valley where Macra and his men had died, Reher led them across another shoulder of barren turf. Looking around as he paused to catch his breath, Tathrin observed how this cluster of high hills was fringed with deep valleys. Here they ran down to a broad vale where he could see the silver gleam of a river. On the far side of the low ground, another range of steep summits rose jaggedly into the sky.

"Whoever these bastards are, they're good." Gren was studying the ground. "There's no trail to speak of."

"This way." Reher didn't slow as they crossed the steep rocky slope to the next gully.

Sorgrad scowled. "Tathrin, you're skylined."

Reher had dropped to his hands and knees to avoid being silhouetted against the pale clouds. Tathrin ducked hastily, following Sorgrad in a crouch that made his back ache.

As they slipped down a mossy incline, Reher paused, his eyes disconcertingly vacant. Then his dark gaze sharpened and he pointed to a distant furze brake. "Down there."

"Couldn't it be Arest and his men?" Tathrin wondered aloud.

Reher shook his head. "Not wearing Macra's belt buckle."

Tathrin wasn't convinced, but nor was he inclined to argue the point. Besides, if it was Arest, he would be perfectly safe, wouldn't he? "So what do I do?"

"Walk down there looking like you'll tell all you know as soon as someone holds a knife to your throat." Gren unsheathed two viciously curved daggers. "We'll do the rest."

"Reher?" Tathrin turned to ask the smith. He wasn't there.

"Just get on with it." Sorgrad's voice echoed oddly from the empty air.

"Gren?" Tathrin looked around wildly but the other Mountain Man had disappeared.

"We'll be close by," Reher's gruff voice promised.

Tathrin took a breath to slow his pounding heart. There was no hint of magelight, no rustle of unseen footsteps among the tussocks of coarse grass. How could three men, one of them Reher's size, just vanish into thin air? Wizardry in tavern ballads and festival tales was all very entertaining. No story ever said how thoroughly unnerving it was to be around magical workings.

An unseen hand shoved him hard in the small of the back. He had to step forward or fall over. Gripping his sword, he started walking down the narrow valley.

Where were these murderous spies? He tried not to look too obviously at the patch of spiny greenery that Reher had pointed out. Showing undue interest in one particular furze brake would betray him, surely? Besides, the sentries around Captain-General Evord's encampment could hide behind two stones and a fallen leaf. These spies could be anywhere. He slowed involuntarily.

What if they shot arrows from cover, like hunters stalking a deer? If Macra had already told them everything they wanted to know, then he was just an inconvenience to be swiftly eliminated. He forced himself to walk onwards, breathing harder than the exertion of walking downhill warranted.

Unable to resist glancing covertly at the furze again, he blinked. The spiny tangles were far less clear than they had been. He looked up at the sky. It was still too early for evening mists to be thickening. More magic?

His grip on his sword tighter still, he walked on, bowels clenching, throat dry. The wind blew his hair into his eyes and he brushed it quickly aside.

Halfway down from the head of the gully to the furze brake, he saw movement out of the corner of his eye. Movement coming uphill, not down. Tense as a hunted hare, he startled as the branches of a stunted blackthorn shivered on the other side of the track. He heard the sound of a boot nail on a stone. He searched the undergrowth desperately. Who was lying in wait? He didn't dare turn and see if someone was creeping up behind him. If he did, he was convinced someone would rush to attack him from the front.

The brambles vanished in a white haze. For a horrible instant, Tathrin thought Sorgrad was sweeping him away with his magic again. In the next breath, he realized it was just mist wrapping around him. But magecrafted mist, it had to be. No normal fog would rise this fast. Already he couldn't see his feet.

Somewhere behind him, a scream tore through the whiteness. Tathrin whirled around, sword at the ready. Cries of alarm sounded on all sides. He tried to make out the shouted words, but to no avail. Every voice was twisted, not merely by the fog but magically muffled, he was sure of it.

His hair was sodden, water trickling down his forehead and stinging his eyes. He desperately tried to wipe it away as shadows loomed through the fog. Was someone intent on killing him? Had Sorgrad and Gren taught him enough sword-work to stop them? Fear and damp chilled him equally. His fingers were numb and clumsy.

"Tathrin?"

Fast as it had arisen, the mist vanished. Reher was standing in front of him.

"Where's everyone else?" Tathrin turned a hasty circle.

"Over here." Sorgrad was kneeling on the back of a mercenary who was trying not to smother as his face was pushed into the damp earth. Sorgrad's vicious hold on his twisted arm ensured he wouldn't be getting up.

"Gren?"

"Coming." The younger Mountain Man emerged from the furze, a curved dagger in one hand dripping red. He had his other fingers knotted in the curly brown hair of a weaponless man, forcing him to scramble along on his hands and knees. Both of them were liberally spattered with blood, drops clotting on the prisoner's shocked white face.

"How many dead?" Reher looked up and down the gully.

"Four." Sorgrad twisted his captive's contorted arm hard up his back. "Is that all?"

"Six of us, that's all!" the man yelped.

"All present and correct." Gren forced his prisoner to kneel on the damp grass, pressing the bloody knife to his throat.

Tathrin realized that he and both spies were still sodden from the fog. Reher, Sorgrad and Gren were all bone dry. That was hardly fair. He sheathed his pristine sword with a shove of resentment.

"Who are you working for?" Sorgrad leaned on his captive's twisted arm.

The man whimpered but pressed his face down into the dirt. "No."

"Him over there eating mud, is he a pal of yours?" As Gren spoke, he drew his curved blade lightly across his own prisoner's throat. "Will he answer to save your neck?"

Tathrin saw fresh blood trickle through the drying splashes on the man's white skin.

"No." The curly-haired man screwed his eyes tight shut.

Gren shrugged. "We'll just have to use you to show him what we'll do to him, then. Unless you have the answers we want?" he offered as an afterthought.

"Don't," the man lying face down warned.

"You saw me rip your mate's tripes out with this," Gren said reasonably. He waved the gory knife in front of the curly-haired man's eyes. "That was quick because I only wanted to kill him. I can keep you alive till sunset. Then I'll truss you up with your own guts and you can wait for the wolves to come and put you out of your misery."

Shivering, Tathrin had no doubt he would do it and sleep soundly afterwards.

"But we don't know anything," the man said desperately.

"We don't know anything," the prisoner being held face down insisted.

Gren sliced open his captive's shirt. "You're lying."

How did he know? What if the man was telling the truth? What if they had already murdered the only man who could answer their questions? Tathrin had to clench his jaw to stop himself protesting.

Sorgrad leaned over the man he had pinned to the ground. "The only reason you're not dead already is you're wearing my dead friend's belt. If you got the pick of the spoils, you've got the rank to know what you're doing."

Tathrin wouldn't have thought it possible to feel any colder than he already did. Sorgrad's tone proved him wrong.

"I'll get your answers." Reher pulled the hammer he'd been using earlier out of the breast of his jerkin. He knelt by Sorgrad and stretched the pinned man's free arm out, clamping his elbow to the ground with his own strong hand.

"Tell us what we need to know and I'll break your arm just the once so you can't raise a sword for a while. Try to be a hero and I'll smash every bone in your hand. You'll never scratch your stones again."

"Go piss up a rope," the man snarled, clenching his fist.

Reher shook his head. "Doing that only makes it worse."

Tathrin winced as the hammer smashed the man's knuckles.

Sorgrad's hold tightened as the man shrieked, writhing in a vain attempt to break free from the agony. "Who are you working for?"

"No." The man drove his face into the soil. Sorgrad grabbed his hair and wrenched his head back before he could smother himself.

Impassive, Reher brought the hammer down a second time. Tathrin had to turn away. He tensed, waiting for the third blow. This time he saw the man's raw scream startle a flurry of small brown birds from a distant thicket.

"I'll tell you what I know!"

Tathrin turned to see the kneeling prisoner begging, wide-eyed.

"A man called Karn paid us to follow some mercenaries north," the curly-headed captive said hastily.

"Who's he, this man Karn?" Sorgrad sat back on his heels and let the tortured man loose. Reher rolled him onto his back.

"That's all we know." The injured man was in far too much pain to think of resisting, never mind fighting back. Tathrin saw he had bitten through his lip, blood and tears mingling with the dirt smeared across his face.

Reher brought the hammer down on the man's uninjured forearm with an audible crack of bone.

"No!" Tathrin protested, but no one was listening to him.

"Whoever Karn is, he's from Triolle," the curly-headed captive said desperately.

"Is he now?" Sorgrad looked interested. "Where did you meet up with him, and how are you supposed to be telling him what you've learned?"

"It was the tail end of Aft-Summer." The curly-haired man was gabbling now. "Around the Greater full moon. We were looking for a hire in the camps between Carluse and Marlier. He told us to leave word of whatever we found out at the Silver Spear Inn in Abray."

"You won't be doing that." Gren abruptly threw the man forward onto his face and held him down with a boot on his neck. "Reher?"

"Coming." The smith rose to his feet with a sigh.

"No!"

The prisoner choked on his plea as a dark stain spread in the seat of his breeches.

"He told you what you wanted to know," Tathrin pleaded.

"So?" Sorgrad was unbuckling Macra's belt. The whimpering man could hardly stop him.

As Reher quickly broke both the curly-headed man's arms, his screams cut through Tathrin's protests. It was a good thing the magic had already made him so ill, otherwise he'd be emptying his stomach again.

"That'll do." Reher stood up, as unemotional as if he'd just finished shoeing a horse.

"What now?" Sickened, Tathrin looked at the two injured men huddled in their misery.

"They're free to go." Reher began walking back up the gully.

"We go back to camp." Gren stabbed his knives into the damp turf to clean them. "We tell Arest what happened and where to find Macra and the other bodies."

Sorgrad was coiling Macra's belt round one hand. "These two had best hope they get far enough away before Arest and his men start hunting them."

That got the injured men's attention. Slowly, they stood, painfully cautious, broken arms crooked against their breasts. The first man's smashed hand was already grotesquely swollen, darkening with lurid bruising.

"Come on." Gren gripped Tathrin's shoulder and urged him up the hill.

He didn't resist, silent until they reached the scramble up to the summit linking this line of valleys. Looking back, he could just make out the tiny figures of the tortured men slowly walking away.

"Why didn't you just kill them?" he asked bitterly.

"Reher said not to." It was plainly a matter of complete indifference to Gren.

"Isn't this as good as murder?" Tathrin rounded on the smith. "Leaving them out here in the wilds without a hand to raise to defend themselves? How will they hunt for food?"

"I didn't break the skin, so they have no wounds to fester." Reher looked steadily at him. "Broken bones will mend with time and care. They can take whatever food and water their friends were carrying if they don't mind suffering to get it."

Tathrin recoiled from the thought of trying to plunder dead bodies with such injuries.

"Dead men feel no pain. If those two have to live with it for a few months, they might think better of making a trade out of other people's suffering." Reher showed no remorse. "This isn't the first time I've broken a man's bones for the sake of keeping Guild secrets safe. There's more brutality goes on in Lescar than you know of, lad."

"Don't think I don't know it!" Tathrin shivered, disgusted. He couldn't stop, chilled and wet as he was.

"'Grad!" Gren shouted to his brother. "The lad's still soaking. We don't want him taking a chill."

Sorgrad reached out, but Tathrin shied away. "I don't want your magic."

"Then take mine." Reher clapped him on the shoulder with one broad hand.

Angry and frustrated, Tathrin saw the smith leave a dry handprint on his leather-clad shoulder. As he watched, the pale shape spread down his front and presumably down his back, wisps of steam rising from the creeping edge of the subtle magic. Warmth slid between his chilled skin and the sodden shirt that had been clinging to his ribs.

"Better?" Sorgrad was watching him.

"What will you do now?" Tathrin challenged. "Will Arest's men hunt those two down, when they can't even fight back? Where's the honour in that? Or will you just drink yourselves stupid like you did after Jik and the others died, and forget them by the next morning?"

"Whoever told you there was honour in being a hired sword?" Sorgrad looked quizzically at him. "Come on, we've a long walk back."

He didn't move, not until Tathrin grudgingly took a step and then another. Reher had gone on ahead, Gren at his elbow, his quicksilver cheerfulness in contrast to the smith's looming presence.

"I don't hold with torture, not as a rule." Sorgrad walked companionably beside Tathrin. "You can always break someone, but you never know if they're telling you the truth or just what they think you want to hear. We could have got that man Karn's name out of those two without leaving a mark on them if we'd wanted to. But Reher's choice was a fair one. Once that tale spreads, there'll be fewer curs keen to take this man Karn's coin and come sneaking about these hills. Those two won't be fighting us in Sharlac, either." He smiled dourly. "Remember that, long lad. You can take more men out of a battle by injuring a handful than you can by killing twice that number."

He sighed, more solemn. "Yes, they'll drink themselves stupid tonight, Arest and the others, to blunt the sting of knowing their comrades were ambushed, killed, robbed and thrown into that hollow to rot. To blunt the sting of knowing it could just as easily have been them. To stop themselves lying awake in the darkness and thinking of all the evil deeds they'll have to explain away to Saedrin, one day sooner or later. If they can find a woman willing to sheath their sword between her legs, some of them will rut till daybreak, just to feel alive. While they're inside a woman, inside the circle of her arms, they don't have to remember that every dawn could see them dead by nightfall. Chances are, if the captain-general can spare them, yes, some will go hunting for those men we left maimed back there. Before you waste your breath being outraged, just remember they took coin from this man Karn and all the risks that went with it.

"Beyond that," he continued coolly, "no, Arest and the others won't grieve overmuch for Macra. The only ones who would have truly lamented his loss died alongside him. Mercenaries only have two or three close friends for the most part, their tent-mates usually, because that's as many friends as you can stand to have and still hope to survive their loss. So don't imagine there'll be many tears shed if you get yourself killed."

That provoked Tathrin into a response. "I have friends and family who'd mourn my loss."

"I'm sure you do, long lad," Sorgrad said equably. "You're not a mercenary. So stop judging everyone else by your own very limited experience of life. In the meantime, make sure you're ready to tell Aremil everything we've learned today. Tell him to pass everything on to Charoleia at once. She needs to find out who this man Karn is and who he reports to in Triolle. And to chase up any letters sent from the Silver Spear in Abray."

CHAPTER THIRTY-THREE

Branca

Eshelwen Manor, in the Lescari Dukedom of Sharlac, 31st of For-Autumn

"*Reniack has unearthed spies in Parnilesse who are reporting back to Triolle.*"

Aremil's voice echoed from the stone walls of the same vaulted hall that Branca had found the first time she looked into his mind.

Was this a childhood memory of some banqueting hall in his father's castle? What did it mean that he still chose to meet her here? Didn't he realise he could remake any place in his imagination? Though she noticed there were windows now, tall lancets patterned with coloured glass in a style that Tormalin's nobles had scorned for half a generation. What had prompted that?

Didn't he wonder why he always saw her in whatever bedchamber or withdrawing room she was truly in instead of some imagined sanctuary? Had he even perceived the veils that Branca wrapped so carefully around her innermost self? Though of course, he always saw his friend Tathrin where he really was. Perhaps it hadn't yet occurred to him that those adept in Artifice could control such things when those without such skills could not. Not so long ago, she could easily have seen the answer to that question. Now, that wouldn't be so easy.

Branca concentrated on the matter in hand. "Do we know if this man Karn sent any more spies sniffing around Carluse before he was killed, besides the ones he sent chasing those mercenaries?"

With that portion of her intellect still here in Sharlac well aware that she was sitting in the morning parlour in this comfortable manor house, Branca listened for Lady Derenna's approach. The older woman sought news from Vanam and from their fellow plotters at least three times a day.

"*Kerith says there's no sign of anyone showing undue interest in them, though Failla jumps at every shadow.*"

"If she's discovered, Duke Garnot won't be overly interested in Nath or Kerith."

In her mind's eye, Branca saw Aremil sitting in his chair, his twisted body awkward, tremors shaking his left hand. Behind him, indistinct in the gloom, she saw a second reflection, pacing back and forth on strong, straight legs. Did he realise how he betrayed his frustration with his crippled condition? How could she warn him without revealing such humiliating knowledge?

Was she the only one who saw this shadowy double image? Neither Kerith nor Jettin had mentioned it. Surely Kerith would have found it a curiosity worth discussing in his search for undiscovered aspects of

Artifice? While Jettin would simply have thought it too good a joke not to share.

She addressed herself to Aremil in his chair, the strongest reflection of how he saw himself. "You're sure all these threads trace back to Triolle?"

"*We're certain. Every spy we've identified has been passing word back to Master Hamare. Charoleia is doing all she can to unravel his webs, to find everyone who might threaten us.*"

Both Aremils stopped still, looking intently at her.

"*Are you certain Lord Narese is to be trusted? That none of your letters are being intercepted?*"

"I am, and all our letters are wholly discreet. Unless Derenna is face to face with someone, she only writes as if they are discussing natural philosophy, alchemy and the like. They're all scholars of one sort or another, so she appears to be keeping them informed about experiments with rare earths and metals planned in Vanam. Warning them against adding anything to such a volatile mix."

"*Tell her to warn them everything's coming to the boil.*"

A rich chuckle ran around the fan vaulting. Branca wondered if Aremil's real laugh would sound like that, or would it be distorted like his speech? It would be so strange to hear the hesitation, the hollowness in his words, when she returned to Vanam. She'd become so used to the ready fluency that aetheric enchantment granted him.

His amusement was fleeting.

"*You must be careful. We cannot afford to lose you.*"

The force of Aremil's emotion momentarily showed Branca the image of her that he held in his own mind.

She was never more than an anonymous maid in Kerith's opinion, vague enough to be any one of a hundred women. Jettin did her the courtesy of remembering her features clearly, but when his attention wandered, he was inclined to picture her in her shift. Not that he'd ever seen her thus and Branca knew better than to mistake this for desire. It was merely the first thought Jettin had about any woman, and in her case, his imagination did not flatter her.

Aremil did not flatter her. The face she saw through his mind's eye was the one she saw in any looking glass. She was no taller, no prettier, no more slender as she sat before him on a chair much like his own.

But in Aremil's imagination, she wore silken gowns, expertly sewn to show her as shapely rather than dumpy. Her hair was long, as if it had grown uncut since girlhood rather than being regularly cropped to fit tidily under a linen cap. As if she were one of those pampered noblewomen with the leisure to have a maid brush such vanity with a hundred nightly strokes.

She looked down at her hands. At least they were less red and chapped than they had been. Travelling as Lady Derenna's maid involved precious little scrubbing and washing and the herbalist Welgren carried at least as many cosmetics and ladies' lotions as he did palliatives and tinctures. Her most arduous task was biting her tongue to curb opinions out of keeping with her supposedly servile status.

"*Branca? Are you there?*"

Aremil tensed in his chair, looking this way and that. "I am."

The coloured patterns of light on the flagstoned floor brightened, as if the sun had come out from behind a cloud outside this hall of Aremil's imagining.

"Forgive me; I'm distracted. Lady Derenna is constantly on tenterhooks lest Duke Moncan discover something that implicates her husband in disloyalty."

The coloured patterns darkened and Branca caught an echo of Aremil's smouldering resentment that his own father had so easily discarded his living son.

"Isn't His Grace still shut up in his castle with his grief for his dead son?"

"Supposedly." Branca frowned. "But Welgren keeps coming across patients who suspect Jackal Moncan is planning something. That's something Lady Derenna wants Charoleia to look into."

"Charoleia has already traced the rumour back to Carluse. It goes no further and she suspects it's just Duke Garnot's malice. So she's been putting her own gloss on such tales, to keep Triolle's spies looking at Jackal Moncan rather than in our direction. That'll be prompting whatever speculation Welgren is hearing."

"Good," Branca said, relieved.

The distant Aremil began pacing.

"If Lady Derenna is so concerned with discretion, is she spreading word of our purpose widely enough? Evord's army is marching down from the north now. They'll be crossing into Sharlac any day. We must be certain that the local lords won't raise their vassals to fight them."

"She's made sure of every noble she says we can trust," Branca assured him. "We must have visited every second manor house throughout the dukedom." She hesitated. "You will tell us, when the fighting starts? Where it's happening?"

She was sorely apprehensive, even though she'd only heard her parents' nightmarish tales of bloodshed. Those were bad enough. Lady Derenna's dread was incalculably greater. She and her family had suffered the loss of loved ones, the ruin of their properties and the anguish of failing in their duty to care for their vassals. Branca reminded herself of this whenever the noblewoman's aristocratic arrogance became too abrasive. Aremil wasn't the only one struggling with petty emotions, she acknowledged ruefully.

"*You'll know every step Evord's men take, I promise. Charoleia's insisting I come with her and Gruit to Abray, to be certain we hear all the news that we need to send on to you, Kerith and Nath as soon as possible. We set out on one of Gruit's river barges tomorrow.*"

Was it her imagination or was the distant shadow of Aremil now armed with a sword and armoured like some knight from a tapestried joust? She blinked and the image vanished as if it had never existed.

"*What are you going to do now?*"

Branca could feel Aremil's reluctance to break off their conversation. Equally she could see that other half of him walking towards a door in the far wall. That hadn't been there before.

"I should be packing. We're travelling again later today. Lady Derenna has letters to deal with before we leave and Welgren is spending his morning treating whatever interesting ailments he can find among Lord Narese's household." Branca allowed herself to enter the image Aremil held and rose from the chair in the echoing hall. "If either of them learns anything important, I'll tell you this evening."

Yielding to a frivolous impulse, she curtsied. The magenta brocade of the unreal gown whispered across the flagstones.

As the seated Aremil inclined his head, the shadowy figure behind him turned at the door to face her and swept a handsome bow. "*Until later.*"

Branca drew a deep breath. The unreality of the vast stone hall faded and her whole attention returned to the padded stool in Lord Narese's curio room. She looked at her dim reflection in the glass-fronted cabinet housing carefully catalogued specimens of pressed leaves and flowers.

It would be so easy to turn Aremil's admiration for her into adoration. She could easily secure a share in the funds that kept him in such comfort. She could even grow her hair longer. Just like one of the bewigged prostitutes who strolled the road where she had her lodgings in Vanam. With a snort, she turned her back on the reflection and went to find Lady Derenna.

The Sharlac noblewoman was in her bedchamber busily writing letters. She looked up as Branca knocked and entered. "What's the news?"

"That we must be on our guard for spies from Triolle." Branca sat on the bed uninvited. At least Lady Derenna didn't stand on tiresome ceremony like some of the noble ladies she'd encountered on this trip. Those ladies who weren't eager partners in exploring the alchemy or natural philosophy that fascinated their husbands. "Duke Iruvain's intelligencer is causing Charoleia some concern."

"Master Hamare?" Lady Derenna blew on the glistening ink to dry it. "I hear he's very astute." She folded the page carefully. "You can burn those." She nodded at a pile of discarded papers on the floor beside the table.

Branca took them over to the small fire. Did Lady Narese's maids wonder at the quantities of feathery ash they cleared away each day? There wouldn't be much they could make of it. She and Derenna always made sure every page was completely burned before breaking up the blackened shadows with the fire irons just to be sure.

"Duke Moncan will find precious few vassals answering any call to arms." Lips tightening, Lady Derenna pressed her ring into a drop of sealing wax. Stowing the letters in her writing desk, she closed it up and locked it with a key from the bunch hanging at her waist. "Let's see what Welgren has learned this morning." She snorted. "Besides how easy it is to burn oneself in a kitchen or to get a housemaid pregnant by tumbling her in a hayloft."

Unfortunately Welgren's patients did tend to confirm Lady Derenna's low opinion of ordinary folk, Branca reflected.

She followed the noblewoman out of the room, her eyes modestly lowered as befitted a noblewoman's personal maid. That gave her another good look at the frayed carpets along this corridor. The guest-chamber curtains were faded by the sun and the furniture would have been long out of style in Lord Narese's childhood.

Though everything was polished and dusted daily. Most of her ladyship's share of the base Lescari coinage received in quarterly rents paid the paltry wages of a remarkable number of maids and menservants. The housemaid Branca was sharing a garret with had told her how the raw wool that could be easily sold for Tormalin silver was carded, spun and woven on Narese lands instead, with the cloth distributed to the tenantry at Solstice and Equinox.

She'd also confided how Lord Narese's son and heir had nothing but contempt for his father's generosity. The whole household dreaded him inheriting. Fortunately, though grey-haired and portly, their lord was still in the prime of life.

How could they expect any different, when the youth had been schooled by his mother's distant cousins in Tormalin and never taught any loyalty to those who'd become his vassals? And for all their generosity, Lord Narese and his lady always dressed in velvets and expensive lace. This trip had shown Branca plenty to confirm her low opinion of landed nobles; easily as much as argued in their favour.

Branca followed Lady Derenna down the wide staircase. The manor had once been a single square stone keep that had defended Lord Narese's ancestors from attack. Now that keep was a tower dominating the northern face of a quadrangle built from humbler brick and plaster. All these newer rooms were lit with generous casements rather than narrow slits, the place grown into a family dwelling instead of the fortification it had once been. But a solid outer wall still ringed the residence, defending the stables, storehouses and the well-stocked kitchen garden. Solid gates were barred at dusk and every man of the household took his turn standing sentry, pacing the battlemented walkway that looked out over the streams and fishponds making up a further line of defence.

Lady Derenna acknowledged a passing maid's curtsey as she went out into the garden in the hollow square's heart. Lord Narese was tending an apple tree espaliered across the warm brickwork.

"Lady Derenna, have you come across this particular fruit before?" He twisted a ripe apple free and offered it to her.

Lady Derenna used the small knife on her keychain to cut a slice. "No, my lord," she said after some consideration. "What a wonderful flavour."

He nodded, satisfied. "We just have to breed some hardiness into it, so it survives our winters in an open orchard."

Branca had learned some curious things on this trip. She'd known animals could be bred for vigour but it had never occurred to her that the same could be done with plants.

"Lord Coelle had some interesting results when he grafted tender plants onto more robust rootstocks. You should write to him." Lady Derenna smiled. "Now, if you will excuse me, I must speak with Master Welgren."

Lord Narese nodded. "Tell him to call on me this afternoon, if you please. I want to discuss his ideas on the healing properties of rosemary."

"He'll be at your disposal," promised Lady Derenna.

What gave Lady Derenna the right to answer for Welgren? Branca followed the noblewoman out of the garden and around the house towards the stable yard. It didn't matter that the herbalist would be just as keen as Lord Narese to debate how plants could be used in healing. What gave any noble the right to assume everyone else was at their beck and call?

"Good, he's nearly done." The noblewoman surveyed the few humbly dressed men and women still waiting outside the storeroom that had been given over to Welgren. She knocked on the door and went in. "A moment of your time, if you please."

"A moment's silence, if you please, so I can listen."

to strike Lady Derenna's head. She fell like a sheep stunned for slaughter.

Welgren sprang up from his stool. Wounded or not, Karn was ready. But Welgren wasn't trying to seize him. Instead, he threw a glittering shower of liquid all over the Triolle man's face and naked chest.

"Don't touch him!" Welgren stretched out a hand to hold Branca back.

She dodged around him to help Derenna. Acrid vapours caught at her eyes and throat, rising from the floor where the liquid had landed.

Moving away from the door, she gave Karn his chance. He snatched at the door handle, wrenching it open. Branca saw raw redness spreading across his bare skin as he ran into the yard. She tried to shout but the fumes from whatever Welgren had thrown were scouring her throat. All she could do was cough. Helpless tears streaming from her eyes, she saw Karn knock down a groom with a single punch and scramble into the saddle of the horse he'd been holding.

"Stop him!"

Stronger voices took up her feeble cry but the men by the gate were taken unawares. The sound of Karn's steed was lost amid confused questions before another groom thought to find a horse and give chase.

Welgren managed to stop coughing. "Let's get her out of here."

Lady Derenna was already stirring as he slipped his arms under her, raising her from the dirty floor. Branca went to help support her. "What was that?"

Welgren wiped his watering eyes on his shoulder. "Vitriol solution."

Outside, the mounting block was conveniently close. Between them they half-led, half-carried Lady Derenna to sit on it.

"What do we say to my lord?" An agitated woman caught at Branca's sleeve.

"I don't know," she snapped.

The woman backed away, affronted.

"Just sit still." Ignoring the discolouration spreading across his own hands, Welgren carefully felt along the vicious bruise running from the corner of Lady Derenna's eye into her hair. "Branca, who was that?"

"Ow." Lady Derenna winced.

Branca looked around but no one was paying much attention to them amid the uproar. "A Triolle spy. His name is Karn. He's supposed to be dead."

"How did you know he was here?" Welgren parted Lady Derenna's hair with gentle fingers.

"We didn't." Branca stifled another cough. It was just too painful. "We only came to warn you to be on your guard."

"How did you recognise him?" Lady Derenna glared at Branca, her eye swelling.

She saw Lord Narese hurrying into the yard. "Later."

"My lady." He came over to clutch Lady Derenna's hand, aghast. "Who did this?"

The men and women of the household gathered round, all loudly insisting that the attacker had been a stranger.

"Enough!" Lord Narese's rebuke silenced the clamour.

Welgren spoke first. "Her ladyship needs to lie down quietly in her room."

Lord Narese clapped his hands. "Bring a hurdle!"

"I can walk," Lady Derenna insisted.

Branca dutifully offered her arm.

Lord Narese nodded unhappily. "Very well."

Everyone obediently backed away. Branca had to admit that this Lescari habit of servility had its uses. In Vanam, a double handful of people would still be offering advice and taking offence when they were ignored while a crowd of onlookers ten deep would all be noisily revelling in the excitement.

It seemed to take three times as long to get back to Lady Derenna's bedchamber as it had to walk down to the stable yard. The noblewoman was leaning ever more heavily on Branca as they negotiated the final flight of stairs.

"My lord." Opening the bedchamber door, Welgren balanced due deference with the authority of his profession. "May we have some warm water and a clean cloth to bathe her ladyship's injury?"

"Of course." Lord Narese hesitated.

"Go and see if your men have caught the scoundrel," Lady Derenna hissed.

"Indeed." Spurred to action, he hurried away.

"Lie down."

Lady Derenna did as Welgren commanded, a faint groan escaping her.

"How badly did he injure your hands?" Branca went to draw the curtains.

"He may have cracked a bone or two but it's not as bad as I made out." Welgren turned his attention to Lady Derenna. "As for you, my lady, I don't believe your skull is cracked, though your head will feel as if he split it like a ripe melon for a day or so."

"What about his wounds?" she asked, her eyes tight shut.

"The vitriol solution will leave him sore." Welgren flexed his bruised hands with a grimace. "But I'm amaze⸳ he can walk with that gash festering in his back, r⸳ver mind steal a horse."

"You said he's supposed to be dead." Lady Derenna squinted at Branca. "What did you mean, and how did you recognise him?"

"Charoleia said he had been snooping around her affairs in Vanam," Branca said flatly. "Later she found out he'd sent spies hunting mercenaries for Master Hamare of Triolle but by then, she had word he'd been killed."

Welgren nodded. "Anyone leaving him with that wound would think so."

"You saw him in Vanam, I take it?" A tear escaped Lady Derenna's swollen eyelid.

Branca nodded rather than lie outright. She had seen Karn's face when she was brushing as lightly as she could against Charoleia's thoughts. The beautiful woman's willingness to encompass the man's death had unnerved her more than she had dared show. Trusting in the honesty of Aremil's motives was one thing. Trusting all of their fates to Charoleia was something else. At least she hadn't learned anything too dreadful, not so far anyway.

"I think he's been on our trail for a while," Welgren said unhappily. "Last market day, one of Lady Shaptre's grooms asked if I'd tend a man who'd been injured by a pitchfork during haymaking. That's who this man Karn claimed to be."

"We can just thank Halcarion I happened to see him." Branca wondered if the goddess was favouring them with good luck or bad. "What did he ask you? What did you tell him?"

"Nothing." Welgren shook his head. "I'd only got as far as cleaning that wound and listening to his heart and lungs with my sounding rod. Neither sounded overly healthy and that infection will probably be the death of him anyway."

"Let's hope so." Lady Derenna shifted her head on her pillow, her eyes still closed. "But we must leave, before he can tell anyone we've been here."

"Unless Lord Narese's men catch him." Welgren looked at Branca.

"I don't think we can count on that," she said reluctantly.

Welgren bent to look at the lurid bruise spreading across Lady Derenna's face. "I'll make a poultice for that, and find something to ease your headache."

"Tend your hands," she said faintly. "We need to ride on today. Branca, tell Aremil what's happened."

Welgren ushered Branca out of the room and shut the door gently. "Stay with her until I come back. She shouldn't try riding today."

"Then we'll have to ask Lord Narese to lend us a carriage. She's right, we can't stay here." Branca looked down to see her hands were shaking. "Can you do that? Then when you get back, I must warn Aremil that this man Karn is still alive."

"I imagine his lordship will try to talk her out of leaving." Welgren managed a wry smile. "Not that he'll succeed."

Branca watched him go along the corridor. Her hands were still shaking. How long would it be before she was calm enough to reach through the aether to Aremil?

It was all very well using Artifice to knot the different threads of their plotting together. But warfare was coming, any day now. Aremil had said so. She hadn't thought about it before now, but her only weapon was Artifice. After the horrid shock of the day's events, she had better give some serious thought to using it for protection and, if need be, attack.

Derenna could have been killed. They all could have died. Karn's merciless threat echoed in her memory. He would have driven that rod through her eye and into her brain without a moment's hesitation.

She looked down and saw that her fists were clenched. Once she'd warned Aremil, she decided, she'd see what Kerith could tell her of the harsher, more aggressive enchantments that fascinated him so. What might Jettin know that she could use to defend herself and those travelling with her?

What could Master Tonin tell her of those more aggressive enchantments that the ancient races had linked to the merciless north wind? She'd have to think carefully how best to phrase such a request if she was to win his help rather than his censure. Or perhaps those Mountain Men could tell her something useful. Their tales of the mysterious *sheltya* working up in the remote mountain valleys might serve to illuminate some of the puzzles that still teased Vanam's scholars. She should ask Tathrin to speak to them on her behalf.

She spread her fingers and saw that her hands were still. As soon as Welgren returned, she'd shut herself away in Lord Narese's curio room and work her Artifice.

Chapter Thirty-Four

Failla

The Three Pigeons Inn, in the Lescari Dukedom of Carluse, 38th of For-Autumn

"What brings you back this way?" The innkeeper set the platter of roast pork and turnips down. "You were heading west, weren't you?"

"You remember us?" Nath poured ale into his tankard.

"I never forget a pretty face." Red-faced and rotund in his long apron, the man winked at Failla, more paternal than hopeful.

She managed a dimpled smile and sipped her drink.

"We come and go where the work is." Nath shook his head ruefully.

"If that's what learning gets you, you can keep it," the innkeeper joked. "I'll take ignorance and being my own master. Well, enjoy your dinner."

As he walked away, Nath speared two slices of the succulent pork with his belt knife and transferred them to his plate. "We shouldn't have stopped here again. Pass the bread, please."

"We'll be leaving in the morning." As she handed the bread basket over, Failla felt the letter hidden in her bodice crackle. How could he not hear it?

Kerith dropped into the third wooden chair around their small table and helped himself to meat and vegetables. "Aremil tells me curious folk have been getting far too close to our friends travelling to the north." He looked covertly around the taproom.

Failla tore a piece of bread into fragments. "Who's curious?" she managed to ask.

"Those same folk from the south that we were warned about," Kerith said quietly. "Thankfully, there's no hint that anyone hereabouts suspects us."

Failla tried to look relieved.

Kerith hooked a slice of meat with the tip of his knife and dropped it onto her crumb-strewn plate. "You don't eat enough to keep a bird alive. Have some of this."

"Thank you." If she tried to eat it, she knew she would choke. Would these two men see that as a sign from Ostrin that she hid some guilty secret? Had that superstition travelled to Vanam and to Tormalin along with those who'd fled Lescar?

"If news does travel south, there's scant time left for those who might hear it to act." Nath looked to the scholar for reassurance.

Kerith shrugged as he chewed. "That depends who he tells. Rouse the boar or the stag even this late in the day and our friends could find their hunt cut short."

Why did Kerith insist on referring to Duke Garnot and Duke Moncan by the heraldic beasts on Carluse and Sharlac's blazons? There was no one close enough to hear them anyway.

Irritated, Failla pushed her chair back from the table. "I had better write a letter to warn my uncle." Courteous habit threatened to bring both men to their feet. "No, don't get up. People will look. Finish your meal. I have a headache. I'm going to bed. Don't wake me when you come up, I beg of you," she added hastily.

If they thought she was unwell, it was all too likely one of them would look in on her with inconvenient solicitude. As she pressed her hand to her breast, she felt the hateful pressure of the folded paper. Could she go up to her room and burn it? No. She was probably already late and the sooner she went, the sooner she'd be back. Hopefully before Nath or Kerith finished eating.

At least she didn't have far to go. Ignoring the stairs in the inn's rear hallway, she slipped out of the back door as if she sought the privies in the yard. She kept going, past the silent pigsties. The lingering scent of blood from an outhouse where the freshly killed meat hung curdled her empty stomach and she was glad she hadn't eaten.

Obedient to some long dead duke's command, the tavern claimed the largest of the plots marked out along this side of the high road while the others had been granted to craftsmen. At the front, their workshops opened to passers-by, their dwellings, vegetable gardens and chicken runs all tucked behind. A narrow alley ran between the stout stone walls marking their boundaries and the ramshackle fences defending humbler cottagers' patches from foraging animals or hungry vagabonds.

Failla hid in the shadow of a sprawling elder bush for a few moments to be certain she wasn't followed. Satisfied, she stepped over a foetid ditch and hurried into the darkness. At least the dusk quickly gave way to night's concealment now that the Autumn Equinox was so close at hand.

The alley took her to a wider road leading down from the highway to the heart of the little town. There were a few people here and there. Failla kept to the side of the marketplace rather than cutting more swiftly across. With luck anyone seeing her would think she was just slipping from one house to the next. She wasn't wearing a cloak, after all.

She wished she'd fetched a shawl from her room, though. The skies were clear and the night was growing cold. She looked up to see both moons at their waning quarter, the stars of Halcarion's Crown bright between them.

Inside a handful of days, both moons would be gone and the sun would set on the darkest night in this whole latter half of the year. No one had told her, but that must be when Captain-General Evord would lead his army down from the hills, taking advantage of the dim nights to follow. How else could they hope to reach Sharlac's borders undiscovered?

On the far side of the marketplace, the road led away beyond the houses towards a little bridge humped over the modest river. A fire-basket burned on the end of the stone balustrade to guide late travellers to the crossing. Failla couldn't see anyone tending it but someone must keep it fuelled.

Her steps slowed to a halt. Perhaps she should have left a note for Nath or Kerith. But how could she have warned them without betraying herself? If she was discovered, she would have to face the consequences. Regardless, she had better do what she must as quickly as possible.

She began walking. If she was caught, she could only hope Nath and Kerith had the sense to run as far and as fast they could. With luck they could lose themselves in the uproar once Evord's army overwhelmed Sharlac. Surely there was nothing Duke Garnot or Duke Moncan could do this late in the day? Not even if Duke Iruvain's intelligencer sent some courier bird winging back northwards once he got word from his spies.

As she passed the smouldering fire-basket and reached the crest of the bridge, she saw another brazier burning bright on the far side. The shrine to Trimon stood dark and silent beyond it. The door was on the far side, facing the open road. As she reached it, the shadows closed around her.

Between her breasts Failla felt the hilt of the dagger that she'd slid into the front of her stays in place of the wooden busk that normally stiffened the heavy cotton. Drawing it out, she hid the weapon amid the folds of her skirt as she pushed the shrine's door open. Whatever Duke Iruvain of Triolle learned of Evord's army, his intelligence master wouldn't be hearing from this spy again.

"Pelletria?"

The vile old woman liked to wait in the dark. Failla tensed, waiting for the rasp of flint and steel, narrowing her eyes against the expectation of a freshly lit candle.

Neither came. She took a step into the darkness. "Pelletria?"

She'd kill the old woman and drag her body into the woods. It would doubtless be found inside the next day or so but it would take a while longer for word to spread. Whatever letters Pelletria had written betraying Failla couldn't reach Triolle before a handful of days had passed.

Long enough for her to give Nath and Kerith the slip. Then she would ride to Lathi's farm and claim her daughter. As long as she could reach Uncle Ernout and secure her gold before the fighting reached Carluse, they could both be lost for good in the confusion of this new war.

But where was Pelletria?

She heard a footfall outside. Darting to the far side of the door, Failla pressed herself against the wooden wall. A shadow crossed the faint moonlight falling where the door stood open. She heard the chink of metal on metal. A lantern's glow slipping between the hinges drew a golden line down her gown. The old woman was late. Failla clutched her dagger, ready to strike.

Whoever was outside shoved the door hard, knocking her off her feet. She fell against the stone plinth in the centre of the dark shrine. Shocked into a cry of pain as the unyielding edge bruised her ribs, she lost hold of her dagger.

"Failla?" Nath stood in the doorway, lantern held high. "Are you alone?"

He walked quickly around the shrine, shedding light into every nook. The lantern struck a gleam from the glazed and painted pottery of the funeral urns. There was no one else there. The statue of the god stood alone on his plinth.

On the dusty floor at Trimon's feet, Failla drew up her knees and buried her face in her skirts.

"There's no sign of anyone else." Kerith appeared at the door.

"What are you doing here?" As Nath moved his light, the dagger blade glinted. "With a knife that you stole from me?" His voice rose angrily as he bent to retrieve it.

"I need to warn my uncle." Failla tried for a tremulous smile, thinking with desperate haste. "You know I send him letters through the shrines."

"You usually ask one of us to escort you." Kerith's face was rigid.

"Since when do you leave letters that could be the death of your uncle for anyone to find?" Tucking the naked dagger through his belt, Nath reached towards the statue.

Failla was horrified to see him pluck a folded sheet of paper from the carved wooden strings of Trimon's harp.

"What's that?"

Kerith was blocking the door. If she did get past him, where would she run?

The paper wasn't even sealed. Nath lifted his lantern to read the brief message aloud.

"*F, you've lied to me. I told you what would happen if you did. P.*"

"Who've you lied to, besides us?" Screwing the paper up, he threw it angrily at her.

Failla barely heard him, numb with horror. Pelletria knew she'd been lying. Duke Iruvain of Triolle would know about her daughter. How long before he told Duke Garnot? How long before Duke Garnot sent his mercenaries to ransack every house where she had kin, to beat answers out of anyone who might have helped conceal such a secret?

She scrambled blindly to her feet and tried to force a way past Kerith.

He pushed her back into the shrine, kicking the door shut behind him. "Who's that note from?"

"You don't understand." Frantic tears ran down her face.

"You can stop your weeping." Nath set his lantern down on Trimon's plinth. "It won't fool either of us."

"You don't—"

Failla gasped as Nath ran rough hands over her. He felt the hidden letter and pulled her bodice laces awry to get it.

"Trimon's shrine by the bridge after dusk, P." He shook her by the shoulder with unexpected violence. "In the same handwriting."

"I saw the maid give you that at the inn." Kerith leaned on the door, implacable as the carved statue.

The disillusion in their eyes made Failla feel sick. She shoved Nath's hand away and straightened her clothing, trembling. "We agreed I wasn't going to share my uncle's secrets with you."

"This has nothing to do with your uncle," Nath said with ominous conviction.

"This isn't the first time you've slipped away this past turn of the moons," Kerith added. "Don't think we haven't noticed."

"Tell us the truth!" Nath stepped closer, raising a hand.

"I've been beaten by better men than you," she spat with futile rage.

"Enough!" Kerith stepped forward.

Failla saw her chance and snatched the naked dagger from Nath's belt. She stepped back, holding it tight, the hilt against her breastbone. "I don't want to hurt either of you but you have to let me go."

"I don't think so," Kerith said quietly.

She gasped as searing pain shot through her head. The knife fell from her nerveless hands to clatter against the stone plinth.

"Catch her!"

She heard Kerith's alarm dimly through the dizziness overwhelming her.

"What have you done?"

Nath's voice was fainter still.

The last of the lantern light faded and she was floating away on a tide of anguish.

Kerith's voice was all around her in the darkness. "I'm sorry, Failla, but we have to know what you have been doing. If you don't resist, this will go more easily for you."

If you relax, it doesn't hurt as much.

Bemused recollection echoed down the years. That's what Lathi's sister had said, when she'd told Failla how she'd given up her virginity to the master of the house where she worked. For the sake of the new gown that the other girls had envied. Only the merchant's wife had found out and Anise had been dismissed. Gossip had blackened her character from one end of Carluse Town to the other.

"What are you doing?" Far away, Nath was shouting at Kerith.

Failla was still falling helplessly through a maelstrom of memory.

What was so shameful about Anise's choice? Any girl holding out for marriage was still trading her body for a man's money and protection. Exchanging vows before a priest didn't stop a man tiring of his bargain and taking to the high road, never to be seen again. Her father had abandoned her and her mother both. Only the generosity of relatives had saved them from destitution. That same charity alone kept her cousin Serafia from starving, her and her little boy Kip, after her beloved Elpin had been dragged off to fight for the duke and never came home.

Her mother always told her how grateful they must be. Failla hated the burden of such gratitude. She never wanted to know the grief that hollowed Serafia's heart. She'd been determined never to fall in love, never to make herself so vulnerable. Only later had she realised her mistake.

"Failla, what have you been doing this past season?" Kerith's stern voice cut through her swirling confusion.

She could feel him inside her mind. She didn't want him there. But she didn't dare fight back. No more than she'd ever dared resist Garnot. She'd chosen her bed and she had to lie in it. Her mother had said so as she lay on her deathbed and turned her face to the wall.

Lie back and let his hands go behind, between, within. Never flinch as he used his mouth and his manhood, gentle or brutal, as he saw fit. That was the price she paid for the gifts and the gowns that she turned swiftly and discreetly into gold. She wouldn't be left destitute when his ardour cooled. When she was ordered to quit his service, Uncle Ernout would give her the money hidden in the shrine and she would start a new life far away.

"I'm sorry. I can't." Kerith's voice was drawing away, strangled with emotion.

"You must." Nath was suddenly loud with anger.

She couldn't feel her hands or her feet, her arms or her legs. She couldn't feel the pain in her head that had felled her, nor the ache in her ribs where she'd fallen against the statue's plinth.

When was it that taking Duke Garnot's coin for the use of her body had no longer satisfied her? What had Uncle Ernout seen in her eyes that prompted him to ask her to pass on whatever she overheard of the duke's private councils that first time? When had she begun deliberately seeking out information, listening at doors, copying letters?

How had Duke Garnot never noticed she had borne him a child? Had her desperate prayers to Drianon been answered? It had seemed that way when Duchess Tadira had ordered her from the castle, just when she feared her new plumpness would be seen for what it truly was.

She should have taken the herbs after missing her first courses. She'd counted the days till the moons turned in her favour again but Aunt Derou had been ill just when she needed her. Then it was too late to do the deed discreetly until the next time. She knew Duchess Tadira's women kept one eye on the Almanac and the other on her intimate laundry. Tadira might not want her husband's mistresses presenting him with bastards but she'd see Failla whipped and thrown out of the castle gates in her bloodied shift for presuming to deny him his offspring.

Then she had been sent away, far from any woman she could trust to help her. Had Drianon, goddess of all mothers, been protecting her and the unborn babe, seeing to it that Duke Garnot didn't visit her? He'd written and explained he was intent on educating his son while Carluse was safe from Sharlac's malice, as long as Duke Moncan stayed shut away with his grief. She'd wondered if he'd found a younger, slimmer mistress. She'd prayed so fervently that he had once she felt the baby quicken within her.

Drianon hadn't answered her prayers. He had sent word at the turn of For-Spring, telling her she was to play the queen at his Spring Equinox celebrations. So she had sent for Lathi, still nursing her last-born. Aunt Derou had come, tight-lipped with disapproval as she mixed the draught of bitter herbs. They had held her hands and wiped her brow as the birth-pangs racked her, forcing her daughter into the world half a season too soon. Whatever she thought of Failla, Lathi had tended the tiny girl with all the care and love she'd show a child born of her own flesh.

Then Lathi had gone, taking the baby, and Derou had bound her breasts and her belly with unforgiving flannel. She had ground herbs and goose grease into salves that stripped the colour from those few marks the curtailed pregnancy had left on Failla. She had choked down the pungent tisanes that dried her milk and shrank her womb. Then she had gone back to Garnot's bed, taking twice and thrice the care that she had before, to keep herself from conceiving. What else could she do?

All her pains returned: the ache in her side, the bruises on her shoulder where Nath had seized her, the throbbing in her head. Along with the sickening heat of her swollen breasts and the vicious cramps as Derou's draughts forced the last of the birth blood from her.

"No, I can't. I'm sorry."

Failla opened her eyes to see Kerith, his face twisted with self-loathing. He knelt beside her, one hand resting on her hair, the other holding her icy hand. Nath stood at her feet, holding the lantern, his face unforgiving.

Shifting, Failla was surprised not to feel the sticky warmth of blood between her thighs or dampness oozing from her breasts.

"She has a child," Kerith said shakily.

"What has that to do with anything?" demanded Nath.

"I'm sorry."

Failla saw Kerith's eyes were wet with tears. She wondered if he was apologising to her or Nath.

"We have to find out who she was meeting," Nath insisted.

"I told her lies," Failla managed a whisper.

"Who was she?" Nath sat down on the plinth. "What did you tell her?"

"Pelletria." Failla cleared her throat. "A Triolle spy. I told her the Guilds were bringing exiles home to defend Carluse against Sharlac."

"She's telling the truth. I saw that much." Kerith helped her sit up.

"You've betrayed your uncle." Nath was aghast.

"She already knew what the priests and the guildsmen are doing," Failla said wearily. "She said she wouldn't tell as long as their plots had no bearing on Triolle's affairs."

Kerith looked at Nath. "Remember those rumours that Charoleia's been trying to pin down? About Duke Moncan of Sharlac planning an attack?"

Nath still looked baffled. "But why tell her anything?"

"She knew about my baby," Failla said savagely. "She said Duke Iruvain of Triolle would tell Duke Garnot. If he finds her, he'll give her to that cold bitch, Duchess Tadira."

"Why didn't you tell us?" cried Nath.

"She doesn't trust us." Kerith's voice shook. "She doesn't trust any of us."

"I came here to kill her tonight," Failla said, desolate. "I knew she'd realise I'd been lying when the fighting starts in Sharlac. But she knows already."

"I'd have cut her throat for you," Kerith said hoarsely.

Nath stared at him. "Saedrin save us."

"What would you do if someone was threatening your child?" Kerith challenged.

"All I want is to see my daughter safe." Failla felt hot tears trickle down her face. "But now she'll be taken to Garnot."

"But you believe in what we're doing," protested Nath. "You want to see an end to Lescar's suffering?"

"I've known you less than half a season." Failla shivered, chilled to the bone. "And your friends kidnapped me."

Kerith lifted her up, his hands too strong to resist. "How far is it to Lathi's farm?"

"What are you talking about?" Nath rose to his feet. "You think we can trust her now?"

Failla shied away, afraid of feeling the pain of Kerith's presence inside her head again. It didn't come.

"Forgive me." He looked unhappily at her. Unbuttoning his long tunic, he draped it around her shoulders. "Nath, this Triolle spy is threatening Failla's daughter and those who've cared for her. We must make sure they're safe, as quickly as possible. Otherwise they'll betray us to the duke's men to save their own necks. They'll have no choice. We'll all be captured and Saedrin save us then."

The warmth in the wool tunic helped calm Failla's trembling. Her thoughts were still in turmoil. "But I lied to you."

"Not really. You just didn't tell us the truth." Kerith managed a strained smile. "Vanam's logicians would say that's not quite the same thing."

"Where is your daughter?" Nath asked finally, reluctantly concerned. "What's her name?"

"I don't know." Failla's tears rose again.

"I know where she is," Kerith said. "We can be there by daybreak."

"Wait here while I get the horses and our gear." Nath spared Failla a more sympathetic look. "We can't take you back to the inn in this state, not without starting some scandalous rumour, and who knows how fast this spy might hear the tale." He looked at Kerith. "Tell Aremil what's happened, so he can tell Charoleia."

"Tell them I'm sorry." Failla wiped tears from her cheeks with shaking hands. "I'll go as far away as I can. I won't say anything, ever."

"Never mind that." Nath frowned. "We need to warn your uncle, in case this spy gets her revenge on you by betraying him, too."

Failla bit her lip. "Lathi can get word to him as quick as anyone."

Could a warning reach Uncle Ernout fast enough for him to act? Would Pelletria make good on her threats to betray the guildmasters' deceptions? Would Uncle Ernout ever forgive her?

"Nath, get the horses." Kerith handed her the lantern. "Failla, keep watch while I work the Artifice to rouse Aremil."

As Failla stood in the doorway and watched Nath disappear across the bridge, she felt oddly calm. Now everyone would know what she had done and why. Whatever Uncle Ernout thought of her, he'd still give her the gold she'd hoarded. She could take her daughter somewhere where no one knew them. Where would be far enough away to be sure no one could ever tell her little girl how her mother had first abandoned her and then betrayed family and allies alike for the sake of getting her back?

Soft in the stillness, she heard faint whispering. Glancing over her shoulder, she saw Kerith sitting on the far side of Trimon's statue, his head buried in his hands.

The road was empty. She wondered how late it was, but the wind was in the wrong direction to carry any chimes from the town. Feeling cold once again, she slipped her arms into the tunic's sleeves and buttoned up the front.

The fire-basket on this side of the bridge burned down to a sullen glow of embers. No one came to replenish it. Presumably no one thought travellers would be on the road so late into the night.

"Before we try any more forceful Artifice, we need to know a good deal more about what we're doing. I will not violate anyone, man or woman, like that again!"

Failla whirled around, startled. An instant later she realised Kerith's angry words had rung inside her head rather than aloud inside the shrine.

He was standing, his back to her, his fists clenched at his sides. The murmur of enchantment faded into nothing.

"Garnot's men would have done far worse." Failla looked at the empty road. "They'd have raped me, even before they began asking questions."

"That's not the point," Kerith said through clenched teeth.

Neither of them spoke again until Nath appeared, hooded and cloaked, leading the horses laden with their baggage.

"I said we'd met friends who'd had bad news from home," he explained breathlessly.

"That's not so far from the truth." Kerith clambered gracelessly onto his mount's back.

"Your tunic." Failla hastily began unbuttoning it.

"Keep it," he said harshly.

"What did Aremil say?" Nath cupped his hands so Failla could step into them and threw her up into her saddle.

"That we ride as fast as we can to make sure we're the first ones to find Failla's child. Then we send Lathi and her family to Abray." The scholar shook out a cloak slung across his saddle and flung it around his shoulders. "Aremil says the men that Master Gruit has bringing supplies across Caladhria will make sure they're taken safely to Vanam." He looked at Failla. "We must tell your uncle to flee, along with anyone else this spy could have betrayed."

Nath looked doubtful. "Won't that prompt questions? If so many people disappear at once?"

Kerith shook his head. "Not when half of Sharlac starts running to stay ahead of the fighting."

Nath bit his lip. "What if we get to wherever Failla's hidden her child and find someone's already taken her?"

Kerith hesitated before answering. "Then Aremil will tell Tathrin and he will ask those two Mountain Men who seem to think so highly of her to devise some plan to take her back."

Failla stared at him. "After all I've done?"

Kerith looked her in the eye for the first time since Nath returned. "It'll be payment for everything you're still going to do."

"No." Failla's hands tensed on her reins. Her horse shook its head. "I'll take my daughter and go."

"Aremil says you know too much to be let loose. We cannot risk Triolle or Carluse catching you alone and unprotected." Kerith's face was implacable in the moonlight. "We've still got too much ahead of us to lose what assistance you can offer. You know more about the Guild conspiracies in Carluse than anyone. If Ernout and the rest are captured, that knowledge will be more valuable than ever." He turned his horse away from the bridge and kicked it into a brisk walk into the night.

"I can't argue with that and neither can you." Nath gestured for Failla to follow. "I'll bring up the rear."

Failla's horse readily took up its usual place between the two men. She let it find its own way through the darkness.

Was there anyone she could turn to now?

Chapter Thirty-Five

Litasse

**Triolle Castle, in the Kingdom of Lescar,
43rd of For-Autumn**

"What is it?" Litasse swept past the lackey into Hamare's study.

The intelligencer waved an impatient hand, silent until the man shut the door again.

"Well?" Litasse demanded. "I don't appreciate being summoned like some maidservant." Uncurled, her hair was drawn back with a single ribbon and she wore a green gown whose moment of fashion had passed several years past. Ink stained the lace at her right wrist. "I have no end of nonsense to deal with if we're to accommodate Their Graces of Draximal and Parnilesse in the luxury they expect."

"Iruvain's not going to spend the festival playing peacemaker," Hamare assured her. "Not when he hears what I have learned. Where is he?"

"Hunting," Litasse said acidly. "What else would he be doing on a dry sunny day at this season?"

"Do you know when he'll be back?" Hamare rifled through the papers on his table.

"When it's too dark to see a deer's rump, as any one of the stable lads could tell you." Litasse turned to go. It was already halfway through the afternoon and she hadn't achieved half the things she'd hoped to have done by noon.

"No, wait." Now triumph was overtaking relief in Hamare's tone. "I have news from Sharlac."

"From my father?" Litasse turned back, her face eager.

"No, forgive me." Hamare halted in his search among the letters, penitent. "But it concerns him. There's been rumour that he's planning a new campaign against Carluse."

"To make Duke Garnot pay for my brother's murder? Why haven't you told me?" Why hadn't her father told her? Litasse hid a pang of betrayal. Because this was Sharlac's business and she was only concerned with Triolle affairs now. "Where will he strike first?"

"Nowhere." Hamare set the paper down. "It's only rumour. Nothing more. That why I've said nothing to you. Pelletria has just confirmed my suspicions."

"You've called me here to tell me nothing's going on?" Litasse set her hands on her hips, exasperated.

"There is plenty going on in Sharlac," Hamare assured her. "There's an army gathering in the hills between the headwaters of the Palat and the Rel."

"Garnot of Carluse," hissed Litasse. "I said he couldn't be trusted."

Hamare shook his head. "He has nothing to do with this. This army is as much a threat to him as to Sharlac."

Litasse knew what had obsessed Hamare all summer. "Is it those mercenary bands that you couldn't account for?"

"Them, a quantity of Mountain Men and Dalasorians, and a goodly number of exiles coming from Vanam and other towns in Ensaimin." He looked down at a map. "It all goes back to Vanam, just as I suspected. By the end of festival, I should know who's behind it."

"We must warn my father, and Iruvain will want to warn Duke Garnot of Carluse," Litasse realised with scant enthusiasm.

Hamare nodded. "If half what I suspect is true, Sharlac and Carluse will need to stand shoulder to shoulder to stop this army."

"So Iruvain must play peacemaker after all, just between different foes?" Litasse sat down, her pretty face thoughtful. "So I'm to turn away Their Graces of Draximal and Parnilesse in favour of inviting Carluse and Sharlac instead?"

"Their Graces of Carluse and Sharlac had far better stay where they are and make ready to repel these invaders," Hamare said firmly, "while Duke Secaris and Duke Orlin must come here to hear certain proof that neither was behind the assault on the bridge at Emirle." Rueful, he ran a hand over his close-cropped hair. "Iruvain was right to insist I ferret out the truth behind that. It was all a feint by another band of mercenaries."

"To keep everyone distracted while this army was gathering in the hills?" Litasse didn't imagine Iruvain would acknowledge that Hamare had been at least partly right.

Hamare nodded. "I was right to suspect that rabble-rouser Reniack. I've traced his links to these plotters in

Vanam and he's behind a blizzard of pamphlets sweeping right across Lescar now. He's spreading even-handed malice against all the dukes to entertain the commonalty and making more measured arguments for those who fancy themselves Rational thinkers. One of your noble father's vassals is involved, Lord Rousharn. Or at least his lady is, Derenna—she has been travelling among the manors of Sharlac spreading discreet disaffection. While those priests and guildmasters who've been undermining Carluse are now bold enough to say openly that Duke Garnot doesn't show sufficient care for their concerns to warrant their fealty."

Litasse was still thinking about Draximal and Parnilesse. "So those tales of wizardry burning the bridge at Emirle were all lies?"

"I can't find any trace of a mage being involved." Hamare opened a box and began sorting out the fine silver lockets that fastened to courier birds' leg rings. "Believe me, I know every wizard Caladhria's barons have tried to suborn. Now, you must write to your father a message he cannot ignore, in your own hand."

"So we need not fear wizardry attacking Sharlac?" That was scant relief. Litasse looked at Hamare, bemused. "So who's behind this? Duke Ferdain of Marlier?"

"No." Hamare sighed. "He's turned his back on Lescari rivalries completely, intent on profiting from trade with Relshaz."

"You'll be hard pressed to convince Iruvain of Duke Ferdain's innocence," Litasse warned, "if you cannot show him the true culprits."

"At your service, my lady," an amused voice said.

"We can't take all the credit," a second unseen speaker amended.

The air by the fireplace shimmered iridescent blue and in the blink of an eye, two Mountain Men stood there, one perfectly calm, the other grinning cheerfully.

"You've nearly put all the pieces together." The calm one made an infinitesimal bow to Hamare, though his eyes never left the spymaster's face.

"How did you get in here?" Litasse gaped. "How long have you been there?"

"Wizards." Hamare picked up his cane and moved to stand between her and these intruders.

"Lady Alaric would send you her compliments on unravelling our plots." The calm one drew a sword. "But she's sent us to kill you instead."

"With her apologies," the cheerful one added sincerely.

As he spoke, the key turned with a soft metallic scrape to lock the door.

The cheerful one beamed with pride. "A friend just taught him how to do that."

Litasse screamed as loudly as she could. "Murderers!"

The calm one winced. "You don't imagine we'd be doing this if anyone could hear us?"

"I believe I owe you an apology." Hamare drew the sword concealed inside his cane. "I take it you were at Emirle Bridge?"

"We managed that nicely, didn't we?" The calm one smiled mockingly.

"You overreached yourselves." Hamare shook his head, his eyes staying fixed on his opponent. "Every hand will be raised against you once word spreads that you've brought magic into Lescari affairs."

"Who's going to spread the word once you're dead and there's no proof?" The Mountain Man gestured and every piece of paper on Hamare's table flashed into scarlet flame. In the next breath, only drifts of black ash lay on the scorched wood.

The Mountain Man attacked as Hamare recoiled from the fire. The spymaster was too quick for him, smashing aside his broader blade with his thin sword. Using the cane scabbard in his other hand, he swept up ash from the table to blind his attacker.

Litasse saw her chance and dashed for the door. Magic or not, the key was still in the lock.

The cheerful Mountain Man was there, blocking her way. She raised her hands, fingers crooked to claw at his face. He laughed and tripped her with a sweep of his boot.

With a yelp of surprise, she stumbled. He caught her, pinning her arms to her sides in a loathsome embrace. She winced and twisted her face away, struggling in vain to free herself. No taller than she was, he was simply too strong.

"Quick as you like, brother," he said conversationally.

Litasse opened her eyes to see the calm one and Hamare exchanging a flurry of sword-strokes. Sunlight flashing from their blades crackled with azure brilliance. What vile wizardry was at work?

A scream rose in her throat. No, she couldn't risk distracting Hamare. Nearly choking, she stifled it.

How could he win? No speck of ash sullied the calm Mountain Man. Instead, Hamare was wiping sootiness off his face with the back of one hand. They circled in front of the fireplace, each man looking for an opening.

"Wizardry and perfidy." Litasse spat her contempt in her captor's face.

"Behave," he reproved, wiping the spittle from his cheek onto the shoulder of her gown.

Litasse stiffened as Hamare kicked a chair at his enemy. As the Mountain Man stepped aside, Hamare swept his narrow sword around to slash at him. The Mountain Man ducked and in a move Litasse could not have imagined, he brought his own sword up and across over his head to meet Hamare's blade. As he did, he stepped forward. Hamare's blade slid harmlessly away behind him. The two of them were standing close as lovers. The Mountain Man wrapped his free hand around Hamare's arm, trapping the spymaster's sword hand against his body.

He still had his own sword free. Unable to retreat, Hamare only had the cane in his other hand to fend off the stroke. It survived the first blow, splintering and falling away under the second. The third time, the Mountain Man's blade bit deep into Hamare's forearm, a spray of blood staining them both.

Hamare's cry of pain mingled with Litasse's scream. She struggled furiously to no avail.

The Mountain swordsman still had Hamare's sword-arm trapped. He clenched his empty fist and punched upwards against the back of the spymaster's elbow. There was a nauseating crackle of cartilage as the joint tore. Hamare's sword fell from his hand with a clatter.

The Mountain Man's blade hit the boards at the same time. His knees bent and he sank towards the floor, still entangled with Hamare.

Relief left Litasse momentarily breathless. She redoubled her efforts to break free even though she couldn't see what Hamare had done.

Then she realised her mistake. The Mountain swordsman, still calm, was lowering Hamare's limp body to the floorboards. As he stood up, he withdrew a bloody dagger embedded between the spymaster's neck and shoulder. Blood spurted briefly as Hamare's head lolled. He looked past Litasse as all life in his eyes faded away.

Litasse was too shocked even to cry out. The Mountain Man holding her relaxed his embrace, catching hold of her wrists instead. She barely noticed.

"I'm sorry, Your Grace." The man who'd killed Hamare sounded genuinely regretful. "We had hoped to catch him alone."

"Then we'd have killed him, set fire to the room and been on our way with no one the wiser," the one holding her explained.

His grip tightened as she tensed. "Just kill me quickly without dishonouring me," she said tightly.

"Of course." The man holding her sounded offended.

"We're only being paid to kill Hamare," the other one observed thoughtfully.

The one holding her frowned. "To kill Hamare and leave everyone here chasing their tails trying to find out who did it. She can just say it was us."

"Do you think anyone will believe her?" Hamare's killer cocked his blond head. "Don't you think it'll cause just as much confusion if everyone thinks it's her?" He smiled with chilling satisfaction.

"If that's what you think best." The one holding her shrugged. "But I just heard the gates," he warned, "and horses."

Litasse couldn't hear anything but the pounding of her own heart.

"That'll be your husband hurrying home." The one holding her was clearly pleased. "I said the news would reach him today, didn't I?"

"You win your wager. Congratulations." The killer looked contemplatively at Litasse. "Which hand do you suppose she leads with?"

"The one with the ink-stained lace," the one holding her said confidently.

Now Litasse could hear shouting voices down in the courtyard and the crunch of hooves on the gravel.

"I think you're right." The killer brushed the bloody dagger blade across her skirt and reached for her hand. Between his strong grip and the strength of the man holding her, she was helpless. As the killer wrapped her fingers around the hilt, the warm stickiness made her palm crawl.

"There should be more blood on her," the man holding her complained.

"It'll suffice." The killer's gaze met Litasse's. "I am sorry, my lady, that you had to be caught up in this."

How could he offer her so earnest an apology with Hamare lying dead at their feet? Litasse's first instinct was to spit in his eye but her mouth was as dry as funeral ashes.

"I'll tell everyone." Her voice was as hollow as the threat.

"That unknown assassins arrived by means of wizardry and killed Triolle's spymaster?" The killer shook his head regretfully. "When everyone can see he tried to force himself upon you and you had to fight to defend your virtue?"

He gestured towards the table. A branch of candles waiting for the evening burst into flame and toppled forward. The ashes of the already consumed papers began burning afresh. Fiery tendrils spread and spilled to the floor, turning from the unnatural red of wizardry into ordinary flames. The carpet began to smoulder.

"Till I get a chance to make amends, Your Grace."

Halfway through his elegant bow, the killer vanished in a flash of azure lighting. They were both gone. Seized with revulsion, Litasse hurled the bloody dagger away. It hit the wall and rebounded to thud onto the floorboards beside Hamare's lifeless body. The acrid stink of burning wool caught in her throat.

"Help me!" she screamed.

"Your Grace?" Startled, the servant outside tried to enter, only to find the door locked against him.

Litasse ran to turn the key. Her fingers slipped, slick with Hamare's blood.

"Your Grace?" The man stood there, astounded.

"Murder." Litasse felt her heart pounding, her chest heaving. She hardly had breath to speak.

The man gaped as he took in the scene. "Saedrin save us, fire!"

He grabbed her hands and hauled her out of the room. Litasse tried to pull away, but dizziness assailed her and she sank to the floor. The servant let her go and ran away down the stairs. She tried to call him back but could manage no more than a feeble gasp. Sprawled gracelessly, she tried desperately not to faint. Footsteps thudded up the stairs amid a confusion of shouts.

"Litasse?" It was Iruvain.

She managed to raise herself up, horribly lightheaded. "Hamare, he—"

"Hush." Iruvain swept her into his arms, as he had done when he'd carried her over the shrine's threshold on their wedding day. "Not a word!"

She looked up to see no solicitude in her husband's face, just cold anger.

A handful of men rushed past to beat out the flames threatening to take hold of Hamare's room. As soon as the stairs were clear, Iruvain carried her down to the courtyard and across to his own apartments. His steward hesitated on the threshold of the tower's audience chamber.

"Out," Iruvain barked. "Close the door." He dropped Litasse hard onto a chair.

The courtyard's cooler air had helped clear her head. She pressed her hands to her chest and concentrated on breathing calmly enough to speak.

Iruvain spoke first. "You couldn't manage to end your affair without stabbing the man? At such a time? When I'm about to broker peace between Draximal and Parnilesse? How am I to do that when you've cut Hamare's throat, you stupid bitch?"

Litasse stared up at him. She didn't know what shocked her most—that Iruvain knew of her adultery or that he thought she had killed Hamare.

"I didn't," she protested.

"His blood's on your skirts, my lady," Iruvain said, scathing.

"They put the knife in my hand." Litasse protested. "There were two men—"

Iruvain's brutal slap cut her short. "Entering a room unseen when a man was guarding the door?" he snarled. "What manner of fool do you take me for? More of a fool than you've already made me with your faithlessness?"

How had he found out? How long had he known? Her head ringing and her cheek stinging, Litasse rejected such questions. She had to convince Iruvain she was telling the truth. "They were Mountain Men, and wizards besides. At least, one of them was. They used magic to come here."

"Why don't you just say they were Eldritch Kin and have done with it?" Iruvain threw up his hands.

She recoiled, fearing another blow. He turned away instead and dropped heavily into a chair.

"Since we'll be telling lies for the sake of your threadbare honour and my tarnished dignity, let's at least make the falsehood believable. All anyone need know is that Master Hamare tried to force his attentions on you and paid the price. I can only thank whatever goddess looks kindly on adultery that you were at least discreet," he added contemptuously, "because there's no chance I'm setting you aside, not now."

What did he mean? Litasse pushed that thought away as another meaningless question. "Master Hamare has news from Sharlac." She corrected herself with a spasm of grief. "He'd had news."

"Yes, he would have." Iruvain surprised her with a heavy sigh. "Though why that should provoke a quarrel between you, I don't know." He shook his head. "Believe me, my lady wife, I am sorry for your losses, but how we're to find a way through all this with Hamare dead, I really don't know," he said with renewed wrath.

Now Litasse was puzzled. "My losses?"

"We may at least hope your lady mother is safe, and those of your sisters who were travelling with her." Iruvain sprang up and began pacing around the room. "As for Lord Kerlin, Saedrin only knows."

Litasse's perplexity turned to alarm. "Why should my mother not be safe? What about Kerlin?"

"You said Hamare had told you the news from Sharlac." Iruvain glared at her. "I suppose we might be able to convince people you struck out at him, distraught with grief."

"What news?" cried Litasse. "What grief?"

"Maewelin's tits, you don't know?" Iruvain was momentarily disconcerted. "I'm sorry, my lady wife, but His Grace your father is dead. Which at least saves him the grief of learning his daughter's a whore," he added spitefully.

Litasse had no time for his petty malice. "My father's dead? Has he been ill?"

"He's been killed in a treacherous attack on Sharlac Castle." Iruvain overrode her urgent questions. "An assault was launched in the dead of night by mercenaries who've been hiding out in the hills above the border."

Litasse stared at Iruvain. "His guardsmen didn't save him?"

"His guardsmen have been getting fat and lazy, confident their lord and master had no need to call on them." Iruvain shook his head.

Litasse pressed shaking hands to her face, heedless of Hamare's blood on them. "My brother Kerlin?"

"He may have fled south." Iruvain looked a little sympathetic. "Of course, if Carluse men capture him, we'll see him married to one of Garnot's daughters before the end of the Autumn Festival. If he's dead, believe me or not as you choose, I'll be sorry for it and not just because we will have to come to some accommodation with His Grace of Carluse."

He began pacing again. "It seems you were right to mistrust Duke Garnot. Whichever of your sisters he manages to catch and marry off to his own heir, you're still Duke Moncan's eldest daughter. With both your brothers dead, that makes your claim on Sharlac the strongest. I'm sure Duke Secaris of Draximal will support your claim." He scowled. "It would be easier if we had a common border with Sharlac."

"This attack has nothing to do with Carluse." Litasse clenched her fists so hard that her fingernails dug into her palms. The pain helped ward off the anguish threatening to engulf her. "That's what Hamare was telling me. That the army poised in those hills threatens Carluse, too. It all stems from the plot he was pursuing in Vanam!"

She sprang to her feet. "You wouldn't listen. Whoever's behind this, they're in Vanam. They're the ones who set Draximal and Parnilesse at each other's throats. They have wizards doing their bidding and that's who came here and killed Hamare because he had learned too much. They were Mountain Men, Iruvain, same as half this army." Grief clawed at her heart but her anger burned too hot for tears. "Did whoever brought you this news tell you that? Wasn't it Mountain Men and Dalasorians who killed my father?"

"That's the rumour, but I wasn't sure if such reports were true." Iruvain looked searchingly at her. "What do Mountain Men and Dalasorians hope to gain by attacking Sharlac and Carluse?"

"They killed Hamare before he could tell me and they burned all his papers," Litasse said, despairing. "You saw the fire destroying all his records, all his ciphers. Why would I do something so ruinous to Triolle?" she demanded with new fury. "Have your men bring you the knife that killed Hamare. You won't know it, my lord, and you'll find no one in this castle who owns it. It's not mine. It's not Hamare's. It belonged to the Mountain-born wizard who killed him!"

"So you're a slut but not a murderess," Iruvain sneered. "I have rather more urgent concerns. Sit down!"

Litasse subsided onto the chair again. She looked at the stinging crescents her nails had made in her palms. Fresh blood mingled with the clotted stains of Hamare's murder. There would be time enough to weep for him later, she told herself fiercely. Just as there would be time to grieve for her father. She would mourn her mother and sisters, her brothers, dead or alive, when she had firm news of them, for good or ill. In the meantime, Iruvain was her only means of avenging any of them. She looked up to meet her husband's eyes.

"I know the names of some of Hamare's enquiry agents and he told me something of their current quests. Give me a little time, and peace and quiet, my lord, and I'll write down all I can remember. They will know who the others might be, and where we can learn more of what Hamare had discovered." She tried to curb her tears. "That's how we first grew close, because he trusted me with Triolle's secrets. I found precious little companionship or tenderness in my marriage, my lord, to draw me closer to you."

"Don't excuse your faithlessness, my lady." Iruvain's lip curled. "Or I'll send you back to Sharlac in disgrace. You can take your chances with whatever mercenaries are plundering your father's castle."

Litasse saw that he meant every merciless word. She looked down at the floor.

Iruvain walked over to the far side of the room. "White brandy?" Glass chinked. "So, is our castle ready to receive the dukes of Parnilesse and Draximal and all their retinues?"

"Very nearly." She took the golden-stemmed glass he offered, disconcerted by this sudden courtesy.

Iruvain downed a generous measure of the clear liquid in a single swallow. "If Sharlac and Carluse are both under attack, we must make common cause with Parnilesse and Draximal. They must surely abandon their quarrel over that cursed bridge."

"That's what Hamare said," Litasse said hesitantly.

"You will not muddy the waters with this tale of Mountain-born wizards killing Hamare. You will take the blame for his death and perhaps Saedrin will weigh it in the scales against all your other guilt." Iruvain shot Litasse a dark glance. "But if these villains are fool enough to use magic in Sharlac, I might be convinced that you're telling the truth. That you're a trollop, not a murderess."

"I will admit to whatever you see fit, my lord." Litasse sipped her brandy and felt the liquid fire strengthen her resolve.

"What of Marlier? Did Hamare say anything about Duke Ferdain?"

To Litasse's relief, her husband sounded more curious than suspicious.

"Only that he was certain Marlier was not involved," she said.

Iruvain sniffed. "He'll be fast enough to take advantage of the situation."

"Then take the initiative," Litasse suggested quickly. "Invite Duke Ferdain of Marlier to discuss this crisis as well as Secaris of Draximal and Orlin of Parnilesse."

"Putting Triolle at the centre of all councils?" Iruvain looked at her before returning to the side table and refilling his glass. "Whoever these attackers are, whatever they intend, they cannot push much further south before winter ends their campaign." He drank thoughtfully. "If Carluse's militias are as formidable as Duke Garnot likes to boast, he may even force this first assault back. So we have until the turn of For-Spring to plan a counter-attack."

Could they plan such a thing without Hamare? Litasse looked at the bloodstains on her gown and a shudder wracked her. "How can we counter magic, if they have wizards on their side?"

"We demand that Archmage Planir strikes them down." Iruvain slammed his glass down so hard he snapped the narrow stem. He stared at the remnant still in his hand before hurling it into the fireplace. "Write down everything you can remember Hamare telling you. There's paper and pens in the cabinet. Don't talk to anyone until I come back, not even the servants."

With that, he strode from the room. As the door opened, Litasse heard Valesti's voice rising hysterically. Iruvain dismissed her with curt finality, slamming the door behind him. Litasse heard the key turn in the lock. She sat quietly, finishing her white brandy.

Would these attackers be foolish enough to use their magic as they plundered Sharlac? Whether or not they did, whether or not Iruvain believed her, she knew the truth. Whoever these unknown assailants were, they were defying all custom by bringing magic into Lescari affairs. Waiting for them to use wizardry again and relying on Archmage Planir's retaliation was foolishness. Whatever they did next might win them victory in one fell swoop. Hadn't Iruvain thought of that?

What could curb them before they could launch some new attack? She frowned. What had Hamare said, when he was telling her there was nothing to rumours of wizardry loose in Draximal and Parnilesse? That he knew every mage who might be bought or coerced? Could she find out who they were? If she were ever to have her revenge on that Mountain-born wizard, a mage in her own service would surely be essential.

Would Iruvain ever agree to retain such a renegade? Litasse doubted it. No matter. Who could help her find one? Who could help her keep such a secret? Who had Hamare trusted most? Karn, but he was dead. Which left Pelletria. Though she was a hundred leagues or more away in Carluse, the last Litasse had heard.

She walked slowly over to the correspondence cabinet and found pen, paper and ink. Could she persuade Valesti to smuggle a letter out for her without letting Iruvain know? Would Valesti be able to find anyone to carry it north and west, when news of this attack on Sharlac would be throwing everything into such disarray? What would Iruvain do if he found her deceiving him again? Was it worth the risk?

Litasse sat at the table and began writing down as many of Hamare's secrets as she could recall. That at least was a first step towards avenging his death.

Chapter Thirty-Six

Tathrin

**Outside the Gates of Losand,
in the Lescari Dukedom of Carluse,
45th of For-Autumn**

TATHRIN LOOKED ANXIOUSLY at the eastern sky where the predawn grey was lightening to gold. "Aren't we leaving it a little late?"

"No." Beside him in the hazel thicket, Sorgrad studied the tumbledown houses outside the walls of the town. More than half were still roofless, their broken walls stained with burning. Common grazing between the hovels and the coppiced woodland lay empty.

In the couple of years since he'd been here last, Tathrin saw that some houses had been rebuilt amid the indiscriminate destruction wrought between Wynald's Warband in Duke Garnot's service and whatever mercenaries had attacked for the sake of Sharlac's coin. More still stood half-ruined. Nevertheless, tendrils of woodsmoke rose from broken chimneys and, here and there, through shattered rafters.

"Why haven't those people fled into the town?" he wondered aloud, his breath misty in the cold air.

Sorgrad didn't answer. The Mountain Man had barely favoured Tathrin with five words together since they'd left Sharlac.

Had the iron-bound gates been barred against the paupers living in the derelict houses? On whose order? Tathrin looked at the pennants hanging limp above the battlemented tower guarding the high road's entry into Losand. Until a breeze strengthened along with the light, he had no hope of seeing the blazons on them.

"Bread? Cold sausage?" Gren appeared at his elbow with a muted chink of chain mail. "Did you sleep well?"

"Well enough." Shaken awake for this last march, Tathrin had been surprised to find he'd slept at all, even after the punishing pace they had set right from Sharlac's devastated gates. Even knowing Evord's tent was the safest place he could be, with hundreds of swords between the captain-general and harm.

Dreams of the sack of Sharlac had haunted his sleep, mingled with memories of the horrors he'd seen the last time destruction had been visited on Losand and the villages all around. Every time he had closed his eyes on the journey he had seen the slaughter Evord's army had wrought among Duke Moncan's men before spreading out to wreak calculated havoc through Sharlac's proudest town.

Every step of the three days' forced march along the Great West Road brought him closer to seeing the same atrocities repeated. How much worse was it going to be here, when he knew Losand, when he knew people living there? He wondered, with sick apprehension, if any of his family could possibly have been caught inside the walls.

He turned to Gren. "Isn't it too late to attack now?"

Gren shook his head as he tore a lump of coarse bread into thirds. "This was never going to be a night assault."

"Why not?" Absently taking a bite, Tathrin found he was hungrier than he realised.

"Because they'd be expecting it, after Sharlac." Sorgrad reached for his share of the bread, still not taking his eyes off the broken houses. "And we needed every advantage of surprise we could get there. Here? They know we're coming."

"They've spent a wakeful night seeing Poldrion's demons in every shadow while we've been tucked up snug in our blankets." Beneath the dull steel of his round helm, Gren smiled. "I'll wager my silver salver against anything you pick up here that their sentries are too dog-tired to see us sneaking up."

Tathrin wondered how much plunder the two Mountain Men had gathered amid the smouldering ruins of Sharlac Castle. And he'd lost track of them for more than half a day on the road. Gren had said they'd needed to make certain some informant of Charoleia's had got safely out of the city. Tathrin was certain he had been lying.

He looked to either side as he ate the rest of his bread. He could barely make out the silent forces mustered all along the edge of the undergrowth, and unlike Losand's hapless defenders, he knew they were there. Was that just the mercenaries' skills at work or something more? "Where's Reher?"

"Back with the baggage wagons." Gren shrugged. "Mending gear and shoeing horses like an honest smith."

"All we need today are swords." Sorgrad was still intent on the distant walls of Losand. "Gren, did you say something about sausage?"

"What are we waiting for?" Gren took a muslin-swathed lump as thick as his forearm out of the sackcloth bag he'd had hanging at his hip since they'd advanced on Sharlac. "There's already enough daylight to tell friend from foe." He offered a generous slice of the marbled sausage to Tathrin.

As Tathrin took it, he looked around to be sure no one was close enough to overhear them. "Sorgrad, couldn't your talents, and Reher's, be used to take the town more easily than Sharlac?"

When the day following that horrific endless night had finally dawned, Tathrin had seen the outer courts of Sharlac Castle literally running with blood. The stench of burning flesh as the dead were thrown on fires fed with broken furnishings had been still more nauseating. Recollection killed his appetite and he dropped the lump of sausage discreetly into a bush.

"This won't be a slaughter like Sharlac." Sorgrad turned momentarily to take a meaty lump from his brother. "Evord was intent on killing as many of the duke's good troops as we could, as quickly as possible."

"Which will get everyone's attention," Gren pointed out, chewing. "Charoleia always says you never get a second chance to make a first impression."

"Sharlac's fate will have every duke shitting his breeches." Sorgrad smiled for the first time since they'd left Sharlac. "Today, we show the common folk we have no quarrel with them, just the mercenaries who take the coin their liege-lords screw out of them. So we want enough light to know we're slitting the right throats."

"Has Evord announced the field sign and word?" Gren enquired.

"Not yet." Sorgrad looked at Tathrin, pale brows raised. "Heard from our Vanam friend yet?"

"No," Tathrin said unhappily. He'd been waiting to hear Aremil's voice since he'd woken. It wasn't like him to be late.

Gren cocked his head. "Wasn't he supposed to be sending you cross-eyed at first light?"

Tathrin swallowed his last mouthful of bread. "What do you mean?"

Gren chuckled. "You should see your face whenever Artifice touches you." He turned as boots crunched through fallen leaves crisp with the first frost. "Arest!"

"Field word's 'Talagrin's bow'." The heavily armoured mercenary held a bunch of bright orange rags in one scarred fist. "Here's your field sign."

Gren wiped greasy fingers on his leather breeches and took one. "Where did you find this?"

"The Duke of Sharlac's private apartments." Arest grinned. "His late Grace's curtains."

"I never did reckon much to Jackal Moncan's taste." Sorgrad abandoned his study of the town to thread the scrap of cloth through the buckle of the belt drawing his hauberk tight to his hips.

"Tie it tight so it won't fall off," Arest advised Tathrin, "and kill any swordsman not wearing a yellow or orange cloth token before he kills you."

"Wynald's men will soon start picking rags off the dead," Gren warned. "Make sure you hear the field word before you trust anyone you don't recognise."

Tathrin was about to point out that he'd had the whole business of field signs explained to him before the assault on Sharlac when Sorgrad interrupted.

"The lad's staying well away from the mayhem. He'll be with Evord and his banner company just like last time."

Thank Talagrin for such mercies. Tathrin knotted the orange rag into the leather thong laced tight underneath his chin. Regardless of where he'd be seeing out the battle, as at Sharlac, Captain-General Evord had insisted he wear a boiled-leather jerkin heavy with steel plates sewn between the outer skin and the padded linen lining.

"Who's out there for the rest of us to fight?" Gren demanded impatiently.

"Outside the walls, the duke's militia are pissing themselves for fear of savage Mountain Men and murderous Dalasorians," Arest said with a low chuckle.

"You sent men in among them during the night?" Gren was affronted. "Why didn't you call me?"

Arest snorted. "After hearing how you people strip the flesh from your dead and eat it raw for a funeral feast, one glimpse of your yellow head would have sent every man running to hide behind his mother's apron."

"Wouldn't that have been best?" Tathrin protested.

"If the militia had fled in the night, whoever's defending the walls would just drive the townsfolk out to blunt our swords when we attack," Sorgrad said sardonically. "At least militiamen have weapons and some notion of how to defend themselves. Arëst, who's up on the walls?"

"What tall tales did you spread about the Dalasorians?" Gren demanded.

Arest grinned viciously. "How they tie a captive's feet to one horse and his hands to another before whipping both beasts into galloping in opposite directions."

Gren nodded with satisfaction. "The best tales are always the true ones."

"They do that in Dalasor?" Tathrin was horrified.

"To execute criminals." Sorgrad was studying the walls again. "It's quick enough and there are precious few trees fit for a hanging out on the grasslands."

Tathrin could only hope the revolting tale of Mountain funerals had no such basis in truth.

"Did you get anyone inside the walls while the militia were busy jumping at shadows?" Sorgrad asked.

"We did, and Wynald's Warband are garrisoning the town," Arest said darkly.

"You owe me a gold mark, long lad." Gren's face brightened.

"I didn't take that wager," Tathrin pointed out.

Evord and his captains had long expected to face this particular mercenary company. Even Tathrin knew they'd been in the Duke of Carluse's service for several years. Sure enough, Evord's advance scouts had confirmed that Duke Garnot had had them patrolling his northern border all summer, as he nursed his suspicions of Sharlac.

"This should make for a good fight," Gren said enthusiastically before remembering an earlier grievance. "I wasn't much impressed with Duke Moncan's personal guard."

"You should have been fighting for the outer bastions instead of disappearing to go hunting for strongboxes." Arest scowled. "Jackal Moncan's chosen men might have got fat and lazy polishing their armour while he locked himself away, but the rot hadn't spread far from the centre. I hope we see an easier fight today."

"We know the tactics that Wynald's men favour and our horses are fresher than theirs. Does that soothe your sore feet?" Sorgrad surprised Tathrin with a grin before addressing Arest once again. "Did you get a man inside to talk to the pewterer?"

Arest's scowled deepened. "I got a man into the town but he couldn't find the pewterer."

"He wasn't at home?" Now Sorgrad was frowning. "Or did your man lose his way?"

"The pewterer's being held by Wynald's men, on Duke Garnot's orders." Arest shook his head. "Him and several other guildsmen and half the town's priests."

"Duke Garnot won't be popular if he lets his hired hounds loose on people the common folk respect." As Sorgrad ran a hand over his chin, sparse golden stubble caught the first true sunlight. "But we need to do something about the gates."

"*Tathrin, are you with the captain-general?*"

Aremil's voice echoed urgently in his ears.

"Sorgrad, it's—"

"You're not feeling well?" Gren's solicitous arm around Tathrin's waist hid the way he jabbed his other hand into his ribs. Even through the metal-plated red jerkin, the blow made Tathrin hunch over as if some cramp had seized him. "But that sausage is perfectly good."

"You've been carrying it around for two days," Sorgrad argued. "This weather's not as cold as you think it is." The Mountain Man shot Tathrin a ferocious look to silence him. "Arest, we'd better ask what Evord wants done about the gates."

"I'll see you at his tent, quick as you like." The massive mercenary strode away.

"*Tathrin?*" Aremil was puzzled by his lack of response. "*It's about the gates.*"

"Arest says the pewterer's been taken by Duke Garnot's mercenaries," Tathrin muttered, hugging himself as if his stomach pained him.

"*I know—I heard.*"

Aremil could hear conversations Tathrin was having before he even realised the Artifice was touching him?

Tathrin straightened up. "Then there's no one to secure the gates for us."

"*Yes there is. Failla's inside the town, with Nath and Kerith. They've seen to it.*"

"Failla?" Tathrin was startled.

"What about her?" Sorgrad demanded.

Tathrin waved him away. "What is she doing here?"

"*They had to come. Duke Garnot has learned of all the Guilds' conspiracies.*"

Tathrin didn't understand Aremil's burning anger. As soon as he wondered about it, he felt Aremil's emotions abruptly dampened.

Sorgrad snapped impatient fingers in front of Tathrin's face. "What is he saying?"

"That the gates will open as planned."

"That's a relief." Sorgrad narrowed his blue eyes. "What's this about Failla?"

"She's in the town, her and Nath and Kerith." Tathrin couldn't hide his concern.

"That's not good." Sorgrad was alarmed for a different reason. "We can always find another map-maker, but we've too few Artificers to risk losing Kerith. And Failla knows ten secrets for every one that Wynald's men can beat out of the pewterer."

"It's a good thing you buckled on your sword this morning, long lad." Gren ate the remainder of his bread in swift bites. "We'll be making sure they're safe?" He looked expectantly at his brother.

Sorgrad nodded. "Ask Aremil to bespeak Kerith as quickly as he can, to find out where they're hiding. We'll come to defend them as soon as our side holds the gates."

"Aremil, we—"

"*I heard. Good.*"

Why didn't Aremil share his relief?

"Gren, go and tell the captain-general." Sorgrad picked his helm up and took his metal-backed gauntlets out of it. "He can tell Arest. You meet us at the foremost oak."

"Quick as you like," Gren said agreeably, fastening his own helmet as he ran off.

"Why is Failla here in Losand?" Tathrin demanded of Aremil. "If Duke Garnot's men are hunting conspirators, surely hiding in a town held by his mercenaries is pure folly?"

"*Later.*"

Tathrin felt his distant friend's evasion. "Aremil?"

"*Why are your feet so sore?*"

"What?"

"*Your feet, they're sore.*"

"Because we walked here from Sharlac to give the Dalasorians who'll ride into battle as many remounts as possible," he snapped. "Why is Failla in Losand?"

Sorgrad snapped his fingers in front of Tathrin's face before drawing on his armoured gloves. "Tathrin, can Aremil use his Artifice to see when we're at the foremost oak? I want him to tell you what we need to know when we get there and not before. I don't want to be crossing open ground and find you slack as a marionette with cut strings."

"*I can do that.*"

With an abruptness that left Tathrin reeling, Aremil was gone.

Sorgrad caught his elbow to steady him. "Are you all right?"

"Yes." Tathrin snatched his arm away. "Aremil will find us at the oak tree."

"Put your helmet on." Sorgrad began moving silently through the trees. "Keep your head down."

Aremil probably knew the lie of the land as well as anyone fighting here, Tathrin reflected. He had felt his presence time and again the previous evening, as Evord had summoned the various captains to his tent, using Nath's maps to show them exactly which prominent landmarks they should use to muster their men and drilling them in the order he wished them to launch their individual assaults. The captain-general was as calm as if he were talking them through a game of white raven. Tathrin had noticed that he gave each company commander a range of alternative instructions, anticipating unforeseen difficulties or unexpectedly high losses to wounds or death.

Though Tathrin had been more concerned with what might happen if any substantial band of mercenaries escaped the massacre Evord planned. If they fled in disarray back along the highway towards

Abray, would his family's inn fall victim to their indiscriminate plundering?

Now more urgent questions nagged at him as he tried to emulate the Mountain Man's stealth. Why was Failla inside the town with Nath and Kerith?

"On your knees." Sorgrad dropped down to crawl through the long grass where the town's cattle had shunned the uncertain shadows of the trees.

Conscious of his height, Tathrin crept along on his belly, the scabbard of his sword scraping along the ground beside him. His helmet's padding felt like a vice around his temples and the metal plates in his jerkin kept digging him in the ribs. Despite the morning chill, he was sweating when they reached the oak tree standing in solitary splendour out in the grazing.

"Talagrin's bow," Sorgrad said clearly.

"I'd know you anywhere, 'Grad." A Soluran voice amid the branches was amused. "New orders?"

"Not for you." Sorgrad crouched behind the wide trunk. "Any movement on the walls?"

Tathrin scrambled to join him. Cricking his neck as he looked up, he couldn't see who was keeping watch. The branches were still thick with leaves, the dull green barely tinged with brown.

"They know we're out here." The voice was unconcerned. "But precious few of Wynald's scouts are getting back to tell them what to expect."

Sorgrad chuckled. "How many arrows and how many kills?"

"A handful of each," the voice said casually.

So the killing had started already and these men just treated it as a game. At least it was only mercenaries dying so far.

Tathrin edged cautiously around the tree to look towards the walls. The banners on the gate tower were fluttering now that the breeze was picking up, though he still couldn't make out the blazons. On the road he saw a flutter of black wings as crows squabbled over something. One of the dead scouts?

"If Evord doesn't want a slaughter, our men will try to spare the militia, won't they?" he asked with faint hope.

"Our men will do whatever keeps them alive." Sorgrad took a drink from the silver flask he carried in his belt pouch.

A whistle floated across the fragrant air, answered by a shrill chorus. Men ran out of the woods, pelting across the open ground in twos and threes, dodging this way and that. Archers instantly appeared on the battlements, arrows hissing through the air to fall down in a lethal rain.

Tathrin winced as he saw men fall. Some stumbled, shouting as they clutched at embedded arrows. Others were simply knocked silently off their feet to lie motionless in the faded grass.

The first shower of arrows had barely ended when quarrels from crossbowmen advancing from the edge of the woods slammed into the stonework. Tathrin couldn't see how many of the archers on the walls were hit, but the second flurry of arrows was more ragged. By the time the third hail fell, the swiftest attackers had gained the shelter of the broken houses beneath the walls.

"Wynald's men were too lazy to clear that ground." Sorgrad passed Tathrin his flask. "They'll pay for it now."

He took a swallow. The warm bite of strong wine surprised him and then he was glad of it. Then he coughed, startled by Aremil's voice.

"*It was the townsfolk. They were supposed to bring down those houses yesterday but they refused. Ten men were hanged for it.*"

Had they realised what Captain-General Evord was planning? Or had they just trusted that whatever the mercenaries wanted, the townsfolk would be better served by denying them?

"Sorgrad. Your flask."

When the Mountain Man looked round, Tathrin tapped his own ear meaningfully before handing back the wine.

"Right." Sorgrad glanced behind them, towards the woodland. "If Gren doesn't hurry, he'll miss all the fun."

Men were pouring out from among the trees. Arrows from the battlements continued to cut them down. But the attackers had crossbowmen inside the ruined houses, finding vantage points and picking off anyone incautiously exposed on the walls. In the rubble-strewn lanes, the Carluse militia were fighting hand to hand with Evord's men. Swords flashed in the sunlight before their bright steel was dulled with blood. Shouts and yells mingled with the raucous cries of the alarmed crows wheeling high above.

"*You need to go up the high road to the fountain square. Take the street running past the covered markets to the horse fair. Follow the lane between the brewhouses to the back of an inn called the Griffin. They're there.*"

With that, Aremil was gone, leaving that same cold anger echoing inside Tathrin's head.

"I know where they are." Tathrin swallowed and found his throat dry.

The gates in the great tower stayed obstinately closed.

"What if they sit tight and just dare us to besiege them?" Tathrin hadn't been bold enough to ask this question when Evord was so calmly detailing his plans for the battle the night before. "Maybe this man Wynald is cleverer than you think."

"Wynald was cut down by his own lieutenants when you were still getting up the nerve to borrow your father's razor." Sorgrad kept his eyes on the gatehouse. "No, whoever's in charge, they'll know Duke Garnot won't pay them in bent nails if they let us pen them up here. That would leave Evord free to plunder the rest of Carluse. This is where His Grace wants us broken." He spared Tathrin a glance, utterly serious.

"This is a more important battle than Sharlac, long lad. No duke will shed any tears for Jackal Moncan, and if we'd stopped to take his castle for ourselves, well, Carluse and Draximal could live with that. As long as they could pen us up there and hold the Great West Road securely for themselves. No doubt they'd encourage Sharlac's vassal lords to fight us but they'd hold off and wait to see what was left by way of pickings once we were defeated. Or if Evord won through to proclaim himself duke, they'd soon send their messengers looking for an alliance." He smiled without much humour.

"If we take Losand, then all the runes are still rolling. Duke Garnot of Carluse is fighting inside his own territory and Duke Secaris of Draximal won't come to his aid. They hate each other and besides, Duke Secaris will be wondering if he might be able to edge his border north and carve off some of Sharlac's unguarded lands. Duke Ferdain of Marlier will be waiting to see what transpires. With Losand secure on our western flank and Sharlac garrisoned in the east, we'll hold a thirty-league stretch of the Great West Road, near enough. That'll cut all trade to and from Tormalin. Duke Ferdain will happily profit from all those merchants sending their goods down the River Rel instead, so he'll be in no hurry to come to Carluse's aid."

He turned to look thoughtfully at the walls and the fierce fighting in front of the solidly closed gates. "As long as we take Losand. If we don't, if we can't hold it, this scheme of yours to turn Lescar upside down for the sake of peace is dead as a doorpost."

Chapter Thirty-Seven

Tathrin

**Losand, in the Lescari Dukedom of Carluse,
45th of For-Autumn**

"WE'RE MISSING ALL the fun." Gren threw himself down beside his brother.

"Wait," Sorgrad ordered. "There they go," he said with satisfaction.

The Carluse militiamen who had been defending the broken houses around Losand were running, utterly routed. Faced with attackers vastly more experienced in waging war after a sleepless night plagued with horrifying rumours, the reluctant recruits were throwing away their pikes and quarterstaffs, some even tossing aside their helmets as they fled.

There were more of them than Tathrin had expected. He breathed more easily as he watched them run: the mercenaries had heeded Evord's instructions to drive the Carluse men out of the ruins rather than just cut them down.

The sound of their panic-stricken flight was lost beneath the drumming of hooves. Tathrin felt the ground tremble beneath him as the Dalasorians rounded the concealing coppices and galloped towards the ruins, stirrup to stirrup. Lances at the ready, they looked like the riders he'd seen hunting the feral pigs in Vanam. That Spring Festival felt a lifetime away now. He clenched his fists. These Dalasorians were bearing down on running men with their merciless spears, not pigs. But he couldn't look away as the horsemen drew closer and closer to the terrified men seeking the shelter of Losand's walls.

The great gates swung open beneath the pennant-crowned tower. Iron-shod hooves sounded loud on the cobbles of the echoing passageway. A force of horsemen equal to the Dalasorians charged with single-minded intent.

"Here they come," Sorgrad said, relieved.

So he hadn't been the only one wondering, Tathrin thought, when Evord had insisted that Wynald's horsemen would seize such a tempting opportunity to charge out of the gate and strike their enemy's mounted warriors in their unprotected flank.

What would have happened if Wynald's men had stayed safely inside Losand's walls to watch the Dalasorians cut the Carluse militia to pieces was a question that could forever stay unanswered. Stomach churning, Tathrin rose as both Mountain Men got to their feet.

"They'll be sending out this year's recruits first." Gren drew his sword.

Sorgrad was moving, half-crouching, his weapon ready. "Anyone who lives signs his name on the permanent muster roll."

"Only if they win." Gren was staying close to Tathrin, his blue eyes flinty. "Let us do the fighting, long lad."

"Gladly," Tathrin said fervently.

They ran along the cattle track towards the gate. Tathrin held his breath as the charging mercenary cavalry drew closer to the Dalasorians. With astonishing fluidity, the solid mass of Dalasorian horsemen broke apart to evade the slashing swords. Fearless, the riders drove their mounts across the uncertain footing of the grazing land. Some stumbled and pulled up lame. Tathrin saw more than one rider fall headlong over his horse's shoulder. Most regrouped safely behind the mercenaries and whipped their horses towards the town's open gates.

"Come on!" Sorgrad broke into a run.

Gren whooped with glee as he did the same.

The burden of chain mail hindered neither. With the weight of his armoured jerkin sapping his strength, Tathrin was hard pressed to keep up despite his longer legs.

On the road ahead, the bulk of the mercenary riders had been taken by surprise. Slow to rein their horses back, their gallop carried them towards the woods just as a fresh force erupted from hiding. Evord's men threw bundles of stakes into the mercenary horsemen's path, cross-tied so that sharpened points stuck up whichever way they landed. Blond archers pierced men and beasts alike with murderous shafts. As the mercenaries fought to manage their maddened horses, Evord's swordsmen rushed in to attack.

A few at the rear managed to pull up before they were embroiled into the chaos. Dragging their horses' heads around, they spurred them back towards the town.

Reaching the road, Tathrin was running for his life. He didn't care that he was outstripping Sorgrad and Gren. He just wanted to reach the shelter of the gate-house before one of Wynald's returning horsemen plunged a lance into his back.

Ahead he saw desperate fighting in the shadows. Failla and Nath had indeed got word to the guildsmen inside the town, he realised with distant relief. They had explained how Captain-General Evord needed the townsfolk to stop the mercenaries slamming the gates shut after the first wave of Wynald's horses had been lured out by the Dalasorians.

Beaten earth underfoot gave way to cobbles. Tathrin's feet slipped on blood and the clash of swords in the confines of the gatehouse was deafening. More of those thrashing in the shadows wore broadcloth than armour, the townsmen fighting with swords, spades and pry-bars. He couldn't stop to give way to his horror. Not this time. He had a job to do.

"Which way?" Sorgrad ripped his sword across the shoulder of a man who'd mistimed his thrust. The mercenary reeled away, his arm hanging limp.

"Up the high road to the fountain square." Tathrin braced himself to meet a downward stroke launched by a mail-shirted swordsman.

Gren was there, knocking the blade up and follow-ing through to thrust the point of his sword into the man's eye. He wrenched his weapon free. "Come on, then!"

Hacking blindly at the press of bodies, Tathrin fought through to the daylight on the inside of the gate, Sorgrad and Gren flanking him.

The first of the mounted Dalasorians had already pounded through the arched passageway to attack those mercenary horsemen who'd been waiting in reserve. In the open space, the fighting was ferocious. Any man who slipped from his saddle faced death just as readily from some stray blow as from the frenzied kicks of a panicked horse.

At least they were all too engrossed in their own battles to look for new foes. Tathrin followed Sorgrad's lead, keeping his back to the wall of the nearest house.

Gren peered around a corner into a side street. "I'd give a lot to know my way around these back alleys."

"Go." Sorgrad shoved Tathrin.

They dashed across the open street to shelter in a doorway as the first of the swordsmen who'd fought their way through the broken-down houses came rushing into the town.

"Talagrin's bow!" Sorgrad shouted.

Tathrin could only hope his orange cloth token was clearly visible. He didn't think he could unclench his jaw to speak.

"Come on." Gren was moving again, glancing forwards and back, swords in both hands.

Tathrin hadn't seen him pick up the second blade. A blood-curdling yell behind him raised the hairs on his neck and he whirled around.

"No." Sorgrad knocked his sword back down as a handful of Mountain Men raced past.

Three mounted mercenaries pursued, spitting curses. The Mountain Men cut down an alley. The horsemen chased them. Tathrin couldn't see how the Mountain Men could possibly escape. Then all three riders flew backwards out of their saddles to land heavily on the cobbles.

"Always good to have townsfolk on your side," Gren said happily.

Tathrin saw that a chain had been thrown from an upper window to the one facing it across the street. Pulled up taut, it had swept the men off their horses. One lay deathly still as the other two struggled up.

The door of the opposite house slammed open and two men and a boy attacked the stunned mercenaries with sledgehammers and a cudgel. Their women-folk screeched high-pitched encouragement from the windows above.

"This is the fountain court. Where now?" demanded Sorgrad.

There was at least as much wrestling as swordplay going on around the broad basins fed by the town's main conduit. Bodies floated in two of them, tainting the water with blood and ordure.

Tathrin saw the open arches and angled roofs of the covered markets and pointed with his sword. "This way."

His sword had blood on it. How had that happened?

He had no time to wonder as he ran across the flagstoned expanse, the brothers on either side of him. One man made a half-hearted attack on Sorgrad, only to stumble backwards as the Mountain Man deftly sidestepped to hack at his legs.

Once they were in the street running alongside the market halls, there was no one to be seen. Sweat running down his forehead stung Tathrin's eyes, so he shoved his helmet back to wipe his brow. He could hear the sounds of battle behind them, by the gate. Here all was stony silence.

"Where now?" Gren was circling around, his back to Sorgrad. Both were alert for any sign of movement, never mind some hint of attack.

"To the horse fair." But as Tathrin spoke, he saw two brewhouses just ahead, on either side of a narrow entry. What had Aremil said? Take the street leading to the horse fair. Had he meant that the brewhouses were on the horse fair or on the way to it?

"This way." He ran down the alley regardless. If he was wrong, it would be easy enough to retrace their steps.

It was a dead end. An iron-studded gate wide enough for a wagon blocked their way. It was set deep into a solid wall, the mossy tiles of an old roof just visible behind it.

"Tathrin?" Gren looked at him.

"Gren," Sorgrad warned. He was still facing the other way, watching the street.

Tathrin turned around to see armoured men advancing on them. Five abreast, they blocked the windowless alley. None wore any sign of a yellow rag. He pulled his helmet back down. With Sorgrad and Gren on either side, he could only hope they'd be able to fight clear of this trap he'd inadvertently led them into.

Or had he? He looked at the gate again. There was a griffin carved into the pitch-stained wood. "This is it." He threw his head back and yelled. "Aremil!" It had to be worth a try. "Tell Kerith we're here!"

The advancing mercenaries shared a bemused look but didn't waste their breath talking.

Tathrin gripped his sword with both hands. If he could account for one of them, surely Sorgrad and Gren could bring down two each? His hands felt slippery with sweat inside his leather gloves.

"Cut them down, quick as you like." Sorgrad made a throwing gesture with his empty hand.

Fiery specks swirled through the air, bright as sap spat from an unseasoned log in a hearth. The sparks flew straight at the mercenaries' eyes. Cursing, the men flinched and dodged but the magical embers followed them, burning through leather gloves to sting their hands, searing their bearded faces.

Sorgrad and Gren were attacking before the mercenaries could recover. Gren hacked one man's head nearly from his shoulders before smashing the pointed pommel of his sword into the next man's face. As he fell with blood gushing from his smashed nose, Gren buried his blade in the man's throat.

Sorgrad brought his first opponent down with a sidestep and a slice to the man's hamstrings. As he collapsed, Sorgrad kicked him into the second mercenary on that side. As the second man stumbled, incautiously raising his arm, Sorgrad thrust his sword through the aperture in the armpit of his hauberk.

The last one was still attacking Tathrin. He slashed at the man's arms, the blade sliding harmlessly along the mail rings. At least his hacking strokes forced the mercenary back half a pace. Before Tathrin could congratulate himself, the mercenary recovered with another smashing blow. Tathrin could only parry with a desperate effort. Their swords locked at the hilts. Feeling the wooden gate pressing into his back, he pushed against it, using all his height and strength to throw the man backwards. The mercenary slipped and Tathrin wrenched his sword free. Before the man could attack, Tathrin ripped his blade across his throat. Blood sprayed all over his face and stung his eyes. He choked on the metallic smell of it as the dead man collapsed at his feet.

"Well done." Sorgrad was cleaning the dagger he'd just used to cut the throat of the man he'd crippled.

"Finally got you blooded." Gren nodded with approval.

Shaking, Tathrin stepped away from the body and wondered if he was going to be sick. He looked at Sorgrad. "I thought you weren't going to use magic."

"Only where someone might see." The mageborn Mountain Man shrugged. "It's only a few sparks. Anyone wondering at the marks will just think they got a faceful of some housewife's ash pan."

"Fighting fair's for fools and nobles." Gren clapped Tathrin on the shoulder and went to hammer on the gate. "All safe now. Open up."

"What's the word?" a voice shouted on the other side.

"Talagrin's bow."

Tathrin was about to ask how they knew to request the field word when he realised Aremil must have told them.

The small porter's door in the gate opened to reveal Kerith, holding a venerable pole arm with incongruous proficiency.

"Master Scholar." All courtesy, Sorgrad extended a bloody gauntlet.

"Are you all safe?" Tathrin stepped forward. "Is Failla here?"

"She is," Kerith said guardedly. "You had better come in."

Tathrin hurried past him towards the open door on the far side of the stable yard. Two ostlers stood irresolute, hayforks in their hands. One retreated at the sight of Tathrin and his bloody sword. The other stepped forward, ready to try skewering him.

"They're friends!" Nath appeared in the doorway. "And very welcome," he added with profound relief.

"You put that down before you get hurt, pal," Gren advised the courageous ostler. The hayfork clattered to the ground.

"We're upstairs." Nath retreated a pace and indicated the steps.

Tathrin caught a glimpse of a frightened huddle in the taproom, men and boys all wide-eyed with apprehension. He took the stairs two and three at a time. On the landing above, a linen-capped woman, her face as pale as her apron, hurriedly slammed a door.

"Failla?" Tathrin didn't want to try the bedchambers at random.

"In here." Her voice was tremulous.

The others were coming up the stairs behind him. "I take it we wait here, till Aremil tells us everything's safe?" Nath asked.

Kerith was less sanguine. "Unless we have to get ourselves safely out, if Evord's men lose the day."

"Not likely," Gren scoffed.

Tathrin opened the door to see Failla sitting with her back to him, in a chair by the window. "Are you all right?"

"I am." Her voice broke as she turned around.

Tathrin saw she was cradling a little girl. Against all the odds, the child slept peacefully on. There could be no doubt this was Failla's daughter, her dark hair curling across her bodice.

"Someone's got some explaining to do," Gren observed with lively interest.

Words failed Tathrin completely. He had never guessed. Had anyone?

"We've got a good deal to tell you all," Kerith said grimly.

"A tale always goes better with food and drink," Sorgrad said practically. "What's this inn got to offer?"

"My lady?" Gren offered Failla his arm, as if he were about to escort her into a banquet.

"No." She looked at the floor, shamefaced. "You'll have things to tell Nath and Kerith that I shouldn't hear."

"What?" Tathrin was bemused.

"Failla was forced into some indiscretion by a Triolle spy," Kerith said coldly. "We've yet to decide if we still trust her."

"I was trying to keep my daughter safe." Failla raised her shadowed eyes to Tathrin with desperate appeal. "I only told lies to the spy."

"So she says." Nath scowled. "Half the Carluse guildsmen have been seized regardless. And she lied to us, time and again."

Tathrin had feared he might see the map-maker looking at Failla with desire the next time they met. Or worse, with proprietorial content. He hadn't imagined he'd see such contempt in Nath's eyes.

First things first. That's what his father always advised when he couldn't decide what to do. Tathrin looked down at his stained gloves and felt the drying blood stiff on his cheek. "Is there anywhere I can wash?"

"My room's next door." Kerith nodded towards the back of the inn. "Come downstairs when you're done and we'll find you some food."

They all filed out of the room, leaving Failla still sitting by the window hugging her sleeping child.

Tathrin found half a ewer of cold water on Kerith's washstand and a chunk of pale soap. He scrubbed the gore from his face. Aremil had turned angry and evasive when Failla had come up in their aetheric conversation. He must know what she had done, or rather, what she was accused of. Why hadn't he said anything? Tathrin dried his face slowly. Not so long ago, Aremil wouldn't have been able to hide something like this. What other secrets was his friend keeping from him now?

He walked quietly back to the room where Failla sat looking blindly out of the window.

"What's her name?"

She would have jumped, startled, but care for her child stilled her. "Anilt," she said softly.

Tathrin knelt by the chair and stroked the little girl's cheek with a gentle finger. "She's beautiful."

"The woman from Triolle, the spy, she said she'd tell Duke Garnot I'd borne her." Failla's whisper cracked with anguish. "He'd have taken her, used her, disposed of her as he saw fit."

"I know." Tathrin knew the fates of the duke's other bastards. Everyone in Carluse did.

"I only told her lies," Failla insisted. "She already knew about the Guilds' conspiracies. I never betrayed them."

Tathrin scowled. "I'm sure we'll soon prove that."

"Kerith knows, even if Nath won't believe it." A tear spilled from Failla's lashes. "They both rode through the night with me, to make sure Anilt was safe. The Triolle woman hadn't betrayed her. I don't know why."

"If this spy baulked at such vileness, surely there's hope for all of Lescar." Tathrin brushed the glistening tear from Failla's face.

"Tathrin!" Gren bellowed up the stairs from the tap-room. "Hurry up!"

"What happens now?" she asked tentatively.

"We wait for Evord to win this battle." He hesitated. "There can't be much more fighting before winter comes. As soon as it's safe, I want to send my family to Vanam." He'd been thinking about that all the way from Sharlac. Once Sorgrad had explained the importance of taking Losand, he was convinced. Everyone he loved must be as far away as possible before this war resumed in the spring. "You can go with them."

Faint amusement lightened Failla's weary face. "Do you think your mother would welcome Duke Garnot's whore and her bastard?"

"That's just what you were, not who you are now," Tathrin said firmly. He rose to his feet. "I'll look after you," he promised. "Both of you."

Chapter Thirty-Eight

Aremil

**Losand, in the Lescari Dukedom of Carluse,
48th and Last Day of For-Autumn**

"I PROMISED I'D have you here before festival."
Charoleia pointed out of the carriage window.

Aremil craned his neck to see the walls of Losand
indistinct ahead. "You're a woman of your word." He
spoke as courteously as he could with the cramps tormenting him.

She challenged him with a smile. "You had your
doubts."

"Losand was barely under attack when we set out
from Abray," he protested.

"Any number of things could have delayed Captain-
General Evord's victory here." Sitting opposite, Master
Gruit supported him. A slow smile spread over his wrinkled face. "But we've done it, haven't we, lad? And I
don't just mean getting here in time to eat sausage and
apples. Lescar can finally look forward to peace!"

"There's no going back now, is there?" Aremil allowed himself a crooked grin. "Did you ever think it would come to this, when you berated Vanam's furriers last spring?"

"I had no notion." The old wine merchant chuckled. "But here we are, with Sharlac fallen already!"

"I told you to be patient and you'd see our plans come to fruition with the harvest," Charoleia reminded him. "But Sharlac is merely one dukedom and, in many ways, the most vulnerable. We have a long way still to go."

Jolted, Aremil winced. Charoleia's associates and Gruit's coin had procured a luxurious coach but they could do nothing about the uneven road. He tried to make light of it. "His Grace of Carluse hasn't been insisting his vassals keep up the highway lately."

"Are you very uncomfortable?" Gruit looked concerned.

"I'll be glad to stop travelling for more than a night's rest." Aremil managed a half-smile.

"This apothecary, Welgren, he's here?" Gruit looked at Charoleia. "I'll welcome some nostrum to ease my aches and pains." He shifted with a rueful expression. "I'm not as young as I was."

"I'll settle for hot wine with a shot of white brandy," Aremil said with feeling.

"Shall I close the window?" Master Gruit reached for the leather strap that would lift the glass back up to close the narrow gap.

"No, thank you." While Aremil was uncomfortably cold, the fresh air helped stave off nausea provoked by the motion of the coach.

The horses slowed for the third time that morning. Aremil heard voices as their escorts exchanged passwords with the horsemen patrolling the high-way on Evord's orders.

If he didn't have Master Gruit's coin or Charoleia's mysterious connections, at least he could speed their travel by learning the passwords from Branca and making sure the captain-general's men were expecting them.

Charoleia folded gloved hands inside her fur-lined cloak. "When were you last in Lescar, Master Gruit?"

"I left Marlier to try my luck in Peorle thirty-some years ago." The old merchant gazed out of the coach window with a distant expression. "I travelled back and forth for a few seasons but every time I came home, I only heard tales of woe. After I moved to Vanam I left the journeying to my apprentices."

"Did you know Losand?" wondered Aremil.

Gruit shook his grizzled head. "In those days Marlier and Carluse were at each other's throats. The only way to pick up the highway going west was to cross the Rel into Caladhria and go north on that side of the river. If you wanted to go east, you had to travel all through Tri-olle and Draximal paying tolls at every turn. I lived near Cotebridge, so heading west was easier and cheaper, with just the fee for the bridge." He smiled reflectively. "If I'd been born further east or nearer the sea, I might just have taken a ship to Tormalin and never seen Vanam."

"I've found little profit in looking backwards, Master Gruit," Charoleia remarked serenely, "and none at all in regrets."

Aremil coughed as smoke slipped through the gap at the top of the window.

Gruit pulled on the leather strap to raise the glass, securing the loop on its brass hook. "The pyres are still burning."

"Were there so many dead?" Aremil wondered with misgiving. Charoleia might disdain regret but he still felt a share of responsibility for those who had fallen here.

"It's Mountain Men boiling something." Gruit peered out, mystified.

"Their fallen," Charoleia said with a mischievous glint in her eye. "They don't believe in burning the dead. According to their customs, bones should rest underground, since all mankind and the land were made by Misaen. In the Mountains, they lay their dead in stone tombs." She held a fold of her cloak over her nose as they passed fires ringing steaming vats. "On some long journey, they can hardly ship a corpse home. They dismember the bodies, strip the flesh by boiling them and pack up the bones until they return."

"Poldrion save us," Gruit said faintly.

"Hence those ghastly rumours spread before the battle," Aremil realised.

"Quite so." Charoleia smiled.

Aremil tried to ignore the insidious smell. Hopefully Branca had heeded his urging to stay safely inside the town while everything beyond the walls was still so uncertain.

They travelled onwards in silence through the significantly reduced ruins surrounding the town. Aremil noted that brick and building stone had already been salvaged and stacked in neat piles.

"I see Evord's had all this ground cleared," Charoleia remarked.

"Did he do that?" As they reached Losand's walls, Gruit pointed at the broken-necked bodies dangling from the battlements.

Aremil was thankful that his indifferent eyesight spared him the repellent details. "I thought most of the mercenaries surrendered?" He looked at Charoleia.

She shrugged, quite composed. "I'm sure Evord can explain."

"I'm sorry I have found it so difficult to work sufficient Artifice to keep you fully informed of late," Aremil said stiffly.

Pain and weariness provoked by the rigours of the journey had severely limited his recent aetheric communications. Though Aremil couldn't be wholly sorry. Seeing the distress of Sharlac and Carluse through everyone else's eyes had taxed him sorely.

Leaving all the gruesome sights behind, the carriage rattled through the archway of Losand's great gate tower.

"Some people are planning on celebrating the start of the festival tomorrow." Gruit looked more hopeful as they saw doors decorated with garlands of red and golden leaves.

"What do you suppose they're thankful for?" Aremil wondered.

He caught sight of a flag in Carluse black and white trampled in a gutter, just as Tathrin's recollections had shown him Sharlac's russet and green cast down in the filth.

An importunate hand hammered on the door as the carriage slowed once again. It opened to reveal Reniack's weather-beaten face.

"If you're going to see the captain-general, can I beg a lift?" Without waiting for an answer, he hauled himself inside.

"What brings you to Losand?" Gruit edged over to give the pamphleteer some space.

"Finding out what really happened here and in Sharlac." Reniack waved an airy hand. "To make sure the truth reaches ears where it'll do most good, while convincing lies terrify all those we want quaking."

Charoleia inclined her head. "You've already done a fine job in Draximal and Parnilesse."

"Thank you." Reniack accepted the compliment as his due. "My broadsheets will be circulating around every festival bonfire, castigating Their Graces, or should I say, their scapegraces." He pressed a grimy hand to his faded blue jerkin, his expression appalled. "How can Duke Secaris and Duke Orlin leave hapless vassals to be slaughtered in their beds by marauding Mountain Men while they frivol with the Duke and Duchess of Triolle?"

Charoleia laughed. "Have you seen Sorgrad and Gren?"

"Not today, my lady." He reached inside his jerkin and produced a sheaf of inky paper. "Now, what do you think of these?"

Charoleia unfolded the page he handed her. "Omens and predictions for the second half of autumn?"

"Based on the ancient and proven principles of Aldabreshin fortune-telling," Reniack said with relish.

"It's all the fashion in Toremal," Charoleia commented, "since one of their warlords visited the Emperor last year."

"An inventive man can read anything he chooses into patterns in the sky or the flight of startled geese." Reniack rattled the papers. "All these prophecies are carefully devised to suit our purposes." He grinned wolfishly. "Wait till you see my almanac for next year's calendar."

As Gruit read the pamphlet, his bushy eyebrows rose to his white hair. "Garnot of Carluse will have his militiamen throw such sedition onto midwinter's bonfires."

"They can make themselves all the more unpopular by doing so." Reniack nodded.

Aremil frowned. "People won't rush to buy books that will get them flogged."

Reniack dismissed his concerns. "My people will sell my almanac in every town across Ensaimin and Tormalin where more than five Lescari families live. As for spreading insurrection across Lescar, we need not commit that to paper." He stood up and thumped on the roof to get the coachman's attention. "We're setting up the presses in the Exchequer Hall. No one objected to us throwing Duke Garnot's reeve out on his arse."

"What have you done with all the records and correspondence?" Charoleia asked quickly.

"Everything's safe with the captain-general." Reniack reached for the door. "Along with the coin, though there was little enough of that. Solstice revenues were sent to Duke Garnot long since and as we attacked before festival, no one has paid their autumn dues yet."

"They won't have to." Charoleia tucked the prophecy pamphlet into her glove. "Make sure everyone knows they can thank Master Evord and his army for that relief."

"Certainly," Reniack assured her.

He stepped out of the slowing coach, barely waiting for it to come to a halt. Through the open door, Aremil could see a broad square with fountains at the centre.

Gruit was still reading the pamphlet. "If nothing else, we can rely on Reniack to confuse our enemies."

They soon drew up in front of a broad stone hall. Bicoloured pennants and a creamy banner with a hovering black wyvern mingled with the guild flags. Hanging from an upper window, he saw the bold standard of Evord's new army. The ring of hands clasping the honest tools used by the humble men and women of Lescar was even more striking than he remembered, brilliant as sunshine against the unbleached linen.

A man-at-arms stepped forward to open their carriage door. Gruit stepped stiffly down and offered Charoleia his arm. She descended with her usual grace. Aremil adjusted the crutches she handed him and accepted Gruit's help out of the coach.

Branca was there, laying her hand on his arm, brushing a kiss on his lean cheek. She looked into his eyes with veiled concern. "How are you?"

"Well enough." He wished he could lay his hand over her hers but that would risk dropping his crutch. "Better for seeing you."

Charoleia was stripping off her gloves. "Can we see the captain-general?"

"He's with his company captains," Branca apologised. "We have wine and cakes while you wait."

"Excellent," Gruit approved. "Lead on, my dear."

The double doors of the Merchants' Exchange opened into a flagstoned hallway. Aremil braced himself to tackle the wide oak staircase ahead. Instead, Branca opened a side door to reveal a large room fitted out with a trestle table and a selection of mismatched chairs.

"Good day to you all." Kerith, his scholar's tunic distinctly travel-stained, bowed courteously. The apothecary, Master Welgren, did the same.

"And to you." As soon as Branca untied his cloak, Aremil headed for the nearest seat.

Gruit and Charoleia exchanged greetings with the two men. She draped her travelling cloak over a convenient chair. "Where is Nath? Drawing up more maps?"

"For the moment. He says he wants to go home," Master Welgren said awkwardly.

Charoleia frowned and drew him to one side. Aremil couldn't hear what they were saying.

He had other concerns. "Where's Lady Derenna?"

"In Sharlac." Branca stepped away for a moment to fetch a cup of wine. "With Jettin."

"What's she doing there?" Seeing the others all engaged in an eager conversation, Aremil allowed Branca to hold the goblet to his lips. The warm wine was fragrant with spices and very welcome.

"She wanted to find the decree confining her husband to his lands." Branca took a sip of the wine herself.

"To burn it?"

Branca shook her head. "She wanted it properly rescinded, but Duke Moncan is dead along with his heir."

"That's certain now?" Aremil grimaced as she nodded. He didn't like to think of Lord Kerlin's death at the hand of some unknown mercenary. "What's to be done?"

"The duchess and her daughters are under guard at one of Her Grace's dowry manors just outside Sharlac Town." Branca held the goblet so that Aremil could drink again. "Derenna is there too, with her husband. The duchess has issued a decree under her own seal suspending his confinement and another forbidding any vassal to raise a militia until the question of the succession is decided."

"Was that Derenna's idea or her husband's?" Aremil frowned. He couldn't think of any precedent for such an action.

"I believe some of the lords Derenna visited over the summer suggested it." Branca cradled the goblet between her hands.

"Are they likely to persuade the duchess to issue any more decrees?" Aremil didn't like the idea of unknown nobles making decisions that could affect them all. Where would Lady Derenna's loyalties lie now that she was reunited with her husband?

"Jettin will tell us if they do." Branca looked uneasy. "Captain-General Evord says it should keep the Sharlac vassal lords quiet, at least until Duke Garnot or Duke Secaris launch a counter-attack."

Aremil could hear Kerith explaining the situation to Charoleia and Gruit. "Let's hope neither Carluse nor Draximal can get their militias mustered this side of winter."

Would the leaves still be falling or budding newly green when warfare reached Draximal? Would his own father and brothers die like Duke Moncan and Lord Kerlin? Aremil had spent the journey's long leagues wondering what their fate would mean to him. He was as good as dead to them, after all.

Branca nodded towards Charoleia. "Evord is relying on her to find out what the rest of the dukes intend, and the sooner the better."

"Do you wonder what we've started?" Aremil asked quietly.

"I do." Branca looked troubled.

"What is it?" He reached for her hand.

"You know how Halcarion's priests warn us all to be careful what we wish for?" She took another swallow of wine. "When I agreed to help with all this, I was looking to learn more about Artifice. Kerith was, too. We didn't realise what we were hoping for."

"Is he still troubled by what he did to Failla?" When the scholar had told Aremil everything he'd learned of her betrayal, Kerith's disgust with himself had echoed across the aether.

"He is, and particularly by the way he was so caught up in her distress until they reached the child. Then he says we should have searched her thoughts much earlier." Branca bit her lip. "He feels we could have saved at least some of the priests and guildsmen from Duke Garnot's brutality. The captain-general says it'll be much harder to push on into Carluse without their help. Kerith says we must set our personal feelings aside and consider how best to use Artifice to find out what people choose not to tell us, whether they like it or not."

"We will have to discuss that." Aremil had felt the strength of Kerith's determination. Personally he was torn between revulsion at the notion of wielding such invasive enchantments and reluctant agreement with the scholar. He was certainly tempted to ask Jettin to look into Lady Derenna's unspoken thoughts. Would the younger man agree to do that?

Before he could ask Branca what she thought, the door opened and the mercenaries Sorgrad and Gren entered, warlike in chain mail hauberks, swords at their hips.

Aremil watched them greet Charoleia and Gruit with delight. "Have you learned anything more of Mountain enchantments?"

"We hear no end of tales about these *sheltya*." Branca wrinkled her nose. "According to some, they can read how a man died from his bones. But no one can tell us by what Artifice."

"I thought necromancy was an elemental art." Aremil looked at Sorgrad laughing with Charoleia. "Does Evord plan to use our friend's wizardry to further the rest of the year's campaign?"

"Sorgrad claims the captain-general still doesn't know the whole truth about him, or Reher." Branca looked sceptical. "I wouldn't be surprised if Evord did. Regardless, he's adamant that our use of Artifice remain a closely guarded secret, in case that draws the Archmage's eye this way. I cannot imagine him sanctioning open use of magecraft."

"Planir has no authority over Artifice," Aremil reminded her.

"Wizards from Hadrumal work closely with the scholars trying aetheric enchantments in the Tormalin Emperor's service," countered Branca.

Aremil recollected one of Charoleia's concerns. "We must convince Emperor Tadriol not to interfere. Charoleia will be travelling on to Tormalin within the next few days."

Branca nodded. "Evord says we must also send envoys to Caladhria and to Relshaz as soon as possible." She found the silver memorandum case he had given her and made a note in the smooth wax.

Before Aremil could remark on it, the door opened and Tathrin entered.

Aremil had seen him change so much over the course of the summer, growing more muscular, more tanned. He had felt Tathrin's resolution strengthen, his endurance for hardship and fear. In these last few days, he had seen the younger man set aside his horror at the sack of Sharlac and refuse to yield to his fears when he was called on to enter Losand as the battle raged around him. He had always admired Tathrin, now so more than ever. But he no longer envied his friend his place in the bloody vanguard of this struggle.

He also knew how much Tathrin resented his role as the passive conduit for communication between those in Vanam and the captain-general. How the notion of Artifice reading unwilling minds outraged him.

Knowing how bitterly Tathrin would resent him knowing such things, well aware how many of his own thoughts he now concealed from his friend, Aremil was left uncertain. The enchantments that had brought them so closely together had opened a gulf between them.

"I'll get some more wine." Branca tactfully withdrew as Tathrin came over.

"Fair festival." Tathrin contemplated Aremil for a moment. "You look different."

"I'm not sure your mentors would recognise you," Aremil said with a crooked smile.

"Probably not till I get a haircut." Tathrin's smile was fleeting. "I didn't expect to see you so soon."

"You can thank Charoleia." Aremil looked around the room. He hesitated, but the question had to be asked. "Where is Failla?"

"She keeps to her rooms, with Anilt. I wanted to send her safely away but Captain-General Evord says she must stay here, to share what she knows." Tathrin glowered, though not at Aremil. "I hope you're going to understand her situation rather better than Kerith and Nath."

That was a conversation for another time, after he'd spoken to Branca. "Where is Nath?"

"Copying fresh maps for the captain-general." Tathrin folded his arms, his scowl deepening. "He says he cannot forgive Failla's treachery." Tathrin's dark eyes challenged Aremil.

"Her situation was appallingly difficult," he said carefully, fervently hoping his Artifice had concealed his own dismay at learning of Failla's betrayal.

"All she wants is to be free of people using her for their own ends." Tathrin set his jaw.

"She has endured a good deal." Aremil cast about for something that might turn the conversation to safer ground. "Your family live within half a day of here, don't they? Have you seen them?"

"They're furious with me." Tathrin's suppressed anger faltered. "When I told them I was part of all this."

"So is Lyrlen," Aremil said ruefully. "She says I've betrayed my family and all who've ever cared for me. She said that if I was set on coming here, I would have to do it without her."

Should he let Tathrin see the old woman's grief, and her dismay when he had defied her to set out on this journey, to show him he wasn't alone? But how was he to do that now they were face to face, with no call to use Artifice?

"My father says we are just bringing down death and mayhem on innocent people." Tathrin looked at him, stony-faced. "He says he sent me away from home because Duke Garnot was having men hanged by the roadside for unproved crimes. Now I march with an army that's hanging bodies from Losand's walls."

"Wasn't he at least glad to see you safe?" Sudden anger warmed Aremil more than the wine. "See what he says when we carry this whole enterprise through to success. Let him weigh Lescar's new peace against whatever suffering it might cost to achieve it."

"As long as the final balance doesn't tip against us," Tathrin said dourly.

An armoured man opened the door before Aremil could respond. "The captain-general will see you now."

"Let me help you." Tathrin held out his arm.

"Thank you." Aremil relinquished one of his crutches to accept it. "What do you make of the captain-general?" he asked quietly. He wanted to know if anything had changed Tathrin's opinions now that warfare had truly begun.

The tension in Tathrin's face eased a little. "If we are to win through, he's the man to make it happen, and quickly enough to save too much suffering."

They climbed the broad stairs slowly, the last to arrive in the upper hall where Evord had his headquarters. Tables on all sides were piled high with papers and ledgers and the walls were hung with maps. Aremil saw Charoleia already taking a keen interest in these.

"Please, be seated." Evord was dressed in a plain grey doublet and broadcloth breeches, as unremarkable as any sober citizen of Vanam. As he spoke, armoured men were quitting the chairs around a half-circle of tables.

"Introductions are superfluous, I take it?" Aremil was surprised to find the captain-general shorter and rather older than he had expected. He had looked different through Tathrin's eyes.

"We're all friends, and too busy to waste valuable time." Evord smiled. "I assume you have questions?"

"What do the townsfolk make of the Mountain Men's customs when dealing with their dead?" Gruit was plainly still bothered by the charnel vats.

"They find Mountain Men disconcerting, regardless of their death rites," Evord replied frankly. "We're turning that to our advantage, suggesting that the sooner they prove they can keep the peace in accordance with our wishes, the sooner they'll be rid of such perilous guests. Lady Derenna is making that case to the vassal lords of Sharlac quite forcefully."

"Master Welgren's been finding out how bones fit together," Gren chipped in.

All eyes turned to the apothecary. "The articulation of the spine and hips has its mysteries," he ventured apologetically.

"Will you be making your headquarters here or establishing yourself in Sharlac?" Gruit enquired.

"Neither." Evord shook his head. "I don't want anyone claiming I'm setting myself up as the new duke."

"Was such destruction there necessary?" Gruit still looked unhappy.

"It was," Evord said calmly, "to convince as many other towns as possible that surrender is preferable to ransack."

"What of the mercenaries you've hanged here?" demanded Aremil. "I thought they had surrendered."

"Another object lesson." Evord looked at him, clear-eyed. "The other dukes will find it harder to retain mercenaries now that company commanders suspect defeat means a noose rather than the chance of buying their way to freedom. Besides, there wasn't a man of Wynald's Warband without innocent Carluse blood on his hands. Ask the Guilds. The fate of all such captives was debated by the townsfolk in front of Raeponin's shrine."

"It was," Tathrin confirmed with a grim nod.

"The dukes will be raising their militias now, with the lash if need be." Gruit shook his head doubtfully. "And bleeding the rest of their people for the coin to buy mercenaries."

"We will be intercepting as many ducal paychests as possible." Evord looked at Sorgrad and Gren with a slight smile.

"We've done it before," Gren confirmed, irrepressible.

Evord continued, "Whatever the Lescari may think of the Mountain Men and the Dalasorians, they will find that none of our forces plunder their farms or villages. Whatever we need, we will pay for handsomely, with honest gold, and yes, the dukes' lead-weighted silver once we capture it." He glanced at Gruit. "In the meantime, I take it you will ensure we have sufficient coin on hand?"

"That's all arranged." Gruit looked happier.

"Do you know if the other dukes have heard of Sharlac's fate yet?" Charoleia enquired.

Evord shook his head. "I don't know and I don't much care. We'll be marching again before they have time to do much beyond tell themselves it can't be true. Though Duke Iruvain of Triolle may have heard. I suspect Moncan's duchess had some means of getting word out to her daughter, Litasse of Triolle."

"These things happen." Charoleia shrugged. "Henceforth, Duke Iruvain won't be nearly so well informed as he has been. His spymaster Hamare is dead."

"Is he?" Evord looked at her with mild surprise.

She looked at Sorgrad and Gren. "You didn't say?"

Sorgrad shrugged. "We thought we'd let you explain."

"It seemed the obvious thing to do." Charoleia looked at Evord with faint challenge.

He met her gaze levelly. "It might be best if we were to discuss such decisions before acting upon them."

"Of course, as far as is practicable." She smiled serenely.

"If Lady Derenna has Sharlac's duchess in her keeping, what's to prevent her doing whatever she sees fit?" Aremil asked quickly.

Kerith spoke up for the first time. "Jettin is keeping us fully informed."

Given the scholar's expression, Aremil concluded he wasn't the only one with reservations about the noblewoman.

Evord acknowledged Kerith with a nod. "All correspondence under Sharlac's duchess's seal is to be read."

"Don't you trust Derenna?" Gruit was looking uncertain again.

"Trust isn't the issue," Evord said mildly. "Staying informed is what matters."

"Do you know what Carluse intends?" Charoleia asked. "Now that Duke Garnot has broken the Guilds' conspiracies, has he been able to make any preparations against your advance?"

"He's aware of some of those who've been working against him," Evord corrected her politely. "We still have allies to call on in Carluse. Mistress Failla is eager to help us contact them, to make amends for her forced indiscretions."

At least Tathrin had the captain-general on his side defending Failla, thought Aremil, even if the Soluran was keeping his eye on her.

Captain-General Evord was still speaking. "For the moment, I suspect Duke Garnot will be more concerned with the immediate threat of our army. Word of Losand's fall should be reaching him just about now."

Gruit cleared his throat. "It's the first day of Autumn Festival tomorrow. Will you be spending it here?"

"I will be marching onwards at first light tomorrow, now that the scouts I sent out have reported back." Evord looked steadily at them all. "We will pursue this campaign as far and as fast as we can through the autumn and into the start of winter if need be. I intend defeating all Lescar's dukes well before Solstice."

"What?" Gruit was astonished.

Aremil saw that Tathrin was equally astounded, along with Kerith and Welgren. The only people who didn't look surprised were Charoleia, Sorgrad and Gren, and even then, Aremil didn't think they had known about this beforehand.

"We march on Carluse." Evord smiled thinly. "I have no intention of giving our foes any more time than I absolutely must to gather their forces to oppose us."

"How long do you suppose you can campaign into autumn before the weather breaks?" Gruit asked doubtfully.

"Mountain Men and Dalasorians are well used to harsher climes than these. They won't baulk at fighting in rain or snow if needs must," Evord assured him, "when our advantage over whatever militias the dukes can whip up will be all the greater."

The merchant wasn't convinced. "My wagons will be hard pressed to keep up with you when all the roads are axle-deep in mud."

Evord was unperturbed. "We waited until the harvests had been gathered before we attacked. Every granary and storehouse is full, so we will buy provisions and forage as we go."

"If you can find any stores, after the dukes have plundered their vassals to feed their militias." Gruit shook his head doubtfully.

"In doing so, the dukes will merely make themselves more hated," Evord pointed out. "While we will offer a share of our supplies to anyone we find starving. We are fighting for the wellbeing of all Lescari, after all. Mountain Men and Dalasorians are well used to living off the land in far less fertile regions," he added with an unexpected grin.

"You have thought all this through." Despite all his aches from the journey, despite all the uncertainties he could still see lying ahead, Aremil felt his spirits rising.

"That's why you retained my services." Evord cracked his knuckles briskly, the sound startling in the silence. "If you have no more immediate questions, I have work to do before we march tomorrow. I suggest you retire to your accommodation to recover from your journey and you can ask whatever new questions occur to you at dinner."

The door to the upper hall opened and the captain-general's men filed back in. How had he summoned them? Aremil wondered.

He set that question aside as he looked at everyone else. Charoleia was contemplating something with half-closed eyes while Gren was tugging at his brother's elbow, whispering eagerly. Aremil found Sorgrad's face as impossible to read as Tathrin did.

Gruit and Welgren were already on their feet. Judging by the way the old wine merchant was pointing to his back, the two of them were discussing medical matters. The apothecary answered with animated hands.

Branca was sitting beside Kerith, listening politely as he spoke. The scholar looked as stern as any mentor at the university. Aremil was determined to discuss the arguments for and against the harsher applications of Artifice with Branca before giving Kerith any answer. He had questions of his own for Kerith too, sure there was more to Nath's antagonism towards Failla than he'd learned so far.

He must talk with Tathrin, openly, just the two of them. They had started this whole enterprise with their earnest discussions back in Vanam. Aremil couldn't bear to think of their friendship breaking under the strains of putting their hopes into motion.

"Master Aremil?" Evord stepped forward to offer his hand. "I'm glad to make your acquaintance."

Aremil braced himself for a soldier's crushing grip only to find the Soluran offering the lightest handclasp. "And I yours."

"I wanted to thank you for all you've done with these aetheric enchantments to keep our schemes marching in step," Evord said.

"I'm glad to be of service," Aremil assured him.

Evord smiled briefly. "As soon as we resume this campaign, you can expect my orders along with everyone else. Until dinner, then."

Seeing Evord step away, Tathrin rose and came over just as Branca appeared on Aremil's other side.

"Can I help you down the stairs?"

"I was just going to say the same."

To Aremil's inexpressible relief, Tathrin shared a wry look with Branca. Whatever other tensions had arisen, the two people closest to him had apparently reached a friendly understanding.

He managed to get to his feet. "It seems the captain-general has plans for me and my Artifice, as soon as the campaign resumes," he confided.

"That doesn't surprise me," Tathrin said frankly. "He won't let anyone sit idle."

Branca nodded. "As he keeps saying, we have a great deal still to do."

The three of them made their way slowly towards the door.

Aremil recalled his sense of achievement as the carriage had reached Losand. That was undimmed. He and Tathrin had first brought all these disparate people together. Through all the unexpected twists of late spring, both halves of summer and early autumn, they had worked together. Now everything was moving towards bringing lasting peace to Lescar.

Deep in his innermost thoughts, he couldn't help wondering what the autumn and winter ahead would see. Just what had they set in motion?

DUKEDOMS OF LESCAR

VANAM
One of the leading cities of Ensaimin, a realm of independent city states and fiefdoms.

Tathrin: Originally from the Lescari dukedom of Carluse. Now apprenticed to Master Wyess.

Master Wyess: A prosperous fur trader.
Eclan: One of his senior apprentices.

Master Malcot: A cloth merchant.
Master Garvan: A master blacksmith.
Master Kierst: A less successful fur trader.

Master Gruit: A wine merchant, originally from the dukedom of Marlier.

Aremil: A nobleman crippled from birth living a retired, scholarly life.

Lyrlen: His loyal nurse.
Lady Derenna: A noblewoman exiled from Sharlac where her husband, Lord Rousharn, fell foul of the duke.

Reniack: Originally from Parnilesse, born to a whore in the mercenary enclave of Carif. A rabble-rouser and pamphleteer.

Charoleia: An intelligent and beautiful information broker. Her origins are obscure and her aliases include but are not limited to Lady Alaric, Mistress Larch and Lady Rochiel.
Trissa: Her maid. Extremely discreet.

Tonin: A senior mentor at the university. A noted scholar engaged in unravelling the secrets of the ancient enchantments called Artifice.
Branca: His student, Vanam born of Lescari blood. Adept at Artifice.
Kerith and Jettin: Also his students, also of Lescari origins,
both skilled in using Artifice.

CARLUSE

A dukedom of the fractured and war-torn country of Lescar.
Insignia: a black boar's head on a white ground.
Colours: black and white.

Duke Garnot.
Lenter: His valet.
Corrad. His horse master.
Duchess Tadira: Born sister to the Duke of Parnilesse.

Lord Ricart: Heir to the dukedom.
(Veblen: Duke Garnot's bastard son, killed in battle two years ago).
Failla: Duke Garnot's mistress.
Vrist and Parlin: Grooms.

Ernout: Priest of Saedrin at the shrine in Carluse town and Failla's uncle.
Lathi: Failla's cousin.
Nath: An itinerant mapmaker with links to Charoleia.
Welgren: A travelling apothecary with links to Charoleia.

Wynald's Warband: A mercenary company retained by Duke Garnot.

DRAXIMAL
A Lescari dukedom.
Insignia: a golden brazier on a blue ground.
Colours: red and gold.

Duke Secaris.

Sorgrad and Gren: Originally born in the mountains, mercenaries who have been involved in shady dealings the length and breadth of Einarinn.

Arest: Captain of the Wyvern Hunters company of mercenaries.
Ziel, Jik and Macra: Mercenaries in his company.

Reher: A mageborn blacksmith originally from Carluse.

TRIOLLE

A Lescari dukedom.
Insignia: a green grebe on a pale yellow ground.
Colours: green and yellow.

Duke Iruvain: Succeeded his father Duke Gerone less than a year ago.
Litasse: His duchess, born daughter of the Duke of Sharlac.
Valesti: Her lady in waiting.
Hamare: Spymaster and erstwhile scholar of Col's university.
Karn: An enquiry agent. Born in Marlier and orphaned as a child.
Pelletria: An enquiry agent.

SHARLAC

A Lescari dukedom.
Insignia: a russet stag on a green ground.
Colours: brown and green.

Duke Moncan.
(Lord Jaras: Heir to Sharlac killed in battle by Veblen of Carluse.)
Lord Kerlin: Second son and now heir.

Lord Narese. Friend and associate of Lady Derenna.

MARLIER

A Lescari dukedom.
Insignia: three silver swords on a scarlet ground.
Colours: silver-grey and red.

Duke Ferdain.
Ridianne: His mistress, lady of Sanlief Manor and captain of mercenaries.

Ulick: A mercenary serving with Beresin Steelhand.

PARNILESSE
A Lescari dukedom.
Insignia: a green wreath overlaying black sword and halberd crossed on a blue ground.
Colours: green and black.

Duke Ostrin.

THE KINGDOM OF SOLURA
An ancient kingdom beyond the Great Forest that borders the west of Ensaimin.

Evord Fal Breven: Retired captain-general of mercenaries now living peacefully at Castle Breven.

ABOUT THE AUTHOR

Juliet E. McKenna has been interested in fantasy stories since childhood, from Winnie the Pooh to *The Iliad*. An abiding fascination with other worlds and their peoples played its part in her subsequently reading Classics at St. Hilda's College, Oxford. After combining bookselling and motherhood for a couple of years, she now fits in her writing around her family and vice versa. She lives with her husband and children in West Oxfordshire, England.

Chronicles of the Necromancer